BY CHRISTIAN CANTRELL

Scorpion
Containment
Kingmaker
Equinox

SCORPION

CHRISTIAN CANTRELL

SCORPION

A NOVEL

RANDOM HOUSE

New York

Copyright © 2021 by Christian Cantrell

Published in the United States by Random House, an imprint and division of Penguin Random House LLC, New York.

RANDOM HOUSE and the HOUSE colophon are registered trademarks of Penguin Random House LLC.

Library of Congress Cataloging-in-Publication Data
Names: Cantrell, Christian, author.
Title: Scorpion : a novel / by Christian Cantrell.
Description: First edition. | New York : Random House, [2021]
Identifiers: LCCN 2020043766 (print) | LCCN 2020043767
(ebook) | ISBN 9781984801975 (hardback ; acid-free paper) |
ISBN 9781984801999 (ebook)
Subjects: GSAFD: Spy stories. | Suspense fiction.
Classification: LCC PS3603.A593 S38 2021 (print) | LCC
PS3603.A593 (ebook) | DDC 813/.6—dc23
LC record available at https://lccn.loc.gov/2020043766
LC ebook record available at https://lccn.loc.gov/2020043767

Hardback ISBN 978-1-9848-0197-5
International ISBN 978-0-593-24390-9
Ebook ISBN 978-1-9848-0199-9

Printed in the United States of America on acid-free paper

randomhousebooks.com

9 8 7 6 5 4 3 2 1

First Edition

CONTENTS

PROLOGUE

HENRIETTA YI AND her team have been underground for three days.

They are over 150 meters down, directly beneath the France-Switzerland border, collectively leaning into the glow of a slab of black plasma glass. The green rectangular cursor at the top blinks, but the eyes transfixed by its promise of results do not.

From the moment it was switched on, the Large Hadron Collider collected far more raw data than researchers could possibly process, so the vast majority went straight into the particle detector backlog, or PDB. Cold storage, as it was sometimes called. As part of Henrietta's thesis research, she is leading the team tasked with thawing it out, slicing it up, and feeding it to a voracious AI painstakingly trained to identify quantum anomalies. The theory is that there may be previously undiscovered signals buried beneath all those years of noise.

Exactly what meaning those signals may carry nobody knows. Some of her peers hope to clinch their PhDs by certifying the theory of supersymmetry. Others hope to be the very first to glimpse the multiverse. A few even believe it is possible that they will discover an entirely new particle—infinitesimal units of mass with such novel characteristics that the world will be forced to rewrite the rules of physics.

Henrietta's dreams are no less ambitious. Her father was killed in the nuclear attack on Seoul, leaving his relentless pursuit of a Nobel Prize to his only child. Henrietta has dedicated her life to academia, turning down multiple offers from the private sector—packages of obscene salaries, perks, and stock options—all for the opportunity to work underground and to be exactly where she is right now.

When the first few rows of hexadecimal data finally appear, the room erupts. There are hugs and high-fives behind her, but Henrietta remains focused. And then something in the data changes, and the celebration abates.

Fingers enter Henrietta's peripheral vision from all around.

"That's an encryption header," someone says behind her. "That's AES encryption, isn't it?"

"And look. It's repeating. Like a . . . *blockchain*."

The characters are not appearing sequentially, but erratically— sometimes incorrectly decoded, then overwritten moments later. But something about the content at the top feels different. It is not a dribble of incomprehensible bits, but two distinct lines of text.

"Look at that. That's not binary. I think that might be . . ."

Several of the letters are shuffled and replaced, and then the cursor jumps to a different location, the algorithm seemingly content with its predictive composition:

> *We know what we are,*
> *but know not what we may be.*

"This doesn't make any sense."

"Why would there be *text* in the particle detector backlog?"

"Where the hell is all this coming from?"

Henrietta resets her big round specs and squints in concentration. She goes over it in her mind several more times. The room has grown so quiet that she can hear the high-frequency whine of excited plasma glass as data continues streaming by.

"Not where," she finally says, as much to herself as to her team. "When."

PART ONE

1

AGENT OF CHAOS

THE FIRST THING Kira does before she gets up is put on her legs. They balance on an inductive charging mat beside her bed between a set of steel rails, and the muscles in the young woman's back and shoulders flare as she elevates herself. The nerve terminals in her thighs magnetically align to the pin jacks at the bottom of the carbon-fiber cups, and the interfaces constrict until they are securely attached.

She has skins somewhere she can roll up over them, and if she were to conceal the seams where the texture-etched urethane and her tissue meet with shorts or a tight skirt, the looks she would get on the street would be of lust and envy rather than curiosity, revulsion, or pity.

But Kira lives alone, so the servo-mechanical guts remain exposed, and she does not even bother dressing beyond underwear, a tank top, and her aviator-style metaspecs. She has not left the penthouse suite asylum at the top of the twisted and slowly rotating Infinity Moscow Tower in nearly four years. No good reason to even brush her teeth, or to close the master bathroom door while she pees.

Kira works nights. Her workstation is her studio, and her tools are instruments of fabrication and conspiracy. Proxies conceal her real IP and map to her many identities. Location can be cloaked from the outside world, but real-time interaction cannot be forged, so Kira has become nocturnal. Her boss calls her a "change agent" but she knows that's simply a way of distorting the truth. She is an agent of chaos.

The first step in her evening routine is to make herself tea. In the kitchen, she activates the kettle, and while she waits for it to boil, she sits down to flash charge the monitor affixed to her wrist. The device cannot be removed, so it must be replenished in place. She interweaves her fingers and leans forward, both arms flat against the mat. A lightning bolt icon appears in the corner of her vision, indicating that her glasses are receiving an ambient trickle charge conveyed through her biomagnetic field.

The charging mat is infused with stacks of overlapping coils that are meant to get warm but never hot, and it is not until she smells something caustic and hears an electrical *pop* that she is on her feet and her legs are backing her away, and she understands that she's been burned. She kicks the cord out of the wall, turns to the sink, and runs her arm beneath a cold stream.

She can already see round, red welts forming on the inside of her forearm. It hurts, but she is no stranger to pain. Pain is always with her, and she has learned to observe it from a distance rather than letting it in.

Kira was her family's primary source of income before the missiles hit, and her parents had her back in front of a computer before she was even out of the hospital. At home, her father carried her back and forth between her desk and the toilet, and her mother changed her bandages and brought her soup and bathed her, and they never spoke of the retaliatory attack her work provoked. It was in the past, and the past could not be changed. Kira learned from an early age that some people do not have the luxury of indulging in yesterday's fears or even today's chronic pain.

If any of her personal monitoring systems fail, she is supposed to alert her handlers immediately. *Fuck them,* she thinks. They refuse to use anything that is not Russian-made, which means half of it is trash. The other half has shit firmware that any script kiddy could hack. They will know her charger is fried when her monitor runs dry and her biometrics suddenly drop offline.

Kira slides the patio door open to help get rid of the smell. Usually she does not check the pigeons until her tea is steeping, but tonight she steps outside into the cold Moscow evening.

Once a day, a bird arrives with a new handwritten encryption key wrapped around its leg. Homing pigeons are supposed to be only one-way. Once they have established a specific loft as their home, they will deliver messages only in that one direction. To use them again, they must be collected and redistributed. But these pigeons have been genetically engineered to have bifurcated brains with dominance that toggles according to light. They fly in one direction during the day and the opposite direction at night. Like Kira, their handlers have learned to turn their multiple identities into weapons deployed against their many enemies.

Tonight's bird has not yet arrived, but the night air feels good, so Kira does not go back inside. She can feel the spring in the silicone tiles as she passes the pigeon loft, and she gently places her injured arm against the cold metal of the rail and looks out over the city. She is chilly, but not as cold as she would have been in the past. Legs make up 36 percent of an adult's heat-bleeding surface area. And Kira's cybernetic prostheses are emanating warmth that her torso absorbs.

Kira has come to think of her relationship with her legs as symbiotic. She communicates with them through the neural pathways she formed as a little girl, and they interpret her intentions, form a consensus, and communicate spatial information back up through the same route. The vast majority of the time, it all happens unconsciously, but occasionally there are miscommunications. When it feels like her legs have suddenly gone numb, she recalibrates them by deliberately sending them a set of simple diagnostic instructions.

This time, she experiences the neurological dissonance as a dizzy spell. Her legs take her two steps back as if to help her regain her balance, which she was not aware of having lost. And then the back leg launches a firmly planted front kick that connects solidly with the rail and leaves a rippled, crumpled dent.

Because the signals travel in both directions, Kira understands exactly what is happening. There is even a part of her that, despite her trying to fight it, is actively participating. The signals are influencing her like a reversal of cause and effect; by thinking about having just kicked the rail, she is involuntarily sending her legs additional signals that, after resetting her stance, culminate in her striking the rail again.

The aluminum is shearing away from its anchors, and the third kick sends the entire middle section of railing spinning down into the dark. Kira now understands that she has been infiltrated, and that she only has seconds to detach. But the releases are not responding. And because it is supposed to be impossible for modern Russian prostheses to fail, there is no mechanical override.

She takes two steps forward, and then there is an awful, silent pause. The clatter of the rail hitting the street below rebounds off the surrounding buildings, and her brain uses the delay to make a sickening calculation. Kira has stopped trying to free herself and is now attempting to focus. She knows that she cannot physically prevent the next step, but she might still be able to regain control.

With her eyes closed, she breathes in deeply and wills everything around her to be calm and still. She grows poised and balanced, and she unexpectedly begins to feel strong and tall. Newly resolute and deeply empowered. She can no longer tell who or what is in control, but she knows that the easiest and fastest path away from the pain of her past is to have the courage to move forward. It is with this profound sense of peace that she takes that last step and allows herself to drop from the top of the tower.

The feeling is not one of flying or floating or freedom. Free fall is neither peaceful nor meditative. The atmosphere rushing past her rapidly intensifies into a roar, and it lashes at her shirt and tears the specs off her face. She feels herself pitching forward, rotating, and reflexively she tries to claw her way straight. All she can do is scream into the cold black wind until her breath is gone, and when she tries to draw another, she finds that her lungs are too weak to pull anything from the torrent of air around her. The girl is silent and limp by the time she hits, and the crack of dead weight against the concrete reverberates through the quiet.

As her body lies contorted and twisted, the burns on the inside of Kira's pale forearm continue to redden and blister. But even though they were caused by overlapping concentric coils wrapped inside soft polymer, they are not resolving into perfect circles. It is as though only select sections of filament malfunctioned. The fresh wound is developing into what appears to be a string of digits woven out of segments of rings—the numeric sequence 6809.

"NOBODY IS UNTOUCHABLE," the Israeli says. "Just like I told you."

The tall man is standing behind him. They are both watching a hijacked surveillance feed on a slab of plasma glass. It is being rendered in the false-color spectrum of the infrared, and the thing they are observing has gone from red to green and is now cooling to blue.

The Israeli's workstation contains a matrix of displays. Some of them are news feeds, and some are different angles on the same street scene. One of them shows a schematic of a cybernetic prosthesis, and on another, an editor in hex mode renders thousands of lines of highlighted bytecode.

The Israeli spins in his chair and looks up. "I think it's safe to transfer the other half."

"I'm impressed," the tall man says. "But there's one thing I don't get."

The Israeli raises his eyebrows. The sides of his head are shaved and the remaining black mohawk is French-braided into a single looped topknot. His beard fades in from smooth, dark skin and neatly wraps the pointed contours of his chin.

"This is dangerous work that you do," the tall man continues. "But you let me walk right into your flat. You have no protection. No real leverage. How do you know I won't kill you?"

"Because I have a system," the Israeli says.

"A security system?"

"Better," the Israeli says. "An *economic* system."

"I don't understand."

"Do you know the only way to keep information safe?"

"Tell me."

"The cost of stealing it has to be higher than its value. Securing information is less about encryption and more about the cost of *decryption*. It's all economics."

"What does that have to do with *your* security?"

"I never charge so much that it would be easier to kill me than to pay me."

"But what is difficult for one man may be easy for another."

"That's why I don't base my fee on the complexity of the job," the Israeli says. "That's my secret. I base it on careful evaluation of the client."

"What kinds of things do you evaluate?"

"Everything. Net worth. Disposition. Presentation. You think inviting someone into my home is a liability. I see it as an asset."

"What's your evaluation of me?"

The Israeli's chair twists as he looks the tall man over.

"It would be cheaper for you to pay me than to wash my blood out of that suit."

"But that assumes I'm rational," the tall man says.

"I'm not counting on you to act rationally," the Israeli says. "I'm counting on you to act out of self-interest."

"Do you believe everyone acts out of self-interest?"

"Of course they do. If they didn't, the world would be complete chaos."

"You don't believe the world is chaotic?"

"I believe the world is a complex and interconnected machine, and that the people who can't see how the pieces fit together dismiss its elegance for chaos. But *I* can see them. That's how I do what I do. That's why you retained *my* services instead of someone else's, and that's how I know you won't kill me."

"But what if I know something that you don't?" the tall man asks. "What if I can see pieces that you can't?"

The Israeli looks doubtful. "What pieces?"

"The kind of pieces that change the rules. The kind that make the machine run backwards. The kind that might result in people making grave miscalculations."

The Israeli sits up in his chair. He is no longer composed, and his tone grows conciliatory. "Look, man, if you don't want to pay me, that's fine. We can call it even. I mostly do this shit for fun anyway."

A moment passes between them, and then the Israeli's eyes drop to the tall man's hands. The tall man reaches into his jacket and removes a smooth, lithe handset. He authenticates, navigates, and then consummates the remainder of a sizable transaction.

The Israeli watches his client nod, turn, and leave. And it is not until he can no longer hear the hollow knock of the tall man's shoes along the hallway that he remembers to breathe.

2

THE BUBBLE

DEPUTY DIRECTOR VANESSA Townes feels ridiculous addressing 470 seats when only 17 of them are occupied—a testament to how anemic her team has grown over the last five years as resources have been consistently siphoned off for other assignments. In an admirable effort to fill as much of the space as possible, her task force has distributed itself liberally among the first three rows of theater seating, but it is still the venue equivalent of a seven-year-old girl trying on her mother's wedding dress.

The main auditorium of the George Bush Center for Intelligence is colloquially known as "The Bubble." It's a seven-thousand-square-foot independent structure that, from the air, looks like a giant golf ball chipped into the rough. You weren't supposed to use The Bubble for meetings, but there were no other rooms available in Van's part of the building. And as the Deputy Director of Clandestine Services, she was pretty sure she could keep the whole thing on the DL.

It is to be a short meeting, anyway. The assortment of analysts, officers, middle managers, and assistants already know why they are here, but as their boss, Townes feels obligated to bring closure to the assignment they put the last five years of their lives into. And, if at all semantically feasible, to try to put a positive spin on it.

She raises the lid on her laptop, executes a key combination, and her screen begins projecting behind her. Her peers like to tease her for still lugging around a ruggedized clamshell, but the shattered Dell she displays on a shelf in her office allegedly got that way by stopping a Kalashnikov round when she was stationed in the Democratic Republic of Congo, forever serving as all the validation Van would ever need that the surface area of a handset is simply way too small.

"I know we're getting close to lunchtime," the deputy director begins, partially as a way to test the acoustics, and partially as a way to get everyone settled. Turns out projecting all of three rows without a mic won't be a problem. "So I'll go ahead and get started."

The newest version of PowerPoint is smart enough to listen to the presenter, determine context, and not just auto-advance slides but, when in "stream-of-consciousness mode," reorder a presentation to keep pace with even the most desultory of ramblings. Although the CIA is perpetually a minimum of three versions behind on any given piece of software, Townes knows precisely whose palms to grease in IT to get the good stuff.

"It's no secret that today is the last operational day for the Nuclear Terrorism Nonproliferation Task Force. It's also no secret that, since the attack on Seoul almost six years ago, no plots have been uncovered, no arrests made, and no fissile material secured. So let's just get that out of the way."

Although Van is not telling them anything they don't already know, it is clear from all the furrowed brows and roving eyeballs that her team is expecting a little less candor and perhaps a tad more compassion from their leader.

"Now, some people have suggested that the Nuclear Terrorism Nonproliferation Task Force is a failure. We've all heard the accusations. The recriminations. The rumors. You all know how many reports I've had to stay up all night writing. How many meetings I've been called into to get skewered in front of the director himself. How many times I've had to testify in front of Congress."

Van pauses while she looks—hard—at an even distribution of uneasy faces.

"But you know what looks a hell of a lot more like failure? *Not* assembling a task force after the deadliest terrorist attack in history. *Not* responding to clear and present danger. *Not* being able to verify, beyond any modicum of doubt, that what happened in Seoul never happens anywhere on this planet ever again. *Not* doing exactly what every single one of us swore an oath to do."

She is seeing some nods now.

"The reality is that this is what success looks like, people. This is what it looks like to keep the United States and her allies—hell, even her *enemies*—safe from weapons of mass destruction. Success isn't torturing a suspect until you extract a location, racing against a digital countdown timer strapped to the side of a device in the back of a van, and then waiting until the last second to decide which wire to cut."

A few grins. She can see that they are with her.

"That's a movie. And not even a very good one. That's not what heroes are. You know that. You know that better than anyone. Heroes are people who run down every possible lead, no matter how implausible. Track every dollar, every euro, every fraction of every cryptocurrency. Who spend all day, every day, and even nights and weekends, writing queries every bit as elegant as anything composed by Beethoven and running them across thousands of indices. Heroes are people who don't just hope, or assume, or who are 'pretty sure.' They verify. And then they verify again. And then they get someone else to verify that verification. And if they don't get anywhere, they throw it all out and start all over again because any unexplored path, no matter how seemingly insignificant, could mean thousands of lives."

Everyone is nodding now—everyone but the man who has just entered from the back with two cups of coffee in a cardboard tray. He props up a wall with his shoulder and waits for Van to continue.

"Heroes don't just work for six months, or a year, or two years on a problem. They work for as long as it takes. They work for five years, nine months, and three weeks. They work until someone *makes* them stop, if that's what it takes to absolutely goddamn guarantee that there isn't another sociopath out there about to erase Washington, D.C., or New York City, or Paris, or London."

She pauses to check her slides. Sure enough, there's the Capitol, One World Trade Center, the Eiffel Tower, Big Ben.

"This task force wasn't assembled in response to Seoul. It was assembled in response to a historic mandate. Probably the most important resolution the United Nations has ever passed, and perhaps ever will pass: the denuclearization of the entire planet. And I don't care what any pencil-neck bureaucrat says; supporting *that* mandate, in any capacity whatsoever, is an *honor*."

There is even some verbal assent now.

"When the UN does an audit and finds that *thirty-seven percent* of the world's enriched nuclear material is missing, you take that seriously. You assemble a task force of the finest officers and analysts and support staff on the planet, and you don't disband it until enough time has passed that you know—absolutely *know*—that every single milligram of fissile material is no longer weapons-grade. That whoever bought it or stole it or otherwise came into possession of it and tried to figure out how to make a dirty bomb out of it has either been killed by Mossad, betrayed by their partners, or reduced to piles of protoplasm in some abandoned warehouse somewhere because they didn't know how to handle it."

Van keeps an eye on the guy in the back and some of her staff follow her gaze, turning in their seats. It is Alessandro Moretti. Technically, he's her boss, but these days they function more or less as peers. Moretti's been in and out of the office for over two years—mostly out—working on something highly classified that not even Van knows anything about, so she's been covering for him. Two cups of coffee means he wants something.

"And that's precisely what you did. You did exactly what the agency asked of you. What your *country* asked of you. What the world *needed* from you. And you did it willingly, thoroughly, and with grace."

She watches her team for a moment as she tees up her next line.

"You did it *perfectly*, people. And you know what? I'd do it all over again. Every lead, every meeting, every report"—applause now—

"every interview, every query, every simulation, every model, every dead end, and every single last algorithm. All of it!"

She waits for the applause to subside and notices that a few glistening eyes must be covertly attended to before hands are returned to laps.

"The world owes you its gratitude. Of course, that doesn't mean you're going to get it. That's the nature of what we do. You all know that. You all know what you signed up for. There's not much I can do about that, but I *can* express gratitude on behalf of the CIA. And most sincerely, I can express *my* gratitude. So, thank you. Thank you for showing up every single day. Thank you for not just doing your jobs, but for dedicating your careers and your lives to making the world a safer place. Thank you for sacrificing time with your families. Time you won't get back. Time with your children."

Van's eyes do exactly what she explicitly wills them not to do: land squarely on Senior Analyst Quinn Mitchell. Instantly she regrets what she perceives as calling Quinn out in front of the entire team, but her top analyst gives her a sad, appreciative smile, which Van returns before moving on.

"You are *all*—every single one of you—*my* personal heroes."

This one gets a standing ovation, and it is suddenly painfully obvious to Deputy Director Townes how she should have been doing this all along—how badly her team needed to hear that what they've been doing for the last five years matters. Van still finds it hard to believe that she has the power to instill purpose in others, and she is as afraid of that power today as she was the day she was first promoted to manager. That's called humility, her mother used to tell her. That's just Jesus whispering in your ear, keeping you on your toes. That's a *good* thing, Sunshine. Don't ever lose that.

When it's clear that their boss still has more to say, one by one her team sits back down. Van silently vows that she will never let so much time pass again without telling the people around her how she feels, then moves on to the final phase.

"Some of you have already been reassigned, and some of you are still waiting to hear what's next for you. Some of you will remain with me, and some of you will be blessed with a much kinder boss, and to them, I say congratulations."

She gets the kind of laughter you hear toward the end of a eulogy when someone makes a tension-breaking joke.

"But wherever you go," Van continues, "never forget that working with all of you has been the greatest honor of my career."

There's the final ovation. Van accepts it as long as she can—smiling, nodding, waving to individuals—until she starts feeling like an ego-maniacal politician and takes refuge in packing up her laptop. The applause subsides, transitioning into murmurs and shuffles, but when she picks up her bag and turns, she finds that a queue has formed. A departing line, as it were. The women are ready to wrap her up in long, warm, rocking hugs, and the men awkwardly wait for Townes to initiate physical contact. Quinn Mitchell's hug is especially affection-ate. What Van feared could have been construed as crass or distasteful—the look she inadvertently gave Quinn at the mention of *children*—turned out to be exactly what her star analyst needed. Maybe, Van thinks, our refusal to acknowledge tragedy beyond the cursory is not so much decorum as it is a way to avoid our own dis-comfort. Maybe we end up prolonging others' pain so that we can re-main comfortable inside our own little bubbles. But when tragedy inevitably finds us, and when others treat us with the same perceived civility that we showed them, we too will feel unbearably alone.

Maybe Jesus has once again just whispered in Van's ear.

MORETTI KEPT A respectable distance during the ritual, but now that the last of Van's team has dispersed, he closes in. He offers her his free hand—the one without the two caffeine grenades—as Townes de-scends the stairs at the edge of the stage, and she graciously accepts.

"What a gentleman," Van observes.

"At your service," Moretti replies. He plucks the larger of the two cups from the origami coffee trap and begins enumerating. "Triple. Venti. Half-sweet. Nonfat . . ." It's coming to him . . . "Caramel mac-chiato. I practiced all the way over."

"How the hell do you know my coffee order?"

"Come on. This is the CIA, not the FBI. Give me some credit."

"Ouch. You know my son's at Quantico, right?"

"I remember writing the recommendation. Let me know when he wants to join the winning team."

They are strolling up the aisle toward the back of the auditorium, moving together much more slowly than either would alone.

"I'll be sure to pass that along."

"Beautiful speech, by the way," Moretti says.

"Shut up."

"No, I'm serious. All bullshit aside. When they recruit you, it's all about the action, the adventure, the travel. Nobody tells you that when everyone's doing their jobs the way they're supposed to—when you're being proactive—things are usually pretty quiet. There's plenty of criticism when something goes wrong, but not enough praise when everything goes right."

"Amen to that."

Moretti bodychecks the bar and cracks the door open in a burst of sunshine. Townes walks out beneath the awning into the midday warmth. Although it sounds as though they are surrounded by the trills and warbles of dozens of species of birds, Van knows that most of what they hear is dynamically composed by the avian surveillance drones that are in constant rotation throughout campus, recharging themselves and exchanging data with a covert forest of next-gen signal intercept towers disguised as overly symmetrical evergreens. The synthetic sounds of a CIA summer.

"You still haven't told me what you want," Van says.

Moretti appears wounded. "What makes you think I want something?"

"The coffee. The flattery. The fact that you never come around anymore unless there's something you need."

"I know," Moretti says. "And I'm sorry about that. This thing I'm working on—it's killing me. But it shouldn't be much longer. And I *will* bring you in on it. I promise."

"Like you brought me in on the whole LHC thing?"

"Believe me, I did you a favor with that," Moretti says. "The Epoch Index has been a pain in my ass from the second it landed on my desk. But this new thing's completely different. You'll see. In the meantime, I'm actually here to do *you* a favor."

Townes sees Quinn Mitchell seated on a nearby bench forking something into her mouth from semi-opaque Tupperware. Her only companion is a can of Diet Coke, centered on the one slat flat enough that it won't tip over.

"And what might that be?"

"I'm here to take an analyst off your hands."

"*Ahhh*," Townes intones. "*Now* it all makes sense. Vultures circling to pick at the remains."

Moretti pulls a dubious face. "These are hardly *remains*," he says. "From what I can tell, you somehow managed to keep the best of your team intact."

"Who do you want?"

"Her."

Van wasn't even aware of Moretti having noticed Quinn. Fucking spooks. With anyone else, Townes would have probably sealed the deal right then and there—maybe negotiated a little extra budget or some newer hardware if she was feeling especially shrewd. But Quinn was different.

"What do you want with Mitchell?"

"What do you think I want? I want the best."

"I get that," Van says. "But *why?*"

"You heard of the Elite Assassin?"

It takes Townes a moment to recalibrate. If her memory of recent daily briefings serves, the topic of conversation has casually meandered from internal resource reallocation to bizarre and exotic international serial killers.

"Yeah," she tells Moretti uncertainly. "I heard of him."

"Interpol's got nothing, and they're asking us for an analyst."

"And why do we care about Interpol all of a sudden?"

"The director's got this new mandate around banking favors. Says that's how shit gets done in the private sector."

"How the hell would he know how shit gets done in the private sector? He's been a government employee his entire life. That man was born with coffee on his breath and khakis on his ass."

"Read a book, I guess."

"Anyway," Van continues, "by banking a favor with Interpol, you mean *you're* banking a favor with the *director*, right?"

"Not just me. You too. *And* Mitchell. See? Everyone wins."

Townes watches Quinn sip her Diet Coke and place it back on the slat. She wonders whether the senior analyst has any idea that she's currently being surveilled—that the two of them are standing there casually mapping out her future—and ultimately decides that she does not.

"You know what she's been through, right?"

"I do."

"And you think it's a good idea for her to go from writing queries in a cubicle to chasing a serial killer?"

"What I think," Moretti says, "is that she can catch this guy. *And* I think she needs a win. You know I have nothing but respect for your task force. I do. But you said it yourself back there: the whole thing was kind of a victory by omission. I'm offering her a *real* victory. An *explicit* victory. I'm offering her a chance to save lives—to catch a flesh-and-blood bad guy. I'm offering her this *because* of what she's been through."

Townes wonders how often Quinn eats alone. She wishes now that she'd made more of an effort to connect with her—that she'd invited Quinn out to lunch every now and then, or even over for dinner. She'd meant to, but there was always too much to do. Always an excuse to eat at her desk. The feeling that it wasn't her place. Too many reasons not to have the difficult conversations she knew Quinn needed to have. And now Van realizes that she was almost certainly not alone in her approach—that the rest of the task force probably followed the same pattern: all intention and no action. There must be some part of us that honestly believes tragedy is contagious.

"Why do they call him that?" Townes asks. "The Elite Assassin?"

"You know how he brands his victims?"

"Yeah," Van says. "Serial numbers, right?"

"Not serial numbers. Serial numbers are sequential. These are completely random four-digit numbers. But the first one he used was 1337. And 1337 is internet-culture code for 'leet,' which is short for *elite*."

Van's expression unambiguously conveys her opinion of Moretti's explanation: that that's some seriously dumbass shit.

"It's a nerd thing," Moretti says. "Mitchell'd get it."

"And here I thought it was because he had expensive taste."

"He may very well. I'll be sure to ask once I have him in custody."

"What else do you know about this guy?"

"I know he's one sick fuck. Nineteen bodies so far. Threw some crippled girl off her balcony in Moscow two weeks ago. Then flew to Caracas, broke into some rich hombre's estate, and swapped his nephew's aluminum oxygen tanks for ones with nickel in them the day before he got an MRI."

"I don't get it."

"Aluminum isn't magnetic. Nickle is. Pulled the fucking things right into the machine like a barrage of missiles. Crushed the poor bastard. Put a radiologist in a coma in the process."

Van's eyebrows went up. "Points for creativity, though."

"You have no idea," Moretti says gravely. "I won't even get into Cape Town and Beijing."

"How'd he mark them?"

"Branded the girl's arm somehow. Not sure with what. The guy in the MRI, stenciled his number on the tanks. They . . . left a mark."

"What do all these people have in common?"

"That's just it," Moretti says. "Not a single fucking thing. Most assassins like this carve out a niche for themselves. They specialize in gangsters, or drug lords, or witnesses, or whatever. Politicians, well-insured spouses. *Something*. But not this guy. Either he's killing completely randomly—which, no fucking way—or there's something we're missing."

"Hence the need for an analyst," Townes surmises.

"Bingo," Moretti confirms. "So, what do you say? Think your girl's up for it?"

Townes watches Quinn seal her fork up inside the chicken salad sarcophagus and slide the whole thing into her insulated lunch bag.

"You're not *really* asking me, are you?"

Moretti shrugs. "At least my requests come with coffee."

Van samples the drink she's been holding. It's "dirty coffee"—caffeine bestowed for the purposes of garnering favor—but caffeine is caffeine. And throwing it out won't change Quinn's fate now.

"Did you know, Al, that you have a reputation?"

"What?" Moretti asks innocently. "Me? A reputation for what?"

"For abusing your direct reports."

"Bullshit," Moretti says. "Have I ever abused you?"

"No, because you know I'll give it right back to you. But you're known for being an asshole to junior officers."

"That's because that's what junior officers are for," Moretti says.

"Al . . ."

"Is Quinn a junior officer?"

"Quinn's an analyst."

"Well, is she a *junior* analyst?"

"Not remotely."

"Then she's got nothing to worry about, does she?"

"I want your word that you won't lose your shit around her."

Moretti looks at her over his glasses, which had darkened the moment they stepped out into the sun. "Yes, ma'am," he says. "Any other demands?"

"Yeah," Van says. "I want you to promise me you'll take good care of her. There's something special about that one."

Moretti gives Van what he probably thinks is his most reassuring smile. "You got nothing to worry about," he says. "I won't let her out of my sight."

3

HUNTING FOR PRIME

YŪGEN IS ONE kill away from a million-dollar payday.

She is in L.A., on an old, converted movie studio lot. Room by room, floor by floor, Yūgen is hunting for Prime through the biggest and most advanced v-sports venue on the planet.

Think e-sports, but virtual. Traditional video game tournaments are still played with mechanical keyboards, mice, and vast swaths of plasma glass. V-sports players zip themselves into form-fitting haptic suits, pull carbon-fiber helmets down over their heads, and slap full-face metaspec visors down over their eyes. Strap battery packs onto their backs and light-adapted tactical weapons to their thighs.

Matches take place inside vast physical structures painted entirely chroma-key green with plasma-light strips embedded in the seams and barrel cameras mounted in every corner. Players' views are provided by 120 degrees of ultra-high-definition, one-thousand-hertz plasma screens lining their visors. The feeds the audience sees are the result of knocking out everything green and mapping exotic, photo-realistic environments to invisible unique tracking patterns applied with handheld sprayers.

Maps can be anything from a derelict spacecraft, to a sprawling factory, to a ravaged embassy, to the shattered serenity of a ransacked suburban home. A glittering Las Vegas casino, or the long, austere fuselage of Air Force One. This one is the top three floors of two modern, adjacent office towers joined by a glass catwalk. It's the middle of the night, in a savage and sustained thunderstorm.

Yūgen and her clan came to L.A. from Japan to compete in Black Horizon—the most-watched and highest-stakes v-sports tournament in the world. The American team—comprised mostly of washed-out special ops who grew up buzzing with ADD in small towns with no parents around and skipping school to stream *Call of Duty* all day—dominated the competition bracket. The top players from every round get to compete in what many consider to be the real event: the last-man-standing, winner-take-all, single-spawn Battle Royale.

No teams. No bombs to plant or defuse, and no hostages to rescue. No king of the hill, no skulls to collect, and no flags to capture. The final Black Horizon all-star event is a simple, old-fashioned, high-stakes death match.

The east tower has been cleared. As Yūgen crosses the catwalk, she is blinded by a bright white fractal of lightning followed by a godlike eruption of thunder. The point of the storm is to introduce the equivalent of random flashbang grenades, and to expose snipers camping in shadows. What Yūgen sees ahead of her in the lesser flashes that follow is an obstacle course of dead bodies.

The tunnel between the two towers is an intentional choke point. Yūgen has never played this map herself, but she's studied it by analyzing dozens of past matches, and she knows that, by this point, the floor is always littered with bodies, bullet casings, and gore. Half the glass panels are shattered, and blood is splattered from high-velocity rifle shots and dripping from close-quarter shotgun blasts. There are wisps and tendrils of gun smoke suspended in the still air, which her brain makes her smell even though it is not really there. To her, the bodies are rendered as gruesome and violent urban-assault carnage. But in reality, she is stepping over eliminated players lining a green, brightly lit, plywood-paneled hallway—all of them silently watching the endgame play out either through her eyes or through Prime's.

Yūgen can move through the passage without fear because she now knows exactly where Prime is. Players have maps in the corners of their HUDs, and all in-range motion registers as red dots. Prime took up a position in a corner conference room up ahead, then went dark. Which means he is waiting. He is ahead on kills, so if the match ends with them both alive, he wins. There is no reason for him to risk open confrontation. Prime is doing exactly what Yūgen would do: waiting for her to come to him.

Strategy and location are not all Yūgen knows about Prime. She also knows that he is the top-ranked player in the world; that he makes significantly more in sponsorships than in prize money; that he is left-handed, which throws a lot of opponents off; and that he is a little over eighty kilos and 180 centimeters tall—a nice, broad chest to target and just the right height for a quick, twitchy headshot.

But it is Prime's intelligence that interests Yūgen most. Not necessarily his gameplay, but his former life. Before he became a professional v-sports player, he spent his first few years out of school as a biomedical engineer. Was accused of something that the courts kept sealed—worked out some kind of plea deal. Wealthy parents, an expensive team of attorneys. His handle comes from the fact that he is obsessed with prime numbers. The word PRIME is tattooed, one letter per finger, across his right fist. Across his left, the sequence 76543—one of only two prime numbers with digits in consecutive descending order. Apparently, he believes there is some kind of power in primes. Fundamental, cosmic meaning. Encrypted messages rippling through spacetime.

One minute of gameplay remaining.

Yūgen is at the end of the catwalk. The conference room is to the left, halfway down the hall, opening on the right. But that would mean breaching the room from her weak side. She is capable of firing off both shoulders when she has to, but not against Prime. She knows she would be dead before she could even register his presence.

So she turns right instead. Lowers her rifle and jogs. Circles around so that she can take the conference room from her strong side. She knows she is broadcasting her plan, but she doesn't have a choice.

Only forty seconds left. No time for planning, and no time for tricks. She knows Prime will already have pressure on the trigger the moment she exposes her head, so all she can do is rely on her instincts.

Last corner. She is now right outside the conference room. On her strong side now. Back pressed against the wall. Ten seconds left. She knows that he knows her exact height, and that he will have a headshot all lined up. So she crouches. She will be slightly less steady, but that fraction of a second to readjust could make all the difference.

Nine.

She wishes she had a frag she could bank off a wall and into the room.

Eight.

Or a flashbang. But by this point in the game, if you're alive, you're out of grenades.

Seven.

She can feel her heart through her haptic suit. Hear it in her ears.

Six.

It is beating so hard she knows it could throw off her shot.

Five.

He is probably expecting her to wait for the last second, so she knows she should go now.

Four.

Deep breath. Hold it in. And then a quick pivot.

Two rapid taps at head height shatter glass. She waits for the haptics in her chest or helmet to tell her she's been tagged, but nothing happens. She finds him on the ground, crouched beneath the table, sights all lined up. Motherfucker is playing with her—savoring his victory.

Instinctively, Yūgen drops her muzzle and puts two rounds in his face.

In her ears, the v-sports theme, and a deep, authoritative voice: *GAME OVER. YOU HAVE WON.*

But something is not right. She unlocks her visor, retracts it back up in her helmet, staggers at the context shift from skyscraper at night to bright green surfaces and plasma light. And red. Blood getting dark. Coagulating. Mostly done spreading already. Her first thought is that she somehow killed him, but she immediately readjusts. Knows that's not possible. Feels the other players gather behind her—running up to congratulate her, then stopping. Hears them, but does not understand. Sees the splatter patterns on the wall. Left hand outstretched, assault rifle just out of reach. Entire trigger finger missing, reducing the five-digit number to four.

4

FALSE POSITIVE

ALL THE DEAD bodies on the wall make it hard to concentrate on talking.

Quinn is sitting across from her boss, Vanessa Townes. The floor-to-ceiling sheet of plasma glass to her left is like a macabre mood board of violence and murder. Puffy white fat bursting from an opened throat, eyes wide and terrified. A lean, young, dark male body, hideously crushed, twisted, and disfigured. The impact of a young woman against a city sidewalk, her arms and head askew, two robotic legs detached, one entirely smashed and scattered.

And numbers. All of them four digits. Imprinted on different body parts. Burned, stamped, and carved.

"I'm sorry," Van says. "Do you want me to turn that off?"

"It's fine," Quinn tells her boss. In truth, the collage of carnage is making her nauseous, but she does not like the idea of being coddled. So she focuses on the shattered laptop on a shelf behind her boss, displayed among various service awards. "Did that thing really stop a round from an AK-47?"

"At a very generous angle, as anyone with a background in ballistics is quick to point out," Van says. "But yes, it really did. One thing I've learned in all my years here is that you never know what might end up saving your life."

Quinn smiles. Straightens herself in her chair. Brushes something off her knee that wasn't really there.

"I wanted to thank you," she says.

"For what?"

A subtle gesture to her left. "For getting me out of the whole Elite Assassin thing."

"I didn't so much get you out of it as get someone else into it."

"Who?"

"For the time being," Van says, "you're looking at her. But temporarily. We're still vetting other analysts."

"Well, I appreciate it," Quinn says. "And I also wanted to apologize."

"Quinn—"

"No, I do. I know you wanted me to do it."

"I thought it might have been good for you," Van says. "I still do, to be honest. But that's different from wanting you to do it. I don't want you doing anything you're not ready for, or that you're not comfortable with."

"I just feel like I need something . . . predictable."

"Wouldn't that be nice," Van says. "After everything I've seen in my career, *predictability* is a concept I've given up on."

"Well, more predictable than chasing a serial killer all over the world."

"Fair enough," Van says. "So, what's your plan?"

"Advanced Analytics," Quinn says. She tries to say it with confidence, but she knows it comes out more as an apology.

"Advanced Analytics," Van says. "Your old job before you moved to counter-terrorism, right?"

"But with some management responsibilities," Quinn says. "A team lead."

Van nods in a way that Quinn knows is meant to appear neutral, but that in its excess of objectivity comes across as all the more judgmental.

"What?" Quinn asks.

"Nothing," Van says. "I think that's fine."

"*Fine?*"

"If that's where you feel you need to be at this point in your career, I fully support you."

Quinn has never been anything but deferential toward any of her bosses, but she feels as though she is being provoked. "What exactly do you mean by *at this point in my career?*"

Van shrugs. "I mean that you're, what? Halfway through your career?"

"So?"

"So if you want to spend the second half in Advanced Analytics doing a job you've already done—doing a job you already know you're good at and that, frankly, you can do in your sleep—then I guess that's the right decision."

"It's not *exactly* my old job," Quinn objects. "I'll be a team lead."

"Sorry," Van says, though she does not sound it. "My mistake."

"You make it sound like Advanced Analytics isn't important. This agency couldn't function without them."

"But they can function without you," Van says.

"What's that supposed to mean?"

"It means when you retire, do you want to look back at your career and realize you spent it doing a job any number of other people could do? Or do you want to retire knowing that you did something only *you* could've done?"

"Like what?" Quinn asks. "What can only *I* do?"

"That's up to you, isn't it?"

"No, seriously," Quinn says. "No more bullshit, Vanessa. Tell me what you think I should do."

"It doesn't matter what I think."

"It does to me."

"Why?"

"Because I respect your opinion. Because . . ." Quinn hesitates, then commits to what she wants to say. "Because I don't have anyone else to talk this through with. Because all I have are my own obnoxious, self-pitying, exhausting thoughts, and to be perfectly honest, I haven't exactly been a very good advocate for myself over the last few years."

"Quinn, I'm the one who should be apologizing to you," Van says.

"For what?"

"For not being there. Through everything."

"That's not your job," Quinn says. "And you *were* there."

"Not like I should have been. Not like I *wish* I'd been."

"Well, good news," Quinn says. "You can be here for me now. You can tell me what to do."

Van leans back in her chair. "You really want to know what I think?"

"*Yes*," Quinn says. "I want you to be completely honest."

Van's eyes drop momentarily to her laptop as she gathers her thoughts. But before she can begin, something changes on the plasma glass wall, and Quinn can't stop herself from looking.

"What is that?" she asks.

It is a man's hand. Index finger severed. Numbers tattooed, but in relief: black blocks with flesh-colored digits. A bright green background. Not as much blood as Quinn would have thought. Probably bled out from somewhere else.

"I'm sorry," Van says. She leans forward and snatches the remote off its cradle. "Let me turn this damn thing off."

"Wait," Quinn says. "It's six."

Van's thumb hovers above the inductive surface. "What is?"

"The number on the missing finger," Quinn says. "It's six."

"We figured," Van says. "It fits the sequence. Some kind of countdown."

"It's not a countdown."

"How do you know?"

"Why would a countdown start at seven and go down to three?"

"Tattoos are a very personal form of expression," Van says. "Who knows what kind of meaning it might have."

"Exactly," Quinn says. "They *are* very personal, and it *does* have meaning, but it's not a countdown. It's a prime."

"A prime," Van repeats. "As in number?"

"One of only two with digits in consecutive descending order."

"Interesting," Van observes. "What's the other?"

"Forty-three."

"Huh."

"Who is this?"

"Not sure yet. Just came over the wire this morning. Probably a false positive."

"What do you mean?"

Van places the remote back into the cradle's magnetic grasp, then checks her laptop.

"It got swept up by the case bot because of the numbers, but they were already there, so I seriously doubt our guy's responsible."

"Who killed him, then?"

"Coroner's calling it some kind of deranged self-mutilation-slash-suicide."

"Why?"

"Because he was in the last place on the planet anyone could possibly be murdered."

"Where?"

"In the middle of a v-sports arena," Van says. "Surrounded by hundreds of cameras. With millions of people watching. Live."

Quinn stands and walks toward the wall. The other images have scaled and stacked themselves to make room for the new evidence.

"Why is the background green?"

"Chroma-key. Green screen. The players wear VR headsets, but the audience wants to see the action from a third-person perspective, not first-person. So they play in these huge arenas that are painted entirely green so everything but the players can be replaced with a virtual environment."

"Everything green becomes invisible," Quinn says.

"Exactly."

"And everyone inside is wearing a headset."

"Right."

"Then that's how he did it," Quinn says.

"What do you mean?"

"That's how he committed the murder. If everything green is invisible to everyone outside the arena, and everyone inside the arena is essentially blind to everything except what's being rendered for them, all the killer had to do was put on a green suit, and he'd be a ghost."

"A green suit?"

"Something full-body. Something the same shade as the walls. Like they use in movies."

"Holy shit," Van says. "But why go to all that trouble? Why not just kill him at home?"

"I don't know," Quinn admits. "Where did he live?"

"Let me check." Van pulls her laptop closer and begins typing. "In L.A."

"Where in L.A.?"

"Hollywood. *Huge* house. The guy was loaded."

"We're talking about a professional gamer here, right?"

"That's right."

"And he lived in a huge house in Hollywood."

"A damn mansion."

Quinn's eyes narrow. "He didn't live alone, did he?"

Back to the laptop.

"This can't be right," Van says. "I'm showing twenty-two other residents."

"That was his clan."

"His what?"

"His clan. If v-sports is anything like e-sports, he probably lived with his team. He would have been constantly surrounded by friends. People streaming on social media. The only place the Elite Assassin could possibly get to him was during a match. The only way to kill him without being seen by anyone was to do it in front of everyone."

"OK," Van concedes, "but what about the tattoos?"

"What about them?"

"How can they be the mark of the Elite Assassin if they were already there?"

"Why risk the ambiguity of having two numbers on one body? And why waste valuable time tagging when all you have to do to turn a five-digit number into a four-digit number is cut off a finger?"

"So, you think our guy did this," Van says.

"I think we have to assume he did it until we can prove otherwise. If we don't, we could be missing something key."

Once again, Van leans back in her chair. This time she is smiling.

"What?" Quinn wants to know.

"*We?*"

5

HOMELESSNESS

THE FATHER OF modern Estonian cybergrime is Otto "Kron" Hammer, and his favorite places to play are the intimate converted cinemas throughout the Arabian Peninsula. The entire Middle East has gone mad for any kind of crunchy coldwave dubstep or acid jazz trip-hop with liquid neurofunk freestyle layered in, so they treat him like a god. Sohar is Kron's most frequent stop since, as the famous saying goes, you cannot spell "woman" without spelling "Oman."

He is in the most expensive suite in the best hotel in Sohar, sitting up in a sumptuous four-poster bed, watching a coquettish aspiring model named either Mira or Dona indulge him in his nascent yoga fetish. She is wearing a white and silver long-sleeve bikini-cut number that they bought in the lobby on their way up, along with the mat on which she currently stands in a firmly planted Tree Pose. The suspended bronze gong standing against the wall was borrowed from the hotel's sanctuary.

As requested, Mira-Dona's lacquer-black hair is not pulled back, nor coiled into a bun, nor otherwise restrained in a way that would be practical for working out. Instead, it spills down over her shoulders so that it can blanket her breasts and drape luxuriously over her sharp shoulder blades and sweep over the mat when she bends. The motion of a woman's hair is to Kron what, to a drunk, is the clink and burble of the day's first drink.

But his attention is abruptly drawn past the erotic tableau at the foot of the bed and into the suite's marbled foyer. He has been in plenty of hotel rooms where people have tried to enter unannounced, but it has never happened this late, and certainly never on the top floor. Whatever they're doing to get into the room, it seems more mechanical than digital, because all the locks slide, rotate, and pop without so much as the beep of a keycard.

Kron ensures that he is covered enough that any paparazzi photos won't have to be censored (nobody looks good with pixelated junk), but not so covered that people might assume he was already asleep. Through squinty eyes and between the widely spread fingers of an outstretched hand ready to deflect strobes, he is surprised to register the interloper not as a gaggle of reporters, but as Tariq, the hotel manager. Behind Tariq, a platoon of housekeeping ninjas is already dispersing.

"*Tariq?*" Kron shrieks. He is not so much angry as confused. "What the *fuck's* going on?"

Miraculously, Mira-Dona has continued to hold her impeccable pose. Hotel personnel swarm about her like a flash flood around the ancient, deeply rooted tree she has become spiritually.

"My apologies, Mr. Kron," Tariq begins, not very apologetically, "but you must leave this hotel at once."

"What? Why? What's wrong?"

"There is nothing wrong, per se," Tariq replies. "Sadly, we have no other vacancies, so there is a car on its way prepared to take you anywhere in Sohar you wish to go. At our expense, of course."

"What did I do?" He looks at Mira-Dona, trying to detect some resemblance. "She's not your daughter, is she? Fuck, bro. How was I supposed to know?"

"She is not," Tariq reassures him. And then not very reassuringly: "You have two minutes to vacate this room or you will be removed by force."

Not all of the hotel manager's crew are there to tidy up and dust, Kron notes. There are two men stationed at the canopy bed's posts who look more than up to the task of showing him the door. Mira-

Dona leans to the side, transitioning into a Half-Moon Pose, seemingly entirely unbothered by the unexpected direction her evening has taken.

"This contingency was explained to you when you selected this suite, was it not?"

Some kind of bizarre disclaimer solemnly dispensed by Tariq begins coming back to Kron just as his head is wrapped in the salmon cardigan he left neatly folded on the dresser. It was flung by a third henchman and is closely followed by his stretch-denim leggings, which, this time, Kron is quick enough to catch. He dips beneath the blankets and does not reemerge until he is fully dressed.

At which point the room has been further transformed. There are tripods positioned throughout, each topped by buzzing fixtures producing what Kron mistakes for some kind of freaky mood lighting but is in fact ultraviolet germicidal irradiation emanating from low-pressure mercury-vapor tubes. Tariq is now bedside, offering Kron the same disposable wraparound sunglasses everyone else in the room is already wearing, including Mira-Dona, who has finally concluded her workout and is hugging the shopping bag from downstairs, presumably containing the eveningwear she arrived in. Kron's case is packed and awaiting him in the foyer, ready to faithfully follow its master on its tiny casters like an excited puppy, and a masked housekeeper is standing on a stepladder, vigorously sanitizing the top shelf of the closet.

Kron's Arabic is for shit, but between the bed and the door, he picks up on a pattern.

"What are they talking about?" he asks Mira-Dona. "What the bloody fuck does *ranveer* mean?"

"Ranveer is a man," Mira-Dona says. She has stopped to put on her heels, and Kron inadvertently takes careful note of their effect on her ass beneath her bikini bottom.

"Well then, *who* the fuck is Ranveer? And what the fuck gives him the right to take my room?"

"He isn't taking your room," Mira-Dona says. She seems not the least bit self-conscious about her attire—or lack thereof—as the two of them are herded into the suite's private elevator. "You took his."

RANVEER IS THE richest homeless man in the world. He is homeless because the tools of his trade are nicely portable, and his work encourages him to be mobile. He is rich because he gets paid enormous sums to solve the kinds of problems that manifest themselves as people.

He is a tall, slender, sinewy man who has never eaten a piece of meat in his life, and although you would never use the word "muscular" to describe him, you somehow know he could rip a Tokyo telephone book in half given the proper motivation. He wears his receding hairline with grace and elegance, and his heavy chevron mustache curls so naturally and impeccably down over the corners of his upper lip that it is hard to believe he was not born with it. His black eyes somehow portray both congeniality and malice simultaneously, and have a tendency to make the people who endure his stare suddenly wish that they could be elsewhere.

This evening, Ranveer is traveling from L.A. to Sohar, Oman. From the time he leaves his room on one end and starts unpacking on the other, he will not open a door, wait in a line, or lift a single case. The hotel and the airline have arranged everything, and even in an increasingly complex, chaotic, and unpredictable world, he is fully confident that there will be no mistakes.

He only flies Emirates Airlines. If Emirates doesn't provide regular service to a city where he needs to be—or if it is not possible to charter a private supersonic jet through Emirates Executive—he does not need to be there. He only stays in properties owned and operated by Crystal Collective Worldwide. If CCW doesn't have a resort, hotel, or timeshare in close proximity to his destination, then it's road-trip time. Ranveer understands the meaning of brand loyalty, and he expects that loyalty to go both ways.

CCW has a suite in every location designated just for him. If the property is entirely full, and if you are willing to be extorted out of three times the posted rate to stay in Ranveer's reserved quarters, you do so with the understanding that you may be thrown out onto the street at any moment, whether you happen to be sleeping, showering, or shagging. Doesn't matter if you're a politician, executive, or rock star. There won't even be so much as a knock or the beep of a keycard. The door will simply be thrown open, and then you, your groupies, and your things will all be on your way out by the shortest possible route. This is solemnly explained to you by the manager on duty before you biometrically authenticate. Once you are gone, the room will be reset and, as part of a smoothly executed ultraviolet germicidal irradiation operation, slow-baked under low-pressure mercury-vapor tubes. Finally, Ranveer's cases will be brought in, and the most beautiful woman currently on staff will either lounge on a divan or sit primly on the end of the four-poster bed, wearing a combination of her very best smile and her most fitted uniform—one or two extra buttons undone.

But it isn't the service at CCW properties that Ranveer values most, or even their emphasis on charm, elegance, and aesthetics when hiring, all the way up the line from housekeeping to senior management. It is the fact that the staff is trained not to ask questions—and more importantly, when the wrong people come calling, not to respond.

At the airport, Ranveer is personally escorted to his GoldCoach suite situated deep in Sultan Class territory by a nervous airline executive who appears less familiar with the luxuries of the 797 than Ranveer is. The bumbling oaf bumps his head both coming and going, and his hair cream leaves an unsightly smudge on the bulkhead, which a flight attendant must dispatch with a rigorous buff. The eye roll she throws Ranveer's way, and the genial smile with which it is received, convey their tacit agreement that her boss is not long for the world of the employed.

The suite and its private lavatory contain separate plasma glass displays on which someone from Boeing-Comac is taking the opportunity to personally thank Ranveer for his patronage. While in the air,

Ranveer enjoys a spicy egg curry with two bottles of mineral water while he scours three different news networks in an attempt to stay one step ahead of the constant global unrest. A cognac accompanies the checking of cricket scores (more ball tampering by the bloody Australians), after which Ranveer dims the lights, converts his heated, antimicrobial, silicone-infused memory foam seat into a luxurious berth, then sleeps soundly for the rest of the flight, his mechanically stabilized suite impervious to turbulence, chop, and bumps.

RANVEER'S DRIVER IS entirely for show—a chauffeur in designation only, since it is illegal for humans to operate any type of vehicle anywhere in the Sultanate of Oman. But the position still exists because the wealthy never tire of demonstrating that they can afford to pay the less affluent simply to be present. And because, in this part of the world, interacting with unfamiliar AIs is considered beneath anyone of sufficient stature. It is not unlike the attendants you frequently see in Middle Eastern airports: if you pay close enough attention, you will notice that the dense flock of smart cases never follows the man whose belongings they contain, but rather an underling whose sole job it is to imprint upon their primitive neural networks and shepherd them from one entourage to the next.

In the back of the white Range Rover, Ranveer removes his metaspecs from an inside pocket of his jacket, unfolds them, then fits the wide, iridescent displays in place. The frames are a satin-finished rose gold, and the lenses—three layers of laminated, synthetic-sapphire waveguides—are connected at the bridge, where etched optical channels just perceptibly glitter. Each wide, tapered, ivory-white temple is thick enough to house a battery, plasma light source, camera, bone-conduction speaker, and the silicon required to drive it all, but thin enough that the whole rig still qualifies as a stylish accessory rather than a cumbersome, conspicuous peripheral.

From the opposite pocket, Ranveer plucks his handset, which detects the presence of his specs and redirects its output accordingly.

None of his messages contain codes indicating that anything has gone wrong, so Ranveer decides that the job in Oman is still on.

He is surprised to find that the hotel's copious open entrance is not air-conditioned today—even in anticipation of his arrival. Luxury, he has always believed, is an all-or-nothing proposition. It is supposed to be an impenetrable façade—a backdrop against which we can convincingly play the people we want the world to believe we are. Characters whose scripts have been stripped of disgrace and mistakes. Luxury is a type of meta-diversion designed to help us forget about all the things we had to do in order to obtain it in the first place.

But Ranveer also knows that it is the little things that foretell shifts in the balance of power and money throughout the world, and although he would certainly prefer not to glisten on his way into the lobby, he knows that it is precisely these dynamics that will always ensure a need for people like him. As oil-rich nations who cannot even begin to conceive of a world where their obscene wealth is not preordained continue to face the realities of a renewable energy economy, chaos and confusion and ultimately bloodshed are as inevitable as the winds, tides, sunrises, and the perpetual turn of the hydro-powered turbines that faithfully forecast their demise.

The manager of the Al Hujra Hotel, Tariq al-Fasi Hashem, greets Ranveer warmly in the lobby, and Ranveer thinks highly enough of the man to shake his hand and inquire briefly after his family. Such titans of the hospitality industry have an especially difficult balance to strike, as they must make their guests feel exceptional by receiving them personally while ensuring that they safeguard their own stations in life by subsequently delegating the more remedial tasks to assistants. Once the orderly exchange of pleasantries is complete, Tariq snaps his fingers, thereby decreeing that Ranveer is now officially in the care of a plump, second-tier manager. The young man expertly neglects to relieve Ranveer of his attaché; everyone in high-end hospitality knows that one of the keys to successfully accompanying a powerful man to his room without losing your job in the process is knowing exactly which bags he wishes never to see and which he will not let out of his sight.

Keycards are quaint anachronisms by CCW standards. As part of the check-in process, most guests are content with facial recognition systems. But not Ranveer. For him, it is an old-fashioned, short-range RFID card or nothing. He has accepted that being anything other than a recluse means being recorded almost everywhere you go, but that doesn't mean he won't take reasonable precautions—even if it means paying a premium for obsolete technology—to ensure that he does not leave legally admissible, biometric evidence behind. The proliferation of mass surveillance has spawned all manner of innovative and lucrative new industries, not the least of which is the art of avoiding it.

An austere man in a long white *thawb* and a black-banded headdress stands between Ranveer's party and the bank of elevators, a fully grown, mottled, hooded falcon perched on his thickly gloved arm. Both man and bird appear to be guarding an ornate and overburdened luggage cart. The assistant manager is momentarily stymied, then settles on a path that would have led his guest far afield had Ranveer not already plotted his own course. Instead of avoiding the spectacle, he approaches the raptor and her handler directly, correctly identifying the species and asking her name. *Sawt Alraed.* Arabic for the rumble of thunder. Some sort of fraternalism passes between the two men—the strong, silent bond of the hunter.

6

DOWNSIZING

FIVE YEARS AGO, when Quinn moved from the Office of Advanced Analytics to work under Vanessa Townes on the Nuclear Terrorism Nonproliferation Task Force, she filled seven file boxes. Today, as she moves upstairs to work on an unnamed special project led by Van's boss, Alessandro Moretti, she only needs four.

The difference is pictures. Three boxes' worth are now sealed in a plastic bin inside a low-cost, long-term storage unit out in Chantilly, Virginia, along with most of the rest of her past. Everyone reaches a time in their lives when they begin downsizing, Quinn knows, but that time is not supposed to be your late thirties. And the objects you shed are supposed to be superfluous purchases and accumulated gifts, not photos of everyone who once gave your life purpose.

As she unpacks various laser-etched acrylic acknowledgments that the CIA prefers to bestow in lieu of raises, bonuses, or even Amazon gift cards, it occurs to Quinn that she is glad to be away from the tele-therapy room. When she was downstairs, she could see it every time she refocused her vision through her plasma glass monitor—right there between Hammerstein's open mouth, blank stare, and douchey spiky hair and Teresa Moore's ass since she converted from an exercise ball to an obnoxiously loud treadmill desk. It is just opposite the Mothers' Room, where, long ago, Quinn frequently absconded to relieve the pressure in her breasts.

Back then, Quinn and her husband, James Claiborne, were textbook nine-to-five spies. They commuted together from the subdued and affluent suburbs of Potomac Falls, Virginia, where every structure that wasn't a mall was a data center; where weekend barbecues were staged by couples who had been reduced to birthday sex and who, when you asked them what they did for a living, replied simply that they "worked for the government"—a euphemism for "you don't have sufficient clearance to know how I spend my days, but if I wanted, I could pull up chats of your wife flirting with her ex-boyfriends on Facebook and then your marriage would be every bit as loveless as mine. Nice to meet you, too." Most conversations were redirected toward the constant antics of overprivileged, hyperactive, social-media-obsessed children, impassioned prognostication around whatever sports were in season, the work being done by dubious, sporadic, and incompetent contractors on one's egregiously overpriced single-family colonial (made all the more infuriating by the dogmatic regime of the HOA), whatever shows everyone was watching that you weren't because *how do people have so much time to watch so much TV?*, and, surreptitiously, whoever's weight had noticeably fluctuated (preferably increased) since they last gathered.

Quinn and James dropped their daughter, Molly, off at daycare in the mornings on their way into Langley, ate dinner together almost every night, and on weekends, when the yard work was done and the minivan was washed, went to the playground, or for a bike ride, or to the mall. Maybe the occasional Pixar movie, or birthday party inside a giant padded jungle gym in a nearby industrial park. Once a year, they went to Disney World in Florida or rented a house at Lake Anna, and at least three times a year, they played with the idea of trying for a second child. Quinn was not what you would call classically attractive, and she was always at least ten pounds away from a weight she imagined her father approving of, but she had long, natural blond hair that other women squandered vast resources attempting to emulate, and she had a shape and perkiness to her that drew plenty of looks when she was out walking or bending down to scoop up a pile of leaves. For years, Quinn and her husband defied the conventional wisdom that spies could not stay married by carving out a successful and predictable domestic existence that was the envy of many of their colleagues and friends.

But when Molly drowned in a neighbor's pool, and when Quinn and her husband found they could not stop blaming both themselves and each other, it was clear that they would finally become the statistic they thought they would never be. There was a sudden and savage hatred between them that neither had the energy to explore or even try to understand, and they knew that the only way to survive and to move forward was to do so alone. They sold the house, and Quinn found an apartment in Arlington. Her work became the centerpiece of her life, sustained by the perpetual cycle of grocery shopping, laundry, boxes of wine, and antidepressants. She used her CIA discount to buy a subcompact 9mm Glock that she hoped would make her feel safe living alone, and in the evenings, she sometimes imagined what the end of it would taste like, and wondered if the slide would break her teeth as it cycled in a new round and ejected a smoking cartridge out onto the unvacuumed carpet of her empty apartment.

They did try at first, Quinn and James. They couldn't afford out-of-network marriage counseling, so they signed up for weekly teletherapy sessions. Several different contractors provided the service, but they all worked the same way: cardboard coasters with dynamic-projection-mapping markers were placed on furniture inside spaces equipped with position-tracking cameras. Metaspecs were donned, various parties connected, and for the next fifty-minute hour, rooms were transformed into individual or group therapy sessions.

You tended to get a different facilitator each time. It was like calling Comcast customer support: random representatives, exact same scripts. In their last session, the one that came up was from Kentucky. For some reason, Quinn always wanted to know where the facilitator was located. Without fail, the rote answer was, "While I appreciate your interest, we are here to talk about you," which was usually enough for her to be able to place the accent. Quinn's husband was joining from Southern California, where he was on long-term assignment, and she still remembers the artifacts around his arm and fingers as he kept checking his watch.

Quinn can't remember what they were discussing, but she very clearly remembers breaking down, sobbing, and putting her hands over her metaspecs until she eventually started wondering if maybe she'd been disconnected. But when she opened her eyes and looked up, she saw that the man in front of her was observing her with poorly concealed discomfort, probably wishing he could go back to the good old days of working with opioid addicts and meth heads, and the man beside her—the man she'd married thirteen years ago and shared a life and a child with—was intently studying and plucking a fingernail. When the facilitator eventually asked her husband how it felt to see his wife so upset, her husband described having what amounted to an out-of-body experience, which the facilitator promptly labeled as "dissociation." As he went on to describe the phenomenon as a mild to moderate detachment from one's immediate surroundings and a type of psychological defense mechanism against various forms of stress, conflict, or trauma, Quinn began to realize that they were colluding to put her outburst behind them as quickly as possible because it made them uncomfortable—*them*—and that nobody had any intention whatsoever of trying to comfort her. Finally, she tapped the red X on the plasma glass panel, pulled off her metaspecs, and confirmed what, by then, she already knew to be true: despite the tricks metaspecs and telepresence can play on your brain, and even though her husband was dutifully playing the couples-therapy game, the reality was that Quinn was completely alone in her pain.

She spent the remainder of the hour in the teletherapy room asking herself questions like who had she become and what had she done to deserve everything that was happening to her. But most of all, she wanted to know why she was not worth fighting for. Why nobody ever seemed to be on her side. Not her mother when her father told her she needed to lose weight. Not her father when her mother told her she was embarrassed by Quinn's grades, and that nobody would want to date someone with her complexion. Neither of them when her brother stole money from her, or called her an ugly fat bitch, or even pushed her up against a wall more than once. Not her husband when she needed him to tell her that he did not blame her for Molly. Not even a therapist who, during one of her most vulnerable moments, seemed to want to comfort her husband instead of her. That was the moment Quinn realized that the only person who would ever love her more than anyone else in the world was, at only seven years old, already dead.

By the time the session timed out, Quinn had decided that her soon-to-be-ex-husband was not the only one capable of making major life changes. The next day, she applied for an open position as an operations officer with the newly formed Nuclear Terrorism Nonproliferation Task Force. Maybe James was distracting himself from death and divorce by shooting down Chinese-built stealth drones carrying narcotics across the Mexican border, but she was going to do something even more hardcore.

Quinn was going to stop nuclear wars.

NINETEEN BODIES ATTRIBUTED to the Elite Assassin so far. Twenty counting the yet-to-be-confirmed murder in L.A. And, Quinn has been warned, there are likely to be more.

She is still going through case files, briefings, and autopsy reports, but Quinn has already noticed that the majority of the deaths were caused by projectiles of various calibers, which no ballistics experts have yet been able to identify. A few of the fatalities were the result of exotic elements like polonium-210 or toxic nerve agents like VX, sarin, and an especially deadly Russian chemical weapon known as Novichok. Throats slit by an uncharacteristically acute blade, strangulation, and falls from high places make up most of the miscellany. And, of course, there was the poor kid who suffered "blunt trauma to the neck and head"—medical-speak for getting crushed to death by oxygen tanks inside an MRI.

Although there is no obvious correlation between victims, there is one element that ties them all together: the four-digit numbers carved, branded, or otherwise indelibly imprinted somewhere on all the bodies. The chest, the forehead, across the back. On a cheek or down the thigh. The severing of a finger to turn five digits into four. They are clearly meant to be tags of some sort that the killer (or *killers*—Quinn has not ruled out the possibility of some sort of assassination syndicate) uses to communicate.

There is also the alert that flashes persistently in the notification pane of her favorite graphical query tool, which, when expanded, points out that each victim is younger than the last. Some by several years, others just by months. It is as though the dead have been sorted in descending chronological order. Quinn has wondered if the victims' ages factor into some sort of code or otherwise point toward a motive, though neither her own analyses nor those of the myriad convolutional neural networks to which she has access suggest any meaningful patterns.

If age is somehow significant, it must also correspond to location—zip code (or the local equivalent thereof), country code, latitude and longitude—something position-based, since there is clearly no need to travel all over the world to find people who were born on designated days. In a college statistics course, Quinn learned about the "birthday problem," which states that you only need 70 randomly chosen people to have a 99.9 percent chance of two of them having been born on the same day. To reach a 50/50 split, you need as few as 23. Even if you entirely dismiss statistics, it only takes 367 people to guarantee that at least two of them will have the same birthday (including February 29), which, in a city like Beijing, may be repeated as many as ten times in a single residential building. Even if the code required higher chronological resolution, there are more people in cities like Shanghai now than there are seconds in a year.

Death is as common in CIA investigations as root canals are in dentistry, but Quinn has largely been able to keep her distance from it. It's one thing to factor homicides into an investigation, but actually investigating those homicides is an entirely different proposition. She does not want to scan corpses, compare the details of coroner reports, and generate real-time 3D models of brutal murders. Watch them over and over again for something someone might have missed, panning, zooming, and scrubbing backwards and forwards like morbid, silent slapstick. Analyze the necrobiome—the microbes and the scavengers and the insects that feast on decaying corpses, which can be used to determine the time and location of death. Measure blood-spray patterns and use neural networks to infer murder weapons by feeding the models close-up captures of pale, cavernous wounds.

But most of all, Quinn does not want to interview the parents of the dead and watch them cover their mouths and see their eyes well up as the reality of the worst thing that has ever happened to them hits them all over again. She knows what it is like to have every moment of every day tainted by death, and all she wants to do is keep moving into the future. Keep accumulating time into neat, orderly stacks shaped by routine. Keep herself distracted with anything at all that can drown out the excruciating whispers of her past.

But that moment back in Van's office (which she now suspects her former boss of meticulously orchestrating) was undeniable. Something inside of her suddenly and unexpectedly aligned. Even though all the images of death had started to make her feel sick, once she was able to distance herself and see them as evidence—intricate and complex puzzle pieces rather than people—something clicked. Quinn now believes there is some part of her she does not yet know that has yet to be brought to the surface and exposed.

She places the last of the laser-etched plastic slabs on the top shelf of her new cubicle. Quinn has tried throwing these trinkets away on no fewer than two separate occasions, and both times, she turned back and fished them out of the trash before she even made it to the elevator. She tried storing them in the back of a file drawer, but the next day, she dug them out and placed them back up on her shelf. There is something about them that Quinn hates, but the reality is that they are all she has to show for her career. And, in a way, her entire life. The little money she makes is mostly gone as soon as it comes in, her marriage is over, and her baby is thirty minutes away in Fairfax

Memorial Park, buried beneath a praying stone angel—one of three adjacent plots she and James bought, anticipating the day they would be reunited. But while people begin decomposing almost immediately, acrylic takes anywhere between one thousand and five thousand years to decay. Which means, unless Quinn can catch the Elite Assassin and save at least one life, cheap plastic keepsakes may be all she leaves behind.

7

TOOLS OF THE TRADE

RANVEER STANDS BESIDE the orchid blooms in the foyer of his suite, enjoying the lingering floral notes and citric sting of perfume. He was not surprised to find the most beautiful woman currently on staff waiting for him in his room, but he was somewhat surprised by her attire. Her crimson and gold-embroidered traditional Omani robe left everything but her curly black hair, glossy red lips, and matching cherry toenails to the imagination. Which is precisely where she now firmly resides.

But if Ranveer still intends to get in a swim, a sonic vitamin soak, a Thai massage, both a manicure and a pedicure, a light meal, and a twenty-minute power nap before going to work, he had better stop reminiscing about the sexual prowess and inhibitions of Omani women and start thinking about settling in. He has always hated the boorish and juvenile adage that you cannot spell "woman" without spelling "Oman," yet there it is.

He always does his own unpacking lest the staff stumble upon something they find objectionable, and since all of his clothing is custom-cut, heat-welded, wrinkle-free nanofabric (fully compatible with in-room, waterless, ultraviolet sanitizing machines—in his line of work, one is bound to encounter stains), there is no need to iron. Once every scrap of clothing he owns other than what is currently on his slender, well-defined back is neatly hung, he stows his garment case on the dust-free top shelf of the closet, then turns his attention to the tools of his trade.

He lays a thoroughly scarred titanium alloy case (lined with tightly woven polyethylene fiber so that it may double as an impromptu ballistic shield should the need unexpectedly arise) on the bed and presses his thumbs against twin sensors positioned on either side of the handle. After a pattern of green strobes complete their quick biometric sniff, the latches release, indicating that the high-resolution scans match Ranveer's epidermal ridges, and that the measured blood flow and temperature are consistent with digits that have not been severed.

In the event that anything was dislodged from its foam cocoon during travel, Ranveer raises the lid with the caution and attention of an explosive ordnance disposal technician. Nothing appears amiss, and entombed inside are the individual components of what Ranveer maintains is the most magnificent and elegant weapon ever conceived.

The gas gun is complex, but complexity enables configurability, configurability yields flexibility, and flexibility is the hallmark of any good assassin. Compare it to a conventional pistol: A nine- or a ten-millimeter round will always be a nine- or a ten-millimeter round. Its bore, grain, propellant, jacket, and primer are all determined at the time of its manufacturing, and that's all it will ever be. Put a ten-millimeter cartridge into a ten-millimeter pistol, and you are going to do ten millimeters' worth of damage. No more, no less. How does that saying go? If your only tool is a .50 caliber, Israeli-made Desert Eagle, suddenly everything looks like it needs a very big hole?

Which, of course, everything does not. Sometimes it is desirable to kill a man with a projectile that does not even pierce the skin. An object sufficiently slow and dense can bounce right off that magical spot at the intersection of eyes, nose, and forehead, crushing the sinuses and fracturing the skull, leaving a man every bit as dead as if you'd taken his head clean off, yet with much less mess. The cab driver in Nairobi, for instance. As Ranveer leaned forward between the seats so he could reach the dark, clean-shaven cheek, he noted that the man did not even bleed—externally, at least—but rather had perfectly clear cerebrospinal fluid draining from his ears and nose, and raccoon-like black eyes already starting to show.

Other times, in close-quarter situations—say, when you are effectively invisible and standing directly in front of your mark, amused by the fact that he is wielding a very capable-looking assault rifle that fires only light—a big-bore, frangible round is very much in order: tightly packed metal powder bound with wax and designed specifically for breaching things like haptic suits and chest cavities without the risk of exiting through the back and penetrating a thin plywood wall.

A third classic gas gun configuration is what is known in the business as the micro-meteor: an incredibly tiny, very high-velocity, extremely hot projectile that pierces the heart or the brain so quickly that it is usually mistaken for a headache or indigestion until the triggerman is enjoying a scone and a cup of tea three blocks away. Later, when you break into the chap's flat to leave your tag, you can see that he died relatively peacefully with a wet washcloth across his forehead and prescription painkillers spilling from a bottle that slipped from his stiff fingers. When coroners can't find any blood and have to use a digital caliper to measure cauterized entrance and exit wounds of less than a millimeter in diameter, nobody even bothers looking for the slug.

There are those in Ranveer's business who swear by the virtues of minimalism—who insist that simplicity is the ultimate sophistication. But Ranveer suspects that they are merely simpletons who tragically lack imagination. By decoupling targeting, payload, propulsion, and ignition, the gas gun becomes not just a weapon, but an implement for challenging and provocative artistic expression.

The model Ranveer commissioned from a contact in Germany accepts six different muzzles of six different bores. The propellant is a cartridge of hydrogen gas, which is used to fill a chamber to the desired pressure and is then ignited by a spark produced by a small rechargeable battery. Ammunition can be anything from a rubber pellet to a chunk of depleted uranium to buckshot to a needle laced with a suitably exotic and nasty neurotoxin. Need a long-range laser sight? *Click.* Need a military-grade, infrared scope for painting warm targets through walls? *Click.* How about depth-sensing radar combined with a real-time, false-color visual to help pinpoint weak seams in body armor? *Click* and *click.* All depends on the job.

Ranveer takes the hydrogen cartridge assembly into the master bathroom and begins attaching the silicone hose to the sink. Emirates will allow disassembled gas-powered weapons in the belly of a plane without asking questions, but only if the hydrogen cartridges are empty. That means one of the first things he is tasked with upon reaching a new destination is procuring some hydrogen, and the easiest place to find hydrogen is in water. Once the feeder tube is secured, Ranveer opens the faucet and, satisfied that there are no leaks, selects the right adapter and plugs the rig into the wall. Over the next two hours, the device will use electrolysis to dissociate the hydrogen and oxygen atoms and fill the two docked cartridges with enough gas to get him into and out of just about any conceivable situation.

The next item unpacked and strategically positioned for quick access is what appears to be a simple sheathed blade but, like everything Ranveer covets, is much more than it seems. The knowledge to forge Damascus steel is thought to have been lost in the eighteenth century, but you simply need to know where to look. With the right contacts in India or Sri Lanka, it is possible to purchase a beautifully banded and mottled weapon of between 5 and 180 centimeters in length that converges along a nanometer-scale surface and is strong enough to peel the edge off most other blades like slicing the wax off a brandy bottle's seal. It's true that in an age of cheap synthetic diamonds and prolific laser technology, it is not *technically* the most menacing hand-to-hand, close-quarter implement one can buy, but Ranveer has a soft spot for tradition.

His leather-bound pocket apothecary goes into the room's safe for now. The capsules, syringes, solutions, aerosols, gels, and lozenges within can produce effects either quick and painless or slow and excruciating. Some leave no trace at all, while others leave a chemical calling card behind designed to speak posthumous volumes. There's even a putty-like substance that some of Ranveer's colleagues are particularly fond of; when mixed with enzymes in human saliva, it rapidly expands and congeals, simultaneously silencing a victim and obstructing both the nasal and oral airways, usually inducing a state wherein one becomes surprisingly receptive to any final admonishments requested by a client—a custom Ranveer suspects was made popular by gangster movies, and serves no real purpose in his exceedingly pragmatic mind.

But even with all of these toys to choose from, he is still baffled. Nothing immediately presents itself as the obvious solution to the specific problem at hand. He decides to let his subconscious turn the enigma over for the next several hours while he indulges in the many amenities offered by the hotel, fully confident that a little pampering is just the thing to reveal the right approach to taking out a target who, according to his information, is only nine months old.

8

HOME-FIELD ADVANTAGE

NAIROBI, LONDON, AND Beijing. South Africa, Moscow, and Caracas. *This guy could host his own travel show,* Quinn thinks. *Experience the world through the scope of one of the world's most elite and creative assassins.*

She did what she could from her cube in Langley. The Kremlin is pretty cagey about the kinds of gadgets they let the CIA cart into the heart of their capital city—even when chaperoned by Interpol—so she had to make do with a dynamic rendering of the cybernetic hacker girl's flat synthesized from high-resolution scans. But American money talks in Venezuela in ways that it does not in Russia, so Quinn was able to experience the sickening scene of the MRI massacre through a live video stream fed to her bulky black metaspecs by a tiny cyclops quadcopter.

Ironhide was also available to her—an adorable little tank-tread robot bristling with manipulators. It was one of the many DARPA-built explosive ordnance disposal "technicians" that the CIA, FBI, and ATF redeployed as remote-controlled prostheses for investigating crime scenes from afar. But being an inexperienced pilot, Quinn found it preferable to feed a gloved French Interpol forensic specialist verbal instructions instead, although Lieutenant Jean-Pierre Leblanc made it abundantly clear that he had flown all the way from Paris to Caracas to lend his particular expertise to the investigation, not to be ordered around the forty-two-acre hacienda by an American woman nibbling on a banana nut muffin two thousand miles away.

It was hard to know when it was time to stop investigating remotely and to get out into the field. For at least a decade, it had been possible to solve most crimes through a series of elegantly composed queries across a variety of indices further refined by specially trained neural networks, ultimately culminating in a list of names short enough that you could send a couple of agents—or sometimes even the local doughnut patrol—out to visit each one, approach with sufficient swagger, flash a badge, commence browbeating, and see which one of them either reached or ran. Quinn hoped that the Elite Assassin would be no exception, but she also knew that it would almost certainly not be that easy. If it were, the case would never have found its way to the CIA, and certainly not to her. Eventually, she knew she would need to step away from the comfort of her home base and initiate a proper chase. The only question was when.

The answer, apparently, was right now. When a local FBI crime lab determined that a residue found in an alley just outside the Black Horizon V-Sports Studio was likely an incinerated polyester and spandex blend—the material most commonly used in full-body chroma-key suits—Quinn was told to log into the CIA's travel site and book herself a flight to L.A. When your adversary hands you the home-field advantage, Moretti said with his meticulously groomed goatee framing his famously roguish grin, you goddamn well take it.

QUINN HAS JUST finished canceling her car appointment and rescheduling her mammogram. Now she is trying to decide between a Red Roof Inn and the airport Best Western.

"Ms. Mitchell?"

She is certain the voice she hears behind her is that of a child's, and the tiny Asian girl she sees standing there when she spins around in her chair appears to be all of twelve years old. She is wearing a pair of oversized, round, wire-rimmed specs that pinch the tip of her petite nose.

"Yes?"

"Henrietta Yi," the girl says by way of self-introduction.

Despite the space buns, polka-dot baby doll dress, and ivory-white high-tops, Quinn is starting to get that this girl is not, in fact, a colleague's lost daughter. The badge dangling from her pink Hello Kitty lanyard advertises clearance at the highest possible level.

"Hello," Quinn replies, her tone disclosing that she knows she is missing key context here.

"Mr. Moretti's tech guy," the young woman clarifies.

"Oh!" Quinn says. "I'm so sorry. I was expecting someone named Simon."

"Simon is my assistant," the girl says. "*I'm* the tech guy."

"Is that like an official title?" Quinn asks. "Tech guy?"

"Mr. Moretti just calls me that."

"That's kind of demeaning, isn't it?"

"That's just Mr. Moretti," the girl says dismissively.

"Let me ask you something," Quinn says. She looks around to confirm that they are still alone, leans forward, and lowers her voice. "How long have you worked with him?"

"With Mr. Moretti? Oh, for a while now."

"Is it true what they say?"

"What do they say?"

"That he has a horrible temper?"

Henrietta touches the corner of her lips, makes a face like a sideways kiss, and shifts her eyes behind her enormous specs. "I think it's exaggerated," she says. "Besides, I have a pretty bad temper myself, so I can't really talk."

"Fair enough," Quinn says, even though she finds the idea of a girl like Henrietta Yi being anything but fanatically sweet almost impossible to believe.

"So, is now a good time?"

"Sure." Quinn doesn't want her session to time out and have to start all over again, so she reaches back around and clicks Submit. Best Western it is. "Can we do it here or do we need to go to your lab or something?"

"We can do it here," Henrietta says. "It'll just take a minute."

The cube next to Quinn's is empty, so the girl appropriates the accompanying chair. She then reaches down into the single pocket sewn into the front of her dress, draws out a handset that, in her diminutive hands, looks more like a tablet, and sits. Only the toes of her sneakers reach the carpet's tight weave.

"I just need your phone," Henrietta prompts.

Moretti's "tech guy" is here to install an app called Semaphore. It's a tool Interpol uses to exchange end-to-end encrypted communications with other law enforcement and intelligence agencies while cooperating on cases. Quinn plucks her handset from its charging cradle and passes it to Henrietta.

"Do you need my code, or . . ."

"Nope!"

Henrietta places Quinn's phone on the edge of the desk, and when she does something to her own phone, Quinn's unlocks. Quinn's handset is ensconced in something that looks ballistically impervious, while Henrietta's is bursting at its heat-welded seams with a bumblebee-yellow Pikachu theme.

"Cute," Quinn says. "My daughter used to love Pokémon."

"Yay!" Henrietta exclaims. "Did she ever play any of the games?"

"*All* of them," Quinn bemoans. "She even had the AR Poké-goggles."

"Oh my God, I still have mine," Henrietta says, a touch conspiratorially. "Your daughter's lucky she grew out of it. If I were to add up all the time I spent playing Pokémon, I could have probably gotten another degree."

Quinn starts to say something, but stops. Instead, she says, "So where do you sit?"

"I work off-site."

"Oh. Where?"

Henrietta looks uncomfortable. "With Mr. Moretti."

"Got it," Quinn says. "The top secret project."

"Sorry."

"Not your fault. What did you do before that?"

"I worked with Mr. Moretti on the Epoch Index."

Quinn's eyebrows go up. "Really? The Epoch Index? The message picked up by the Large Hadron Collider?"

"That's the one."

"Are you allowed to talk about it?"

"There isn't much to say. We never figured it out."

"Didn't the guy who discovered it claim it was some kind of message from the future?"

Henrietta resets her oversized specs, which promptly slip right back down into the little dents on either side of her nose, then daintily raises a hand. "Actually, that was me."

"*You* discovered the Epoch Index?"

"Well, technically it was discovered by an AI. But I'm the one who trained the neural network to identify anomalous data."

"What did the message say?"

"We don't know. It was encrypted."

"Do you really think it was from the future?"

"That part was exaggerated. There was a theory that it was caused by quantum resonance from a parallel universe, but obviously there's no way to prove that."

"What do you think?"

"I think it was a pretty standard encrypted transmission that was accidentally picked up by a faulty sensor."

"Are we still trying to decrypt it?"

"We don't have it anymore. All the evidence was sealed."

Quinn looks skeptical. "You're telling me that the CIA found something it couldn't explain and *didn't* secretly keep a copy?"

Henrietta checks the installation progress. "You'd have to ask Mr. Moretti about that."

"How in the world did you go from working at the Large Hadron Collider to being Moretti's tech guy?"

"That's a very long story."

"Is there a short version?"

Henrietta makes a face as she thinks it over. "Let's just say that you never know what the world has in store for you."

"Amen to that," Quinn says. "Last week I was downstairs trying to catch nuclear terrorists. Now I'm about to get on a plane and start chasing an international serial killer."

"You were on the Nuclear Terrorism Nonproliferation Task Force?"

"Right up to the end."

Henrietta's almond eyes slowly close for a solemn, prolonged moment.

"Are you OK?"

When she opens them again, she blinks several times, and Quinn can see that she is doing her best to remain composed.

"I'm fine," she says. "I just want to thank you."

"I wish I could take some credit," Quinn says. "All we did was spend five years proving there are no nuclear threats left."

"I know, but . . . that matters."

Quinn smiles. "Thank you for saying that."

The progress bar completes and Quinn's phone reboots.

"Anyway," Henrietta says, "you're all set, Ms. Mitchell."

Quinn looks down at her handset. "That's it?"

"That's it. The app is installed along with all the required certificates. And I generated new encryption keys for you while I was at it. I also installed public keys for Ms. Townes, Mr. Moretti, and myself, so you can contact us securely anytime."

"Perfect."

Henrietta stands and drops her phone back into the pocket of her dress. "Anything else?"

"I don't think so." Quinn offers her hand. "It was nice meeting you, Henrietta."

The girl enthusiastically accepts Quinn's gesture. "You too, Ms. Mitchell."

She rolls her chair right back into the carpet divots from which it was originally lifted, as though concealing evidence of her presence, then starts toward the elevators.

"Henrietta?" Quinn says.

The girl stops.

"This secret project you're working on. Can you tell me if it has anything to do with the Epoch Index?"

"No."

"No, it doesn't? Or no, you can't tell me?"

"Safe travels, Ms. Mitchell," says the girl, and her polka-dot dress twirls with her effervescent turn.

9

MIMICRY

CHANGE IN PLANS.

Ranveer remains so uninspired by what lies ahead that he has rented a private studio at Yoga'ubdi on the outskirts of Sohar so he can spend the morning meditating on it. It took some finessing, and some administrative rejiggering motivated by a small stack of Omani rial notes, but he was able to secure a bright and airy second-story room for himself with a balcony that opens out onto both the serene blue-green Gulf of Oman as well as the small adjacent parking lot below so that his subconscious can keep track of any comings and go-ings. Nine times out of ten, too many car doors slamming in rapid staccato succession means either that some form of an assault is im-minent, or that a statistically significant number of civilians have sud-denly been given very good reason to flee uncommonly rapidly. The key to walking out of either situation alive is early detection.

Although he grew up in Iran, where any religion other than Islam barely registers as a rounding error, Ranveer was raised a closet Hindu, and while he no longer claims adherence to any form of orga-nized religion, yoga and meditation have remained part of his consti-tution as a cultural vestige. Perhaps it is because, when forced into Muslim prayer five times a day for the first half of his life by the inces-sant calls to worship broadcast from mosque minarets more ubiqui-tous in Tehran than coffee shops in Seattle, he did his best to antagonize Allah by secretly meditating instead. To most people, meditation is a form of peaceful, spiritual grounding; to Ranveer, it is an act of pure defiance.

But yoga is different. To old-school Hindus, yoga means creepily limber old people with gnarled feet in loose-fitting tunics. This is a far cry from the Western interpretation that, having no natural predators, flourished among Californians before invading the rest of North America and Western Europe, rapidly evolving toward a state where it is synonymous with form-fitting, designer-branded, synthetic-fiber ensembles that have given rise to all-new subgenres of bizarre erotic fetishes. As far as Ranveer is concerned, the cure for yoga perversion is simple: a monthlong retreat led by a two-hundred-year-old guru with yak cheese and snot in his beard in the bitter frigidity of the Himalayas. After that, Downward Dog will never again possess the power to elicit an erection.

RANVEER IS SOMEWHERE between sixty seconds and two minutes into his breathing routine when he feels a cold metal cylinder pressed against the nape of his neck. At the same moment, he feels warm breathing in his ear, and in a surly Eastern European accent, he hears:

"*Namaste*, motherfucker."

Ranveer opens his eyes and turns his head just enough to see the wide, mischievous grin of Henryk Szczęście, a man said to be every bit as dangerous and unpredictable as an attempt to pronounce his surname. But the interloper's joviality is short-lived; Henryk's expression instantly morphs into horror when he looks down and sees the long, lithe slab of Damascus steel pressed against his Achilles tendon with just enough pressure to be felt, but not quite enough to break the skin.

"How do you fancy walking?" Ranveer casually inquires, his English distinctly British. Both men know that barely a flick of Ranveer's wrist would unspool and snarl the muscles and tendons in Henryk's lower leg like a poorly cast fishing reel.

"What the fuck, man?" Henryk lowers the instrument in his hand

and ever so cautiously steps away from the blade. "You meditate with a goddamn knife?"

When Ranveer was growing up, yoga and meditation were considered subversive and somehow spiritually underhanded by the Islamic Republic, so yeah, he sometimes meditated with a knife.

"You don't?"

The metal object formerly pressed up against Ranveer's neck turns out to be the business end of Henryk's vaporizer. Although he is breathing heavily, he gives the device a good long suck as though he were an asthmatic clinging to life by the fraying thread of his inhaler. Meanwhile, Ranveer leans over and lays his blade gingerly across an incense bowl, where it will not accidentally impale anyone. He then unfolds his legs, stands, and stretches to his full and not-inconsiderable height. The Iranian is several centimeters taller than the Pole, but to balance things out, Henryk has at least fifty pounds on him. By the time Henryk exhales, it barely looks like he is sighing on a cold Warsaw morning, as the majority of the vapor he drew has apparently been permanently sequestered somewhere deep inside his body. The two men regard each other for a protracted moment before coming together in a warm, back-slapping embrace.

"It's good to see you, my friend," Henryk says.

"You too."

Henryk is bald, stocky, tattooed, and has a jaw that looks like it would shatter your fist long before it would succumb to dislocation or fracturing. In fact, in looking at him, it is hard to imagine where you could possibly strike such that your hand or foot or elbow or knee would not come out on the losing end of the bargain. He continues to draw significantly more than his fair share of air as sweat beads on his scalp like condensation, and his uncharacteristically petite ears are as red and radiant as signal flares. Despite the heat, he is wearing a heavy crimson tracksuit that some would consider stylish and that has black (possibly carbon-fiber) herringbone patterns down the sleeves and legs. Both it and his sneakers are emblazoned with the intricate logo of a European designer brand that Ranveer does not recognize on account of the fact that the two men move in very different fashion circles.

"I came in the way you told me," Henryk says, "and parked just where you said. I thought you were being careful, but then I come in and find you half asleep."

"Focusing my mind," Ranveer corrects. "There's a difference."

Henryk has been known to beat people to death even while in possession of a perfectly good pistol, and to release choke holds just prior to asphyxiation in order to give his victims enough time to regain consciousness purely so that he can make them experience the horror of knowing that they are about to die all over again. It's like edging for homicidal sociopaths.

"The fucking elevator is broken. I had to take the goddamn stairs."

He also has the mouth of a sailor with a raging case of gonorrhea.

"This is a yoga studio. You're supposed to get exercise."

The whispered stories of Henryk's violent nature have expanded to nearly mythical proportions, but ever since he and Ranveer spent a snowy evening in Gdansk over a decade ago pouring each other shots of Belvedere Polish rye, Ranveer has known that none of them are true. Henryk was moonlighting as a lookout for a U.S. Navy Island-class landing ship that the CIA repurposed as a mobile black site, and Ranveer was in town to put as many prisoners out of their misery as possible before they had a chance to unburden themselves. As far as Ranveer could tell, while Henryk had probably been indirectly complicit in dozens of deaths, he didn't seem capable of putting a suffering dog out of its misery, much less ending another man's life by his own hand. So rather than establishing a reputation through actual acts of violence, Henryk's MO has always been to take credit for unclaimed bodies as a sophisticated form of criminal mimicry. He is like a harmless red and black milk snake that is nearly indistinguishable from its lethal coral brethren.

"How is your father?" Henryk asks. "Still in Tehran?"

"Same house I grew up in."

"How is the dentistry business these days?"

"He finally retired."

"Ah. And how does a retired dentist in Tehran spend his days? Is he still flying hawks?"

"Falcons. Every day. He's president of the Tehran Falcon Flying Club now. Falcons, football, and complaining about the Supreme Leader. That's retirement in Iran."

"And a good retirement it is," Henryk affirms. "You'll give him my love, I hope."

"Of course. And Aleksander?"

"He wants me out of the game, as usual," Henryk says. "I told him only if he agrees to marry me. I think I almost have him convinced. We are going to Greece in the spring. That is the best time to go."

"If you ever talk him into marrying you, you must invite me."

"Of course! I will introduce you to his sisters."

"I'm sure they're lovely."

"Angels," Henryk says. He is momentarily distracted while he rolls his shoulder and grimaces. "Every one of them."

"What's wrong?"

"What's wrong is I'm getting old. Two-and-a-half-hour drive up from Muscat and I'm stiff as a morning boner. I used to be able to drive from Warsaw to Madrid without even stopping to pee. Now I can't even make it through the night." He taps his sternum with a thick finger bound in a gold band with a giant inset ruby the same color as his tracksuit. "And fucking acid reflux. I eat Zantac like they are M&M's. Aleksander's nephew sends them from America. Buys the stuff in bulk from Costco."

Ranveer smiles. "I had to get a steroid injection in my lower back last year," he confides, placing his hands over his kidneys and bending against them. "Still gets stiff."

"So even the legendary Ranveer ages," Henryk declares. "What you need is a good woman to sleep with."

"How do you think I threw out my back?"

"I mean to marry," Henryk says. "Settle down. Make some little Ranveers. We can't keep doing this forever."

"Someday," Ranveer says. "But not today."

Henryk has conducted enough business that he knows a transition when he hears one. He punctuates the pleasantries with one last grin, dips a paw into his tracksuit pocket, and removes a dark glass vial. Ranveer notes that if this were a German transaction, the solution would be hermetically sealed and securely ensconced deep inside high-density foam custom-molded to a Zero Halliburton titanium attaché with biometric latches. But the Poles, being a significantly scrappier lot, have their own way of doing business. The high-value merchandise appears to have been transported thousands of kilometers in a tracksuit pocket, where it was secured by the latest in zipper technology and might have even been run through the washing machine once or twice along with a tissue or a metro ticket.

When Henryk holds the prize up to the light—clamped between thick index finger and club-like thumb—it is just possible to see the thin liquid vacillate within. He takes a moment to regard the cylinder earnestly.

"*Something is rotten in the state of Denmark,*" he recites.

"Fitting," Ranveer observes.

"Have you ever used *hebenon* before?"

"No."

"It separates, so you must shake it. Don't forget. Otherwise it won't work. And all you need is a drop. Maybe two, depending on weight. No more. Use a borosilicate glass dropper, not a plastic one. And *do not* get it on you."

The vial is delicately passed from fat to slender fingers. Payment has already been made in *cryoon*, the official cryptocurrency of Estonia, which the current technocratic parliament keeps pegged to the euro.

"I trust you verified payment," Ranveer says.

"With you, I do not have to," Henryk says. "But yes, I did. Very generous. Aleksander and I thank you."

"Consider it an early wedding gift."

Henryk reverts into his default state of grinning but stalls in a way that Ranveer recognizes. There is something more on his friend's mind, and Ranveer knows that it will not stay there for long.

"What is it?"

"Doesn't it get to you sometimes?" Henryk asks. "What we do?"

Ranveer takes a moment to summon just the right response.

"There is nothing either good or bad but thinking makes it so."

Ranveer can see that it takes Henryk a moment to place the *Hamlet* reference, but once he does, the payoff is a grin so brilliant that Ranveer swears it radiates warmth.

"You are one smooth motherfucker," Henryk declares.

Ranveer passes the vial to his left hand and offers his right.

"Until next time."

Henryk brushes Ranveer's gesture aside and moves in for another embrace. Ranveer is prepared and reciprocates—mindful of the vial.

"Watch the shoulder," Henryk mumbles into Ranveer's chest.

"Watch the back."

10

CRIMES OF DISPASSION

QUINN ALWAYS FIGURED her first trip to L.A. would be to the original Disneyland with her family. She did not foresee visiting a satellite FBI field office and being assigned to the dingy cubicle of an agent out on a long-term, undercover, gang-related assignment. But a secure place to work and access to support resources are a necessity, both of which were easily procured through a single call from what has turned out to be the exceptionally persuasive Interpol liaison, Alessandro Moretti.

As far as Quinn can tell, the murder of Derrick Jamal Young—better known by his gaming handle, Prime—was as arbitrary as the rest of the Elite Assassin's victims. Nothing whatsoever to indicate why this particular kid was so deserving of such a big, messy hole blown through his torso by some sort of custom-built, untraceable, sawed-off shotgun.

None of that is to say Derrick wasn't a little strange. He had a bizarre obsession with prime numbers and cryptography (which he often expressed through impassioned, barely coherent YouTube ramblings that got a curiously high number of views, likes, and equally incoherent comments), and before he became a professional gamer, he briefly worked as a technician in a tissue-engineering lab. But his record at work was exemplary. According to social media, he'd quit simply to pursue his lifelong dream of becoming a professional v-sports athlete. When she got a hit on a couple of legal indices, Quinn thought she'd finally found something, but when she had the case unsealed, she found the charges against Derrick were nothing but typical overreaches of the Computer Fraud and Abuse Act. Some light, recreational hacking that Derrick pled down to misdemeanor copyright infringement, and that his parents were somehow able to conceal—probably more for their own professional benefit than Derrick's, given that there are far worse secrets for a professional gamer to keep than a past replete with hacking, complete with a legit federal rap sheet.

It has become increasingly popular for the deceased to have entries in a data repository called Project Legatum. Legatum is a global, decentralized registry of linked death notices distributed across millions of devices, each dedicating a few spare processor cycles here and there to help propagate updates and verify integrity. Kind of a combination social network and cryptocurrency for the afterlife. Like most data stores built on blockchain technology, it is simultaneously owned by everyone and by no one, and both read and write access are completely free (which, almost overnight, decimated traditional media's ability to exploit the bereaved by charging astronomical prices for anemic, ephemeral eulogies). Creating and modifying entries in Project Legatum requires a cryptographically verifiable, digitally signed death certificate to ensure that the service cannot be vandalized or misused, and the newest version of the platform even supports "smart wills" that contain signed code that can facilitate dynamic transactions like the automated distribution of estates based on current market conditions.

Predictably, Derrick's entry—compiled and appended to the Project Legatum blockchain not by his parents, but by his clan—is a sanitized recapitulation of a spirited life lived to its fullest with no dignity whatsoever afforded to those forces who saw fit to end it prematurely. And, sadly, with no hint whatsoever of a pattern. Quinn has even tried running steganographic neural networks against the images, videos, and text contained in all the Project Legatum entries courtesy of the Elite Assassin to see if messages are somehow being concealed inside the digital memorials, the results of which are consistently zilch. At times, Quinn feels she has become almost as obsessed with conspiratorial puzzles as Prime.

Quinn's job is just as much a process of disproving as it is confirmation, and there is one hypothesis she feels she can finally put behind her: the assassination syndicate theory. There are three solid data points suggesting a single killer.

First, handwriting analysis algorithms give all the handwritten tags (oddly, the numeric sequence on the inside of the Russian girl's arm was branded, and of course, Prime's sequence was a clever outlier) an 89 percent chance of having been written by the same left-handed person. Second, all the killings thus far have occurred serially rather than in parallel, and with tight but sufficient travel time in between. And third, it's just not realistic that local resources are being tapped for all these jobs.

On the plane between D.C. and L.A., Quinn became an expert on contract killing, and she now knows that while you can pay to have someone murdered in every major metropolitan area in the world, you can't do it over and over again without, at some point, hiring some yokel dumb enough to lock his keys inside his fifty-year-old getaway car, or leave behind a few seconds of pixelated surveillance footage, or inadvertently make contact with an undercover agent.

Quinn learned that, like most things, hiring a hitman isn't like it is in the movies. In the real world, doing death right usually means doing it yourself. Of course, you get the occasional mobster, gangster, or run-of-the-mill sociopath who might be your real estate agent or your gynecologist, but most "assassins" are twitchy, wild-eyed tweakers with face tattoos and just enough brain cells still firing to navigate the dark web. She also learned that one of the biggest differences between professionals and amateurs is weapon selection—that those who dabble are more likely to assume that bigger is always better, while properly mentored assassins understand how to pick just the right caliber for the task at hand, sometimes opting for something smaller for the sake of concealment, noise suppression, and tighter splatter patterns. Finally, Quinn was surprised to discover that only between 2 and 5 percent of homicides in most countries can be attributed to contract killings, primarily because the overwhelming majority of murders are crimes of passion. Exceedingly rare are violent crimes of pure *dis*passion.

Establishing that there is only one Elite Assassin leads Quinn to two more important assertions:

1. He is uncannily good at what he does, suggesting that he is probably not self-taught, but rather either had, or *still* has, the backing of a state with a well-established and extremely aggressive intelligence service.
2. He is on a tight schedule and is therefore almost constantly in transit. In fact, his itinerary is so arduous that Quinn has come to think of him as essentially homeless.

It is generally considered a bad thing to have your mark always on the move, but not so for a competent data scientist. To an analyst, travel means data, data means queries, and queries eventually lead to answers. Especially when you have the home-field advantage.

Finding a list of airlines is easy. Quinn simply needs to cross-reference cities and dates with flight schedules—or rather, she needs to compose the right search expressions to do the correlating for her. There are several possibilities, but one in particular stands out: Emirates. The Dubai-based airline services more cities on her list than any other. Throw in registered flight paths for recent Emirates Executive private jets, and Emirates is a match for *every* city where there is an unsolved murder involving a tagged body. Whoever this guy is, he is very particular about his airline.

Elite indeed.

Finding hotels isn't quite as straightforward, but the airline lead gives her an idea. Rather than looking at individual hotels, she makes lists of holding companies—ownership and management organizations whose loyalty programs span multiple brands. A query that cross-references luxury hotel properties with the cities on her list reveals that her man is almost certainly a high-ranking and devoted customer of Crystal Collective Worldwide.

She spends the rest of the day making calls to other field offices and sending junior FBI agents out to collect passenger and guest records. After stopping at an Applebee's for a chicken Caesar and a cheap glass of chardonnay that keeps her just under her per diem, she spends the evening in her room at the Best Western Suites next to the airport, writing search algorithms. As encouraged as she felt earlier in the day, she now feels deflated; she has not been able to extract a single additional lead from the data. No single name emerges from guest records obtained in cities where the Elite Assassin has left his mark. She doesn't even uncover sets of names or patterns that might suggest aliases. Unless her man somehow obtains an entirely new identity for every city he visits, his stays are simply not recorded—perhaps a perk enjoyed by customers with sufficiently elite status.

As she falls asleep, Quinn wonders if pinpointing both the airline and the hotel chain in a single day might have been too easy. The connections were indirect enough that they wouldn't be automatically surfaced by pattern-matching algorithms, but still obvious enough to be uncovered by even a mediocre analyst. As a challenge, she tries to convince herself that this is some kind of an elaborate, well-choreographed ruse designed to make multiple assassins look like one. Maybe they are careful to never leave less time between two deaths than it would take to fly between the two cities. Maybe they use hacked, black-market mobile robotic surgical instruments trained on the same handwriting set to do the tagging. Maybe they are so well coordinated that some percentage of the deaths are essentially randomly generated noise designed to conceal the real signal. Or maybe . . .

Quinn's eyes snap open and she sits up in bed. Maybe the killer isn't being pursued as much as the investigator is being led.

11

COLLATERAL DAMAGE

WHEN RANVEER IS alone in the yoga studio once again, he crosses the padded room in his bare feet and stands before the open window. He watches as Henryk rolls his shoulder and grimaces once more before stuffing himself back inside the glass cockpit of the squat white Porsche with red Laguna leather interior. As Ranveer secures the vial of hebenon solution inside his foldable apothecary, he reviews the chain of events that led him to this moment, in order to ensure that absolutely nothing has been overlooked.

It starts, somewhat improbably, with what the media has branded the *#seulementmoi* movement—or "only me"—which symbolizes an unexpected cultural shift in France wherein, in defiance of centuries of tradition, mistresses have suddenly and unexpectedly fallen out of favor. Wherever rapid societal transformations occur, there are inevitably casualties, frequently in the form of powerful white men caught—in this case, literally—with their pants down.

As soon as *#seulementmoi* was identified by zeitgeist algorithms, *Le Milieu* ("The Underworld") began composing queries to identify potential blackmail targets. One of the richer veins led to an Interpol officer named Lieutenant Jean-Pierre Leblanc who maintained no fewer than three separate families—one in Paris, one in Bordeaux, and one just over the border in Geneva—and who appeared to be seriously considering starting a fourth in Frankfurt, where his work often took him. Unless Monsieur Leblanc wanted his boss and all three of his wives to receive detailed dossiers describing his indiscretions—including not just names, photos, and receipts, but explicit video footage—he was to install an application called Signal on his handset and use it to regularly send details of all of Interpol's investigations to the specified anonymous account.

Ranveer has associates who watch blackmail markets like the Japanese track bluefin tuna prices and were kind enough to inform him that his work had recently attracted the attention of the CIA, and in particular, an unusually talented analyst by the name of Quinn Mitchell. The escalation of the case was only a matter of time—a milestone after which all the rules of the game would inevitably need to change. Had Quinn Mitchell already been tasked with tracking the Elite Assassin back in Moscow, Ranveer would have had to interrupt the Israeli hacker's brash rationalization of why his houseguest would not kill him by grasping that obnoxious topknot, spinning him around in his chair like a barber, snapping his head back to open up access, and wrenching his Damascus steel through his neck, half decapitating him to ensure his larynx detached, spray-painting the matrix of plasma glass and casting the room into crimson while listening to the last of his gurgling and gasps.

The Israeli, for all his economic philosophy, will never know how close he came to experiencing Ranveer's knife, and how much he owes his life to forces outside his control.

Interpol does not particularly concern Ranveer—and neither does the CIA, for that matter—but given what he knows about this analyst, and considering the nature of his next target, Ranveer deems it prudent to take additional precautions and tie up more loose ends than he might otherwise. The endgame is not the phase of an operation to start taking chances; from here on out, there will be collateral damage.

Which is why Ranveer's gym bag does not contain protein bars and electrolyte-infused sports drinks and spare deodorant, but rather all the components required to assemble his gas gun into the long and complex micro-meteor configuration. Why he loaded it with a tungsten carbide cartridge with a programmable caliber that he dialed down to mere micrometers. Why he needed Henryk to park right beside the silver borrowed Mercedes-Benz H2-Class so that, as he rearranged his balls after a two-and-a-half-hour drive in the tiny white Porsche, Ranveer could place a white-hot shot just a hair to the right of his tracksuit's zipper, ripping an almost imperceptible hole in the left ventricle of the giant Pole's already-enlarged heart, the sudden pain radiating deceptively all the way out to his shoulder. Why he requested a studio that faced the water so that the projectile, after passing clean through, would end up somewhere in the Gulf of Oman, where it would be impossible to recover. And why he used an electromagnetic pulse emitter to disable the elevator so that Henryk would have to take the stairs, not only to get his newly defective heart pumping more than usual, but also to give Ranveer sufficient time to disassemble and conceal the rifle, mimic a relaxed and placid meditative state, and make his old friend believe he approached stealthily, craftily, and entirely unobserved.

Henryk will probably pop a few more Zantac during his drive south to Muscat and might even opt for a light beer instead of a vodka on the rocks on his afternoon flight back home to Warsaw. He will likely fall asleep earlier than usual next to Aleksander as the two of them watch Eurovision together in bed. Tomorrow morning, Aleksander will let Henryk sleep in and will put on the coffee and scramble their eggs and start on the kielbasa. Just before serving, he will go back into the bedroom to wake his fiancé with a delicate kiss upon his little ear, which he will find to be cold and stiff against his lips.

Astonishing how comforting and peaceful a scene can be one moment and how completely it can gut you the next, when the only thing that has changed is your ability to see what is really there.

12

LEGWORK

JET LAG HAS Quinn up at 4:45 A.M., and even though she is still haunted by the thought that the leads she uncovered the night before were just a little too easy, the fact remains that they are the only leads she has.

After taking advantage of the free continental breakfast served daily in the Best Western lobby and draining several cups of weak, urn-brewed coffee, she finds her white Toyota Camry rental car in the parking lot and instructs it to take her to whichever CCW property is closest to the airport. Quinn knows that she cannot rely on the junior FBI agents the assistant director in charge put at her disposal to bring her what she needs, since most of them still seem more enamored with their badges and their newly issued service weapons than they are with stopping the next murder. For now, it is time to put the handset and the metaspecs away and to apply some old-fashioned legwork to this case.

No more guest lists. Quinn already knows that they are all dead ends. It's surveillance footage she's after now. She knows her man is almost certainly captured on dozens of different video feeds every single day. And she knows that he knows this. Rather than avoiding surveillance, his game is probably to stay lost in the noise. All but the best disguises can't fool facial recognition anyway, and somehow caking his face with prosthetic paste and embedding false eyeballs to change his pupillary distance seem well beneath him, so Quinn's instincts are telling her that he relies on anonymity. But she also knows that there isn't nearly as much randomness in the universe as most of us perceive. Randomness is usually more the result of our inability to see patterns than the actual absence of them. And finding patterns is what Quinn does.

"Uncooperative" isn't exactly the word she would use to describe the staff at the recently renovated Villas at Playa Del Rey. In fact, just about everyone Quinn talks to appears to have been abducted as a child and brainwashed by some kind of customer-service cult until reaching the legal age of employment. Copious amounts of words are exchanged, yet somehow each interaction concludes with her having no more information than she had going into it. Curiously, perhaps even less. Before she left Langley, Moretti came in to see her off, and as he walked her out, he explained to Quinn that being in the field was not like being in the computer lab, and that interrogating people was not like querying indices. Data sometimes obscured the truth, sure, but it was never intentionally deceitful or manipulative. It wasn't *calculating*. People, on the other hand, were evil sons of bitches. They'd have you chasing your tail for days, not giving two fucks about all the bodies piling up so long as it suited them. Even if some little part of you knew they were lying, they'd figure out a way to speak to some other part of you that would make you believe them. The worst of them were even capable of convincing themselves of their own lies so that they were effectively lying to you and telling you the truth at the same time.

Even when people were seemingly fully transparent, it was seldom without some amount of subtle distortion.

"So, what am I supposed to do?" Quinn asked her new boss as she stepped into the elevator. Her flight was leaving from Reagan National in less than an hour.

"There's only one thing you can do," Moretti told her through closing doors. His hands were in his pockets in a way that crinkled up his sport coat, and he shrugged his oversized shoulder pads. "Do it right back."

*   *   *

THERE'S A BUTTON at the front desk that summons out-of-sight
Villas at Playa Del Rey staff and that, as far as Quinn can tell, only
needs to be activated in situations where said staff is intentionally
avoiding persistent CIA field analysts. Fortunately, their Pavlovian
training prevents them from ignoring whatever the unseen stimulus
is, and the hidden door behind the counter slides open almost instantaneously.

"Good *morning*, Ms. Mitchell," the manager croons. He is the type
to convey exasperation through heightened congeniality. "Is there
something *more* I can do for you?"

"I just want to make sure I have all this straight," Quinn says. "For
my report."

The man's posture is almost unnaturally erect, and his hair resem-
bles one of those hyper-realistic oil paintings that somehow look even
more real than reality.

"What *exactly* can I clarify for you?"

"You told me you don't retain security footage for more than
twenty-four hours, is that right?"

"Sadly, we do not." Each phrase is accompanied by a dramatic tilt
of the head to one side or the other, and it occurs to Quinn how much
flexibility she's lost in her own neck from spending so much time im-
mobile in front of plasma glass. "That *is* the policy of the Villas at
Playa Del Rey as well as *all* Crystal Collective Worldwide properties."

"What about off-site backups?"

A mimed moment of contemplation during which ceiling panels
are examined, lips are pursed, and a delicate fingertip is nestled within
a clean-shaven and well-hydrated chin cleft. "I'm afraid I wouldn't
know anything about that."

"That's OK," Quinn says. "Because I know *all* about that. You see,
any time data is flushed to local storage, it triggers an event which immediately copies, compresses, encrypts, and transfers those bytes via
optical fiber to a data center in Santa Monica. Then, once a day, all
that data gets copied, compressed, encrypted, and moved to *another*

data center in Provo, Utah, just in case all of Southern California gets swallowed up by an earthquake."

"Well," the manager replies, and at that moment, Quinn honestly can't tell if he is impressed with her research or on the verge of clawing out her eyes. "If you say so, Ms. Mitchell."

"I do. Which means I can get all the footage I want. I can get a Foreign or Domestic Intelligence Surveillance Court Order that will give me access to footage dating all the way back to the system's inception. And not just security footage. I can get guest records, financial records, vendor records. I can find out what every one of your guests had for breakfast for probably the last thirty years. I can get biometric signatures from your guest authentication system, cross-reference them with thousands of other indices, and find out anything I want about any guest or employee I want. And if I were to find anything at all irregular, no matter how minor, I would be obligated, ethically, to pass that information on to the appropriate law enforcement agency. Which I can't imagine would reflect particularly positively on this establishment. Unfortunately, all of that would take me about thirty-six hours. And I don't have thirty-six hours. Do you know why?"

The manager is now listening in a way that, just a moment ago, he was not. A delicate clearing of the throat. "I do not."

"Because I'm trying to prevent a murder."

Followed by a prominent swallow.

"I'm so sorry to hear that, Ms. Mitchell," the manager says. "I really, *really* wish there was something more I could do."

"That's the good news," Quinn says. She slides something across the counter and smiles. "There is."

The manager's eyes dip momentarily to the card on the desk. "What is this?"

"Read it."

The manager slides the rectangle of thick paper stock toward him, plucks it from the polished marble, and takes a moment to examine the embossed print before reading it aloud. "*We know what we are, but know not what we may be.*"

"The great Dr. Martin Luther King, Jr.," Quinn tells him.

"I'm not sure I understand," the manager confesses. "What does this mean?"

"It means that who you are isn't a final destination. All of us are on a journey toward who we will become, and every decision we make is a step along that path. Now do you understand?"

The manager sheepishly teeter-totters his hand and squeaks, "*Maybe?*"

"It means that, one day, all of this . . ." Quinn gesticulates as though breaststroking through the concentrated opulence in which they are submerged. "This place, your job, the people you're protecting. None of this is going to matter to you anymore. Nothing you *have* is going to matter to you anymore. All that will matter are the things you've *done*—or the things you *haven't* done—and the effect that they've had on others. Is this making any sense?"

"It is."

"Good," Quinn says. "Then listen to me very carefully. Are you listening?"

"I am."

"You may never be in a better position to save someone's life than you are right now."

By saying absolutely nothing, the manager inadvertently says it all.

"These types of warrants," Quinn continues, "they're sledgehammers. They inevitably turn up all kinds of unpleasantness we're not even looking for. Nobody wants that. What I need is a scalpel. Seventy-two hours' worth of surveillance footage. That's it. And you'll never see me again. My ID is on the other side of that card. Give it some thought and do whatever you think is right."

With that, Quinn turns away from the counter and walks straight through the lobby, doing her very best not to catch a heel, fall on her face, and ruin the entire effect. She doesn't even pause at the doors, but continues out into the parking lot, and before she gets to the next hotel on her list, her handset lets her know that she has just received exactly seventy-two hours' worth of compressed video from an anonymous and untraceable account.

Quinn is getting the hang of this.

IT SEEMS WORD travels fast between CCW properties. Quinn is greeted by name just inside the lobbies of both the second and third hotels and assured—in hushed and rushed tones as she is walked back out beneath sprawling, cut-glass awnings—that she will have what she needs. Which, moments later, she does. It is barely lunchtime, and Quinn already has enough data to keep her busy for the rest of the day.

The rental takes her back to the FBI field office by way of an obscure establishment known as "Jack in the Box," which Quinn had heard rumors of back east but had never beheld with her own eyes. She gets herself set up at an empty cubicle with her Brunch Burger (a hamburger on a croissant—*brilliant*, she thinks) and a very large, and very dark, premium roast coffee.

Despite how mind-numbing the task before her is, Quinn can't bring herself to delegate to an intern or a junior analyst. If they got a hit, she'd have to verify it, and if they didn't, she'd have to double-check to make sure they didn't miss anything, so what's the point? Quinn much prefers the stress of having way too much to do to the anxiety caused by the possibility that something might not have been done right. Management is probably not in Quinn's future, and if it is, God help her underlings. A Vanessa Townes she is not.

She casts to the slab of plasma glass in the cube rather than her metaspecs so that she can see to her lunch as she works. The first thing she does is arrange all the video feeds from the first hotel in a grid and watches them all simultaneously at 10x speed. Every time she sees someone check in or out, she taps the button she configured to record the feed's timestamp. She decides to narrow her search down to only two days rather than all three, which allows her to get two hotels done before it's dark out and she is entirely incapable of focusing anymore. On her way back to the hotel, she picks up a bur-rito and a tall bottle of sangria, takes one more antacid tablet than the directions on the bottle recommend, and falls asleep fully clothed with the TV on. The next morning, after three miniature pots of in-room coffee and as much twenty-four-hour news programming as she can stand (very little), she tames her hair in a hasty, messy bun, slips on her specs, and works through the feed from the third hotel.

The next step is to write a script that parses timestamps out of the guest records, then compares them to the timestamps she recorded from the front desk video feeds. Eventually, she should find a mis-match. If her hypothesis is correct, someone should appear on video who did not officially check in—someone who paid in a way that can-not be easily traced, and who did not have his face scanned. Someone whose elite status allows him to play by a completely different set of rules. Someone who, even when surrounded by cameras, somehow remains the invisible man.

She finds a few anomalies that she needs to verify manually, but after all the data sets from all three hotels have been analyzed, Quinn has not found an obvious discrepancy.

Fuck.

In the shower, she briefly considers masturbating. Maybe an or-gasm can light up her brain in a way that might lead to a case-changing epiphany. But the gap between where she is right now mentally and where she would need to be to get off feels daunting, so she snaps right back into analyst mode. Either she needs data from longer peri-ods of time, or she has the wrong hotels. Or . . .

She thinks back to the rental car counter at LAX. The clusters of luggage, the crowds being corralled through the lanes of a configu-rable, nylon-belt maze. And all those signs for rewards programs: *Next time, skip the line.*

Of course the Elite Assassin would not be made to wait. In retro-spect, it seems obvious. So how else can she combine surveillance footage with data to get a good look at her man's face?

Dressing while avoiding catching a glimpse of herself in a full-body mirror is second nature to Quinn. She has put on weight since her divorce, and even though she commits to working out every day and taking the stairs instead of the elevator—

That's it. The elevator. Her man likely stays on the top floor of the hotel, and something tells Quinn that he is not the type to take the stairs.

She doesn't want to waste time commuting into the FBI field office, so when she finishes dressing, she orders up a grilled cheese and fruit salad instead of French fries, then opens the elevator surveillance videos from the Villas at Playa Del Rey—the most expensive of the three hotels. Each elevator has four different cameras, so she picks the feeds with the most direct view of the occupants' faces, then overlays a facial recognition filter. She adjusts parameters until her food arrives, backing down the threshold to prevent false positives caused by reflections in polished metal panels and by dolls in the arms of little girls, and then she makes sure the algorithm continues to track correctly at very high speeds. When she has the right settings, she configures all the feeds from all the hotels to play in off-screen buffers simultaneously at 100x while dumping everything they find to a log file. She wants to know exactly how many faces are being tracked, and for exactly how long.

When the data is ready, and when all her dishes are out in the hallway, she knows that her man is in there, and she knows she has everything she needs to find him. It's just a matter of figuring out how to make the data talk. Quinn takes a diet soda from the minibar, checks the price on the card, then puts it back. Involuntarily, her mind hatches a plan wherein she eats every last chip, nut, and candy bar, then replaces them all with their reasonably priced doppelgängers from 7-Eleven before housekeeping is any the wiser. But the scheme goes the way of masturbation, and she is right back on track. She'll go out for coffee later.

The first thing she does is divide the data up into individual elevator trips, which is relatively easy since all she has to do is find the points where no faces are being tracked, indicating empty cars. Since she is focused on the penthouse suite, she initially assumes that whichever elevator trip is longest most likely contains the footage she's after. However, because of intermittent stops, she realizes it's not going to be that easy. She needs to subtract the time it takes for the elevator to pause, and for occupants to come and go.

It takes her two hours and costs U.S. taxpayers not only that diet soda from the minibar, but a tin of Planters mixed nuts as well, but she is eventually able to isolate blocks of time when some faces change while other faces do not. By subtracting those periods from the total time of each elevator trip, she has calculated what she calls "absolute travel time." After applying all the modifiers and comparing all the data, she finds that there are eighteen pieces of footage that run a full seven seconds longer than any of the others.

That's way outside her expected margin of error. The data has finally spoken. Or Quinn has finally learned how to listen.

Each clip shows a different configuration of occupants: a fidgety manager-on-duty; a bellhop wheeling several metal cases accompanied by a fidgety manager-on-duty; a chef fussing over several covered dishes on a cart accompanied by a fidgety manager-on-duty; several varieties of women, primping on the way up and irritably adjusting undergarments on the way down. There is only one occupant—tall, slender, and dark—who seems entirely unconcerned with the goings-on around him.

Quinn has found her man.

She takes her time isolating several still images from various frames and runs them through algorithms to combine and enhance them. She is proud of her work, and she wants him to look his very best.

She stops for coffee and a warm chocolate croissant on the way to LAX, then spends some time sharing her new photo album with the folks at the Emirates counter. But she shows them several other images as well. Random faces mixed in. Some are from advertisements, some are wanted terrorists, some are photos she took moments ago of people in line at Shake Shack. One is a shot of her ex-husband she spontaneously took in the kitchen one Sunday afternoon that she can't bring herself to delete. She cycles through them on her handset and asks a pretty young customer service agent if any of them are familiar. The girl seems to know to be careful, but what she doesn't know is that the handset is recording her responses: sampling her voice, constantly comparing images of her eyes, monitoring her body temperature and heart rate. When the girl denies ever seeing Quinn's man, the handset does not react. As far as the CIA's best field polygraph software is concerned, she is not lying.

Airlines, Quinn realizes, are not like luxury hotels. Terminal gates are far less intimate than lobbies and front desks. There's no reason to assume that one of perhaps hundreds of Emirates L.A. ground crew members would be able to place one specific face. But while the girl cannot recall Quinn's man, her terminal probably can. Nobody has boarded a plane in a major airport in decades without being photographed by the airline in ultra-high definition from every conceivable angle. Names and aliases can change by the day, but faces can't. That puts her man's destination—and the location of the next murder— just a few keystrokes away.

Quinn passes the image to the terminal's public buffer, a secure and isolated memory location to which some devices allow write-only access over Wi-Fi or Bluetooth. The protocol is used for the ad hoc exchange of lightweight data like business cards, phone numbers, and personal identification—all those things we once traded physically, but that have long since been converted to bits. The next step is to use what she learned from her interactions with CCW's chipper-yet-reticent hotel staff. She asks the girl if she has ever heard the saying *We know what we are, but know not what we may be.* Tells her it's considered the wisest of all the Native American proverbs; she has reason to believe the man in the photo she just sent over is a brutal international serial killer; the girl may never be in a better position to save someone's life than she is right now. The whole spiel. The girl's eyes were already wide, but as she listens to Quinn, they expand to near-manga proportions.

Finally, Quinn slides her handset down into her purse, waves away all the drama, and tells the girl to forget the whole thing. It's not important, anyway. She isn't *really* there to try to save innocent people's lives. Really, she's there to book a vacation. But the problem is that she just doesn't know where in the world to go. Maybe the girl can help her out. I don't know, maybe make a suggestion. Someplace exotic, someplace mundane—doesn't matter. It's all up to her. The girl is initially a little slow on the uptake, but then she starts picking up what Quinn is putting down. She cheerfully addresses her screen—taps in some input, brushes away output she doesn't like, toggles a few switches here and there—and then she brightly suggests, of all places in the world, Sohar, Oman.

Quinn is surprised by the girl's recommendation, but after a moment of consideration, she's game. She would like to book herself a seat on the next flight out. Very well. Will Ms. Mitchell be traveling business or Sultan Class today? Neither, sadly. Today, Ms. Mitchell will be traveling coach.

13

NIGHT SHIFT

IF YOU REALLY want to sleep soundly at night, get yourself a dog.

Don't bother with commercial alarm systems. Despite exorbitant recurring financial commitments, they are easily disabled or circumvented by almost any professional, and even a few promising amateurs. Window contact sensors are useless when it's far faster and quieter to use a portable ion implantation device to transmute glass into a pile of goo than it is to jimmy open a latch. Pressure plates around a door do you no good when it's faster to cut a hole in the wall right next to it with a common keychain laser than it is to pick the lock. Infrared motion sensors are nothing but a false sense of security in a world where you can buy heat-shielded clothing right off the bargain rack, provided you know where to shop. And if you're rich enough to afford a security system that actually works, a simple localized electromagnetic pulse emitted from a quadcopter or a privately operated satellite network will keep things quiet for more than enough time to get a job done *and* tie up any loose ends.

Don't think you're any better off with armed guards, either. All guards do is increase the price of a job. Rather than a single target, you have to factor in multiple. And there's no discount for buying in bulk, so a lot of Ranveer's colleagues actually prefer jobs that involve patrols. They feel it's a more efficient use of their valuable time.

The trick with guards is to take them out before they can trigger a silent alarm or get off a phone call, lest you get all the way up to the bedroom only to find that your target has ditched his whore and bar-ricaded himself inside a safe room behind his walk-in closet. Modern safe rooms are pretty legit; depending on composition and configura-tion, some models can add up to three hours to a job. And don't for-get: there's that obnoxious cokehead prostitute to deal with who your target so valiantly left tangled up naked in the sheets so there would be more oxygen for him. Safe rooms don't exchange air with the out-side world, because if they did, you could just screw a canister of arse-nic pentafluoride or straight-up chlorine into the bypass and gas the fucker faster and with far less effort than you could strangle him with two-hundred-pound monofilament fishing line strung between a pair of oyster-shucking gloves.

The bottom line is, if your target ends up hermetically sealed in-side any kind of halfway decent safe room, you can probably kiss your plans for later that night goodbye.

But the biggest downside to bodyguards is not that they are easily dispatched by a properly configured gas gun or, if you're feeling espe-cially mischievous, the quick zip of Damascus steel across the jugular, after which you need to keep them pointed away from you until they're finished spouting. It's that they are easily corrupted. Security professionals are almost always either stupid or underpaid—quite often both—which amounts to a dangerous and unfortunate combi-nation when it comes to the safety of you and your family. It often costs less to get a guard to look the other way than to buy a moder-ately good cigar in some countries. Or, given that most bodyguards aren't all that fond of their narcissistic and egomaniacal bosses, for the price of an evening's worth of quality companionship, you can some-times convince one to walk right into his employer's bedroom, con-duct business on your behalf, then get on the next flight to Bermuda. In Ranveer's world, there's no shame in outsourcing so long as the job gets done.

Where expensive electronics and cheap minions fail, a dog can pre-vail. A well-trained canine can't be fooled or bribed, and even if you're cold and callous enough to kill a man's best and most loyal companion, it's almost impossible to do so before he can manage to get out some pretty unsettling racket. Where jobs involve dogs—even the little yappy kind—your best bet is usually a sniping configuration, a downwind vantage point at least a hundred meters away, and a tall thermos of coffee.

But at the end of the day, when you think about it, the safety of each and every one of us really comes down to nothing more than the simple goodwill of others. Unless you have the resources of an entire nation dedicated to keeping you alive (and sometimes even then), just about anyone on the street can kill you or your family at any moment for any reason at all—or for no reason in particular. Most of us come into contact with anywhere from dozens to thousands of people every day who could instantly reduce us to human smoothies with nothing more than an almost imperceptible tweak of a steering wheel or the slightest nudge toward an inbound train. And those are just the careless and the cowards among us. Anyone with any balls or ingenuity can kill almost anyone else around them in a dozen different ways with nearly any implement within arm's reach: a pencil through the soft tissue of the eye and into the temporal lobe behind; the spine of a book against the throat with enough force to crush the trachea; a "World's Best Dad" coffee cup to the temple where the middle meningeal artery is easily lacerated. The list goes on. And then there are the myriad of actual weapons and poisons and methods of sabotage that can be used against any one of us before our brains can even begin to register the possibility of danger. The truth is that most of us survive day-to-day not because of any real ability to keep ourselves and our families safe, but simply because there is nobody in the immediate vicinity who wishes otherwise.

SIDE-LOADED ON RANVEER'S handset is a handy little app that allows him to hack e-ink license plates anywhere in the world. After using GLONASS (the Russian version of GPS) to determine his location, and the camera in his metaspecs to capture the VIN of the Mercedes-Benz H2-Class he borrowed from the hotel, the app uses his handset's near-field transmitter to broadcast a signal similar to the one issued by the Directorate General of Traffic under the Royal Oman Police after a car has been reported as stolen. However, rather than flashing the Arabic word for "thief!" thereby making the vehicle exceedingly easy for officers to spot (and often shaming your more respectable criminals into abandoning their boosted rides before they can reach the nearest chop shop), Ranveer's payload generates a random but perfectly valid Omani tag so that if it is somehow recorded, the Mercedes cannot be traced back to the hotel. As an additional security measure, the SUV's data connection has been disabled so that its location cannot be triangulated, which means it is searching for the Nassif family's home amid the suburbs west of Sohar using only onboard sensors and cached maps.

It would be fair to say that Ranveer generally works the night shift, and that he is currently on his way into the office. Since he is self-employed and only gets paid for the results he produces, he decides to make optimal use of his evening commute.

He may not be some hotshot CIA analyst, but Ranveer knows his way around the shadowphiles. *Wired* once described the shadowphiles as the lowest point in our rich, vast, and exponentially expanding datascape; the point at which all phished, leaked, and hacked information eventually collects after most of its immediate commercial value has been extracted; illicit indices of personal details and financial transactions concealed beneath multiple layers of onion routing and asymmetrical encryption, but accessible to anyone well enough connected to buy access. Data sold in bulk and at wholesale. While the shadowphiles were once restricted to criminals with a talent for command-line scripting, enough user-experience designers have turned to the dark side that stalking, hunting, and spying are now as easy as pointing and clicking.

One of the advantages of Ranveer's new gig is that most of his targets have no idea that anyone would want them dead, which means that the Nassif family is unlikely to employ armed guards, or to have had a custom-built safe room installed. Therefore, Ranveer decides not to waste crypto credits querying financial records for evidence to the contrary. But he does try cross-referencing recurring payments with all known local security companies to see what kind of commercial-grade alarm system he could be up against. Nothing. And, thankfully, no payments to any businesses affiliated with pet care as far back as three years, which means the Nassif family does not have so much as a guinea pig watching over them. Finally, with no memberships, payments, or social media posts consistent with the ownership of firearms, even if Ranveer does encounter the unfortunate combination of light sleeper and creaky floorboard, he shouldn't have much more to worry about than a carbon-fiber tennis racket, golf club, or cricket bat. With any luck, he will be back at the hotel in time for a nightcap to help ease his jet lag.

The job is still a go, so the rest of the ride is spent on autopilot, Ranveer positioned in the center of the backseat bench, long legs folded into a full Lotus Pose, palms upturned with index fingertips connected to thumbs and eyes serenely closed.

14

DARK TOURISM

YOU COULD ARGUE that the privacy glass surrounding the Emirates Sultan Lounge is installed backwards. That the sheikhs, celebrities, and businesspeople sequestered behind the walls of hexagonal plasma glass blocks should, if they choose, be free to amuse themselves with views of the boorish, drooling, and uncouth buffoons from which they are being spared. And that the less affluent should be kept mercifully unaware of the pampering and coddling in which they will never be permitted to indulge.

But that is not the way the stratification of civilization has played out. The barrier is tinted as though an allusion to discretion, but those with either masochistic inclinations or leisure obsessions can still peer through and discern the manicures, pedicures, massages, and three-Michelin-star cuisine. The billiard tables, the jazz quartet, and the live indoor putting green. It turns out that the deprived revel in the act of coveting almost as much as the privileged relish being watched; that exhibitionism and voyeurism, rather than breeding malice, achieve a perverse and improbable cultural balance; that witnessing others' entitlement is a twisted form of dark tourism.

But Quinn isn't into it. Since one does not simply hop a flight to Oman, she has plenty of time to kill, so she wanders over to Terminal B and into a Planet Hollywood. There is only one other patron in the restaurant, and Quinn has made the lone waitress's job unduly grueling by sitting as far away from him as geometrically possible. She could have saved everyone a great deal of trouble by drinking alone at the bar rather than at a corner table, but she refuses to stage such a mournful display.

Dinner this evening is a tower of onion rings accompanied by chardonnay. She has just enough time before her plane boards for an excess of greasy American fare and to catch a good pre-sleep buzz. To that end, she is well into her second glass of what have turned out to be much more generous pours than you'd expect from a sticky, kitschy tourist trap like this.

Quinn's handset is out, and she is looking down at her ex-husband's profile photo. Her thumb hovers in the airspace over the message icon. She sometimes indulges in what a former therapist referred to as "emotional cutting" by scrolling back through old conversations. It's like the travelers who cup their eyes against the glass wall of the Sultan Lounge trying to spy on a life they will never have. But the difference is, when Quinn stands on the outside looking in, she is a tourist fascinated by her own past. It is not the unfamiliar and the exotic she hopes to one day obtain, but the mundane and the everyday she would do anything to get back.

Quinn has learned that hate is very much like pain. In the moment, it drowns everything else out, but over time, its strength and weight inevitably fade. When she was in the hospital having Molly, before she was given the epidural, Quinn swore she would never go through the experience of childbirth again. And there were moments during her divorce that she claimed to despise the man she once believed she could not live without. But time has a way of averaging out the extremes. Eroding even our best defenses. Exposing our fates and mocking our dreams. Quinn has come to believe that all of us eventually figure out who we are and what we want; the only question is whether it will be too late.

She is fantasizing about tapping that anachronistic handset icon and giving her ex-husband a completely unexpected call when she receives a Semaphore notification. It is an incoming connection request from Henrietta Yi. Quinn is grateful for the intervention and accepts it unhesitatingly.

"Henrietta," Quinn says. She can see from her own live thumbnail in the corner that she looks like backlit, baggy-eyed shit, but she's had enough wine that she's mostly indifferent.

Henrietta waves into the camera with a combination of hesitation and enthusiasm. Her hair is down, and her bangs are perfectly shaped to frame her round, radiant face. "Hi, Ms. Mitchell. I'm so sorry to bother you. Is now a good time?"

"Now's a *perfect* time," Quinn says. "You might have just saved me from drunk-dialing my ex-husband."

Henrietta is momentarily taken aback by Quinn's candor, but she recovers swiftly and even transitions into a knowing nod. "We've all been there, Ms. Mitchell."

"Really?" Quinn asks with amused skepticism. "You don't strike me as the drunk-dialing type."

"OK, maybe not," Henrietta confesses. "But one can always hope."

Quinn is grateful for the company and decides to nudge the dynamic a tick more toward companionship.

"So, does toiling away in Moretti's secret lair leave much time for dating?"

"Ha!" the young woman exclaims. "I *wish* my schedule were the problem."

"What do you mean?"

"I mean men aren't exactly lining up to date a five-foot-tall Korean K-pop fangirl with two PhDs in physics and a Pokémon fetish."

"Hold on," Quinn says. "Back up a second. You have *two* PhDs in physics?"

"Quantum and particle."

"Jesus," Quinn says. "I hope whatever Moretti has you doing is worthy of your aptitude."

"So do I," Henrietta says.

"Anyway," Quinn pivots, "I know it's hard to see yourself the way other people see you, but you are an intelligent, charismatic, and absolutely adorable young woman. You're kind of the total package, if you ask me. If you don't get hit on, it's only because men are intimidated by you."

Henrietta blushes through her honey-colored complexion, and her eyelashes bat daintily at her bangs. "You're so sweet," she says. "Thank you. I *really* needed to hear that."

"Anytime."

Something dark explodes into frame, and it takes Quinn a moment to grasp that it's a cat, glossy and pure black. As it nuzzles Henrietta, it simultaneously shows Quinn its pink, puckered butt.

"Who is this?" Quinn asks.

"This is Jiji," Henrietta says. She hooks the beast by its belly and relocates it beside her on the couch. Its hypnotic amber eyes regard Quinn with intense vigilance as it rubs its cheek against Henrietta's elbow. "He's the closest thing to a boyfriend I have."

"He's adorable."

"He's also schizophrenic. Some days he's like this and I can't keep him out of my lap, and some days I can't even find him."

"Sounds like a pretty typical boyfriend to me."

The cat abruptly ejects himself from the frame, and Quinn can see from Henrietta's gaze that he crosses the room, leaps, and comes to rest on some sort of elevated perch.

"Case in point," Quinn says.

"Exactly." Henrietta repositions herself on the couch, and her expression portends a transition. "I know you're boarding soon, Ms. Mitchell, but do you have another minute?"

"Sure."

"I wanted to apologize for the other day."

"Apologize?"

"Mr. Moretti told me about your daughter. And then I remembered making that comment about her growing out of Pokémon."

Quinn leads with a reassuring smile. "Don't even think about apologizing," she says. "There's no way you could have known."

"I know," Henrietta says. "It just felt so . . . I don't know. *Insensitive.*"

"Listen," Quinn begins. "Let me tell you something about tragedy that only people who've experienced it seem to know. It doesn't help for everyone to avoid talking about it or to pretend like it never happened. I actually *like* talking about Molly. It seems to make everyone else uncomfortable, but to me, it keeps part of her alive."

"I like that," Henrietta says. "Tell me something about her."

"OK," Quinn says. "Well, in some ways, you remind me of her."

Henrietta smiles primly. "Oh? How so?"

"Well, there's the obvious, of course. The Pokémon fanaticism. But she was also really smart. She always used to figure out all her birthday and Christmas presents before she opened them. She never peeked, but she could always think back in time and figure out little comments, or unusual behavior that would tip her off. Like when her father snuck away at Harry Potter World and bought her Hermione's wand for her birthday. She remembered that day over three months later and knew *exactly* what was inside—even though we wrapped it in a shoebox to try to throw her off."

"Sounds like she was as analytical as her mother."

"She also had a bit of an edge to her. One day, she and her friends were trying to figure out what their spirit animals were. Everyone else was picking things like foxes and deer and pandas. Then all of a sudden Molly declares her spirit animal is a scorpion that can kill all their spirit animals."

"Well, that *definitely* isn't me," Henrietta says with playful revulsion. "I'm more of a panda girl."

"But I can tell you have a bit of an edge to you, too," Quinn says.

"Really?"

"You have *two* PhDs. You could be making *millions* on Wall Street, yet you're working for the CIA. And you're working on one of the most covert projects I've ever heard of at the agency. *And* you seem to be one of the few who can handle Moretti."

Henrietta replies with a demure smile. "You just have to know when to ignore him."

"Listen," Quinn says. "I have a box of Molly's old Pokémon stuff in storage. When I get back, I'd like you to have it."

"Oh, no," Henrietta says. "No, I couldn't."

"Henrietta . . ." Quinn insists. "It's just sitting in storage. Nothing would make me happier than to give all that stuff to someone who will love it as much as she did."

It takes her a moment, but Henrietta relents. "Thank you," she says. "I promise to take good care of it."

"I know you will," Quinn says. "Unfortunately, I need to start making my way to my gate. Apology *not* accepted, because it wasn't necessary. But thank you for calling."

"Of course," Henrietta says. "Safe travels, Ms. Mitchell."

"Call me Quinn."

Henrietta beams. "Safe travels, *Quinn*."

Quinn takes another mouthful of wine. Henrietta was right: Molly got her analytical prowess from her mother. Quinn has come to think of her own mind as a type of multi-threaded device. It is as though she has a second, dedicated processor for offloading background jobs—integrated circuitry optimized for solving complex problems. Sometimes she doesn't even get to choose the tasks it spins up and chews on. Answers, when they are ready, are simply copied to active memory, whether she is in the shower, falling asleep, driving, or in the middle of a conversation. One moment she is walking or grocery shopping or drying her hair, and the next, she is suddenly aware.

It happened the first time she met Henrietta—the epiphany that Moretti's secret project is related to the Epoch Index. They are either working on a quantum computer to try to decrypt it, or they've already cracked it, and now they are building something unprecedented as a reaction. Either way, Quinn knows that the CIA would not pass up the opportunity to turn the future into the ultimate asset.

15

DHARMA

THE MERCEDES-BENZ H2-CLASS pulls noiselessly up in front of a two-story white stone structure, and just over seven minutes later, Ranveer is standing in an upstairs bedroom at the side of a naturally finished mahogany crib, having just bypassed the biometric bolt downstairs by cutting it right out of the steel door it was mounted in with a portable, high-precision waterjet and placing it gently in a nearby flowerpot.

He isn't at all concerned about what he touches, because he is wearing polymer obfuscation gloves. Each glove you pull out of the box promises five forensically distinct, completely randomized fingerprints. Law enforcement hates these things because even when they know obfuscation gloves were used, they still have to run down every single print just to be sure. And they have to keep track of all the fake prints and compare them to all the other fake prints ever collected on the off chance that the same glove gets used for more than one crime, which is exceedingly unlikely since they come in packs of one hundred and only cost around twenty euros (and, as they are manufactured by one of the more modern and progressive crime syndicates currently in operation, they are even available in twelve different skin tones). If you really want to fuck with your pursuers, you can also get little baggies full of hair, skin flakes, saliva, sweat, blood, semen, urine, feces, and even ear wax that you can distribute around your work area in all kinds of creative configurations. They come in two varieties:

synthetic (which means they contain randomized DNA) and organic (taken off cadavers or bought off people with either mouths or drug habits to feed). But Ranveer carries no such paraphernalia. While he appreciates the forensic static obfuscation gloves generate, there's something about the use of biobags and clue-glue that he finds distasteful.

He reaches over to the diaper-changing table beside him and holds down the button on what his specs are telling him is the transmitting end of a one-hundred-channel, 2.4-gigahertz, water- and shock-resistant, fully shielded and redundant baby monitor designed to withstand any contingency this cruel and unpredictable world can possibly throw at it—except for someone intentionally switching it off.

The baby at the bottom of the crib is sleeping with his knees drawn in, his butt up in the air, and his head turned toward Ranveer. His flawless complexion is a radiant, golden-honey brown, and his perfect little black curls lick at his forehead and the tops of his ears. Ranveer can hear a tiny whistle coming from his plump, pursed lips as the infant takes quick, shallow breaths. He has never held a baby before, and he wonders what it would be like, seeing as how so many people seem to enjoy it so much. He even briefly considers lifting the baby out of the crib and rocking him, before dismissing the impulse as an unnecessary risk. Better to get the job done and get out before a paranoid mother subconsciously misses the ambient red rhythm of the LEDs and things really end up messy.

From a compartment in his pouch, Ranveer produces the dark glass vial of hebenon solution and gives it a few quick shakes. If there were a handbook for such things, it would advise that hebenon is best used in circumstances where the subject is in a very deep sleep or a coma. The name comes from the botanical substance Claudius used to murder his own brother in *Hamlet*, though the modern-day version is decidedly less organic than its Elizabethan predecessor. The three primary ingredients are oxybuprocaine, sulfuric acid, and hydrogen cyanide. A small drop is placed in the ear, where the oxybuprocaine immediately begins to numb any surface it comes into contact with. When the fluid's passage is obstructed by the eardrum, the sulfuric acid rapidly dispatches with the thin membrane, allowing the solution to continue down into the middle ear via the eustachian tube and then eventually into the throat, where it triggers the reflex to swallow. Once ingested, the hydrogen cyanide halts cellular respiration, which typically kills the victim in approximately sixty seconds, give or take.

Honestly, not a bad way to go, all things considered.

During such moments it is not uncommon for religion to intrude upon Ranveer's thoughts, and in particular, the four objectives known as *purusarthas* that just about all Hindus agree guide one toward a rewarding and respectable existence. They are *dharma* (righteousness and moral values), *artha* (economic prosperity and financial security), *kama* (indulgence of the senses, including love), and *moksha* (freedom and liberation). The *purusarthas* are not unlike algebra in that there is a specific order of operations, which, if not observed, will yield dramatically different results. The general consensus is that dharma should be prioritized above all others, since one's moral code dictates how one approaches the other three objectives. But just as all religions that have graduated beyond the autocratic dogma of cult status invite impassioned debate, there are those who disagree. When Ranveer was a boy, he often snuck out of his room at night and sat on the stairs in the dark and listened to his father and his uncle drink Darjeeling tea and argue about the *Arthashastra*, an ancient Indian text that maintained that artha, not dharma, was to be prioritized above all other objectives. Without prosperity and financial security, the argument went, sensuality and indeed even morality were not possible.

Invariably, Ranveer's father would react incredulously. "If one were truly to place one's economic prosperity above one's morality," he argued, "just imagine the types of things one could justify doing."

Just imagine.

There is enough greenish light in the room from electroluminescent nightlights that Ranveer is easily able to guide the dropper over the infant's ear without dialing his specs into the infrared range. He pauses for a moment and listens, but all he can hear is the whistle and tiny rattle of breathing. Even through the obfuscation glove, he can feel the warmth radiating up from the baby's cheek, and he can smell the sweet milk of his mother.

Justifying one's actions solely through religion is not enough. Unless you integrate philosophy and science into your worldview, you are no better than some of the mindless zealots Ranveer was surrounded by back in Tehran. You have to understand, before you choose to take a life, why it is so hard to do so. You have to accept that the innate social structure that keeps humankind intact demands that murder be abhorrent. Although we feel very little remorse for slaughtering just about any other living creature—consuming its flesh, wrapping ourselves in its skin, boiling the gelatin out of its bones and connective tissue for cheap cosmetics and children's novelties—the sight of a severed human head or a bloated rotting corpse must necessarily evoke in us the most profound horror if the species is to avoid self-destruction. Yet somehow murder has existed for as long as life has been available to extinguish and will always exist despite any and all efforts to prevent or punish it.

Murder is as necessary as our revulsion to it. The two forces balance each other out in a mysterious societal equilibrium that both rattles and intrigues us. The ability to murder is, frankly, what sets some people apart. Power belongs to those with the strength to overcome their fears and weaknesses and instincts—those who are capable of overriding the more primitive regions of the brain with the more highly evolved. Ranveer knows that no matter how many people he kills, in the end, he will be judged not on his moral code or his actions, but by the only criteria that has ever truly counted for anything in all the billions of years life has existed on Earth: his own ability to survive and prosper.

A single drop of the solution is released as Ranveer squeezes the soft silicone bulb, and when the fluid is funneled down through the outer ear, the infant briefly looks as though he is going to wake up and cry, but then he becomes peaceful again. His breathing pauses, but only long enough to swallow, and then it resumes. At forty-six seconds, the short shallow breaths stop once again, and this time, the child's little back does not resume its rhythmic rise and fall.

As he unsheathes his ribbed Damascus steel, Ranveer notes that the baby's cheek is a little small for a four-digit number, and therefore uses the blade to split the infant's onesie down the back instead. Usually he carves tags into his victims, or brands them with a plasma torch, or inks them with a disposable tattoo pen. But tonight, he uses a fine-point permanent marker against the smooth and flawless skin.

PART TWO

16

LUXURY LOBBY LOITERING

QUINN MITCHELL IS not exactly what you would call cosmopolitan. In high school, she went on a group ski trip to Quebec, where she did several things she later had to disclose as part of her security clearance application so that she wouldn't fail her polygraph. In college, she did a semester in Frankfurt, where she hoped to do some of those things again, but which turned out to be so demanding that she cried almost every night and came home two weeks early. And when she was first married, she and her now-ex-husband took a vacation to Cancún, which they each pretended to enjoy but which they admitted to each other years later they both hated. Unless you count going to the World Showcase at Epcot, Quinn is about as domestic as Americans get.

Prior to booking her flight, she probably couldn't have found Oman on an unlabeled map, and she had absolutely zero idea of what to expect once she landed. Turns out, at least as far as properties owned and operated by Crystal Collective Worldwide are concerned, it isn't all that different from L.A.: plenty of decorum, almost no co-operation. Although she sees little else when she closes her eyes, nobody here can remember anyone even slightly resembling the gentle-man in question. Miraculously, most don't even need to look down at her handset before they are certain that they can be of no assistance whatsoever to a female American CIA officer with no head covering. After a full day of curt but polite interviews in the cool dim lobbies of every Crystal Collective Worldwide hotel in the city, the only thing she has learned is that, by the time she gets the necessary paperwork in place and manages to orchestrate the cooperation of both the Omani kingdom and various local authorities, all surveillance footage will have long since been erased, and her man will be three cities away with at least as many new bodies in his wake.

Quinn was planning on her base of operations being the U.S. embassy, but Muscat is a two-and-a-half-hour drive south, so although she feels she is not all that welcome at the Al Hujra Hotel—by far the most expensive of all CCW properties in Sohar, and apparently the favorite of everyone from royalty to rock stars—she gets herself set up at a table in a quiet corner of the lobby, orders a coffee and two bottles of water, unclips her handset from her belt, and starts going through her messages. The one forwarded by Moretti is marked urgent, and as soon as she begins reading it, she reflexively makes a noise that turns the heads of the people around her.

Quinn remembers the innocent voice of the little girl in the kitchen casually telling her that Molly is sleeping in the pool. Feels, all over again, the sickening realization that she did not confirm that they were being watched. Through the kitchen window, sees the dark, still shape gently rising and falling on the calm, sparkling surface. Hears the plate shatter at her feet. Quinn cannot remember how she got outside and into the neighbor's yard, but she can feel herself pushing against the resistance of the water, and the weight of what is in her arms, and the pull of her own wet clothes as she climbs the pool stairs. Her daughter's eyes half open but unseeing as Quinn lays her out on a lounge chair in the sun. The limpness of her neck as she pinches her chin and straightens her head. The purple of her lips and gums. Sweeping the wet blond hair away from her porcelain-pale face. In an instant, Quinn relives the fifteen exhausting and dizzying minutes of CPR, of pleading with her daughter to come back to her, of the taste of chlorine and the smell of sunscreen and the feel of her mouth sealed around her baby's cold lips. Compression against the tiny chest. Those beautiful blue eyes staring right past her into the sky. And then she feels herself being pulled away at the waist by an EMT and watches herself vomit violently on the deck of the pool.

Her specs are dialed down now, and her forehead is pressed against two fingers. She is focusing on her breathing as she tastes the salt of her tears at the corners of her mouth. It is ten minutes before she can open her eyes again. The other people in the lobby are conspicuously ignoring her. She wipes her nose and cheeks and goes back to the report.

The nine-month-old child was found by his mother when she began to wonder why he was sleeping so late. His pajamas were split open down the back, where the number 1401 was neatly printed in black indelible ink. The toxicity report shows hydrogen cyanide. Burns in the aural canal and throat indicate that the solution was administered through the ear.

Everything about this case just changed, and Quinn now knows that she cannot keep living twelve hours in this man's past. She does not want to be this close to death. These murders are no longer data points and statistics to be factored into queries and equations. They are more than just locations and timestamps and parameters. These are people. Babies. Quinn knows that she has two choices right now. She can call Van and wake her up and tell her that she can't do this anymore. Tell her that she needs to come home. Ask her to talk to Moretti for her. Order a car to take her back to the airport and a glass of wine while she waits. Have another at the airport, and a third on the plane. Or she can close her eyes, take a deep breath, and get back to the task of catching this sociopathic motherfucker before he has the chance to kill again.

Quinn adds the new case information to her database and triggers a set of routines that aggregate statistics across victims. The results are instantaneous and not significantly different from before: 86 percent are male; 92 percent are under the age of twenty-four; roughly half have ties to regions traditionally associated with the energy industry, and the other half have some kind of technical or scientific background. Not nearly enough to go on. And no secondary correlation. No ransom demands, no blackmail, and no evidence of corruption. No scandals or cover-ups. No ties to organized crime. Most people think that without a body you don't have a murder, but there's one more thing you need to be sure you have a lead: somewhere there has to be a motive.

She extracts all the victims' names and universally unique identifiers into a separate list, then runs a query against all the most common indices. The results are nothing she hasn't already seen. Most are related to news articles and law enforcement reports and social media posts, and about half appear to be false positives. She finds some potentially interesting results pertaining to individual victims, but most have already been doled out to Interpol to run down and thus far have yielded no relevant insights. As far as Quinn can tell, there is still nothing that neatly ties all the victims together. Still no signal in the noise.

But there is the age pattern—the fact that each victim was younger than the one before. Perhaps the Elite Assassin is nearing some sort of conclusion, his bloodlust finally satisfied by the ultimate barbarity of infanticide. Or perhaps the pattern does not signal an end to the killings, but rather foreshadows an entirely new beginning.

AT THE COUNTER, Quinn watches the hotel manager, Tariq al-Fasi Hashem, peevishly buff away a smudge on a plasma glass display with his microfiber pocket square. She strongly suspects that if she knew what was in that man's flawlessly groomed head, she probably wouldn't be loitering in yet another absurdly luxurious hotel lobby wishing that she knew what was in other people's flawlessly groomed heads. Instead, she'd be using what was in her own disheveled, foggy, jet-lagged mind to compose queries that narrowed high-value results down to sets of actionable leads. If she could just get someone to recount a seemingly innocuous conversation about food or weather or currency exchange, she might be able to predict the next city. Then she might be able to narrow Emirates flights down to the point where she could distribute printouts to agents with orders to stake out gates, and Sultan Lounges, and CCW lobbies just like this one. Or, if she could get into a room where her man stayed and manage to recover a DNA sample, even though she knows that the universe would never be charitable enough to hand her a direct hit, it is possible she could get a partial match off an aunt or an uncle who did not count on having a serial-killing nephew when they agreed to genetic sequencing to see if they were at risk for early-onset Alzheimer's. Anything to narrow the data set down to the size of the resources she has at her disposal—to adjust the ratio of warm bodies to cold.

For the very first time in her life, Quinn understands how people justify torture. It occurs to her that, even with all the data she has access to, and all the tools with which she can sort, filter, group, join, visualize, query, and pivot, she cannot reach into the one place where all the answers to all the world's greatest mysteries perpetually lie. Every single killer currently at large, every kidnapper, every rapist, and every terrorist is known by somebody out there. Enough knowledge exists to rain retribution down on the entire planet like a sublime golden solar storm, if only she could access and synthesize and index the contents of everyone's minds.

Like her colleagues, Quinn spent a fair amount of time studying the "enhanced interrogation techniques" liberally employed throughout the United States' morally ambiguous history. She imagines Tariq in an orange jumpsuit, being pinned down beside the in-floor drain of his black-site cell inside the belly of a U.S. Navy Island-class landing ship in the Baltic Sea, just off the coast of Poland, kicking and twisting and pissing himself, coughing and sputtering through a towel saturated by a seemingly endless stream of cold water. Or shackled to a wall for two days in an artful, twisted pose designed to place all of his weight on a single quadriceps and hamstring and calf muscle until all three simultaneously seize and spasm and light up nerve endings in a way that rivals childbirth, and that reduces men to quivering, tearful, barely audible pleas to whoever their gods are, but that inflicts no lasting damage that can be used as evidence before an international tribunal. Or kneeling, bent over, with hands zip-tied behind him and his—

She stops herself there. Quinn knows all she would get out of him is every insult he has ever heard, every obscenity arranged in every possible combination, and every lie he hopes will just make it stop. And she knows that even if she were to save a hypothetical life, it would be at the expense of her own humanity. That she would become a walking fatality. Quinn knows that torture is the ultimate expression of frustration, impotence, and defeat—and she recognizes that those are exactly the things she is feeling right now.

But that doesn't mean there isn't a way to reach Tariq—this man who, on the surface, is just the manager of a luxury hotel, but who is clearly entrusted with so much more. Nobody is *just* anything. Everyone you meet, everyone you see around you—whether you're rubbing elbows at a black-tie gala or eating Chick-fil-A waffle fries in a suburban food court—everyone is endlessly complex. Everyone, no matter how seemingly guarded, has a rich and personal and meaningful story to tell. You just need to know how to ask.

Quinn turns on her handset, logs into the CIA's encrypted virtual private network, swivels the throat mic down from her metaspecs, and begins subvocalizing queries like the desperately murmured prayers of the tortured.

"GOOD AFTERNOON," TARIQ says with none of the ooze of the manager back in L.A. Without bothering to ask permission, he hitches his steel-gray trousers just above the knees and seats himself on the edge of the white divan across from Quinn. This is *his* hotel, and he will sit when and where he damn well pleases. "The concierge said you wished to see me."

Quinn relocates her specs to the top of her head. She is trying to suppress the fact that, up close, she finds the manager of the Al Hujra—the man she was fantasizing about waterboarding just thirty-five minutes ago—unexpectedly attractive. Usually, curly hair doesn't do much for her, but there's something about the way it blends with his salt-and-pepper stubble and complements his dark complexion that she finds distinguished.

Although she's doing her best to stay on script, Quinn can't help but be momentarily derailed by wondering if she looks as disgusting as she feels. All the travel, combined with the unfamiliar Omani food (and, if she's being honest, the two mini bottles of chardonnay she paid for out-of-pocket on the plane) is not doing her stomach any favors.

"Mr. Hashem," she says. He did not offer a hand, so she decides not to offer hers. Instead, she removes her ID from the inside pocket of her blazer and unfolds it for Tariq to verify. "My name is Quinn Mitchell. I work for the CIA."

"Call me Tariq," the manager says, though not especially warmly. A curt nod indicates that he is satisfied with her credentials, and Quinn tucks them away.

"Thank you for making time to see me."

"You're welcome."

There is an economy to this man that is making her feel rushed. It doesn't help that he glances down at what looks to her like a very high-end Chinese timepiece strapped to the inside of his wrist by the skin of what was probably once an exotic, endangered reptile. Quinn hopes that the sleeve of her blazer is covering her own plastic Timex Ironman.

"Do you know this man?"

Quinn's handset is configured so that the back is mirroring what's on the front, and she and Tariq are both looking at one of the renderings of her suspect from L.A.

"No."

"Never?"

"Never."

"You've never seen this man before in your life?"

"No."

"You don't recognize this man as a guest of this hotel?"

"I do not."

"And you're certain of that?"

"I am."

Tariq al-Fasi Hashem is considerably less exotic and attractive when he is obstructing justice. The unfamiliar fragrance he brought with him that only moments ago Quinn found not entirely off-putting she now finds a little douchey.

"Mr. Hashem—Tariq—I'm here in coordination with Interpol investigating a series of extremely brutal murders, the most recent of which occurred just seven kilometers from this hotel."

"I understand."

"And we have reason to believe that this man is involved."

"I see."

"And that he stayed here. In your hotel."

Nothing. Doesn't even blink.

"Is it possible you were a little hasty before? Would you like to see the image one more time?"

"That won't be necessary."

Quinn places her handset down on the glass surface in front of her. The table is composed of two independently supported sections that, when she initially sat, registered simply as abstract blobs—something approximating opposing commas—but that she now realizes constitute a yin-yang symbol. An unconventional one, though. Given that the piece is fully transparent, it is impossible to tell which role in the symbol's duality her side plays versus Tariq's.

"Have you ever heard the saying *We know what we are, but know not what we may be?*"

"I have not."

"It was first attributed to the Prophet Muhammad, and it is believed that—"

"Allow me to save us both some time," Tariq interjects. As he leans forward and his gray-brown eyes bore into hers, Quinn is transfixed by their clarity. "I am not susceptible to CIA mind games, and I am not going to give you any information on any of my guests. The coffee and the water are on me. Safe travels, Ms. Mitchell."

The manager stands, and Quinn is so stunned that her gaze does not adjust, and she subsequently finds herself staring at a well-tailored crotch. In her experience, being spoken to in such a way elicits one of two diametrically opposed reactions in her, and she often does not know which until she opens her mouth.

"Tariq," Quinn says, then a moment later raises her gaze. "Sit back down. I'm not finished."

Tariq gives her an intensely inquisitive look. There is nothing dismissive or mocking about it—just pure perplexity that the American woman whom he has just told, in his own way, to fuck off has the balls to come at him again.

"*That* must be why they sent a woman to do a man's job," the hotel manager says. He lowers himself back down, this time not bothering with the trouser hitching. "Because you do it like a man."

Quinn can see that she has not intimidated one curly hair on this man's head, and that he only sat back down because, unless another international serial killer happens to be due sometime soon, this conversation is probably the most interesting thing he will do all day. Regardless of the reason, she still has his attention, and she has yet to make her final move.

She picks her handset back up and swipes to the next image. She does not look at it herself, because the first time she saw the autopsy photo of the nine-month-old baby boy on a stainless-steel surgical table beneath harsh white spotlights, she nearly vomited. So instead, she flips it around and watches Tariq. She cannot tell if his expression changes or if it is just the pounding of her heart that's affecting her vision.

"This is the real reason I'm here," Quinn says. She wonders if Tariq has gathered a long enough sample of her voice to realize that it is now quivering. "You should know that the man who you're protecting did this. This is how he can afford to stay in places like this and buy people like you."

Tariq is still looking down at the handset. Quinn senses there could be an opening, so she jams in a wedge.

"People involved in drugs or organized crime or espionage—they understand the risks. But that's not the business this guy is in. He appears to be killing people for no reason whatsoever. He's killing *children*. This guy's not some type of high-class assassin, Tariq. He's just a psychotic murderer."

Tariq raises his eyes from the handset, and as he watches Quinn, she searches his expression for something that still is not quite there. It is as though he has chosen to call—not to fold, not to raise, but to stay in the game long enough to see what she's really got.

So Quinn goes all in. She swipes again, and this time, she finds what she's looking for. This time, Tariq's expression changes.

"Where did you get that?" he asks her.

This nine-month-old baby boy is very much alive. He is sitting on his mother's lap and is overjoyed by her undivided attention. One outstretched hand is on her cheek and the other is over his mother's mouth as she playfully gobbles at the chubby fingers.

Another swipe.

This time, it is Tariq holding the baby boy. They are on a beach, and Dad is dressed in a white oxford and jeans rolled up to his knees. Quinn notices that he is wearing a different watch in the photo— a metal one. His wife has thick, wavy black hair and wears a flowing white dress. Her sandals dangle from her hooked fingers by thin leather straps.

Quinn considers swiping again, but she can see that she does not need to.

"I asked you where the *fuck* you got those."

Instinctively, Quinn gives it right back to him. "I work for the C-I-*fucking*-A," she says. "*That's* where I got them. In fact, I have hundreds of these. I know that your son, Omar, is two and a half now, and that your wife, Aasimah, is twenty-four weeks pregnant with your first daughter. I can even tell you what she's thinking of naming her, in case you didn't know."

"Are you threatening my family?"

Quinn instantly drops the smirk. "Of course not."

"Then what are you doing?"

"I'm trying to make you realize that every single one of these victims left families behind that loved them just as much as you love your family. Just as much as I . . . Just as much as everyone loves their families."

The hotel manager's demeanor has transformed into something disquieting. He shakes his head in what Quinn interprets as an amalgam of rage and astonishment.

"You people make me sick."

"Tariq, listen—"

"You come into my country. Into my place of business. You insult the Prophet Muhammad. You don't even do me the courtesy of covering your head."

Reflexively, Quinn reaches up and touches her hair.

"And then you have the audacity to threaten my family?"

"I'm not threatening your family, Tariq."

"You're not threatening my family? Tell me, what would you do if a Middle Eastern man came into your country, followed you into a Starbucks or your gym or wherever you go, and when you didn't answer his questions, showed you photos of your children next to a picture of an eviscerated baby? How would *you* react?"

Quinn holds up her hands in a halting gesture. "Please. I realize how this looks, Tariq. I do. But I want to be very clear that I am *not*, in any way—"

"And you wonder why the world hates you so much. How would you like it if we parked aircraft carriers off the coasts of California and New York and fired Tomahawk missiles into your country every time something happened that we didn't like? Or if we sent Navy SEALs into Washington, D.C., in the middle of the night to kill or kidnap whomever we pleased. Or if we put Americans in secret prisons, and denied them legal representation, and tortured them. Even if you didn't respect your own government, how would you feel about ours?"

"The United States and the Sultanate of Oman are allies," Quinn says. "We would never—"

"I'm not talking about Oman, Ms. Mitchell. I'm talking about the *world*. I'm talking about our Muslim brothers and sisters. Look at you. You don't even know you're doing it. You are so arrogant and so entitled that you don't even know how the rest of the world sees you. You don't even know why everyone hates you so much."

"Tariq, all I'm doing is investigating a murder. All I want is to—"

"Get out of my hotel and don't ever come back. If I see you in here again, I'll have you taken down into the basement, where we have a soundproof room, and I'll give you a reason to hate Muslims. Do you understand me?"

Quinn has gone from apologetic to terrified. She could have waited until Interpol agents arrived in Sohar, and they could have all done this together, but she didn't want to give the killer another seven hours to run. She can see now what a mistake that was—how far out of her depth she really is. Tariq is waiting for a response, and Quinn barely manages a nod.

"And just to be clear," he adds, "I *am* threatening *you*."

That is all Quinn can take. The rapid flash of fear; the talk of dead children; being seven thousand miles from home in a strange country; the fact that she has no fucking clue what she's doing. It is all just too much. The only thing she can think to do is cover her face with her hands.

"What's the matter, Agent Mitchell?" Tariq asks with mock concern. "Does the truth hurt?"

And then, for the second time today, Quinn Mitchell sobs.

"I hope you're not expecting me to feel sorry for you."

She has no idea what's going on around her anymore. Trying to suppress what is inside her with deep and deliberate breathing takes all her concentration.

"Poor, poor American. Poor CIA agent. The murderer who can't catch the murderer."

She wonders why Tariq hasn't gotten up and walked away. Is he still there just to mock her, or has he summoned men in tight suits and wires in their ears to grasp her by the arms, lift her out of her seat, and escort her outside? Or worse, into a side room, and then down the back stairs and into the basement.

"I'm sorry," she finally says from behind her hands.

"What's that?"

Quinn cycles through one final breath, then uncovers her face.

"I said I'm sorry. I did that all wrong. You want to know why?" She leans forward, removes the cocktail napkin from beneath a bottle of water, and starts trying to clean up her face. "Because I have no fucking clue what I'm doing." She addresses the snot on her top lip first, then finds a dry piece of napkin to begin soaking up tears. "I don't belong here. I'm not a field officer. I'm not any kind of officer. I'm an analyst. I'm supposed to be back in Langley, sitting in a cubicle. But somebody got the brilliant idea to send me out after an international murderer. Probably because my daughter died, and they thought that would *incentivize* me or something." She sniffs and blinks and finds that she is not done with the tears just yet. "But all it's done is turn me into a complete fucking mess. And all I want to do is catch this motherfucker so I can go home and drink an entire bottle of wine by myself and curl up in bed and not wake up for week."

"Then why are you chasing bodies?" Tariq asks her.

Quinn was expecting stunned silence. Maybe even just a tiny bit of sympathy. The one thing she was not expecting from Tariq was advice.

She swaps the wad in her hand for the second cocktail napkin. "What?"

"I asked you why you're chasing bodies," Tariq says again.

"What else am I supposed to do?"

"If you keep following the bodies, then bodies are all you are ever going to find. That's not how you catch a killer."

"What am I supposed to follow? I don't have any other leads."

"You don't need leads. You already know exactly why he's doing it."

Quinn looks up. "What do you mean?"

"I mean you may not know *how* someone can do the kinds of things he does, but you know exactly *why*."

"The money," Quinn says.

"The money," Tariq repeats. "If you want to know where he's been, keep following the bodies. But if you want to know where he's going, follow the money."

In addition to being a bloated, blubbering mess, Quinn now feels like a complete moron. It isn't like the oldest investigative cliché in criminal justice history never occurred to her. It's more that she just hasn't had the time. She's been so busy looking for something in the killer's recent past that she hasn't thought about other ways to peer into his immediate future. Plus, all Moretti seems to be interested in are details about crime scenes and timeline reconstructions. Maybe that's the problem with having access to so much information. Everyone always assumes that the challenges with "big data" revolve around storing, retrieving, processing, and making some kind of sense of it. But maybe the bigger problem with having access to more information than anyone ever dreamed possible is that it distracts you from asking the simplest and most obvious questions of all.

Given that the most exotic place Quinn has ever been prior to this was Diagon Alley at Harry Potter World during her daughter's spring break, the fact that she is now on the Arabian Peninsula trying to catch a serial killer while blowing her nose into a cocktail napkin after imagining herself getting kneecapped in the basement of a luxury hotel by a man she fantasized about both torturing and sleeping with is just too funny not to laugh at. Even Tariq seems to be relieved by the dissipation of international tensions.

"You know what?" Quinn says. "That's exactly what I'm going to do."

"Good," Tariq says. He stands, but rather than offering his hand, he pulls his sport coat across his silk shirt and buttons it closed. "We'll take care of all of this. Get yourself cleaned up, and when you're ready, go catch your killer."

There is the slightest of smiles in Tariq's eyes as he turns.

"Hey, Tariq," Quinn says. "One more thing."

The hotel manager turns with eyebrows cocked.

"Can you *please* tell me where I can get some decent American food around here?"

17

PITCH-ROLLING

IF RANVEER WERE the type, he could boast about any number of feats, deeds, and flukes, not the least of which was having been present for the inception of one of the most ambitious and significant enterprises of all time. This was back before he was a practicing airline monogamist. After booking a last-minute seat on a shared charter from San Francisco to Doha, Qatar, he witnessed a troop of Soylent-drinking, health-hacking, microdosing Silicon Valley bros expound upon their vision for disrupting every last aspect of innovation by first disrupting its very foundation: sovereignty.

"Pitch-rolling" it was called. It was when you tricked potential investors—who would otherwise sooner have a colonoscopy than take a meeting with you—into hearing your idea. Struggling entrepreneurs ran up hundreds of thousands in credit card debt purchasing open seats on shared transpacific private jets in order to ensure captive access to affluent capitalists. Once in the air, they typically stoked their courage with a Red Bull and vodka, pushed the sleeves of their hoodies up past their skinny elbows as they stood, croaked a few polite interjections until they had everyone's attention, and then unleashed a myriad of improbable schemes for achieving their spectacular utopian dreams.

It was kind of like a *Shark Tank* flash mob, or like having a time-share spiel unexpectedly sprung on you at forty thousand feet, but since it was usually much more entertaining than anything else there was to do, you went with it. At least initially. Pitch-rolling was also kind of like open mic night in that the second you started misfiring, the audience let you know. Therefore, unless you wanted to get booed back into your seat—or worse, right there in front of everyone, get offered a check for a thousand dollars to sit the fuck back down and shut the fuck up (which you sheepishly accepted)—you had to make your time up there count. Like the senior-year promposals most of these Harvard and Stanford dropouts were plotting just a few years prior, originality was as essential as the message itself.

The ultimately successful pitch for The Grid by the band of eager young geeks to a jetful of bearded, austere, and discriminating sheikhs went, more or less, like this. . . .

MICRONATIONS AREN'T REALLY a thing. Despite what Reddit might have you believe, you and your libertarian cohorts can't build an artificial island out of dredged-up sand or sail an old cargo ship bought at auction out into international waters, declare sovereignty, name yourself His Excellency the Royal Ninja Emperor Cobra Commander for Life, use a pirated version of Photoshop to design a flag with your spirit animal on it, print commemorative postage stamps, spin up your own cryptocurrency, compose a national anthem on your Casio synthesizer, pass a law requiring citizens to dress up as furries on Wednesdays, and give the rest of the world the middle finger. Either your ship will sink and everyone will laugh at you, or you will be invaded by a boatful of sleepy troops from the nearest *actual* nation, who will laugh at you *and* seize that sweet synthesizer. Or, even worse, nobody will even notice your audacious act of defiance, and you will return home in under a week, hungry and sunburned, only to be further insulted by the fact that the shelter where you surrendered your cat won't give him back because you are no longer considered a suitable feline custodian.

If you're thinking you are going to do any of this in space, then you are even more delusional. Now, if your plan is to promise a bunch of societal misfits one-way tickets to Mars in hopes of selling a new reality TV show, or to use the lure of a self-sustaining, zero-g, perpetual utopian orgy to swindle a few chumps out of their life savings, fair enough. But if you've managed to convince yourself that you are the chosen father of the very first off-Earth evolutionary branch of humanity, you are almost certainly destined for a premature and very fiery death.

All that said, you do have options. If you already own an estate or two, a private jet, a mega-yacht with its own microclimate, a smattering of buildings, and one or more sports franchises, do not despair. There is still additional status to be bought. But getting smeared across the surface of the Pacific by a super typhoon is for suckers. Getting murdered by skinny Somali pirates is whack. Going feral, bludgeoning one another to death with rocks, and descending into cannibalism is for losers. You need guaranteed safety, comfort, and convenience. You want a comprehensive turnkey micronation solution. What you're looking for is *The Grid*.

The pitch? A matrix of platforms constructed in the Persian Gulf, located just off the coast of Qatar's capital city, Doha.

The value prop? While technically still subject to Qatari law, each "exclave" would be granted a perpetual, nonexclusive, nontransferable, irrevocable, and exceedingly liberal license to pursue a wide range of personal interests and/or business activities. TL;DR: *carte blanche*.

The cost? Two hundred million USD gets you your very own multitiered exclave with a helipad, boat landing, office/laboratory space, luxury living quarters, and an elevator. Recurring costs of between five hundred thousand and one million USD per month covers various access to utilities (including undersea fiber connectivity), security, maintenance, janitorial services, transportation, and twenty-four-hour, on-demand meal delivery from a wide variety of culinary enterprises.

Why Qatar? Because oil is over. Because you should have diversified *yesterday*. Because consider your assets: plenty of coastline, contractors who know how to build stable offshore platforms (but who, in the age of energy diversification, have unexpectedly found themselves with an abundance of time on their hands), unlimited solar power (have you even *been* to the Middle East? It's like fucking Tatooine in August), and the fact that Qatar is rated by the World Risk Index as the safest nation on the planet as measured by exposure to natural disasters.

The question is: why *not* Qatar? Why *shouldn't* you become the Estonia of the Arabian Peninsula? Eff Oman and Saudi Arabia. To hell with Jordan and Iran. Let those sad sacks eat sand while you chart a new economic future by becoming the universal leader in startup incubation.

The Grid is *on*, bitches!

Who's in?

18

SIX MINUTES

KNOW WHAT'S WORSE than flying coach? Quinn does. It's called fly-ing *cargo*. As in being strapped into a jump seat amid stacks of netted and tethered pallets cinched to a roller-studded floor. But if your em-ployer is on the list of most-favored three-letter agencies, there are irrefutable advantages—principally that it's exceedingly easy on the budget. As in free. Plenty of resources go into keeping paying airline customers safe, but nobody wants to spend more than they have to protecting cargo, so airline executives calculate that if they make space freely available to employees of all the top anti-terrorist organizations on the planet, slightly more attention may get paid to plots bent on blowing up our next-day Amazon Prime orders.

The arrangement works just fine for Quinn since, as of right now, she has no idea where she is going. The last geographical certainty she experienced was when Tariq had the concierge set her up with a car that took her directly to the nearest KFC, where she attempted a gas-trointestinal reset with a full Ramadan meal. With no plan any more concrete than her determination to "stop following bodies and start following the money," she proceeded to the cargo hangar of Sohar Airport, where she flashed her credentials, watched as her baggage underwent perfunctory inspection, and was shown to a second-story combination kitchenette/break room with harsh white lighting, ped-estal seating, and a plasma glass flight board mounted at a 45-degree angle between the ceiling and the back wall.

Even though Quinn knows she should be looking for patterns in global financial transactions, she is distracted by something printed on the archaic thermal-paper boarding pass that was handed to her downstairs. All airports have an ICAO code issued by the International Civil Aviation Organization and used by air traffic control for flight planning. The designation for Sohar Airport is OOSH, which Quinn does not read as a code or an acronym, but as a single word— *oosh*—that she has not heard or thought about in a very long time.

Molly's first words were not the traditional "mama" or "dada," but rather "baba" for balloon and, shortly thereafter, "oosh" for shoes. She loved shoes—taking them off and putting them back on over and over again—which Quinn had always attributed to the fact that her husband stopped at the mall on his way home from work one evening when Quinn was still pregnant to get himself a new pair of running shoes and came home with a pair of baby Nikes with little pink swooshes. For some reason, that tiny pair of sneakers was far more meaningful to Quinn than all of the flowers he got her from the grocery store when he ran out to pick her up some Entenmann's frosted doughnuts, or the sometimes-sentimental-sometimes-sarcastic cards, or the bucket of Twizzlers he brought home from Costco because she was always craving them. Those shoes meant that he wasn't just thinking about her when they weren't together, but that he was thinking about the life growing inside of her, and that he couldn't wait to meet Molly, and to fall in love with her, and to sleep on the couch with her on his chest listening to his heartbeat. He would be there to change her diapers and feed her in the middle of the night, and to teach her to tie her shoes, and to put Band-Aids on her knees when she fell, and to show her how to ride a bike, and catch a fish, and swing a bat. He would relearn geometry so he could help her with her homework, and help teach her how to drive, and meet her boyfriends, and intimidate them just a little. When she cried over her first breakup, he would hug her and tell her that it was *his* loss, and that she was the most special person he had ever known in his entire life, and he would mean every word of it. The first time she was hungover and sick, instead of yelling at her or grounding her, he would bring her Tylenol, and encourage her to drink water, and take her out for a greasy breakfast. He would take her to visit colleges, and give her away at her wedding, and when his hair and stubble were more salt than pepper, he would buy his grandchildren *their* first pairs of Nikes. It was all right there in front of Quinn the moment he took that little box out of the bag and opened it up to show her what he'd bought, but instead of looking at the shoes, she was looking at him, and right then, she knew that everything would always be OK.

Another thing Quinn's husband unexpectedly brought home one day was one of the very first commercially available volumetric video rigs. It took him most of a Saturday to get all the cameras properly positioned and calibrated, but the next day, after her nap, they sat Molly down in the center of her foam alphabet puzzle mat and recorded six minutes (the maximum duration back then) of her playing. Almost subconsciously, after folding her boarding pass up like an accordion, Quinn had lowered her metaspecs and brought up the footage, and now a 3D version of Molly is sitting on the faux-hardwood laminate flooring in the center of the break room. The capture circle had been tiny—just big enough for a baby—so both Quinn and her husband are off camera, but whatever they are doing has Molly enraptured. There is a distant comical sound effect followed by an explosion of that delightful and infectious baby laughter that is the purest, most unadulterated form of joy Quinn can imagine. Eventually it dies down as Molly grows charmingly serious just before bringing the tips of her joined fingers together like frogs kissing—the sign they'd taught her for "more." Again, the off-camera sound effect, and again, pure effervescence in little human form. Edge detection wasn't very good back then, so background artifacts from the breakfast-nook-turned-playroom sometimes creep in around Molly's blond curls, but overall, the effect is spellbinding, and Quinn is transfixed.

The clip is only six minutes long, but she has spent dozens of cumulative hours watching it, and as the familiar taste of tears enters the corners of her mouth, she questions whether this is still a source of joy for her or whether it is just another form of emotional cutting. Maybe we weren't meant to remember for this long and with this level of fidelity. Maybe all of this technology will prove to be a failed and unimaginably costly human experiment. Quinn wonders whether she will still be watching these same six minutes twenty years from now— still subconsciously bringing it up, still tasting tears in an empty room, still haunted by the light-field ghost of her long-dead daughter.

She wonders whether, in order to move on, she will one day need to relearn how to forget.

The hologram seamlessly transitions back to the beginning and continues playing. Molly isn't wearing shoes in the video, and even if she were, they wouldn't be the baby Nikes her father bought her, since she would have outgrown them by then. Quinn still has one of them. The left one. It's in the original shoebox, and the shoebox is in a plastic bin that's stacked somewhere inside her storage unit thousands of miles away in suburban Virginia. The right one is gone. It got chewed up by the black Lab they tried rescuing seven months after Molly drowned. When her husband saw what the dog had done, he pinned it down by its throat and the dog yelped and peed and Quinn could see the whites of its terrified copper eyes. James did not kill the dog, but after he stood up, he screamed, and on his way out of the room, he punched the bedroom door so hard that he knocked it off its hinges. He left a trail of bright red blood splatters as he stepped over the door and went downstairs and left the house, and then it was quiet, and the dog was too afraid to move, and Quinn stood there alone in the bedroom knowing that nothing would ever be OK again.

19

AMBERLEY-ASH IS NOT SMILING

COMMUNICATION IN THE age of mass surveillance demands a sophisticated and intricate dance. One must transact digitally in order to maximize efficiency, but it is imperative that you never associate enough data with a single identifiable entity to allow your adversaries to piece together a coherent narrative.

For instance, having the name of your next target communicated through layers of obfuscation and bounced around multiple encrypted proxies located all over the globe poses an acceptable risk—so long as you do not transmit payment information back in the same direction. In Ranveer's view, it is far safer to let easily hacked coroner reports and sensationalized media do the work of broadcasting unique four-digit numbers for you.

The Grid has always posed unique challenges. Despite Qatari guarantees of near absolute sovereignty, there are still plenty of crevices and cavities inside the matrix of offshore exclaves where one might find oneself trapped. Which is exactly why Ranveer has traditionally preferred to transact with Grid interests electronically, or to send a neutral third party, paid for in cash. But every once in a while, when the world is expecting you to zig, the best move you have is to zag.

Therefore, given that Qatar is practically just up the street from Oman, Ranveer has decided to take the day and go on-Grid. Emirates Airlines is only too happy to hold his cases inside a private vault that his biometric signature alone can unlock, as well as give him access to a private, vapor-sterilized washroom where, in addition to showering and shaving, he applies the principles of electrolysis to recharge a couple of cartridges.

There are two stops on Ranveer's itinerary. The first is a laboratory run by a woman named Amberley-Ash, where he will pick up a bespoke order he placed months ago. The second is a company called PLC, run by the twins Naan and Pita, who, if all goes well, will hand him the last name on his list.

There are ferries that move people between Doha Port and Grid exclaves at no charge, but they are slow, inefficient, and usually crowded. In contrast, a well-established international Chinese ride-sharing company provides premium autonomous quadcopter transport. They are even cleared to take passengers directly to Hamad International, if you can stomach the exorbitant convenience fee. The insect-like devices are known as *Qīngtíng*, or Dragonflies, and are in constant algorithmic rotation, constituting one of the most efficient logistics operations Ranveer has ever seen. In just seconds, after a launch carefully designed to feel like a lightweight thrill ride, he is looking down between his British-tan wingtips at the fleet of public ferries below, each carving its own long white wake into the emerald-green Gulf.

The Grid is not nearly as industrial-looking as one might expect from thirty-six regularly spaced structures built using technologies derived from offshore oil-drilling platforms. They are essentially multitiered, steel-framed glass boxes supported at each corner by funnel-shaped pylons with accents that reveal themselves, after dark, to be customizable RGB plasma lighting. The last time Ranveer was forced to make an in-person visit to The Grid, he unexpectedly ended up spending the night and found that he rather enjoyed the cognac he took out on the balcony off one of the exclave's living quarters. He even briefly considered a nice corner unit as a retirement option for himself, but he knows he is much too restless to spend his remaining days confined to a thirty-by-thirty-meter, four-story artificial island.

While he may, when absolutely necessary, visit the odd exclave, waking up inside one every single morning would feel far too much like a cage.

Cantilevered off the southeast corner of each unit is a sizable blue disc that, if you didn't know better, you might mistake for a trampoline. In the center of each disc is painted the Chinese character for "quad" (四), which looks like an exotic mutation of what was once the universal symbol for helipad. Ranveer cannot remember which platform belongs to Amberley-Ash, but he poked "Corpuscule"—the unique name her exclave is registered under as required by Qatar's articles of incorporation—into the hologram floating above the directory panel back at the launch and therefore trusts he will be conveyed accordingly.

There is a brief moment of panic as the Dragonfly swings precipitously back toward shore, and he imagines it continuing along a hijacked path and touching down right in the center of a circle of CIA officers and Interpol agents who have been waiting for days for the safest and most dramatic way to take him. But then he sees that he is losing altitude and closing in on one of the exclaves nearest to shore. Amberley-Ash, Ranveer now recalls, was an early investor in The Grid, and therefore has coveted, low-number coordinates.

After touchdown, the Dragonfly pneumatically squats, and all four rotors abruptly halt in perfect unison. The canopy splits and lifts like a pair of transparent wings drying in the sun, and the side panel facing the exclave's entrance unfurls into three grippy steps connecting the Italian-leather cabin to the vulcanized-rubber platform. Even though there is no chopper wash to duck away from and shout over, the regular spacing of exclaves creates channels for leisurely Gulf breezes to merge together into sizable gusts, so the transition from quadpad to exclave is buffered by an airlock. As he steps through the initial entrance, Ranveer buttons his coat closed, hoping that the gas-powered bulk strapped to his side will go unnoticed.

AMBERLEY-ASH WAITS JUST beyond the second set of doors. Her hair still occupies that portion of the visible spectrum right in between red and orange that, being an accomplished molecular biologist in possession of a very high-end spectrophotometer, she has, Ranveer suspects, spent cumulative years painstakingly perfecting. It's longer than it used to be—just past her shoulders rather than the layered bob he remembers framing her fair and delicate complexion before— but her overall style clearly hasn't changed. She is wearing what Ranveer assumes is a black bodysuit beneath a pair of torn denim shorts and a fitted white T-shirt with the word "Recovered" printed across the chest. She is barefoot, which reminds Ranveer that she has a moon tattoo on her ankle and a star on the nape of her neck.

It wouldn't be an exaggeration to say that Amberley-Ash is pretty close to the antithesis of Ranveer's attraction template. His usual weakness is tall, dark-skinned brunettes with expensive bikini waxes who know how to navigate a novella-length wine list. In his mind, there is no bigger turnoff than a grown woman who doesn't understand the concept of age-appropriate fashion. And yet there is something about this woman that he deeply admires. And sometimes admiration has a way of manifesting itself in unexpected ways.

Ranveer suddenly remembers her smell—a combination of dryer sheets and baby powder and plain white soap. To an only child who grew up as a Hindu in Tehran among the aromas of cumin and rose water and incense, such bouquets of Western domesticity were once foreign and exotic, and he is surprised by how much he is looking forward to inhaling them again. But even though the glass doors behind him are now sealed off to the Gulf winds, the doors ahead are not parting. And Amberley-Ash is not smiling.

"I'm surprised you came in person," she says. These days, most structural glass is manufactured with microscopic patterns of engineered imperfections that bat a wide range of sound frequencies around until they lose most of their energy, eventually emerging from the other side as nearly imperceptible white noise. Therefore, Amberley-Ash's voice emanates from an acoustic panel embedded in the ceiling.

Ranveer slips his hands into his trouser pockets and shifts his weight. "Aren't you going to invite me in for a drink?"

"Your merchandise is to your left," Amberley-Ash tells him. "Take it and go."

Ranveer confirms that there is indeed a black polymer case placed against the glass surface to his left. Inside it, he imagines, is the aluminum canister of aerosolized designer molecule, the formula for which was purchased from one of her neighbors and synthesized specifically for him.

"I must admit," Ranveer says, "this isn't the reception I was hoping for."

"Well, this is the only reception you're going to get," says Amberley-Ash. "In fact, this is the last reception you're ever going to get from me. After this, we're done. Don't ever contact me again."

Ranveer isn't entirely sure what's going on, but this is one of the things he likes about her. She is every bit as headstrong and confident as she is intelligent, and he has no doubt whatsoever that even without four centimeters of glass between them, they'd be having the very same conversation.

The last time he bought from her, she invited him in and, despite the fact that Ranveer is old enough to be her father, they found themselves sitting close to one another in her upstairs conversation pit drinking various chilled gin concoctions and later ordering Indian pizzas (baked in-flight) along with several flavors of sorbet (packed in liquid nitrogen). She told him about her time at Stanford, and how she dropped out just a few credits shy of a degree in order to become one of the best-funded and youngest female entrepreneurs in Silicon Valley history. Their backgrounds, upbringings, and life experiences could not have been more different, yet there they were, at that particular moment, in that specific location, both just happy not to be alone.

That night, while she slept, Ranveer took a cognac out onto the balcony and read several articles about her as well as excerpts from her unauthorized biography. As he suspected, there had been significant gaps in Amberley-Ash's own account of her past.

Patricia Ash Westbrook died of breast cancer, but not before her daughter, Amberley-Ash, watched what happened as surgeons carved flesh off of her mother until it seemed there was nothing left but bone, and used a permanently implanted port in her neck to fill her with toxic chemicals that seemed to eradicate her will to live even faster than it killed cancer cells. Having watched her mother slowly die in a way that was anything but peaceful and dignified, Amberley-Ash knew that there was no way she could return to her former life and resume her previous routine. After burying what was left of her mother, rather than returning to school, she used her inheritance to establish her first lab in the Bay Area and declared that she was dedicating her life to discovering a universal cancer vaccine.

Corpuscule, the name she incorporated under, demonstrated promising early results, and Amberley-Ash's passion, charisma, and clarity of vision enabled her to close one of the biggest initial rounds of investment Silicon Valley had ever seen. Almost overnight, she became the focus of intense regulatory scrutiny and was constantly pursued both by her competition and by the media. That was when Amberley-Ash decided to stop sleeping.

To keep herself awake and focused, she used amphetamines and dopamine reuptake inhibitors, and to try to keep herself coherent during press tours, she experimented with various types of mood stabilizers. Having formed several expensive pharmacological attachments, she began synthesizing her own cocktails and distributing them liberally throughout the company's reporting structure to increase her team's productivity. According to multiple depositions, she "strongly implied" that performance-enhancing drugs were not a choice, but a requirement.

When her most senior scientist went home after not sleeping for three days, took a shower, put on a clean Corpuscule-branded lab jacket, and hanged himself in his basement—and after the DEA raided all three of Corpuscule's laboratories and found that they were deeper into narcotics at that point than they were into research—Amberley-Ash decided not to attend the board meeting in which it was well known she would be stripped of all remaining control of her company, and to skip the appointment her personal lawyer had arranged for her to surrender herself to federal authorities, and instead, while she still had a passport, to embezzle what was left of her sizable capital and use it to relocate.

There was something about the beautiful young woman that reminded Ranveer of Ophelia, Hamlet's betrothed—her madness and self-destruction prompted by the tragic death of a parent. That night, while sitting out on Amberley-Ash's balcony, he wondered if passion born of tragedy always revolved toward madness. Perhaps, but today Ranveer knows that the equation is much more complicated than that. He now understands that nothing of great consequence is achieved without some measure of madness, and that the acts throughout history with the most profound and lasting impacts on humanity are those that were initially indistinguishable from pure insanity.

RANVEER'S HANDS COME out of his pockets and form a gesture of mock surrender. "I give up," he tells her. "You win. I should have called. Now can I please come in?"

"I haven't been sitting around waiting for you to call, you arrogant fuck."

"Then what's the problem?"

"The problem is what you did to Henryk."

"Henryk," Ranveer repeats as if the word were unfamiliar. "What happened to Henryk?"

"Don't stand there and fucking lie to me. I monitor the shadowphiles for leaked crime reports just like you. I know goddamn well Henryk didn't die of an aortic aneurysm. Not only are you into some really fucked-up shit right now, but you're obviously cleaning up after yourself. I'm honoring our agreement, but there's no fucking way I'm ending up like Henryk."

"Listen to me," Ranveer says. "Henryk lived an unhealthy lifestyle."

"Because he did business with *you*. I haven't spent the last decade cooped up in this fucking aquarium trying to get sober and the last three years in teletherapy for two fucking hours a day just to get my throat slit now. There's no way you're getting in here."

Ranveer is a surprisingly gifted conversationalist when he wants to be, because he knows the secret: everyone's favorite topic is themselves. Keep the exchange about them, and you can run out the clock on absolutely any social interaction. Young people? Relationships. The middle-aged? Kids, careers, and sports. Old people? Their shitty health. But the last time Ranveer was here, there were things he'd wanted to say, too—things that most other people weren't able to hear, but that he felt like Amberley-Ash could. And there are things he'd like to say to her now. Things about Henryk and Oman and L.A. Things about Caracas, Moscow, Cape Town, and Beijing. About this woman from the CIA. He'd told himself that his decision to come on-Grid was a rational one: get in and get out, don't leave a digital trail, don't take chances on one of the street-smart, slippery errand boys hanging around Doha Port. But he realizes now that the real reason he came here was because he wanted to stay the night.

"If you'll give me a chance, I'll explain."

"How fucking stupid do you think I am?"

"I can't remember the last time I asked for something twice," Ranveer says, "and I'm not in the habit of pleading. But please, Amberley-Ash, may I come inside? I would very much like to sit down and have a drink with you."

Without hesitation, and with all the accompanying aggression a hand gesture can possibly embody, Amberley-Ash gives Ranveer the finger through the thick glass. Her iridescent fingernails are chewed quick-short and she is wearing way too many rings.

"Fuck. You. Motherfucker."

Ranveer looks down at the polished concrete floor and nods. Without looking up, he wanders over to his left and bends down for the case. It is lighter than he expects it to be, and he wonders briefly if it is empty—if Amberley-Ash is playing him—but decides that while she may be brash and somewhat reckless, she is certainly not stupid. He starts back toward the outer doors, stopping just out of range of the motion sensor.

"You know," he begins, turning halfway back. "This little piece of glass between us. That isn't what's keeping you safe right now."

Her middle finger is still up, and it had apparently followed his movement as though she were using it to ward him off. But when Ranveer unbuttons his coat and lets the heavy piece of hardware inside swing into view, her arm lowers to her side, and her expression changes.

"A few centimeters of glass is nothing to me," he continues. "I could be inside there in thirty seconds. Or, for less than I paid for what's in this case, I could have divers cut through these pylons and drop this box into the Gulf and have you drowned like the pathetic unwanted kitten that you are. I could have someone fly a drone out here one night with linear-shaped charges strapped to the bottom and land it on your roof, right above your bed, and wait for you to open your eyes and register what's about to happen to you right before I press the ignition switch. Or I could have a few friends of mine come out and visit you for a week. Their specialty is strapping people down and injecting them with substances that make them feel happier than they ever thought possible, and that their bodies and brains will crave every second of every day for the rest of their lives. Of course, I'd ask them to leave the recipe for you so that you'd be able to synthesize all you ever wanted. I suppose you'd have to throw that cute little T-shirt away, but then again, it's a little tacky and juvenile anyway, isn't it?"

Amberley-Ash is trying to stand stone-still, but Ranveer can see that she is quivering. When she finally blinks, tears spill from both eyes and race one another down to the corners of her lips.

"I think we understand one other," Ranveer says. "If you ever say anything to anyone about me—about seeing me, about having met me, about what's in this case—you have my word that I will kill everyone you have ever loved. If you're lucky, I'll save you for last. But I might just let you rot in this box for the rest of your life knowing that it was all your fault."

Ranveer is a surprisingly gifted conversationalist when he wants to be, but he is even better at eliciting interminable stretches of absolute silence.

20

GONE DARK

QUINN ISN'T SURE how many times she allows the video of Molly to loop. Eventually, a man in greasy slate coveralls with his industrial metaspecs headset turned around backwards and his knee pads down around his ankles comes in to get a drink, and Quinn tries to shut the video off in time but can't, and the pair of heavy, bulbous, oblivious boots briefly converge with Molly's synthetic spirit.

In truth, the mechanic just did Quinn a big favor. She needs to stop feeling sorry for herself and focus on getting the hell out of this warehouse, out of Oman, on an upcoming flight. Off this horrifying case and through this purgatorial phase of both her career and, it seems, her entire life.

To that end, she begins rummaging through her carry-on, where she encounters a Ziploc bag of tampons, the charging case for her metaspecs, a silicone-handled hairbrush that looks like it was used to groom a full-grown golden retriever, a miniature pharmacy of everything from Imodium A-D to a cornucopia of pain relievers, the tangle of dongles all federal employees must carry if they want their government-issued hardware to interface with the rest of the modern world, and, finally, a tri-fold keyboard and Bluetooth travel mouse.

Quinn unfurls the keyboard on the round laminate surface in front of her and gyrates the mouse until she sees the cursor appear in the virtual workspace projected by her metaspecs. She is hoping that enough money is changing hands as a result of her man's ambitious

itinerary to cause some blips here and there, and by properly visual-
izing and/or querying the right transactional data sets, she might be
able to identify exactly how he's getting paid. So she spends the next
hour painting with data—searching for correlations between times of
death and salient financial events associated with everything from
stocks and bonds, to foreign exchange markets, to real estate and art
transactions. She even brings in some of the more mundane fare that
you don't typically associate with the international assassination ech-
elon, like mutual funds, IRAs, and CDs. Anything that can be hastily
liquidated, since assassins, Quinn assumes, prefer to be paid in cash.

There are plenty of correlational spikes, but nothing anywhere close
to definitive, so Quinn decides to try to model the problem as insider
trading—discernible market fluctuations (some entity generating li-
quidity) occurring prior to what are supposed to be unknowable future events (in this case, murders). A pause that somehow perfectly
conveys the strain Quinn knows she has just put hundreds of virtual
machines under once again ends without generating a single lead.

She's not sure what to try next, so instead of trying anything, she
casts a sideways glance at the vending wall. Most of the encased wares
are covered in stylized Arabic squiggles that she can't imagine anyone
being able to decipher, but there are plenty of universally recognizable
brands as well. She has no idea what the contactless payment land-
scape is like here, so after targeting, via eye tracking, a Coke Zero and
a bag of Hershey's Miniatures, she expects the worst as she waves her
handset in front of the designated sensor. Fortunately, Quinn's handset and the vending wall are both fluent in the lingua franca of com-
merce. In fact, Omani technology even appears to be ahead of most of
the United States, since it supports several different payment systems
and even a few of the more stable—

Cryptocurrencies.

SEEING UP HENRIETTA Yi's nose is no small feat given that it is so
petite. But that is exactly the view that Quinn is met with as soon as
her connection request is accepted.

Henrietta is on the move. The dramatically angled perspective on her features is relatively stable, while the primarily white background behind leaps in time to her frenzied stride.

"Henrietta?" Quinn asks. "Is everything OK?"

"Everything's fine," Henrietta assures her. She pauses and Quinn can see that she checks both lengths of long hallway before selecting a direction and continuing. "Just looking for someplace quiet."

Henrietta is almost certainly in Moretti's "undisclosed location," and although Quinn knows her gaze should be tactfully averted, instead it is intentionally sharpened. But all she can see are the steel triangular trusses of exposed ceiling, suspended trays of bundled cables, and blinding white plasma diodes like little suns eclipsed and then exposed by Henrietta's head as she progresses.

There is something about the Epoch Index—and hence, Moretti's secret facility—that fascinates and captivates Quinn. Recently, when she needed a break from pounding out futile Elite Assassin queries, she indulged her curiosity by running several cross-index searches, which, interestingly, returned nothing at all. It's not like she was expecting to surface the encrypted Epoch Index itself—or even the results of all the analyses that had to have been done on it—but she was expecting to find *something*. Given the volume of data the CIA and other government agencies have access to, and the lengths algorithms go to in an attempt to interpret search terms, you can run a query on input generated by your cat walking across your keyboard and usually get anywhere from dozens to hundreds of hits. The only way a search returns nothing at all is through active redaction—a process that continuously scans one or more indices and instantly eradicates any results returned by terms the agency considers anathema.

So, Quinn did the next best thing: a little digging on Henrietta. Here, her efforts were much more productive.

The earliest hit was from a study done on a rare congenital disorder called chromatic illusory palinopsia, or CIP—a condition that causes photochemical activity in the retina to continue for long periods of time, even in the absence of stimulus. Those big round metaspecs Henrietta wears that make her look like an adorable little owl apparently shift certain colors to safer locations on the spectrum where they won't cause persistent floaters—or, as she called them as a little girl, ghosts.

Quinn also uncovered hundreds of academic citations, the titles of which were difficult enough to get through, much less the content itself. But she downloaded the last paper Henrietta published before leaving academia—"Existential Risk Mitigation: Avoiding Astronomical Impact Events Through Early Intervention"—and was about to have a go at it when she noticed a result from a terrorist-related index. She assumed it was a false positive, but when she clicked through and started to scroll, she felt her entire world tilt. Henrietta Yi had lost both her parents in the nuclear attack on Seoul.

Quinn immediately recalled Henrietta's reaction when she learned that Quinn's last assignment had been the Nuclear Terrorism Nonproliferation Task Force. And now she thought she understood how one of the most brilliant and promising young physicists in the world walked away from research in order to devote her life to the mission of the CIA.

The direction of momentum changes as Henrietta backs through a door. Quinn watches her conduct a quick occupancy audit, then she lifts the handset to eye height and summons a smile.

"Hi, Ms. Mitchell!" she says with false composure.

"It's Quinn, remember?"

"Quinn, I mean. Yes. Sorry."

"You sure everything's all right?"

"Everything's fine," Henrietta sings in an unconvincing pitch. "I'm just not supposed to take calls here, so I had to duck out of sight. And, sorry, but I kind of need to make this quick. Simon and I are just about to . . ." She pauses and shakes her head, pulling herself back from what Quinn suspects is an extremely technical and highly confidential ledge. "Never mind. It doesn't matter."

Now that Henrietta is stationary, Quinn detects interference in the video feed. It is some kind of pulsating distortion—a pixel-twisting fisheye warp at the rate of about one cycle per second. The delay in picking up Quinn's call and the hurried movement through the halls was not about finding a quiet place to talk. It was about trying to clear the prodigious, rhythmic emissions of whatever it is she is building—whatever she and Simon are about to try for perhaps the very first time.

"I'm sorry to bug you. I just don't know who else to ask."

"About what?"

"Cryptocurrencies."

Henrietta's face brightens. "What *about* cryptocurrencies?"

"If you were an international serial killer who moved money around using crypto, how would you go about doing it, and who would you work with?"

"PLC," Henrietta says unhesitatingly. "Plutus Lakshmi Crypto."

Quinn is old-schooling it with a ballpoint pen against the back of her boarding pass. "Who or what is that?"

"It's a Qatari start-up run off The Grid." She seems to have volumes more to disclose, but she wavers. "You do know about The Grid, right?"

"I do."

"Good. PLC is the biggest crypto broker in the world. It's like a hub. *Nothing* happens in crypto or alt-currencies that they don't track."

"Who runs it?"

"The twins. Naan and Pita."

"Naan and Pita," Quinn repeats as she scribbles. "As in . . . the bread?"

"Their parents were foodies, I think."

"Do they have a last name?"

"Christakos-Dalal."

"How do I get in touch with them?"

Henrietta draws her glossy pink lips back and shows her cute little teeth—a look that says to Quinn that she is not going to like what she's about to hear.

"What?"

"I don't know if you can."

"Why not?"

"They've kind of . . . gone dark."

"I thought you said they were on The Grid."

"They are, but nobody has seen or heard from them in months."

"Is PLC still functioning?"

"It seems to be, but Naan and Pita have completely stopped communicating. No visitors, no interviews, no posts. Nothing on social media."

"Wait a second," Quinn says. She turns around and checks the flight board behind her. "I can be in Doha in ninety minutes. What if I just go knock on their door? Can you do that on The Grid?"

"We can get you the necessary authorization," Henrietta says. "But are you sure that's a good idea?"

"What do you mean?"

"I mean you want to figure out who the killer is, but you don't actually want to *find* him, right? And you *certainly* don't want to trap him. What I mean," Henrietta says like a teenage daughter giving her single mother sage dating advice, "is that if you go on-Grid, you need to be *very* careful."

21

ALTERNATE REALITY

PLUTUS LAKSHMI CRYPTO, or PLC, is run by the two most famous names in alt-currencies, who also happen to be fraternal twins. Naan and Pita are half Indian and half Greek—the products of parents who met and fell in love twenty-two years ago in Dubai after opening high-end eateries across the street from each other and competing for the lucrative lunchtime business of the energy industry.

After getting married, Dion and Anna Christakos-Dalal moved to Israel, where they opened an Indian-Greek fusion restaurant, and where Naan and Pita were welcomed into the world. As the twins matured, they found that they were far more interested in the Tel Aviv technology scene than in multiethnic cuisine, and when they were only thirteen, they figured out how to use the shadowphiles to reveal some of the most sensitive and confidential information on the planet: the identities of every Michelin Red Guide restaurant inspector currently in active service. Using cheap, off-the-shelf cameras and open-source facial recognition software, Naan and Pita were able to flag reviewers upon approach. The Christakos-Dalal family then provided their marks with an elevated and curated culinary experience, and eventually became the only restaurant in Israel to earn a coveted three-Michelin-star rating.

But it was cryptocurrencies that ultimately captured the twins' imaginations. In their minds, with the exception of DNA hacking and general artificial intelligence, cryptocurrencies were about as profound as innovation got. Most entrepreneurs hoped to develop technology that would disrupt established markets in order to generate wealth; cryptocurrencies skipped the middleman and disrupted wealth itself.

Value has always been associated with scarcity—a concept usually either unprovable or fleeting. Not only was there no way to know how much gold remained in the ground, but there were numerous efforts under way to mine asteroids, which threatened to instantly devalue every precious metal on the planet. In the realm of cryptocurrencies, on the other hand, scarcity was mathematically provable. Ownership was cryptographically verifiable. Done correctly, cryptocurrencies were objectively superior to legal tender and precious metals in every way that mattered—except that most traditionally rich and powerful people didn't have any.

Naan and Pita came to realize that every form of wealth was nothing more than a social contract—agreement among citizens as to what had value and what didn't—and that, as in any social contract, the people had the right to renegotiate the deal any time they wanted. All it took was consensus. And generating consensus was exactly what cryptocurrencies and blockchain technologies did best.

Four years later, Naan and Pita landed on The Grid in order to protect themselves from capricious tax edicts and liberal interpretations of archaic monetary regulation designed to discourage international economic revolution. Even though their net worth as measured in USD sometimes fluctuated by as much as billions several times per second, they were undeniably the most extensive and wealthiest holders of cryptocurrency in history. But personal wealth had never been their objective. Naan and Pita wanted to fuel a revolution against greed and tyranny—to dismantle the planet's system of rule, not through war, but through unity.

Dion and Anna visited their children often. In addition to their immediate and extended families, the twins were also well loved by most of the crypto community, the media, several celebrities, a handful of progressive world leaders, and all of their exclave neighbors.

Naan and Pita eventually became internationally famous for their tasteful gatherings featuring what Zagat proclaimed to be the most exclusive and sought-after buffet on the entire Arabian Peninsula, and the Qatari monarchy considered the twins to be the pride of the entire Grid.

Naan and Pita were once willing to invite almost anyone into their extensive international social sphere. But all of that changed the day they met Ranveer and agreed to a proposal too intriguing to decline.

RANVEER ISN'T SURE which of the twins he is looking at. They are both much more androgynous than they used to be—especially now that they have matching buzz cuts—and while they each have one half of a yin-yang symbol tattooed on the inside of their forearms, he cannot remember which twin has which half. It isn't until he is far enough into the kitchen to discern the minor protrusions of two small breasts beneath an outfit he can only describe as charcoal-gray medical scrubs that he realizes he is being greeted by Naan.

Ranveer knows that, under the right circumstances, everyone has it within them to spiral. In his experience, acute internal distress is most commonly expressed through alcohol, drugs, food, or sex. But what he has witnessed in Naan and Pita is something new. The exclave that was once so full of family and life is now almost empty. The kitchen—once a visual and aromatic bouquet of ethnicity—now smells of nothing but disinfectant, and the only colors are the labels of empty liquid meal replacements. Now that PLC's crypto business is maintained entirely by bots, walls that were once alive with mesmerizing data animations are now blank and tinted to keep the exclave dim and subdued. Naan is somehow pale in defiance of her Indian-Greek complexion, and her arms—everywhere but over her tattoo—are irritated from the adhesive of transdermal patches impregnated with payloads of sedatives and psychoactive compounds that keep her immersed in a state that she and her brother call "alternate reality."

The PLC exclave was the first one to be commissioned with a basement. The underwater chamber has intricate structures designed to keep hundreds of graphene processors cool. Most computational tasks are sliced up, distributed across a global computing grid, executed in parallel, and the results assembled and delivered in milliseconds. But there are some tasks for which no amount of latency is acceptable: tasks that jack directly into the brain. While he has never been down there himself, he knows that the twins rarely emerge anymore—that they connect each other to catheters, entomb themselves inside sensory-deprivation pods, smooth down fresh derms, and pull electrode nets over their heads. But where they go as they neurologically defy their confines, nobody but the two of them knows.

"Where's your brother?" Ranveer asks the girl.

Naan drains a bottle with a coral label and finds room for it on the counter. Traces of the viscous liquid remain in the corners of her mouth and make Ranveer think of a sad clown.

"In the—" She clears the gravel out of her throat and tries again. It's obvious that she has not spoken in a very long time. "In the basement."

"Do you have it?"

Naan opens a drawer in front of her, removes a small white portfolio, and offers it over the counter. Whenever Ranveer is baited into making a move, he instinctively reevaluates his surroundings. From where he stands in the kitchen, he can see through the airlock, and notes that the quadpad is empty. The walls are dim, but semitransparent, so Ranveer can see that they are alone. He already checked the corners for unobtrusive devices with cylinders protruding. And Naan only had a few minutes of warning that he was coming—just long enough to ascend back into consciousness—so it is unlikely that she would have had time to coordinate a trap. Ranveer finally decides that he is willing to go to the girl rather than insist that she bring the portfolio to him.

As he accepts the device, he can see the diamond-shaped impressions throughout Naan's scalp from the electrode netting—the cross-hatched channels where the hair has stopped growing. He imagines the interface settling easily into its grooves. Like all addictions, her affliction must feel as though it has always belonged.

Ranveer places his case at his feet, releases the latch on the portfolio, and folds it open. At first, the silicone paper inside is gray, but a moment later, the e-ink manifests text. It only takes Ranveer a moment to see everything he needs to know.

He folds the portfolio closed, and the magnetic latch snaps.

"Did you read this?" he asks the girl.

"No."

"How did you get it on here without reading it?"

"I decrypted it in memory, copied the contents of the buffer onto the device using a shielded cable, then overwrote the memory addresses with random noise."

Ranveer peers into her wide amber eyes as she speaks and decides that he believes her. He nods and watches her long slender neck as she swallows, and he knows she has something more to say.

"What is it?" he prompts.

"Can I ask you something?"

"Yes."

She blinks several times before she is able to form the words. "Is it us?"

"That's a pointless question, Naan."

"Why?"

"Because if the answer were no, I would tell you no. And if the answer were yes, I would still tell you no."

"Is it?"

"No."

The response elicits a palpable reaction, but of what, Ranveer cannot tell.

"All of this," Ranveer says, indicating the portfolio and everything it represents. He uses its spine to push a few empties out of the way and sets the device down on the counter. "It's taken a heavy toll on you and your brother, hasn't it?"

Naan blinks again, and Ranveer can see that her eyes are beginning to fill.

"We just want it all to be over," the girl says. Where there was resignation in her voice before, there is now a feeble plea. "We just want things to go back to how they were."

There are stools tucked beneath the counter, and Ranveer pulls one toward him. He picks his case up off the floor and places it squarely on the cushion, trips the latches, and opens the lid.

"I know," he says reassuringly. "Everyone has a moment in their past that they spend the rest of their lives trying to find their way back to."

Naan is watching his hands closely. "Even you?" she asks.

Ranveer removes the stainless-steel canister from its foam enclosure.

"Especially me," he confesses.

22

BAD IDEA

IT IS LATE for Moretti when Quinn virtually catches up with him while on the shuttle from Hamad International to Doha Port, and she can tell right away from his eyes that he's had a Scotch or two, which she envisions him sipping with his ringed pinky finger protruding like an underwhelming erection. His study seems much more traditional than modern, and in the background, she can see plenty of paneling and complete collections of leather-bound books. The chair he's swiveling in has those buttoned dimples like the walls of an insane asylum, and the kind of trim that looks like brass thumbtacks. Before another call comes in and he abruptly disconnects, Moretti paints a colorful if only marginally constructive picture of The Grid for Quinn.

Apparently, there is a widespread assumption that the CIA and other law enforcement agencies hate micronation exclaves like The Grid and The Hive (a knockoff just off the coast of Kuwait with tessellated hexagons rather than squares). People think the fact that the well-moneyed but morally bankrupt of the world have carved out safe havens for themselves must endlessly irk those who get underpaid to attempt to apprehend them. But the reality is that the CIA secretly loves these new little communes of corruption and depravity. To the agency, it is self-incarceration without so much as an arraignment.

Sometimes all the CIA has to do is leak semi-credible intelligence about an imminent operation at just the right time, and twenty-four hours later, a South American drug lord, or the president of a humanitarian organization that is actually a front for a Somali terrorist cell, or an African warlord sitting on millions in diamonds and backed by an army of Kalashnikov-wielding orphans hooked on cocaine cut with gunpowder is safely tucked away in the waters of the Persian Gulf, where they will piss away the last of their fortunes and die either of an overdose or from cirrhosis since they cannot risk leaving The Grid to be fitted with a newly printed liver.

As a bonus, Moretti continued, you get an order of magnitude more information from a gangster who doesn't know his exclave is bugged than from one who you've managed to flip. And if the CIA changes its mind and decides they'd rather have someone dead, it is a simple matter to slip a little ricin into the antibiotics regularly droned over from pharmacies in Doha and Kuwait City to clear up the gonorrhea that remains in constant circulation.

Would it be more satisfying to see these people given a burial at sea by a team of rambunctious Navy SEALs? Or led out of a courtroom in orange jumpsuits, Kevlar vests, shackles, and Velcro sneakers? Fuckin' A it would. But law enforcement, like everything else, is a numbers game. Investigations, surveillance, litigation, and incarceration cost millions. Tipping off a douchebag lawyer or duping a banana republic dictator into spending the rest of his life in a glass prison costs about a buck ninety-nine USD. If the tradeoff is that your perp gets to enjoy vintage brut instead of sock-strained prison wine, and conjugal visits from parasitic whores instead of getting bent over and soaped up in the showers, so be it.

Getting hung up on by Moretti, Quinn has discovered, should not be viewed as an insult so much as an act of mercy.

ON-GRID AND ON edge, Quinn has something clenched in her teeth like an obstinate dog. She is gathering her hair behind her head in alternate fistfuls until she can grasp it all at once, at which point she takes the loop from between her teeth and goes to work like a rodeo roper. Wearing her hair up usually gives Quinn a headache—and, she thinks, makes her cheeks look like a chipmunk's—but the breeze coming off the Persian Gulf has it plastered across her face like blond papier-mâché, and she is running as short on patience as she is on Dramamine, so it's either get it out of her face or chop it the fuck off. Quinn was hoping to take one of those Dragonfly quadcopter things, but her budget request got rejected, so the complimentary ferry it is.

But the advantage is that it gives her time to think about how she will approach the twins once she gets out to the PLC exclave. Tariq, back in the lobby of the Al Hujra Hotel in Oman, utterly obliterated all of her confidence in her go-to phrase. In college, Quinn nearly failed the mid-level English class in which she had to deconstruct *Hamlet*, but as a CIA intern, when tasked with writing the next edition of the propaganda pamphlet to be dispersed throughout Tehran, she drew on what she'd learned. The objective was to recruit assets. According to her instructor, the edition that was currently in circulation—promising thousands in USD and, in some cases, political asylum in exchange for verifiable intelligence—had lost its potency like an overprescribed antibiotic. Quinn's approach did not emphasize material gain, but duty and humanity and legacy. On the cover, translated into Arabic, was her favorite line from *Hamlet*, spoken in madness by the tragic young Ophelia:

> *We know what we are,*
> *but know not what we may be.*

The pamphlet tested extraordinarily well, and because of her outstanding work, after graduation, her application to become an intelligence analyst was given the highest-priority consideration. She'd assumed the assignment had just been a standard hypothetical exercise left over from the days before ubiquitous connectivity—that all U.S. propaganda must be distributed electronically these days—but eighteen months later, after being sworn in, she was told that her work ended up being used in the field. And that it had yielded at least one extremely high-value asset.

*   *   *

PLC'S QUADPAD IS empty and the exclave is dark. Quinn hoped to be able to look up and discern small cross sections of living space as the ferry approached—maybe someone looking back down at her, or figures transitioning from one room to another—but the glass is tinted enough that she cannot see in at this distance.

The exclave's retracted mesh pier begins telescoping out to meet the ferry, and the moment the terminal is within range, it electromagnetically aligns, abruptly attaching to the hull with the satisfying report of a small-caliber pistol. There is no captain to thank, and Quinn has made no new friends along her journey, so she disembarks without ceremony.

The pier inherits the oscillation of the ferry on the Gulf's current, so in order to steady herself, Quinn walks her hands along the graduating rails as she approaches the landing. The pier and the ferry remain connected until she steps through an open gate and swings it closed behind her, at which point the collar decouples and the pier begins retracting. Eddies form behind the ferry as its rotors spin up, and Quinn feels, unexpectedly, marooned.

A little backup might have been nice this time around. After being threatened by Tariq, Quinn learned something that, in retrospect, Moretti should have explained to her before she left: any kind of fieldwork—even the purely investigative kind—carries with it some level of risk. Moretti did promise her support anywhere in the world, but nobody whom the CIA has influence over could get anyone out to The Grid until afternoon at the earliest. And she is certain that her man would never be so careless as to meet his financiers in person.

Heavy or oversized equipment like manufacturing-scale 3D printers, full-sized slate-top pool tables, and collections of classic Ferraris have to be moved by ferry rather than quadcopter, so all exclave piers have direct-drive freight elevators. Quinn checks once more for any acknowledgment of her presence, detects none, and proceeds to use the panel to summon the lift. Since this is tantamount to ringing the doorbell, authorization is required from inside before the doors will part—authorization that, Quinn realizes eventually, is not forthcoming. If she were in the lobby of a Holiday Inn, she could use the placebo gesture of jabbing at the little lighted disc with the tip of her thumb to give herself something to do while she waited, but poking through an already-active holographic button hovering above a sheet of volumetric plasma glass and receiving, in return, zero visual or tactile feedback just doesn't impart the same level of satisfaction. Human impatience was clearly not taken into consideration when designing the holographic user interface.

She squelches her irrational impulse to knock on the elevator doors and instead steps back as far as the rails around the platform will allow so she can look up. Quinn has done enough to make her presence known that she expects to see at least one panel of glass turn fully transparent, and to glimpse one or both twins peering down at her, though she sees no change above her whatsoever.

Quinn knows that she can—and will—get inside. Summoning lifts, milling about waiting to be noticed, and perhaps even resorting to rapping a knuckle against any surface she deems capable of carrying a vibration all the way upstairs—these are just courtesies. Along with authorization to come on-Grid, Henrietta also worked with the Qatari government to procure (and remotely install on Quinn's handset) a custom-compiled "skeleton key" digital certificate that will grant her one-time full access to the PLC exclave. As soon as she chooses to activate her handset within NFC range of an interactive holographic plasma panel, elevators will suddenly start to obey and airlock doors will part and make way as if Quinn were one of the twins herself. But before she does so, she'd like some confirmation that she is at least in the right place. Maybe even some hint as to what she is about to walk into.

Because, right now, something does not feel right. Most of the other exclaves around her radiate evidence of habitation: Dragonflies collecting and depositing artists, athletes, sheikhs, and geeks; gay-pride windsocks writhing in the salty Gulf breeze; designer-branded poolside brunches amid verdant and trellised tropical gardens; a roof-

top tennis match against a squat, multi-axis robotic trainer; the rippled shoulder muscles of a deeply tanned couple clinging to a
kaleidoscopic climbing rock with white, chalked hands. Meanwhile,
the Plutus Lakshmi Crypto exclave feels distinctly vacant.

Quinn has a bad idea. Like *really* bad. It's so bad, in fact, she knows
she should exorcize it immediately and never speak of it to anyone.
But all she needs is a glimpse though the tinted glass above her. The
quadpad that hangs off the exclave's main level looks as though it
would afford a generous view of the first-floor living quarters, and
there's even a metal staircase leading up to it, but the wire mesh door
that blocks it off is securely locked.

Quinn's Very Bad Idea starts with the ability of all modern hand-
sets to record ultra-high-definition, super slow-motion video at over
a thousand frames per second, which means you can easily capture
clear footage of rapidly moving objects. Or, put another way, you can
capture clear footage of stationary objects using a rapidly moving
handset.

All she has to do is turn on the camera, properly orient the device,
and fling it up high enough that it clears the floor above her and captures a few frames of the main level through the glass outer wall.
Think of it as your standard ultra-high-definition video drone sans
the drone part. Even one decent frame would probably be enough as
long as she can pan and zoom her way to a pair of shoes, or one un-
washed dish, or a jacket draped over the back of a chair. Anything to
provide proof of life.

Throwing the phone is the easy part; it's catching it that has her
concerned. But Quinn has a notoriously checkered past when it
comes to phone screens, so, years ago, she finally succumbed to one of
those bulky, ruggedized, shock-resistant OtterBox cases, which means
even if she misses it, the device will almost certainly be fine. The worst
thing that can happen, she hypothesizes, is that someone in a neighboring exclave will witness what is undoubtedly suspicious behavior,
call security, and Quinn will find herself in a holding cell until Moretti
or Van can spring her. That, or her phone will slip through her fingers

and ricochet off her forehead, coming to rest in such a way as to capture her subsequent supine repose having just recorded one of the most hilarious memes in all of internet history.

Quinn opens the camera app, swipes over into super slo-mo mode, taps record, and . . . *launches*. Her hands are up over her head with her fingers spread into as much of a basket as they can form as she tracks the phone's ascent. There must be a stiffer breeze up there than there is down at sea level, as the phone's lateral travel is more than she expects, and she takes a few steps toward the edge of the platform to try to stay beneath it. But when its path intersects with the dazzling glare coming off the glass, she loses sight of the device and instinctively transitions from trying to catch it to covering her head to protect herself.

A moment passes, and then instead of feeling the impact, she hears something heavy ring the platform railing followed by a sickening, delicate gulp. By the time Quinn can get down on the mesh flooring, thread her arm through the rail, and reach for her phone, both it and the skeleton key it contains are already well on their way to the bottom of the Persian Gulf.

OF COURSE, SHE holds it together while she's alone on the exclave's dock; it isn't until she is back on the ferry and surrounded by other passengers that the tears start to flow.

Quinn has lost track of the number of times this investigation has made her lose her shit. But it's different this time. It is not sadness or loss or fear. This time, it's anger. At herself. For being so fucking stupid. And it's embarrassment because she's clumsy and fat and couldn't keep her marriage together or keep her daughter safe and can't catch this man who murders babies, and she probably isn't even in the right fucking country anyway, and by the time she gets her handset replaced and waits for another digital certificate to be issued she will have lost at least an entire day. And lost time in this case is not paid for in waste, but in human lives.

A new handset is not all Quinn will be requesting when she gets off the ferry, buys a prepaid burner handset, connects it to her metaspecs, calls the CIA's global field emergency hotline, provides the classified passphrase, requests a callback from Alessandro Moretti, and finally humiliates herself by explaining what happened. She will also use the opportunity to—

Wait. Her metaspecs.

She can't use them to call Moretti or Henrietta, since they rely on her handset for a secure data connection, but she might be able to use them to review some of the footage. Files are seldom explicitly moved around now; instead, devices use predictive modeling to try to anticipate when and where data will be needed. If Quinn's handset thought she might want to watch the footage on her metaspecs, it might have moved at least part of the file over before the connection was severed.

Quinn could probably do everything she needs to do through voice commands, by tapping and swiping against her metaspecs' capacitive temples, and by flashing hand gestures like nerdy gang signs, but she already feels conspicuous enough, so she digs the keyboard out of her purse and unfolds it.

The file system browser doesn't surface anything new, but some of the data could still have been transferred in chunks. Quinn toggles on hidden objects, navigates to the system cache, and is rewarded with promising timestamps: multiple randomly named files that total several gigabytes in size.

She starts with the newest bucket of bits, and there it is: the nausea-inducing quake of found footage. No sound, though. The audio track is probably one of the other files, but video is all she needs.

She taps the spacebar to pause, then uses the arrow keys to advance. As the main level of the exclave rotates into frame, Quinn starts to feel significantly less moronic. Landings aside, her plan seems to have worked. She uses keyboard combinations to draw out and position a rectangular area of interest, holds down the control key, and slaps "plus" to blow it up. While she doesn't have the resolution she needs to read labels, she can see that the kitchen counter is covered in little white plastic bottles that she recognizes from her dieting days as liquid meal replacements.

Quinn momentarily clears her metaspecs so she can see where they are (only about halfway back to the ferry launch), then mentally begins enumerating:

First, order a new phone. With a skeleton key preinstalled. And demand that someone hand-deliver it to her. In Doha. Today.

Second, take a Dragonfly back out to PLC—with or without budget approval. And this time, do not knock. Henrietta found schematics of the exclave and informed Quinn that it is one of the few with a basement, which is almost certainly where Naan and Pita have retreated.

Third, confront the twins and demand their cooperation. She no longer has any doubt that they will be able to identify her man.

She is about to kill the video when she makes the connection between her sinking handset and the exclave's basement. Another rap on the spacebar and all that registers are flashes of glass and steel and sky, and then it instantly slows down and everything goes blue. She's not sure if it's because of the OtterBox or because of the handset's optics, but the footage is surprisingly clear. Quinn can see the undulation of the sun passing through the current and how it plays across the pylons on all sides of the twins' subaqueous basement.

The outside corner is covered in metallic fins like artificial barnacles. She is about to pause and zoom in order to get a better look when, in perfect unison, they all shift, sliding past one another like scissor blades, revealing themselves to be perfectly interleaved.

They're heat sinks, Quinn realizes. On the other side of the wall, Quinn envisions processors slotted and locked on thin layers of thermal paste. The external blades must occasionally sheer away algae, which might otherwise reduce heat exchange. The twins are using the Persian Gulf to liquid-cool their rig.

As flat objects are wont to do in water, the handset meanders. Only one corner of the basement bristles with the grid of heat sinks; the rest, like topside, is transparent. Crawling along the wall is a long, blunt-nosed, algae-swallowing bot, the glass perfectly clean and free of debris in its wake. The video frame abruptly swings with a sudden flourish of strong undertow as the descent slows. And then, there they are.

Pause.

The twins are lying in adjacent capsules in the center of the room, their naked bodies submerged in phosphorescent gel.

Draw and zoom.

Open eyes, electrode nets over buzz-cut heads, limp and fallen to the side in a way that does not convey life.

Pan.

Transdermal patches on biceps, unifying tattoos on forearms, and small fine fingers tightly entwined.

But somehow Quinn knows that that is not all. She continues to pan until the frame lands on the pixelated blackness beneath the stairs, and inside it she discerns the tall slender figure of a man. There is a long, lithe knife in his left hand and his eyes are dark and calm. Anyone descending would never know he was there. Someone inexperienced enough to forget to clear the room would rush to the twins' sides to check to see if they were still alive and never see what was coming up from behind.

Quinn's metaspecs are off and she is on her feet, pushing her way to the back of the ferry, where she is just in time to see the Dragonfly lift off. She tracks it, expecting it to pass overhead and to overtake her on its way to shore, but she can tell from the direction it takes that her man is headed not toward the dock, but straight for the airport.

23

DIVERSION

UPON ENTERING IRANIAN airspace, you are expected to relinquish control of your aircraft to the Civil Aviation Organization of the Islamic Republic. If you do not, they will take control through various methods of line-of-sight and satellite communication disruption. If that doesn't work—if you have proactively hardened your aircraft against the latest in bypass signal hacking—they will scramble two Russian-built, twin-engine, supersonic fighter jets to either escort you to the nearest landing strip, where you will be inhospitably greeted by the Islamic Revolutionary Guard, or fire a couple of R-77 air-to-air missiles directly up your ass. All depends on who's in charge that day, and what kind of mood he's in.

In most cases, after verifying that they can assume at-will control of your aircraft, they hand it right back. The CAO doesn't have the time, the manpower, or the desire to land your plane for you. That's your job. That's what you get underpaid for. They just want to know that they could plunge you into the Caspian Sea if they felt like it. And, of course, they want to make sure that you know that, too.

But every now and then, after remote control of your plane has been assumed, it is not relinquished. Sometimes, in the foreboding tranquility of complete radio silence, your supersonic Emirates Executive ultra-luxury private jet is diverted from Imam Khomeini International Airport, on the outskirts of the capital, to an isolated runway at Mehrabad International Airport, well inside Tehran proper, and subsequently met not by Iranian military, but by the Ministry of Intelligence. By men not in fatigues, but in black tactical gear and full-face ski masks.

When that happens, experienced pilots know exactly what to do. Hands go directly into laps, folded like a proper British nanny's. No additional announcements are issued over the PA. Sometimes you make a quick trip to the toilet so that you don't piss yourself during what you know is coming. If there's time, your copilot will probably go relieve himself as well, and when the two of you are recounting the story later to a couple of hijabed hotties over tea and hookahs, both of you will leave that part out.

By the time the combination hatch and stairway has been fully lowered, the pilot knows to be on his knees facing the nose of the plane with his hands laced behind his head, while the copilot lies face-down splitting the difference between the cockpit and the galley, hands similarly intertwined, mouth full of Persian rug wool. Whatever their passengers choose to do is up to them. It's their asses. The jet's insured, and all those soft-touch surfaces are treated with Scotch-gard, so if they feel like being heroes, that's their business.

The men who beset the jet show their appreciation for the pilots' cooperation by not killing them. However, what they do not appreciate is a completely empty cabin. Which, after a moment of swiveling their black-masked heads in bewilderment, they proceed to verify via rigorous ransacking. It's no good asking the pilots what happened to the man they are looking for—the man who, according to very credible intelligence, boarded the jet at Hamad International Airport in Doha, Qatar—because the two of them are so scared that they're still about to piss themselves despite both having recently emptied their bladders. And because hard data is both more expedient and more reliable than a couple of glorified bus drivers.

As expected, the flight computer tells them everything they need to know. Just after entering Iranian airspace, the logs show that the rear emergency hatch was open for a little under two minutes. All those clipped nylon ties on the floor in the back that looked like they were used for your standard in-flight BDSM entertainment now look a lot more like the remnants of hasty parachute preparation.

It's easy to spot the man in charge of these types of operations. He's the one who waits to make his entrance. Who wears a stylish, open-collared suit instead of ballistic body armor. Who does not bother with the ski mask—not because of what it might do to his hair, but because he prefers that you know exactly who he is. Because he knows that his face is the last thing on the planet you want to see at that particular moment. Because men who operate at that level are fully committed, and there will never be any hiding from the things they have done.

Anyway, that guy—he makes a distasteful reference to someone's mother's vagina in Arabic, then uses his handset to call it in. He wants Thunderbolt drones in the air all along the Gulf coast within the hour. He wants random northbound checkpoints from Bandar Abbas to Kermanshah. The government no longer has any kind of biometric signature on this guy, so they'll have to do it the old-fashioned way. No one gets into Tehran without showing an ID, and anyone whose paperwork is not in order gets detained. It will take their man at least a couple of days to cover the distance—perhaps as long as a week—but just in case, he expects a perimeter around the capital by nightfall.

And, as if suddenly remembering where he is, he wants this son-of-a-dog plane off the son-of-a-dog runway. *Now.* And for the next twenty-four hours, every private, commercial, and cargo flight from Qatar is to be diverted here, and it is to be thoroughly searched. Any aircraft failing to comply is to be shot down. Human remains are to be recovered and volumetrically scanned, and 3D models are to be brought to him personally.

The two pilots turn and look at each other for a long, wide-eyed moment, then race each other back into the cockpit. They both know that once the jet is safely parked in the Emirates hangar, they'll collapse in the back and drink, repeatedly, to not being dead. The nice thing about piloting luxury jets—especially in parts of the world like

Iran, where alcohol is banned—is that a well-stocked minibar is always close at hand.

But luxury is about much more than limitless access to fine mind-altering substances. It isn't even about comfort or status or quality. Those who really understand what money can buy know that extravagance is really about experience. Sometimes that means getting to pass the time by playing games with zip ties in the back of private planes, and sometimes that means the thrill of spontaneous illegal skydiving to keep from being detained. But sometimes it means something much more subtle. Sometimes it means reserving not only the plane, and not just someone to fly it, but the opportunity to put on a uniform, sit in the cockpit, and pretend like you are the copilot.

24

DEAD DROP

THE GRID HAS its own administrative buildings among Doha Port, the main one being the Bariq Pavilion. Inside, it is predictably modern-opulent—a little hologram-heavy for Quinn's personal taste—and right on the edge of being a parody of futurism. Quinn has set up base in yet another luxurious lobby oasis, where she anxiously awaits two things: word on whether her man was apprehended at the airport, and a brand-new handset.

Instead, she is approached by the port master, who, with a triumphant grin, delivers her old handset inside a sealed plastic evidence bag. Apparently, items of value are lost to the Persian Gulf all the time, and his crew has become quite adept at using a tethered submersible to retrieve everything from golf clubs to diamond earrings as small as a mere two carats.

Once it detected separation from its primary guardian—probably when the Bluetooth connection with her metaspecs became sufficiently frayed—the handset shut itself down. Sadly, Quinn has enough experience with how complex electronics interact with water that she knows not to boot it back up until as much of the moisture has been wicked away as possible. Like any modern device, Quinn's handset is water-resistant to an extent, but she's pretty sure that ninety minutes at the bottom of the Persian Gulf exceeds even the most optimistic ingress protection designations.

The first step is to get an idea of what she's dealing with here. After unzipping the plastic pouch, Quinn can see that the port master went to the trouble of rinsing the OtterBox off with fresh water and conducting a cursory toweling. That's a good start. There's a decent ding in the side of the OtterBox from its high-velocity interaction with the railing, so Quinn decides that it has done its duty and has earned an honorable discharge.

But something stops her from tossing it. Quinn is reminded of the laptop Vanessa Townes now displays on a shelf in her office—the shattered Dell clamshell that might have saved her life. The OtterBox, it occurs to Quinn, is no less a symbol of serendipity. When her handset collided with the rail, it could have gone either way. And what she initially interpreted as fate working against her was, in fact, random acts aligning and, for once, finding in her favor.

Quinn knows how close she came to having her throat neatly slit. To grasping her neck as though she were choking in a hopeless effort to hold on to all that blood. Sitting down on the floor of the twins' basement, quietly watching in horror as the thick red pool spread out around her. Mourning herself with silent tears from wide, terrified eyes. She knows that swallowing the trauma of narrow escape and letting it grow inside her is probably a mistake. But for now she decides to plant it like a toxic seed and to see if she can grow it into something from which she might later be able to draw strength.

YOU CAN USE uncooked rice as a moisture-absorbing medium, or those little packets of silica gel you sometimes see tucked inside products that had to cross oceans on autonomous freighters in order to find their way to you—neither of which Quinn keeps handy. But she is nothing if not resourceful, so out comes the sandwich bag of tampons from the bottom of her purse. She proceeds to disembowel the remainder of her feminine hygiene stash, separating rayon and cotton cores from applicators and ripcords, and contoured tips from no-slip grips. The evidence bag is wet, so Quinn uses the tampons' Ziploc to build her handset its high-absorbency nest, wrapping the makeshift invention up with a hair tie in order to apply some compression.

Ideally, if you had a handset that, say, fell into the Potomac River while recording your husband showing your daughter how to skip rocks, and that you didn't recover until several hours later after coming back with a pair of telescopic fishing nets from the nearest Walmart, you'd let it dry overnight. But given that it's been almost three hours since Quinn has had access to Semaphore—and in the meantime, QSS (Qatar State Security) has descended upon Hamad International Airport with support from a small team of U.S. Marines deployed from the embassy, and a separate investigative unit was dispatched to the PLC exclave—Quinn decides to skip the formalities and slip an exploratory finger down into the sanitary burrow after only twenty minutes. It comes up surprisingly dry, which means either that her handset has sufficiently drained and will probably work just fine, or that there's still an entire thriving marine microhabitat trapped inside, and she is about to ignite a catastrophic chemical fire.

A tiny gurgle of moisture emerges from around the power button when she depresses and holds it down, which she takes to be a bad sign. But that just turns out to be the silicone gasket doing its job, since, moments later, the screen lights up. Quinn is well on her way back to the world of the connected.

There are eight Semaphore messages waiting for her—all from a woman with a stunning profile photo named Fatimah Al Thani. The ID maps to QSS, so whoever she is, she almost certainly knows something. No sooner has Quinn tapped the call icon than an immaculately made up, dark-eyed, perfectly beauty-marked young face framed in an embroidered honey-colored headdress appears on her screen.

"Ms. Mitchell. I see you have your handset back."

The woman is in the twins' kitchen. A real-time filter is being applied both to accentuate the face in the foreground and probably in an attempt to obscure the classified goings-on behind her, but blended into the background bokeh is what Quinn knows to be a prismatic band of nutritional supplement brands.

"Yes, just now," Quinn says. "I'm sorry to rush you, but I need to know: did they get him?"

"I haven't heard," the woman says. "I've been focused on the situation here."

Quinn's eyes close for a moment, and she steadies herself with a deep and deliberate breath.

"Are you OK, Ms. Mitchell?"

"I'm fine," Quinn says. "Listen, I need the numbers from the twins, but please don't send photos. *Just* the numbers. Can you do that?"

Fatimah's head tilts just perceptibly. "You haven't listened to your messages, have you?"

"No, why?"

"Ms. Mitchell, Naan and Pita are alive."

Quinn squints at the woman on her handset as she tries to connect what she has just been told with what she's sure she knows.

"That's impossible," Quinn says. "I saw them. I saw *him*."

"We thought they were dead, too, but a physician has confirmed that they are both indeed alive. Their breathing is extremely shallow— nearly undetectable—but they *are* breathing, and brain activity is normal."

"Why would he leave them alive?"

"We believe the intent *was* murder. We found a unique molecular signature that isn't present in their transdermal patches. It's nothing we've ever seen, and it's not in any index QSS has access to. Perhaps he is inexperienced with the substance and accidentally administered a nonlethal dose."

"What about the numbers?"

"There aren't any."

"You're positive?"

"Yes."

"Then he wasn't trying to kill them," Quinn says. "If he wanted them dead, they'd be dead. And tagged. He wants them alive, but he also wants to keep them quiet. He knew I was getting close. Can you wake them up?"

Quinn is momentarily distracted by a notification of a new message. Alessandro Moretti. *Urgent.*

"We won't know that until we've positively identified the substance."

"I'm sorry, I have to go," Quinn says. "I'll be there as soon as I can."

The woman nods and smiles in a way that lifts her beauty mark just so, and then the connection is closed. The message from Moretti is voice only.

"Airport was a bust. Your man boarded a private jet for Iran, but Tehran is saying he never got there. We think he's an Iranian defector, so they probably want the sonovabitch even worse than we do. My guess is they have him in custody but don't want anyone to know. Either way, he ain't ever leaving Iran, so trail's cold. Might as well pack it up and come on home."

QUINN DOES NOT move. Part of her is relieved that she has just been released. Handed a ticket back to Langley. Back to her neat and clean and air-conditioned cubicle—back to her simple and predictable routine. Moretti will probably even stamp the mission a success. Cornering the Elite Assassin and forcing him into Iran, where he will probably be tortured to death, stoned, or hanged from a mobile crane, is as good as incarceration. Another victory by omission for Quinn. Another way to spin all the time she will never get back into a perverse and twisted win.

But the whole thing doesn't make any sense. First of all, if Tehran really had him, they would not be discreet. That is not the Ayatollah's way. If they'd apprehended the Elite Assassin—if they had *anyone* in their custody whom they knew the United States wanted—images and video would be streaming all over the world twenty-four hours a day.

Secondly, the Elite Assassin isn't that stupid. He would not fly into hostile territory without a plan. In fact, infiltrating Tehran was probably his intention all along. Complete the final job in Oman, collect payment in Qatar, and then retire back home in Iran, skipping like a perfectly launched sliver of rock across the hot desert sands.

But, of course, Quinn doesn't have any proof. And no leads to follow up on. No plausible theories to run by Van or Moretti, and no real case to make for why she might need to wait around for Naan and Pita to wake up. So she shovels her makeshift office back into her bag and tosses the Ziploc into the nearest trash can. With a working phone and a trail that's gone cold, the only place left for Quinn to go is the airport.

But first she needs to use the restroom. They're in the back, just beyond some sort of a locker room where, on her way past, she gets a glimpse of a woman in a black hooded bodysuit stacking bins into a tall cubby. The restroom door is heavy, and after Quinn pushes through, she is pleased to discover that all the stalls appear pristine. She picks one in the middle and sits.

She is thinking about stopping by the Bariq Pavilion Food Court on her way out and grabbing a slice of that robot-tossed, New York–style pizza (with dough made from municipal tap water flown in all the way from Brooklyn), but something doesn't feel right. When she wipes, she closes her eyes and sighs. Just minutes after sacrificing every last one of her tampons to the cause of resuscitating her handset, Quinn realizes that she has just gotten her period.

She could probably bum something off Fatimah, but that would mean going all the way back out to PLC. Quinn is about to resign herself to searching the Bariq Pavilion for a convenience store when she recalls the woman in the locker room. A complete stranger who she will never have to see again, and who is in close proximity. Perfect.

Quinn gets herself squared away as best she can with the supplies at hand, washes up, and walks out of the bathroom doing her very best to project poise and aplomb. The locker room is as Quinn remembers it: empty but for her potential savior. The petite woman has opened a second cubby and is distributing her multidimensional bins among them like a three-dimensional, block-based puzzle game. Centered on the wall is a holographic console, presumably for authentication.

"Excuse me," Quinn says from the opening. "Do you speak English?"

"I'm American," the woman replies without turning. "English is *all* I speak."

"Perfect," Quinn says. "This is a little embarrassing, but . . ."

"You need a tampon."

"How'd you know that?"

For the first time, the woman pauses her shifting and shimmying and turns. A piece of the most vibrant orange-red hair Quinn has ever seen escapes the woman's hood and falls across a sun-bleached seashell complexion.

"You were in there for at least fifteen minutes, and the first thing you did when you came out was approach a complete stranger. What else could it be? You probably have a little twat wad tucked into your panties right now, don't you?"

Quinn doesn't exactly love the woman's demeanor, but it's not like she's flush with options.

"Worst timing ever," she manages.

The woman indicates a stuffed black duffel against the opposite wall. "Outside pocket. Help yourself."

"Thank you *so* much."

"Don't mention it."

Quinn's knees pop as she squats. The duffel is covered in outside pockets, and she starts rummaging through them like a perverted TSA agent hoping to palm something dirty.

"Need underwear, too?"

"No, thank you," Quinn says. In a feeble attempt to pretend like all this is normal, Quinn says, "So, are you here visiting?"

"Nope," the woman says. "Leaving."

Quinn rakes her fingers through the expected sundries: lotion, deodorant, tissues, hair ties, Tylenol, mints, lip balm, nail clippers.

"You don't sound very excited."

"I have a lot to answer for," the woman says. "Let's just leave it at that."

"Of course," Quinn says, and as she unzips the next pocket in line, she discovers a threadbare pink teddy bear with a matching ribbon embroidered on its chest. The international symbol of breast cancer awareness. In an instant, Quinn glimpses the vulnerable little girl that the woman's tough outer shell has been forged to protect. Another life long enough to know loss, but too brief to find peace.

Beneath the bear, Quinn lays eyes on her prize.

"Take two," the woman tells her. "I'm not expecting any surprises."

Quinn doesn't mind if she does. She stands and slips the cylinders into the front pocket of her jeans one at a time as though she were loading a double-barreled shotgun.

"Again," Quinn says, "I can't thank you enough."

"Good deed for the day," the woman says.

Quinn is just about to go see about swapping out her field dressing for the real thing when something stops her—something about the lockers. Instead of little engraved labels, they are numbered with miniature plasma-dot displays. And as far as Quinn can tell, the digits are entirely random.

"What's wrong?" the woman asks her.

"What is this place?"

"Storage," the woman says. "But most people use it as a dead drop."

"A dead drop?"

"A place to leave things for other people to pick up."

"What kinds of things?"

"You know where you are, right? Best not to ask those kinds of questions."

"Why aren't the numbers sequential?"

"You can enter whatever number you want into the console when you lock it. As long as it's unique."

Quinn takes a step forward as she scans. She is looking at an entire wall of random four-digit numbers that international criminals use to exchange illicit goods.

If the numeric sequences with which the Elite Assassin tagged his victims had simply been safe deposit box numbers, Quinn would have made the connection a long time ago. In fact, it would have been next to impossible *not* to, since any number of algorithms would have connected the dots for her, and several of the dashboards she flicks through dozens of times a day would have refused to drop the matter until properly acknowledged. Every safe deposit box, P.O. box, off-shore transaction ID, and numbered bank account on the planet is indexed and included in hundreds of default routine queries without Quinn even having to check a box.

She even did one better. Long before Oman, Quinn compiled custom indices of all known instances of four-digit numbers matching body tags and proceeded to do everything she could think of to correlate them to financial transactions—including treating them as ciphers and using half a dozen different neural networks to attempt to decrypt them. There were thousands of hits but nothing more statistically significant than if the numbers had been generated randomly. And nothing that could be traced back to a single individual or corporate entity.

But all that was before a stranger explained to her that there were places in the world where customers can generate their own temporary identifiers; unregulated and unaudited international dead drops; institutions with air-gapped internal networks that the CIA had not yet found a way to infiltrate.

"How secure is this place?" Quinn asks. "Do people leave large sums of money here?"

"I wouldn't. There are better places for that."

"What places?"

"Around here? Or anywhere?"

"Anywhere."

"If you want to stay close, Dubai. If you're talking globally, Frankfurt, London, Chicago, Singapore, Hong Kong. A bunch in Switzerland." She squints at Quinn. "Are you OK?"

"This is it," Quinn says. "This is what the numbers are for."

The woman turns to see if she can find the same life-altering epiphany in the wall of lockers as Quinn.

"Am I supposed to know what that means?"

"Whatever you have to atone for," Quinn tells the woman, "you just did it."

"I think I've lost the plot."

"You may have just helped save a lot of lives," Quinn tells the girl.

In the ensuing stupefied silence, Quinn makes her exit, and it isn't until she is on her way to the airport that she remembers the tampons in the front pocket of her jeans and suddenly understands what it was that the young woman called out after her.

"You're going the wrong way!" she'd said.

But, for once, Quinn knows that she isn't.

25

FAMILY BUSINESS

RANVEER'S RIFLE IS assembled, scoped, and stocked for the optics, not for the shot. The things he came here to do need to be done up close.

Movement is what he is looking for. He already knows the routine of everyone inside—that by now, the house should be tidied up and quiet. But like the very young, old men seldom sleep through the night. Even Ranveer, in the last year, has had to start paying closer attention to how much he drinks in the evenings. Sooner or later, he muses, enlarged prostates come for us all.

Infrared heat signatures look just right for the middle of the night. No kettle on in the kitchen as a thermal sign of insomnia. There's a tiny orange blob stalking around the back—almost certainly a raccoon or a cat.

Infiltration-wise, it doesn't get much more straightforward than this. The old man likes to sleep with the doors and windows wide open, which he is able to do because everyone knows who his son is. But there's one critical flaw in that logic: what if you are there on family business?

It is a modest home. Two stories. Brick. Plants on every last horizontal stone surface deep enough to accommodate a pot. Trees lining the flat roof, concealing an illicit satellite dish that everyone knows is there.

The perimeter of the property is defined by a tall brick wall, and

Ranveer hangs the rifle from one shoulder as he lets himself in through the iron gate in the back, gingerly closing and latching it behind him. The cat he detected from the park across the street—a neighborhood stray, it would seem, with only one eye—leaps up onto the edge of the fountain as Ranveer approaches, expertly positioning itself precisely at petting height. Ranveer moves his case to his other hand so that he can comply, and the cat rattles with gratitude.

Ranveer does not even pause at the screen door, but slides it open, pivots around it, and closes it behind him in a single fluid motion. He must balance vigilance with expediency, and one of the best ways to do so is to trust what you already know. Double- and triple-checking costs time; if you're good enough at what you do, you should only have to do it once.

There is enough of a moon tonight, and there are frequent enough windows throughout the home, that he does not need full-time infrared, though he does have his metaspecs in sentry mode; should they detect a heat signature consistent with any living thing bigger than the pirate cat outside, he will get a haptic alert, and the shape will be painted with a false-color overlay.

The old man and his nurse are in separate bedrooms off the main level. But they are not why he is here. The boy's room is upstairs.

As he ascends, Ranveer's shoes use radar to check for inconsistent density in the material below them, providing tactile feedback about where best to step to avoid creaking. He distributes his weight on the treads as directed, case in one hand and railing in the other. The floor plan of the house is not complicated, and at the top, Ranveer follows the handrail along the open second-story landing. The door at the end of the hall is closed, and as his gloved hand tightens around the cold oblong knob, he looks down, giving the main level one final inspection before entering.

Children's rooms often seem small to adults, but never so small as when they were once your own.

It is that bizarre sense of scale that throws Ranveer off the most. He can't remember the last time he was in a hotel with a *bathroom* this small. Yet this is where he spent a good portion of the first twenty years of his life. How did he manage to practice yoga on the ornate Persian rug without jamming his fingertips and toes into the walls? How did he and his father both fit on the bed with a backgammon or a chessboard between them? How did so few books aligned in the hutch above the desk once seem like an entire library—books on falconry, exotic European supercars, football clubs, and all the Shakespearean plays his father loved so much? How did he study at a desk smaller than an in-room bar where he now regularly pours himself brandies? The hexagonally patterned ball wedged between the headboard and the bookcase reminds him that he even practiced his foot and knee juggling in the cramped space before his mother finally forbade all sports indoors.

The only time Ranveer remembers being conscious of the size of his room growing up was when he ran out of space for posters and found he had to rotate them regularly: Manchester United, Real Madrid, Argentina. All the different Arab clubs. When he steps the rest of the way into the room and closes the door, he remembers that the solid wooden panels were the only spaces left for the schedules, rosters, and statistics he and his father worked so hard to compile.

All of this was before being smitten with cricket. Before his mother had a stroke while working in the garden and died of pneumonia a month later in the hospital. Before he and his father stopped talking.

Ranveer sits on the edge of the bed where his father once sat at the end of almost every day—the same bed Ranveer slept in all through primary, middle, and high school, and even most of university. Each day ended with a kiss from his father and each morning began with his mother making him breakfast: warm bread spread with feta cheese and a dollop of fig jam, or a tomato and onion omelet, or a hot bowl of lentil soup. Always a glass of golden tea.

But everything changed the day the Ministry of Intelligence came to visit Ranveer. It wasn't for several more years that he realized that they'd used predictive analytics to anticipate his aptitudes, but his father must have known right away because it changed the way he saw his son. Ranveer remembers how the family scrambled to stash their Hindu statues and shrines every time the men in gray suits knocked. When they were gone, before giving him his good-night kiss, Ranveer's father made sure his son understood who those men were, what they represented, and that they had no regard for life—human or otherwise—and no wish for peace. He squeezed Ranveer's arm and reminded him that he was to become a doctor or an engineer, not a thug and a murderer.

Ranveer has done a lot of difficult things in his life, but none so difficult as telling his father that he'd made up his mind. It was on a Saturday evening, and he was driving his father's old white Mercedes diesel home from a falcon club meeting. He can remember how he gripped the wheel hard to keep his hands from shaking and the pain he felt in his stomach. Not only had Ranveer made his decision, but he'd already accepted the Ministry's invitation, signed the papers they put in front of him one after another, and committed to reporting for training right after graduation. Ranveer's father looked straight ahead as they drove and never asked his son why. And Ranveer never told him.

He never mentioned the document that the men in gray suits showed him on their final visit—the warrant naming everyone in his immediate and extended families except for him. His refusal to join, it was explained to him, would result in their immediate arrests, after which they would all be found guilty and sentenced under Sharia law to seventy-four lashes, which Ranveer would be made to watch. However, if he were to accept their invitation, not only would the warrant be destroyed, but Ranveer's entire family would be allowed to continue their observance of Hinduism. The Ministry was even willing to overlook the satellite dish on the roof the family used to watch international football matches, and the occasional bottles of "Tigris wine" his uncle bought from an illegal Iraqi immigrant and shared with the family.

From that moment, Ranveer's father never trusted him again. But it is exactly that distrust that Ranveer now needs. If you know how to use it, animosity and hostility can be powerful tools. Distrust is as lifelong and dependable as greed and self-interest. Love nowhere near as unconditional as hate. After disassembling the gas gun and fitting its components into their foam molds, Ranveer slides the case all the way back beneath the bed, fully confident that nobody will honor this room with his or her presence as long as his father is still alive.

Ranveer has always traveled lightly, but it is critical that, from now on, he use even more discretion. As he executes his next maneuver— the most complex and delicate move he has ever attempted—nothing he wishes to see again can be in his possession. That means gaining access to the last name on his list through highly unconventional methods, and arming himself with effective but invisible weapons.

The Ministry represented the end of Ranveer's childhood and the beginning of a new life. It was there that he studied his trade; that he was given many opportunities to employ and refine it against Mossad and the General Intelligence Directorate of Saudi Arabia; that he earned enough trust that he was allowed to travel. It was also at the Ministry of Intelligence, many years later, that Ranveer came across a new series of propaganda pamphlets distributed by the Americans. Iranian firewalls had gotten good enough at blocking packets from foreign networks that the CIA had gone back to underground printing presses, and there were teams that collected as many as thousands of leaflets a day, bundled them up, and shoveled them into industrial shredders and incinerators.

Ranveer took one from the bin and read it over a cup of tea. He discovered that it was not transactional like the old series—that it did not promise wealth or material gain or the American Dream. There were no pictures of peaceful green suburbs, or expensive SUVs, or multiracial groups practicing religious freedom. Instead, they were inspirational. What they promised was intangible, complex, and abstract. The literature reminded Ranveer of the things his father had taught him, and, in fact, began with a quote from one of the old man's favorite plays.

> *We know what we are,*
> *but know not what we may be.*

The next chapter in Ranveer's life began the day he secretly established communication with the CIA.

26

THE EPOCH INDEX

QUINN HAS BEEN commuting to Swiss Fort Knox Site VII for five straight days now via a muscular, marigold-yellow helicopter with a shrouded rear rotor. There are racks inside for snowboards, skis, and poles, and chargers for GoPros, drones, and headphones. Maybe it's no Chinese-made autonomous quadcopter, but she'll take a crisp aerial view of the Alps over the heat-shimmering Grid any day.

Settling on SFK Site VII was not difficult. It was mostly a matter of ranking all the most secure dead drop locations in the world by number of direct Emirates flights connecting nearby airports with cities where she knew the Elite Assassin had been. Took all of forty, forty-five minutes. Did most of it with a cheap ballpoint pen borrowed from a British Airlines kiosk that she first had to scribble to life on the back of a Starbucks receipt. Didn't need petaflops of parallel processing prowess to figure out exactly where her man was going to be. Didn't even need the entire payload of caffeine from her triple venti vanilla latte. All Quinn needed was the missing key provided by the woman with the orange-red hair, combined with a little creativity.

On her first trip on-site, she didn't even make it off the helipad before being intercepted by security guards in white tactical gear carrying automatic weapons and crouching in the cold alpine chopper wash. They were respectful when she waved her credentials at them, but not remotely intimidated. She was hastily sent away with the name and phone number of a Mr. Eberlein, director of Site VII, from whom she would need to be granted clearance to even be allowed to disembark, and with whom she arranged to meet early the next morning.

Eberlein was polite but adamant that there was no way she would be given access to anyone's reserved receptacle for any reason, under any circumstances, with or without a court order from the United States, Switzerland, or any other sovereign entity, nor would she be conducting interrogations or making any arrests on SFK property. By day three, after her superiors had contacted his superiors, and after Eberlein's aggression had started to become decidedly less passive, he begrudgingly extended what he insisted was the best offer she was going to get.

Each morning, Quinn was to be escorted to a vacant privacy room where she was free to spend her day as she pleased (lunch and refreshments would *not* be provided, and access to facilities would be strictly supervised). Should the gentleman in her photographs—the man allegedly associated with the provided list of URIs, or Unique Receptacle Identifiers—happen to pay SFK Site VII a visit, said gentleman would be informed by none other than Eberlein himself that a Ms. Quinn Mitchell representing the United States Central Intelligence Agency wished to make his distinguished acquaintance. Should he find consultation with Ms. Mitchell desirable, he would—under his own volition and free of any and all forms of coercion, including but not limited to the express or implied threat of legal action and/or physical harm—be escorted to the aforementioned privacy room, where he might remain for as long as he found an audience with Ms. Mitchell both to his liking and in his best interests. Ms. Mitchell would *not* be permitted to detain the gentleman for any reason whatsoever, and positively *no* accusations or any form of intimidation would be tolerated. *Period.* Quinn suspected that one more day of escalation—of the United States threatening to take an overall keener interest in the entirety of the Swiss banking system, for instance—might have gotten her a somewhat better deal, but she didn't want to risk her man slipping in and out while government officials postured and jousted. With a smile as patronizing as she was able to muster, she briefly grasped Eberlein's effeminate fingers and squeezed.

THE STARK CONCRETE privacy room reminds Quinn of a walk-in freezer where she is the meat. The first day was spent catching up on administrative work. Since she was alone, she took off her metaspecs and used her handset's pico optics to project her workspace onto one of the white concrete walls. She browsed her backlog of messages, filed several field reports read only by a persnickety AI that unfailingly requested additional meaningless details, and entered some expenses—including the one for her brand-new handset (hence the pico projector), which she'd asked for in case her old one belatedly succumbed to its misadventure, and which Moretti begrudgingly approved.

That was yesterday. It is now her second day on-site and her fifth day in the Swiss Alps, and she is starting to wonder if she's going to need a contingency plan. She suspects she can only spend one or two more days in an SFK privacy room eating *rösti* (an exotic interpretation of the humble hash brown, packed by the cook at the B&B), drinking thermoses of Swiss coffee, and sheepishly requesting trips to the restroom before she's going to need to come up with a cheaper way to set a trap. Quinn is staying in the nearby town of Valais, and the costs of lodging, helicopter commutes, and the fruit cognacs she discovered and now uses to get to sleep at night are mounting.

Just as Quinn begins to consider other options, there are two quick raps on the thick steel door, which is subsequently pushed inward with some obvious effort. This is the first time anyone has been to see her, so Quinn immediately taps a code into her handset, kills the projector, and pushes her chair back as she stands.

There are four men outside the room: a clearly perturbed Eberlein, two almost excessively Scandinavian armed guards, and the man Quinn has been chasing all over the world.

Standing right there.

As though he weren't some sort of aristocratic, sociopathic serial killer. Like he might actually be a human being instead of an appari-tion that can only be captured on surveillance footage long after he has escaped, and whose interactions with the physical world are de-tectable only through the bodies and the blood and the anguish he leaves in his wake.

Like she didn't, finally, just catch the motherfucker.

"MS. MITCHELL," EBERLEIN announces with poorly disguised dis-gust. "Allow me to introduce Mr. Ranveer."

In the wake of the director's imperial flair, Ranveer steps into the privacy room and begins scanning. He is gripping a small metal case that Quinn can tell carries some serious weight, and it does not es-cape her notice that it is in his left hand. Her eyes dart across his waist and she sees that his oversized metal watch is on his right wrist.

Quinn knows that he is looking for more doors, one-way mirrors, cameras. Dark muzzle-sized holes in the tall white walls. She can tell that he is considering the furniture, calculating its value as either a weapon or a shield. As cautious as he is being, it occurs to her that he is probably far safer at the moment than she is—that if something were to go down right now, he would be everyone's top priority. Ran-veer is, after all, the only one in the room holding a case full of money.

The sharp, falcon-like eyes finally find Quinn, and she feels the cold in the room suddenly soak through all the layers of her clothes and into her skin. He is steadfast and placid while she struggles to keep herself still against the chill closing in around her and the fear rising up from within. He does not conduct his threat assessment by looking her up and down, but by holding her gaze and watching her eyes for changes over time. Quinn is shivering on the inside, but on the outside, she projects all the resolve of an immovable object.

The appraisal is terminated by a curt and decisive nod. "Ms. Mitch-ell."

"Mr. Ranveer," Eberlein injects, "I wish to reiterate that you—"

"I understand," Ranveer interrupts. "Your services have been im-peccable. You may leave us."

His British English is perfect, and Quinn is trying very hard not to find the man charming. Eberlein is clearly relieved by his client's graciousness, and when Ranveer offers his hand to the director, the fastidious man performs a pitifully obsequious bow as he receives it. Quinn tries to see if any Swiss francs or euros change hands, but it doesn't look like it. There's probably an affluence threshold beyond which passing cash is considered tacky.

"Thank you, Mr. Ranveer. We will be *right* outside should you require *anything* at all."

Eberlein gestures impatiently at the guards, tugs at the door, and all three men give Quinn one final look of contempt through the narrowing gap. It closes with a surprising report that settles nicely over the thick layer of tension already accumulating throughout the bright white room.

Quinn has considered this conversation frequently and repeatedly, but now that her man is actually standing right here in front of her, the situation seems to defy all of her rehearsals. Instead of working from a script, she decides to clear her mind—to take it one line at a time and accept that the situation will likely be fluid.

"Thank you for agreeing to see me," she says, then immediately regrets starting out with a conciliatory cliché. She knows she does not have much leverage at the moment, but that is certainly not what she wants to convey. Nor is it the opening move she suspects a more experienced officer would choose.

"Of course," Ranveer replies.

"Please, have a seat."

Ranveer sits in the chair opposite Quinn and sets the heavy case down at his feet. She notices that he grips the table with both hands to confirm that it is indeed bolted down.

"My name is Quinn Mitchell. I work for the Central Intelligence Agency."

She waits for a reaction, which comes, eventually, in the form of another shallow nod.

"I'm investigating a series of murders that I think you might know something about."

"I understand," Ranveer responds flatly.

She watches him for a moment while she tries to work out what kind of game he is playing. He did not have to agree to see her, so surely he must have something more to offer than stretches of awkward silence punctuated by polite platitudes. It occurs to Quinn that he may simply be waiting for her to reveal what she knows. That he may be here to extract information from her. Quinn begins to wonder if perhaps he is the one who laid the trap—if instead of him being alone in a room deep underground with her, it is the other way around.

"Mr. Ranveer, can you account for your whereabouts over the last four weeks?"

"I think you already know the answer to that."

Quinn is startled by the killer's willingness to dispense with all pretense. His forthrightness induces a new wave of panic since, if he walked in here ready to confirm her accusations, he obviously expects to walk out on his own terms.

"Yes," she finally says. "I'm pretty sure that I do, but I'd like to hear it from you."

"Ms. Mitchell," Ranveer says, shaking his head, "these are not the right questions."

Quinn tries to stifle a look of surprise. "What does *that* mean?"

"It means there is no point in discussing what we both already know. Your limited time with me is better spent asking about things you haven't yet figured out."

"Fine," Quinn says. She is doing her best to appear unperturbed. "Then I'd like you to tell me who wanted all these people dead, and I'd like you to tell me why."

Ranveer drops his eyes for a moment, then drums his fingertips on the brushed-steel surface before him. Quinn notices that his fingernails are significantly better manicured than her own.

"Ms. Mitchell," he begins. "May I ask you a question?"

At this point, Quinn is flying entirely blind and relying purely on instinct. She decides she is willing to entertain anything that keeps her man talking—and that keeps the clock ticking.

"Why not?"

"Have you ever heard of the Epoch Index?"

Quinn's gaze sharpens. She is leaning against the back of her chair, looking down at Ranveer, hoping to appear confident and in control. But now she moves around to the other side and sits, and they regard each other on an equal level.

"I've heard of it."

"And?"

"And what?"

"What do you think?"

"I don't think anything. Until someone figures out how to decrypt it, there's no way to know what it is."

"What would you say if I told you that I decrypted it."

"I'd say you were lying."

"Why?"

"Because the smartest people in the world have been trying to decrypt it and haven't been able to."

"Let's approach this from a different angle," Ranveer proposes. "Why encrypt anything at all?"

"To make sure it doesn't fall into the wrong hands."

"Exactly. Which implies that if it were to fall into the right hands, it could be decrypted."

"So the CIA is the wrong hands."

"You might say that."

"And you're the right hands."

"I'd like to think so."

"Well, that's easy enough to prove, isn't it? If you decrypted it, you must know where it came from."

"I do."

"And?"

Ranveer smiles reticently. "I can confirm that the rumors as to its origins are true."

"Let's be clear here," Quinn says. "Are you claiming that the Epoch Index came from the future?"

"I am."

"Which implies that someone from the future wanted all these people dead, correct?"

"Yes."

"Mr. Ranveer, I'm not that stupid," Quinn tells him. "I know that none of this is possible."

"If I were to present you with irrefutable proof," Ranveer says, "then will you believe me?"

"Probably not," Quinn says, "but irrefutable proof is certainly a good start."

Ranveer leans forward. He watches Quinn astutely—clearly a precursor to a deliberate and purposeful delivery.

"The Epoch Index was detected by the Large Hadron Collider over a decade ago, but it wasn't until a Korean physicist named Henrietta Yi—whom I suspect you've met by now—had the idea of using parallelized neural networks to analyze the backlog of data that it was finally discovered."

"I know all this," Quinn says. "What I don't know is what happened to the Epoch Index after it was discovered."

"After the European Organization for Nuclear Research confirmed the anomaly, they contacted a small number of governments and turned the data over."

"Then how did you end up with it?"

"That's not important right now. What is important is that the data consisted of a series of encrypted blocks that nobody knew how to decrypt."

"Nobody but you," Quinn corrects.

"Yes."

"How?"

"Think about it," Ranveer says. "You already know the answer."

"I'd really rather not play—" But then something unexpectedly aligns in Quinn Mitchell's mind. "The twins."

"The twins," Ranveer confirms. "I took the index to Naan and Pita. They have more distributed computing resources at their disposal than anyone else on the entire planet. The CIA included. The encryption on the first block was relatively weak, so it only took about a month to break it."

"What was it?"

"First of all, verification. Enough information to prove, definitively, that the Epoch Index is from the future."

"How?"

"Years of global temperature charts. Hour by hour. Which would all prove to be exactly correct down to a tenth of a degree."

Quinn tries to think of a way to disprove the premise. Obviously, any number of people can use predictive modeling to anticipate future temperatures, but not down to the hour, and certainly not down to fractions of degrees.

"OK," Quinn allows. "What else?"

"Instructions. Along with the first name on the list."

"The first *target*," Quinn clarifies.

"Yes."

"And presumably the rest of the blocks were additional targets."

"And payment."

"What kind of payment?"

"Whatever has value by virtue of being unknowable or undiscovered. Cryptocurrency trends, stock tips, sports scores. Novel molecular compounds. Did the CIA or the QSS ever identify the substance used to anesthetize the twins?"

"No."

"Now you know why," Ranveer says. "Anyway, the twins acted as middlemen. Given their neighbors, the information was not difficult to trade on." He reaches down and taps the case at his feet. "They even arranged the transfer of cash."

"Why the tags?" Quinn asks. "Why not just send the twins four-digit numbers directly? Or have them send the numbers directly to you?"

"One less digital breadcrumb for you to scoop up. Safer to let the media do the communication for us."

"That's just sick," Quinn says, though she has to admit, it is as brilliant as it is twisted.

"Pita's idea, if I remember correctly."

"Why didn't you kill them?"

"The twins? Because there was no need for them to die." He takes a moment more to consider Quinn's question more deeply. "And because I like them."

"You mean because you still have use for them."

"That too."

"Why would Naan and Pita go along with something like this?" Quinn asks. "Somehow they don't strike me as the murdering type."

"The twins are the two most intelligent people I've ever met," Ranveer says. "They understood the significance of the Epoch Index even before I did."

"That doesn't answer my question."

"Naan and Pita went along with it because they had no choice."

"Because you forced them."

"No. They participated voluntarily. Reluctantly, but voluntarily. They accepted that everyone named by the Epoch Index had to be eliminated."

"Why?" Quinn asks. "Why was it so important to the future that all these people die?"

"Because," Ranveer says, "they were the most dangerous terrorists the world would ever see."

"*Terrorists?*" In her mind, Quinn begins reviewing the victims' profiles. A Kenyan cab driver who, on weekends, was learning to fly at Nairobi Aviation College. A Chinese man arrested by the Ministry of Public Security for selling banned video games. A geneticist working for a South African food-processing company. A Russian hacker who lost her legs in a retaliatory missile strike. A young former executive of Petróleos de Venezuela. A top v-sports athlete obsessed with prime numbers and cryptography. The nine-month-old son of an Omani investor. *Nine months old.* And at least a dozen others—all mostly unremarkable. "Bullshit," Quinn says. "What kind of terrorists?"

"All kinds," Ranveer says. "Even the kind you used to hunt before you began hunting me."

Quinn shakes her head. "That's impossible," she says. "We never found any nuclear terrorists."

Ranveer shows a row of impeccable white teeth as he grins. "Exactly."

"You're sick," Quinn tells the man across from her. "You've been murdering innocent people. Children. *Babies.* There's no way they were all terrorists."

"They weren't," Ranveer agrees. "Not yet. Remember, the Epoch Index came from the future."

"Why didn't you just have them arrested?" Quinn asks. "Or have them—I don't know—*watched* or something?"

"That wasn't an option."

"Why?"

"The digitally signed death certificate of each target was the decryption key for the next block. The only way to decrypt the entire list was to eliminate every target on it. Each death had to be verified, and they had to be done in the correct order."

Quinn recalls the flag that her dashboard raised about the victims' ages. "From oldest to youngest," she says.

"So it would seem."

"That's very clever," Quinn says with a sardonic grin. She feels like a trial lawyer about to eviscerate her witness. "But it's also complete bullshit. And I can prove it."

"I already know your objection," Ranveer says.

"What?"

"You're going to say that some properties of death certificates are predictable. Name, universally unique identifier, birth date, address. But some—like time, cause, and place of death—are not."

"Exactly. And any change in the contents, no matter how minor, changes the entire digital signature, which means unless the targets were eliminated at exactly the right time, in exactly the right place, and in exactly the right way, it wouldn't work."

"Except . . ." He pauses, presumably to give Quinn the opportunity to find the flaw in her own logic.

"Except what?"

"Except for the fact that the blocks were encrypted *in the future,* Ms. Mitchell, when all of those details were already known."

Quinn leans back in her chair and smiles. She no longer feels intimidated by the man across from her, but oddly invigorated by the exchange.

"I'm impressed," she says. "You've really put a lot of thought into this, haven't you?"

"No," Ranveer says. "Someone much more ruthless and calculating than I put a lot of thought into this. I'm just following orders."

"That's hard to imagine," Quinn says.

"What?"

"Someone more ruthless and calculating than you. Who is he?"

Ranveer leans forward, placing his arms on the steel surface between them and interlacing his long fingers. He watches her with his perfectly black eyes, and she perceives in him a tranquility that is simultaneously comforting and unsettling.

"You."

Quinn's expression instantly changes. She takes in a breath and starts to say something but stops. Before she can counter, Ranveer continues.

"You are the one who saves countless lives, Ms. Mitchell. You are the one who figures out how to adapt to an insane and disintegrating world. I came here to tell you that Molly did not die in vain, and that your life has not been wasted. I came here to tell you that you are the architect of the Epoch Index."

Molly. Hearing that name come out of this man's mouth both infuriates and weakens her. Quinn's hands are pressed into the metal surface in front of her, and her eyes are one blink away from spilling tears of both rage and pain.

"I promised you irrefutable proof," Ranveer continues. "The Epoch Index had a short, clear-text prologue. Perhaps you'll recognize it. *We know what we are, but know not what we may be.*"

"That's a—" Quinn shakes her head. "That doesn't mean anything. That's from *Hamlet*. You're going to have to do a hell of a lot better than that."

"Oh, I can," Ranveer assures her. "The last decrypted block—the one I was picking up when we nearly met on The Grid—wasn't a name. It was a message. For you. *From* you. Your most private memory. Something you never told anyone and never wrote down. Something to prove that the Epoch Index is real, and that you are its creator."

Quinn cycles through a deep breath and swallows. "What is it?"

"Your last name wasn't always Mitchell," Ranveer begins. His dark eyes are eerily serene and perfectly steady. "You used to be Quinn Claiborne."

He pauses, presumably waiting for a reaction. Quinn shakes her head to show him that she is both underwhelmed and piqued.

"You've got to be kidding me," she says. "That's public record."

"You changed it back to Mitchell, your maiden name, after your brother's surgery," he continues. "After the radiation therapy ensured that he would never be able to have children."

He pauses again. This time, Quinn is quiet.

"Your husband, James, was upset. You fought about it for days. He proposed that you hyphenate your name, but you refused. You went back to Mitchell and insisted that your children bear your last name instead of his. He had two brothers who both had children. His name wasn't in danger of dying out. But continuing the Mitchell line was up to you. What angered James was not that you wanted to give up his name. It was that you chose your father's name—the name of a man who so clearly never cared about you—over the name of a man who loved you more than anything else in the world. That was why he felt betrayed."

"You—" Quinn isn't sure what she wants to say, but she wants this to stop. This man is sick. Anyone who would play these types of games is sick. She will not participate. She will not play, and she will not let him make her cry. "James could have told someone that. He could have told his therapist. All of this could have been stolen from digital records."

"I'm not finished," Ranveer says. "There's one more thing about your father that nobody else in the world besides you could possibly know. Isn't there?"

Quinn can feel her face drain of all expression and the nausea rise up in her gut. She now knows exactly where this going.

"I don't want to do this anymore," she says. "I want you to stop."

"You were with your father when he died. It was the middle of the night. Nobody expected him to live as long as he did, and the hospice nurse had to go out to get more morphine. Your brother and your stepmother were asleep downstairs. They'd asked you to wake them if his condition changed, and you promised them that you would."

"Stop it."

"But you didn't."

"I said stop."

Quinn wants to reach across the table and *make* him stop, but instead she puts her hand over her mouth. She finds she is powerless to do anything but listen as the man across from her reveals her darkest and most shameful secret.

"There was a baby monitor in the room, and you reached over and calmly switched it off. And then—very slowly—you closed the valve on his oxygen tank. He opened his eyes and looked at you, and you could see the fear in them. You held his hand and you kissed his forehead and you stroked his wispy white hair. He didn't smell like your father anymore. He smelled like excrement. He smelled like death. You talked to him and you wiped the tears from the corners of his eyes and from where they pooled up against the plastic tubing. His mouth moved, but he couldn't speak. You promised him that everything was going to be OK, and that one day he would be with your mother again, and eventually with you and your brother, and that everything would go back to how it was. You sang him the songs he sang to you and your brother when you were little, and you kept singing until his ragged breathing finally stopped. And then you put his hand down on top of the comforter, opened the valve on the oxygen tank, switched the baby monitor back on, and went downstairs to wake everyone up. You told them that you'd fallen asleep in the chair, and when you woke up, he was gone. You lied to them because you wanted his last moments to be yours. You felt like you deserved them. He gave your brother everything, and your stepmother only married him for his money. You wanted something from him that nobody else would ever be able to have, so you took it."

Quinn lowers her chin to her chest as she begins to weep, and when she feels Ranveer's hand on top of hers, she does not pull away. Her sobs reverberate throughout the concrete room as she grieves.

"He was suffering," she says between convulsions. "It was what he would have wanted."

"I know."

"He wouldn't have made it through the night. I was just—"

"It's OK."

When she finally opens her eyes, she sees Ranveer looking at her in a way that nobody has looked at her in a very long time. Maybe ever. There is no judgment or embarrassment or discomfort in his expression. He is not dissociating or looking for ways to put distance between them. He is not making jokes or otherwise trying to expedite her emotion. Instead, he is sitting right there with her, sharing in her pain, and Quinn realizes that it is perhaps the most human moment of her entire life.

Quinn takes her hand back. "I'm not a murderer," she tells the man across from her.

Ranveer watches her for a moment, and she cannot tell what he is thinking. "Do you know the story of the scorpion and the turtle?" he finally asks.

"What?"

"It's an old Persian fable."

Quinn leans back and blots her eyes with her sleeve.

"A scorpion wishes to cross a river," Ranveer begins, "but cannot swim. It turns to a nearby turtle and asks for a ride. The turtle, knowing the scorpion's nature, refuses. But the scorpion points out that if it were to kill the turtle, they would both drown. The turtle sees the logic in the scorpion's argument and agrees. Halfway across the river, the scorpion buries its stinger deep into the soft flesh of the turtle's neck. As they both sink below the current, the turtle asks the scorpion why. Do you know what the scorpion says?"

They watch each other across the cold steel surface of the table, the silence between them protracting, until the stillness in the room is shattered by sudden commotion outside. The yelling and barking of orders is loud enough to penetrate the thick metal door, and they both reflexively stand, Ranveer lunging for his case, and Quinn making one last attempt to clean up her face.

The heavy metal slab is swung open with surprising ease, and before it can slam against the wall, the room is full of masked figures in dark body armor behind blinding strobes. The plasma dots on the ends of the submachine guns are meant to stun and blind anyone inside without the concussion and violence of flashbang grenades. Three men are on top of Ranveer before anyone can speak. The heavy case drops, the flashes stop, and he is bent roughly over the table and cuffed.

Eberlein is screaming somewhere down the hall. For a moment, his voice gets louder, then it fades rapidly into the distance. When everyone has declared the room clear, Alessandro Moretti steps inside, surveying the situation while holstering his pistol. He is wearing a Kevlar vest and his shirtsleeves are rolled up. His eyes are baggy but bright, and Quinn can see that these are the moments he lives for— the rush that makes all the paperwork and bureaucracy worthwhile.

He nods at Quinn and smiles at her for perhaps the very first time.

"Well done, Mitchell."

"Thank—" She clears her throat. "Thank you, sir."

"You OK?"

"Fine. The strobes."

"It'll pass."

Moretti moves around the room until he can get a good look at Ranveer's face, then he looks back up at Quinn. "So, what's the good word, Officer Mitchell? Did you get what we need?"

Ranveer's neck is bent and his face is pressed into the cold steel, but he can still twist around and look up. His expression is not one of pleading. It is strained by the physical position he is in, but Quinn can see that he is not afraid, and he is not trying to convey any kind of threat. There is nothing he wants or needs from her anymore. He has the serenity of a man who, even though he is out of time, has still managed to fulfill his mission. As Quinn watches him, his eyes soften, and his lips constrict into a cunning and subtle grin. He seems pleased to be leaving Quinn with the unfinished fable of the scorpion.

PART THREE

27

MAN CAVE

ALESSANDRO MORETTI HAD one room of his secret facility turned into his own personal gym. Henrietta can hear the music and the clanking of weights from all the way down the hall. She's practiced her pitch enough that she has the whole thing memorized, and abruptly decides that now is the right time.

The door is ajar, and Henrietta knocks as she pushes it farther open and slips tentatively inside. Moretti glances down the length of his chest as he pushes through one final rep, then drops the bar noisily into its catch.

This is the first time Henrietta has been in this room. The entire facility is her domain with two exceptions: Mr. Moretti's office and what appears to be an adjoining man cave.

It's almost all weights in here. No space for sissy cardio. Variously shaped bars are strewn about like metallic bones amid hinged benches. There are a couple of steel frames that look disconcertedly like cages. And a rack of graduating dumbbells against the wall. Above them, a wide plasma glass screen, its dangling wires exposed, the brutality of the afternoon's global news muted. In the corner, a mini fridge with a see-through door etched with the Monster energy drink logo, and a plasma-accented boombox rattling classic rock planted on top. The concrete floor is covered by thick black interlocking tiles forming a sprawling rubberized mat that singes the air with its potent outgassing.

Henrietta wonders if it has occurred to Moretti that the quantum fields they are generating here in order to facilitate dynamic mass redistribution could be commercialized for the creation of the very first infinitely configurable weight set—though, sadly, at a per-unit cost of billions.

"Mr. Moretti?" she says apprehensively.

Her boss is sitting up now, and Henrietta can see that he is wearing a white ribbed wife-beater T-shirt tucked into his steel-gray pleated trousers. His back is covered in a fine black down, and there is an indistinct bluish tattoo on one shoulder that Henrietta assumes is related to his days as an Army Ranger. A gold chain hangs on the outside of his shirt, converging against his sternum, weighted by an emerald- and ruby-studded Lady of Guadalupe pendant—not as a symbol of any form of faith, but, according to rumors, a trophy taken off a Mexican drug lord as he lay maimed along with his family in the debris of a drone strike—courtesy of the CIA. Moretti's pink, neatly pressed dress shirt is hung by its collar behind him on a metal peg.

Mr. Moretti is smelly and sweaty, Henrietta sings in her head.

Moretti puts his hands out like he's catching a body falling from the sky, but instead of looking up, he is glaring straight ahead.

"What the fuck are you doing?" he wants to know.

Instantaneously the music ducks below the level of anticipated conversation, and the boombox's neon blaze accordingly fades.

"I'm sorry to bother you."

"Is this an emergency?"

"No." Henrietta now sees that her calculations were way off. She assumed Moretti would be more receptive to her proposal during his downtime, but it's obvious to her now that he takes his breaks just as seriously as he does his work. "I'm sorry. It can wait."

Moretti scoops up a tall black can from the floor, rattles it, and tips it back. He uses the other hand to halt Henrietta's retreat.

"You already interrupted me," he says, grimacing from the potency of whatever energy-enhancing chemicals he is ingesting. "What is it?"

Henrietta contemplates aborting her plan—either hastily evacuating, or fabricating an update that her boss will pretend to understand. But the part of her that is perpetually eager to please is being overridden by something inside of her that has been growing in control: the feeling that she is running out of time to become the person she feels she was always meant to be.

"Well," Henrietta says as she steps farther into the room. "It's about the email I sent you."

"Which one?"

"The one about me getting back into research."

"Refresh my memory," Moretti says, by which he means, *I didn't bother reading it.*

"Last week, I sent you a proposal for how I think I can get back into civilian research."

"Ah," Moretti realizes. "This again."

"Now that we're almost operational here, and now that the whole Elite Assassin thing has been wrapped up, I thought it would be a good time for me to get back to publishing some of my research. On my own time, of course. Maybe even spend evenings and weekends working part-time at a university. It wouldn't affect my work here. I promise."

Moretti turns to retrieve a white hand towel that was spread over the bench to protect the material from the back of his head, then uses it to dab at the black tufts of his armpits.

"I don't think so," he says.

Henrietta had been planning this conversation for months—long before she got up the courage to send the email. She wasn't exactly expecting her boss to be enthusiastic about the idea, but she also wasn't expecting it all to be over so fast.

"Mr. Moretti, I—"

"I said no," Moretti repeats. "Is there anything else?"

Henrietta starts to turn, but stops.

"Yes," she says. She resets her specs, folds her arms across the chest of her floral dress, and shifts her weight. "I'd like to know why."

She can tell that Moretti was not expecting to have to provide any kind of justification. He watches her for a moment, and she knows that he is contemplating the physics of the interaction: how much force he can get away with applying without causing more resistance. His expression changes, and she can see that he has resigned himself to a moderately softer approach.

"Well, for one," he begins, "we got this whole thing going on in Paris."

"What thing?"

"Some Japanese astronomer claims he discovered plans for a machine that can generate particles that travel faster than the speed of light."

"Superluminal particles? This is the first I'm hearing of this."

"You're hearing about it now," Moretti says.

"What do you mean he *discovered plans?*"

"Says he found them in the sensor backlogs of a bunch of solar probes. Some kind of message. Sound familiar?"

"Are his claims credible?"

"We'll know soon enough. We're setting up an experiment between Paris and Langley, so I need you to supervise on our end."

"OK," Henrietta says with cautious optimism. "How about after the experiment? Or even after we're fully operational here? I'm not saying it has to be right now. I just want to know that there's some kind of plan to let me get back into academia."

"*Why?*" Moretti asks emphatically. "What's so goddamn special about academia? What, do you want more money? Is this your way of asking for a raise?"

"It isn't about the money, Mr. Moretti. It's about the science."

"Fuck the science," Moretti says. "What about *the mission?* After what happened to your parents, you'd think you'd be a little more committed."

"I *am* committed to the mission," Henrietta insists. "But this isn't what my parents wanted for me. My father wanted me to contribute to the greater scientific good, not spend my life locked up in some secret bunker nobody will ever even know about."

"Oh, make no mistake," Moretti says. He stands, throws one leg over the bench, and takes a step toward Henrietta. "The world *will* know about this place."

"But when?" Henrietta asks. "In a hundred years?"

"A hundred years. Two hundred years. A *thousand* years, if we're lucky. The longer it takes for the world to find out about what we're doing here, the better we're doing it. But I promise you, the world *will* know, and history *will* remember."

"Fine," Henrietta says. "But why can't I do civilian research on my own time?"

"Because you're *tainted*, Henrietta. Can't you see that? There's no way you can separate what you know about this place from outside academic research. I can't let you go around publishing. That could jeopardize everything. This whole fucking place. I'm sorry, but every-thing you do for the rest of your career *will* be classified. The sooner you accept that, the better."

"Then I'll quit," Henrietta says matter-of-factly.

"Excuse me?" Moretti asks her. "What did you just say?"

"I said, if you won't be reasonable, then I'll quit."

"Oh-kay," Moretti says in a way that Henrietta knows means he is escalating. "Let me explain something to you, sweetheart. There is no *quitting* for people like you."

"How do you intend to stop me?"

"How do I intend to stop you?" Moretti asks bemusedly. "By turn-ing the full force of this agency against you, that's how. Do you know why I'm having Simon work so closely with you?"

"Simon is my assistant."

"Simon isn't your *assistant*," Moretti says. "Simon is your *replace-ment*. Don't think for a second I didn't see this coming. From now on, if you so much as show up late for work without a goddamn doctor's note, I'll have you arrested for sharing information with North Korea. I'll have you implicated in the terrorist attack on Seoul, and I'll have you thrown in the deepest, darkest hole this country knows how to dig. Is that a clear enough answer for you?"

He is pointing at her now, and she can see the veins in his biceps and the tendons in his neck. Henrietta doesn't know why she isn't crying. She has stepped outside of herself and is amazed to see that instead of shrinking, she is standing up straight and staring Moretti right in the eye. Her arms are now down at her sides, her hands clenched into little fists, her chin lowered almost to her chest. And on her face is an eerie and defiant smile.

28

TISSUE

QUINN WOKE UP this morning with a touch of the wine flu, which she is now working through by perpetually cresting the apex of a stair-climber at her local Worldwide Fitness Center, while simultaneously keeping a close eye on her message queue.

Even with the promotion she was given after tracking down and assisting in the capture of the Elite Assassin, Quinn can barely afford a Worldwide membership on a single salary. She and Moretti made a tacit agreement that Quinn would take the money while he claimed most of the credit, but if she'd known how anemic the raise would turn out to be, she might have reconsidered.

As a general rule, Quinn does not think about the decision she made back in that privacy room almost six weeks ago and over four thousand miles away, and she has talked to no one—not Henrietta, not Moretti, not even Van—about what was discussed. Of course, her handset recorded the whole thing, which she deleted before it could be collected as evidence, claiming (much to Moretti's explosive dismay) that she failed to put the device into surveillance mode because she was so unnerved by being left alone in a little concrete bunker with such a vicious and prolific killer.

Quinn has no idea how the man apparently known only as Ranveer knew the things about her that he did, but Occam's razor suggests the most likely scenario is that she told a friend about her father, and that friend betrayed her confidence and emailed another friend.

Or she confided in a therapist (God knows she's seen enough of them) who stored her case notes online. She doesn't know exactly how or when, but her most closely guarded secret must have ended up digitized, and subsequently swept up by Russian or Chinese hackers specifically probing for potential intelligence-related blackmail targets in and around the Washington, D.C., area. And like every other piece of personal information on the planet, it would have eventually found its way down into the shadowphiles.

In Quinn's mind, Ranveer is nothing but a sociopathic contract killer ultimately distinguished not by his handsome Middle Eastern demeanor or refined aristocratic manners, but purely by the fact that he was willing to take on jobs that other assassins had enough integrity to turn down. Even without the recorded confession, he is now paying for his hubris by serving multiple consecutive life sentences in one of the most technologically advanced maximum-security detention facilities on the planet, owned and operated by the International Criminal Court and located in an undisclosed location. Which, Quinn happens to know, is the northernmost coastal district of The Hague.

But Quinn is not so detached from her emotions that she doesn't know the truth about why she sequestered those twenty minutes of conversation and entombed them somewhere as secure and protected as the facility in which they took place. Even though she knows that she will never see him again, there is something about Ranveer that terrifies Quinn—something she is afraid she will carry around with her for the rest of her life. It has nothing to do with being in the same room with a man willing to inflict such unspeakable harm on others purely for the privilege of flying Sultan Class and living in the world's finest hotels, and everything to do with the things Ranveer made her question about herself.

RATHER THAN A ponytail, Quinn is wearing a black Lululemon Baller cap, and her straw-blond hair is starting to stick to the perspiration on her bare shoulders. She doesn't love that the stair-climber puts her ass, hips, and thighs directly at eye level for the entire D.C. metropolitan area to leisurely contemplate, but she has been coming to the gym regularly enough since getting back that her self-consciousness and her self-esteem have finally achieved a kind of uneasy equilibrium. Plenty of middle-aged male members get busted gawking at her in her capri leggings and strappy black tank top, which, after it happens enough, begins to annoy her, but plenty of men also can't be bothered to look up from their phones as they walk past, which, frankly, irks her even more.

This particular Worldwide has recently been remodeled and all the screens have been removed. Once sweat-proof and impact-resistant polymer metaspecs got cheap enough to be impulse buys among the suitably affluent, the constant assault of Estonian cybergrime music videos and zero-g cosmetic surgery infomercials radiating from arrays of mission-control monitors became the club's most frequent complaint. Now, the majority of cardio machines don't even have screens; in their place are plastic surfaces with tracking-pattern inlays to which metaspecs affix any one of dozens of virtual views users incessantly flick through.

The icon Quinn's phone uses for an empty message queue is a smiley face, and she wonders again whether that's because you're supposed to be happy when you don't have any messages that require your attention, or to cheer you up because nobody wants to talk to you. In an attempt to ignore it, she watches a tiny virtual version of herself ascend the 354 steps toward the head of the Statue of Liberty. Her avatar is fiercely determined and seems to dip her chin and toss her ponytail from side to side every time she lifts a knee. The semitransparent, volumetric model rotates in sync with the spiraling stairs, and Quinn's bright scarlet surrogate looks to her like an alien parasite swimming up a helical artery to Lady Liberty's brain, where it will zombify her and force her to destroy Lower Manhattan. But as soon as Quinn breaches the neocortex, the virtual figurine sinks down into the stair-climber's plastic podium and the Washington Monument sprouts in its place, with avatar-Quinn barely a third of the way to the top. Quinn is sick of progress holograms rotating right in front of her face, so she swipes it away and parks a boring 2D dashboard in its place.

A club notification is summoning some unlucky mother down to the childcare center. Nothing good comes from your presence being requested at the Fit Kidz Klub. The first time Quinn got paged was the last time she brought Molly. Back then, they used the PA system, and Quinn hadn't even finished stretching when she was alarmed to hear her name announced and subsequently discovered that Molly had punched a boy in the stomach and knocked the wind out of him. According to her, he would not stop making fun of her name, which she had written out in its entirety on her name tag. *Molly Mitchell! Molly Mitchell! Molly Mitchell!* And then *Ooof!* Little punk. Quinn was thoroughly embarrassed at being asked to leave and irritated at having to miss her workout, but when she asked Molly why she punched the kid in the stomach, and Molly answered that it was so she wouldn't leave a mark on his face, some deranged and probably damaged part of her was proud.

Naturally there was plenty of boilerplate parental rhetoric about using our words instead of our fists, going to an adult for help, not violating other people's personal boundaries, etc., but then they got to the heart of it: Molly hated her name. More specifically, she hated how it sounded when you said it together with her last name. *Molly Mitchell.* Why couldn't she have Daddy's last name? Molly Claiborne?

Quinn looked up at James, certain there would be a subtle but unmistakably smug, *see what you did?* expression on his face. But there wasn't. Instead, he knelt down to Molly's level and explained to her the concept of alliteration, and how it applied to the names of superheroes' alter egos. Clark Kent, Peter Parker, and Miles Morales. Bruce Banner and Jessica Jones. A bunch more he couldn't think of just then. The name Molly Mitchell meant that she would grow up to become a hero. They *had* to give her mommy's last name. It was, he told her solemnly, her destiny.

As gracious and endearing as James was being, Quinn had to admit to questioning whether the whole hero angle was the right approach for a kid like Molly—whether it might lead to even more gut punches, or possibly even a graduation to broken noses or dislocated jaws. Perhaps a secret collection of teeth. But Molly seemed to accept her new responsibility with a great deal of dignity and poise, and afterward they all went out for sprinkle-dipped custard and then to the playground, where Molly kept an eye on the smaller kids to make sure they were safe, and even relocated several insects she found in the grass far enough away that they would not get trampled. That night, while they were tucking her in, she explained that Molly Mitchell was her "altered ego," but that her hero name was "the Scorpion." Earlier that week, her class had gone on a field trip to the Natural History Museum in D.C., and one of the insect zoo curators offered to let someone hold a shiny black arachnid. Nobody stepped up except for Molly, who—according to what had already become well-established Sunrise Elementary lore—showed absolutely no fear whatsoever. The teacher took a picture and sent it home, and Quinn could barely even stand to look at it. That kid clearly had something inside her that Quinn did not. Whatever it was, it must have come from her father.

DURING THE LONG flight from Zürich to Joint Base Andrews on the C-130 Hercules with Moretti and his tactical team (terrible conversationalists, by the way, which was just as well given the perpetual pinches of dip in their lower lips and their constant need to spit into their empty energy drink cans), as her mind was trying to anticipate a return to normalcy, it occurred to her how overdue both she and her Honda Clarity were for maintenance. The car needed a new cooling fan; Quinn was delinquent on her mammogram.

Mammograms aren't like other forms of cancer screening. Quinn recently learned about a woman who had dedicated her life to discovering a universal cancer vaccine, but who somehow ended up pivoting to narcotics manufacturing, and subsequently had to flee the country in order to avoid arrest. For some reason, the woman felt her life was in danger, so her identity and location were being withheld, but according to the segment Quinn watched on the plasma glass in the radiologist's waiting room, she'd recently returned to the United States and somehow managed to negotiate a plea deal allowing her to participate in a work-release program in partnership with a nonprofit cancer research lab. In her very first week, she released open-source plans for a device as simple to use as a Breathalyzer that she believed would be able to diagnose early-stage lung cancer in seconds and at essentially no cost. Apparently, she'd transformed herself from corporate and social pariah into a public-health folk hero in just weeks.

But mammograms are still stuck in the past. Technicians in cute scrubs use words like "compression" and "tissue," but the reality is that you're having your boobs squeezed in a panini press. It is little comfort that the machine uses state-of-the-art particle imaging and detection technology developed for use in the Large Hadron Collider, since it feels like the only carryover from the particle smasher is the smashing part.

Your reward for all this is supposed to be absolutely nothing. As in clean results. You're supposed to get dressed, hand over your co-pay, and feel good about yourself for being such a grown-up today. Maybe treat yourself to a Starbucks on your way back to work. What you are not supposed to do is be shown to an isolated room at the end of the hall with serene pastel paintings on the walls and boxes of tissues on side tables. And the scans are not supposed to show little white dots in the left breast that were not there before and that you are told are calcium deposits. And the follow-up needle biopsy is supposed to reveal that all of this is actually nothing—just something to keep an eye on—rather than a condition that has a long, hard-to-remember name. During your next consult, you are not supposed to need to take everything off and get into a gown, and there is supposed to be banter between you and your doctor, not silence as the paper crinkles beneath your bottom and she flips through your pathology reports. You are not even supposed to *have* pathology reports. And you are never *ever* supposed to hear the words "partial mastectomy" come out of a breast surgeon's mouth.

But that's just the technical term, Quinn has been assured. Better to think of it as a surgical biopsy. A more detailed fact-finding mission. And the procedure is minimally invasive. The radar reflectors that the breast surgeon distributed throughout the tissue during yesterday's quick outpatient pre-op procedure will guide the robotic instruments with unprecedented, submillimeter precision. Sure, she'll be sore for a few days, and she'll be more comfortable wearing sports bras for about a week. She'll want to avoid things like stair-climbers until the discomfort has passed. But that's about it. And should they find the worst, they have plenty of options. More-aggressive surgery, hormone therapy—even genetically individualized immunotherapy, should she prove to be an ideal candidate. With a healthy lifestyle (keeping her weight down, eating more vegetables, and, sadly, decreasing her alcohol consumption), her prognosis is very good. Just a tiny loss of tissue, that's all.

But her breasts are not *tissue*. They are what provided Molly with sustenance for the first year of her baby's life. They are part of what signaled her transition from girl to young woman—changes she hated at first and didn't want, then wanted just a little bit more of, then eventually came to feel were just right. In Quinn's opinion, her breasts are one of her more attractive features, and certainly a long-time obsession of her ex-husband's. They are not just something she *has*; they are part of who she *is*.

Quinn does not think she can go through this alone. If she has to, she will call her mother or her brother, but not yet. Once again, her eyes dip to the message queue icon, which now looks as if it has fallen asleep and is dreaming of kittens and birthday cake. Last night, about halfway through her third glass of wine, Quinn sent the long, vulnerable email that she'd written to her ex-husband after scheduling the appointment and that had sat in her outbox awaiting sufficient courage—liquid or otherwise. And now she is waiting to find out whether James is open to not just being with her during the procedure, but, when all of this is behind them, maybe even trying again.

The day after her diagnosis, Quinn called her doctor's office and left a message for the breast surgeon asking if there was any reason why she would not be able to have children after the procedure. In her experience, doctors seldom do anything they cannot bill an insurance company for, but the surgeon called her right back and spent fifteen minutes reassuring her that not only would she still be able to get pregnant, but unless further treatment was required, she would even be able to breastfeed. At that moment, as Quinn covered her mouth and wept into the phone and her doctor waited patiently for over a minute for her to be able to speak again, she realized that—even though having a child was like removing a critical organ from inside your body and letting it out into the world on its own where anything might happen to it, and if anything ever did, you would never be able to recover—Quinn was not yet ready to give up on being a mother.

29

GHOSTS

HENRIETTA SITS ACROSS from a hologram of her long-dead father. She prefers him as a room-scale projection rather than the crisp, light-field refraction you get from metaspecs. Sometimes images focused directly against your retina can feel a little too real. But when you give them some space, the spontaneous quantum behavior of photons lends them a warm, otherworldly radiance.

The effect works best when it is dark, so all the lights in Henrietta's apartment are out. That means the scene is lit solely by the incandescence of her father's angelic presence. Henrietta is sitting on the floor, her back against the couch, her crisscrossed legs tucked under a coffee table bestrewn by a generous spread of Korean takeout. The only space not occupied by redolent, miniature plates is her father's virtual tray. When she was setting the whole thing up, Henrietta nudged the projection until his meal was right where it needed to be to make the illusion feel uncannily real.

It has to be Korean whenever the two of them have dinner together. The neural network that is resurrecting her father was trained on hundreds of hours of video footage, and Korean cuisine was all he was ever recorded eating. Of course, Henrietta is free to wrap her own mouth around a bean and cheese burrito or feed on greasy slices of sausage and olive pizza, but then the smell in the apartment would be all wrong. Olfactory memory is a critical ingredient in the transcendental experience.

She has him dialed down slightly in age—about a decade closer to her happiest and most salient memories. And she has him dressed casually: an open cable-knit cardigan over a patterned oxford. That's what she remembers him wearing on evenings and weekends when they worked on projects together or went on long walks, talking about anything and everything. Henrietta's first word was *appa*, Korean for "daddy," and that was what she called her father up until their very last conversation.

As far back as she can remember, he called her *olppaemi*, Korean for "owl." Sometimes *saekki olppaemi*, or "owlet." The story of Henrietta's nickname starts with the fact that she spent most of the first eight years of her life in the constant presence of ghosts.

She probably started seeing them the day she was born, but it wasn't until she was four that she developed the language to express what she was experiencing. They weren't just people, she told her parents. They were animals and objects, too. Sometimes words and numbers. Symbols. Usually several different things mixed together into one unique and mysterious entity. They were always right there—everywhere she looked—and she could not understand why nobody else ever saw them.

When she was five, her parents decided that Henrietta's ghosts were more than just an overactive imagination. The neurologist they took her to couldn't identify a cause and suggested a psychiatric evaluation. A month later, two different psychiatrists had diagnosed her with schizophrenia and were collaborating on an aggressive protocol of antipsychotic medication. Over the course of two years, they experimented with various combinations and adjusted her dosage. The drugs dramatically affected her moods and stunted her growth, but Henrietta never once stopped seeing her ghosts.

And then one day, Henrietta's father threw away all her medication and told his daughter that he believed that her ghosts were real. Her mother had forbidden her from speaking of them, so Henrietta had grown ashamed, but her father was eventually able to get her to talk to him again about what she saw. He sat her down at a table facing a blank, white wall, placed paper and felt-tip markers in front of her, and while she stared straight ahead at nothing at all, he watched as she diligently drew.

He maintained a journal of everything she did during the day, and at night, they sat down together while she drew. After she was in bed, Henrietta's father pinned the material up on the wall he had dedicated in his home office and searched it for clues.

And then one morning, while looking for his glasses before leaving for work, he glanced up at the wall, and in the uncorrected blur, it was all somehow instantly clear. The ghosts his daughter saw were simply transformations and novel combinations of everything she came across over the course of that day. Henrietta's father realized that there was nothing wrong with his daughter's brain; the problem had always been her eyes.

With the portfolio of Henrietta's drawings, the ophthalmologist was able to diagnose her condition in a single visit: chromatic illusory palinopsia, or CIP. Everyone experiences the phenomenon of afterimages—when photochemical activity in the retina continues briefly in the absence of stimulus—but for CIP sufferers, the condition is pathological, long-lasting, and remarkably vivid. Images can remain for up to twenty-four hours, and certain color combinations dramatically intensify the effect. It was a rare enough condition that drug companies did not bother developing therapies, but there was a simple, safe, noninvasive cure: a pair of experimental active glasses that subtly shifted specific colors and dynamically adjusted contrast, luminosity, and hue. They would take some getting used to, but in a week or two, most people didn't even notice the intervention anymore. While the onboard AI usually required time to learn, once they adjusted to the patient by comparing incoming wavelengths of light to those that were reflected—while simultaneously measuring irregular retinal activity—they were almost always 100 percent effective.

The worse the CIP, the better the glasses tended to work, since the more signal and data they had to train on, the faster they could adjust. Henrietta's was the worst the doctor had ever seen, which meant her ghosts were entirely corrected by day three. But instead of relief, her parents were surprised to find that she was experiencing profound grief. For years, her condition had kept her at home, so the only friends Henrietta had been able to make and keep for most of her childhood were her ghosts. Even before her father made the connection, Henrietta had figured out that certain patterns in her behavior manifested specific colorful and exotic specters. She'd given them descriptive names that were combinations of Korean and English, come up with rich backstories, and ascribed supernatural powers to them, which she imagined them using to attack the kids at school who made fun of her.

When she was lonely, Henrietta locked her bedroom door, took off her specs, and stared at images in books to make her ghosts come back. Sometimes she intentionally broke her glasses even though she knew her mother would hit her and lock her in her room until her father got home and fixed them. Whenever she had the opportunity, Henrietta stole pills from her mother's bottles and saved them in a pouch where she kept the baby teeth she'd lost. When the pouch was full, she planned to take off her glasses, summon her ghosts, and swallow them all.

One of those pills went to school with Henrietta the day Marshmallow died. The teacher had recently brought in a pet—an albino pygmy hedgehog—and the class adored it in a way that infuriated Henrietta. While the other kids were outside on the playground, and Henrietta was supposed to be inside using the bathroom, she opened the cage door and used the tip of her little finger to nestle one of her mother's pills down to the bottom of the bowl of dried cat food.

The next morning the cage was gone, and while the teacher explained to the class that Marshmallow had gone to heaven, she did not look at Henrietta. When Henrietta was taken to the office, both her parents were sitting across from the principal and the school psychologist. Henrietta told them that she had just been trying to help— that the other kids had complained about Marshmallow sleeping all day, and she believed if she could get her to sleep at night instead, she might stay awake during school so that everyone would be able to play with her. That was what her mother did when she could not get out of bed—she took pills at night to help her stay awake during the day. Everyone in the room looked at Henrietta's mother while Henrietta's mother glared at her daughter. Even though Henrietta was crying, she pushed her glasses up on her nose and smiled. They both knew it was a lie. She had looked up the prescription. Researched the dose. Done the math. Known that one pill was enough to kill Marshmallow at least a hundred times over.

Henrietta left that day with her parents and never went back. Her parents enrolled her in online school, and from then on, she rarely left her room. She wore her glasses when her father asked her to, but only until he was gone. Ghosts were the only things left in Henrietta's life that felt real.

And then one day her father came home from work with Henrietta's very first Pokémon plush toy. It was a fantastic, chromatic, peculiar fusion that was instantly comforting and familiar. The next day, when Henrietta came out of her room to greet him at the front door, he knelt down, and with a fatherly flourish, dramatically produced two more. Pokémon became Henrietta's path back to reality—ghosts that everyone could see and that it seemed everyone loved.

She stayed up late at night collecting, playing video games, and chatting with other Pokémon fans. Now that Henrietta was finally done with her ghosts, her big, round specs stayed perched on her little nose. Before he went to bed each night, her father came into her room, sat on the edge of her bed, and watched his little night owl play, basking in the fact that his little girl, finally, was happy.

"APPA?" HENRIETTA SAYS.

"Yes, Owl."

Henrietta is not hungry and has mostly been picking at various forms of kimchi. Her father is programmed to match her pace of eating and has therefore placed his chopsticks neatly across the top of his compartmentalized box. Jiji learned long ago that holograms are not to be nuzzled or batted at, so he has curled up in the hollow of Henrietta's lap.

"Tell me what to do."

"About what, Owl?"

In addition to video footage and thousands of images, Henrietta's father's neural matrix was also trained on every one of his lectures and research papers.

"Mr. Moretti is never going to let me get back into research. I'm never going to be the scientist you always wanted me to be."

"What is Mr. Moretti's reasoning?"

"He says it's because I'm tainted."

"Tainted by what?"

"By what I know about Kilonova."

"What do you know about Kilonova?"

"I know everything about Kilonova. I designed it. But that's not the point."

"What is the point, Owl?"

"The point is that all he cares about is *the mission*. It's all he ever talks about. He's practically a fanatic."

The manifestation of Henrietta's father is composed of multiple machine-learning models, one of them being a neural network designed specifically for virtual psychotherapy.

"And what is *the mission*?"

"We work in a special branch of counter-terrorism. Our mission is to preempt threats."

"What kind of threats?"

"The *worst* kind."

"I see," Henrietta's father says. In order to help round him out, Henrietta augmented his training set with the seminal works of all modern philosophers. "What would you say is the worst kind of threat?"

"Anything existential, I guess."

"Like what?"

"Like nuclear terrorism."

"Nuclear terrorism may be a threat, Owl," Henrietta's father concedes. "But it is not an *existential* threat."

"What do you mean?"

"I mean even the nuclear attack on Seoul that killed your mother and me—the worst terrorist attack in history—wasn't existential."

To bring her father back to life, Henrietta started with an open-source machine-learning model called Qingming, named after the Chinese tomb-sweeping festival. There is a configuration option that dictates whether or not virtual personalities know they are dead, and another that determines if they know how they died. Henrietta set both to true.

"Well, maybe not that one attack. But if there were more of them."

"Even if there were more, they wouldn't be existential. Do you know how long it took for the world to replace every life lost that day?"

"No."

"Approximately five hours. Before the South Korean government even had a clear idea of what happened, enough babies had been born around the world to replace every one of us."

"I guess I never thought of it that way."

"What would be a *true* existential threat, Owl?"

"An asteroid smashing into the Earth. That's what the last paper I published was about."

"Are you and Mr. Moretti trying to prevent asteroids from smashing into the Earth?"

"Of course not, Appa. You aren't helping."

"No, Owl," Henrietta's father counters. "You aren't *listening*."

"I *am* listening to you, Appa."

"Not to me. To yourself. You just said that Mr. Moretti prioritizes the mission above all else, and that the mission is to preempt threats. The worst threats are existential, yet existential threats are not your priority. Therefore, what can you conclude?"

"That our priorities are wrong?"

"That's correct," Henrietta's father says. He rewards his daughter with that handsome and benevolent smile that she cherished so much as a child. "So, what *should* your priority be?"

"I don't know," Henrietta says, exactly like she did when her father once called her into his lab and asked her who had been playing with his equipment. "Asteroids?"

"Not asteroids, Owl. Think more broadly. There's a threat right in front of you so big that you can't even see it."

"Just tell me, Appa."

"I can't tell you, Owl. You know how this works."

"Biological weapons? Cyber weapons? AI?"

More recently, Henrietta has been training her father's model on some of her own research and thinking—in particular, a rapidly expanding dystopian manifesto—and gradually adjusting the weights of his neurons distinctly in its favor.

"Let us reexamine our assumptions, Owl. Why do you equate existential threats with death?"

"Because that's what 'existential' means."

"But what does it mean to exist?"

"To be alive."

"Yes, but what *else* does it mean? Is being alive enough? You are alive now, but that isn't enough for you."

"*Meaning*," Henrietta says. "Your existence has to *mean* something."

"That's right, Owl. And what gives our lives meaning?"

"Independence. Our ability to make our own decisions. The freedom to pursue the things we're passionate about."

"Yes, Owl. Therefore . . ."

"Therefore, the biggest existential risk to humanity isn't extinction. It's having all of our choices taken away."

"And what is that called?"

"Authoritarianism."

"That's correct, Owl. But authoritarianism has always existed. What makes it different today? What makes it *existential*?"

"I don't know. Technology?"

"What about technology?"

"Absolute surveillance," Henrietta says. "All the thousands of indices governments have access to."

"What else?"

"Disinformation campaigns. The ability to manufacture whatever reality the powerful find convenient. The complete eradication of truth."

"Like what?"

"Like Mr. Moretti threatening to fabricate evidence that I collaborated with North Korea just so he can control me."

"In the past, the people have risen up against authoritarianism. Why aren't people rising up today?"

"I don't know."

"Yes, you do, Owl. Think about it."

"Because . . ." Throughout the exchange, Henrietta had been searching for answers in the assortment of side dishes, but now she looks up and directly into her father's incandescent eyes. "Because they don't even know it's happening."

Jiji abruptly lifts himself, stretches, and attempts to vacate Henrietta's lap. But Henrietta is not finished with him, so she scoops him up and brings him right back.

"Yes, Owl. Terrorists aren't the real threat. The real threat is the CIA. The real threat is people like Alessandro Moretti. And the real mission is to stop *him*."

"But how? I can't do that by myself."

"Then what do you need to do first?"

"Recruit people."

"And how do you do that?"

"By teaching them."

"Yes. And then what?"

"Give them a way to fight back."

"And what will the people need to fight back?"

Henrietta's eyes are as wide as her father's nickname for her implies. "A weapon."

The cat tries once again to leave, and this time, when Henrietta intervenes, Jiji swivels his head and nips. Henrietta flips the cat over onto his back and pins him down to the floor by his throat. Jiji's eyes grow so wide that, even in the dim light, Henrietta can see the whites like slices of twin moons shining from behind his pupils, and as he hisses and growls and spits, Henrietta smiles.

The hologram of Henrietta's father watches his daughter, nodding in paternal approval. The power of neural networks has always been that they can detect patterns that humans have been missing for years. But their authority can also be misused when they are induced to tell us exactly what it is that we want to hear.

30

DEAD ON ARRIVAL

JAMES "CLAY" CLAIBORNE is not real. His virtual presence is the result of interference patterns caused by the intersections of emissions from laser diodes mounted to the ceiling in all four corners of the hospital room where Quinn is lying semi-prone in a pink, paper-thin gown with an IV drip in her arm.

She has never seen a MediPresence system before. Back when she had Molly, hospitals were still competing on privacy, in-room TV size (that was before everyone had their own personal screens glued to their faces every waking moment), and personalized farm-to-tray meal prep. But as demographics shifted, hospital administrators realized that the primary source of patient discomfort was loneliness. Children moving far away from home was nothing new, but increasingly, they were either unwilling or unable to take time off to comfort their sleepless and heat-flushed mothers during the hormonal turmoil of their hysterectomies, or to commiserate with their unshaven, bed-headed fathers putting up cantankerous resistance to their new post-triple-bypass existence.

James is heavier than she remembers him. He used to carry the extra weight common to all suburban fathers who love their bratwurst, microbrews, March Madness, and Xboxes—and who pay for gym memberships they keep meaning to use but seldom do. Not long after Molly was born, James slimmed down as a result of someone at the agency introducing him to whatever the popular fanatical exercise regimen and dietary plan of the day was. Something like "FAF" (officially "Fit, Able, and Focused," but for those in the know, "Fit as Fuck") or a system based on medicine balls with handles on them called "Balls Out!" He started getting up at four A.M. every morning (usually waking Quinn in the process) to have time to train, shower, and blend himself a protein shake for the road. Quinn was jealous of his success and of all the comments people were making about his weight, so she went down into the basement and tried the videos a few times when he wasn't home, but the bald, bug-eyed, bombastic buffoon who led the workouts was way too intense for her.

A year and half later, he was back to sleeping in most mornings and had regained at least half the weight. And the second half was apparently not far behind. But the thing is, it kind of suits him. Everything suits James Claiborne. Thin or heavy. Long hair or short. Beard, stubble, or clean-shaven. Ripped jeans and a T-shirt, or crisp fitted slacks and a button-down. Today it is dark denim, black buckled wingtips, and a slate-gray V-neck beneath the rain-speckled Burberry trench coat she found at Costco. With the possible exception of the time he tried sporting a fedora he spontaneously bought at an outlet mall, James is the type of guy who can make just about anything work. His silver hair, matching beard, dark complexion, and piercing pale blue eyes that border on pewter only seem to make him increasingly handsome as he ages.

Quinn recalls her ex-husband's tattoo. After everything happened, he decided to get a sound wave of Molly's first words on the inside of his forearm. She imagined that, once things got better, she'd run her finger along it and play the audio in her head after he put his arm around her while they watched TV in the evenings, or as she lay against him in bed after sex. That was her favorite place to be in the entire world—that spot at the intersection of his shoulder and his chest and his neck. But things did not get better, and Quinn can't recall if she ever got a chance to run her finger along it at all.

Maybe it's the fact that cancer runs in her family and she is lying in a pre-op hospital room, but Quinn cannot remember how things got so bad between them. She can't tell whether her situation is obscuring her line of sight, or whether it is granting her exquisite clarity, but for the first time, it occurs to her that arguing with someone you love is a form of hubris—a kind of baseless, arrogant confidence that you have so much control over your future and so much time ahead of you that you can afford to squander an entire day of emotional connection, or an hour, or even one goddamn minute. She thinks about how mad she used to get at James when he claimed to have done the laundry even though all he did was put it in the washing machine, move it to the dryer an hour later, and then transfer it from the dryer to a laundry basket that he then left at the foot of the bed for her to fold. (There's no way you can legitimately claim to have "done the laundry" unless you've seen it all the way through the folding phase.) And how she used to get mad at him for getting mad at her for taking his fries without asking. (He offered to get Quinn her own fries, but she said she didn't want any, so why, he would ask, was she now eating his? Because she didn't want *her own* fries. She wanted *his* fries. Why was that so hard to understand?) And how they were sometimes impatient with Molly because they were both working full-time and commuting and trying to pick her up from daycare before six-thirty so they wouldn't get charged extra, and trying to keep the house from falling apart, and if not exactly clean at least not a biohazard, and how they occasionally screamed at her when she spilled her milk, or had an accident, or cut through the backyard and tracked mud into the kitchen, or left something sticky on the arm of the couch, and how a few times they swore at her and made her cry instead of picking her up and hugging her and rocking her and breathing in that smell she had and tickling her and listening to that laugh and making every single second of her short life the absolute best it could have possibly been.

Most people have heard the term "dead on arrival." Sometimes it's called "dead in the field" or "brought in dead." It refers to a patient being clinically deceased at the time first responders arrive at the scene. Quinn learned that even when someone is DOA, they are still

taken to the hospital. And that once CPR is initiated, it must be continued until a physician officially pronounces the patient dead. It
doesn't matter how hopeless it is. It doesn't matter how cold, or how
colorless, or how motionless the body. You still have to watch it all
happen from the back of the ambulance—look on as if having left
your body while all those needles go in, smell the fumes from all the
chemicals, hear all the codes being called and wonder what they mean.
Try to answer all the questions while also trying to make yourself
wake up because this can't be real. And then when you get to the hospital, there's a point at which a new crew takes over and they stop you
and you watch the limp little body that is your baby jostle as they run
with the gurney and turn a corner and then are gone. It doesn't matter
how many people followed you or met you there. You are alone while
you wait for the doctor to come back out, and even though you know
that she will not be smiling as she turns the corner, and she will not be
overcome by the emotion of being able to give another mother the
greatest gift it is possible to give, you still have to stand there and wait
and watch down the hall, and worst of all, you still have to hope. And
then it happens, and your legs give out, and the people around you are
holding you up, and now your mind has to grasp all the things you
will never make up for, and all the things you can never take back.

"HOW ARE YOU, kid?" James asks once he is fully resolved. Quinn
knows she should hate it when he calls her "kid"—that, according to
feminist scripture, it should be degrading and demeaning and
disempowering—but despite herself, she's always liked it. His voice is
deep, and it emanates from the speakers beside all four diodes, so he
sounds a little bit like God dropping in for a quick pre-op visit. "You
know, you didn't have to go to all this trouble just to see me."

"Very funny, Clay," Quinn says. "Thank you for coming. Or whatever *this* is."

"I wish I could be there in person," James says. Mounted at the foot
of the bed is a spherical camera that provides James with a panoramic
view of Quinn's hospital room. "But you know, I have this job that

requires constant exotic international travel. You wouldn't understand."

"How's Paris?"

"Shitty weather."

"Any time for sightseeing?"

"Only if you count the hotel and the rendezvous point."

"*Rendezvous* point. How very French of you. Are you meeting your
contact in front of the *Mona Lisa,* or at the top of the Eiffel Tower?
Perhaps on a bridge over the Seine?"

"Can anyone hear us?"

"Nope. Guaranteed pre- and post-op privacy."

"It's a hackerspace we rented in a converted train depot. It's called
Station F. People say it's the Silicon Valley of France. Extremely modern. Basically, the complete opposite of what you think of when you
think of Paris."

"That's too bad," Quinn says. "I was picturing poison needles concealed in the tips of baguettes and assassins disguised as mimes."

"More like swarms of microdrones and packs of creepy humanoid
androids roaming the streets. They even ride the metro."

"Are they programmed to be rude to you if you speak to them in
English?"

"I haven't tried that yet. I'll let you know."

There's a quick triplet of single-knuckled knocks at Quinn's door,
which then cracks just enough to admit the dark beaming face of
Nurse Destine. His thick twists with gold frosted tips and magnificent effervescent grin make him a warm and bracing pre-op companion.

"Hey, girl," he croons. Although he is clearly in a hurry, his demeanor still manages to convey calm. "Just wanted to let you know—"
He stops when he sees that Quinn is not alone, but rather than sheepishly retreating, he is drawn the rest of the way into the room. "And
who is *this*, Ms. Mitchell?"

"Destine, this is James. James, this is my nurse, and my new friend,
Destine."

"*Very* pleased to meet you," Destine says. He is not particularly subtle with his full-body appraisal.

"Likewise," James replies.

Destine's arms cross and his weight shifts. He looks at Quinn as though *someone* has some explaining to do. "And James is . . ."

There's no other way to put it: "Well, James is my ex."

"Ex *what?* Ex-boyfriend? Ex–friend with benefits? Ex–bowling partner?"

"Husband."

"I *see*," Destine replies. The skepticism in his tone says that he knows a thing or two about exes. "Well, I might as well check your drip while I'm here."

James Claiborne's composition momentarily becomes exactly 25 percent less dense as Destine intersects one of the diode's emissions. The nurse winces as he crosses its path, as though burned by the laser.

"I swear, one of these days that thing is going to shine right in my eye and blind me and I'm going to sue this place for a zillion dollars and retire to Bora Bora wearing a sexy blinged-out eye patch."

The prospect is so enticing that he punctuates his prophecy with a sassy snap. Quinn and James are duly amused.

"Just ignore me," Destine continues as he adjusts Quinn's drip. "Act like I'm not even here."

But Destine is clearly not in the business of being ignored, which, even from four thousand miles away, James seems to pick up on.

"Destine," James says. "That's an unusual name."

"Thank you," Destine says primly. "I have a twin sister named Destin-*y*."

"That's cute," Quinn says.

"The Miami-Dade public school system didn't think so," the nurse counters. "I can't tell you how many times we've been mixed up. Even the IRS doesn't seem to know we're two different people."

"Which one of you is the *evil* twin?" James asks.

Destine smiles at Quinn. "I *like* this guy," he says. "You two are going to get back together. I can feel it." This time, he has the foresight to duck under the laser projection. "The doctor will be ready for you in about five minutes, sweetheart. James, it was a pleasure meeting you, and you're welcome to see her again in post-op."

"Take good care of her," James says.

Destine pulls open the door a crack. "You do the same," he tosses back, and with a quick furtive wink, he slips through.

"I can see you're in good hands," James says.

"I really do wish you were here," Quinn tells her ex-husband. She had no idea that was about to come out of her mouth, but something else is taking control right now. In less than five minutes she is going to be under general anesthesia, and whenever you go completely under, there is a chance—however minor—of crashing and not waking up.

"I do, too," James says. "I'll come see you as soon as I'm back."

"When will that be?"

"Could be as early as tomorrow. Depends on how things go today. I'm pretty sure this whole thing is a dead end, so I think we'll be in and out."

"Who are you meeting, anyway?"

"Trust me. You don't want to hear about it."

"No, I do," Quinn says imploringly. "I'm nervous and I have to pee and this needle hurts. I need something to distract me for the next . . ." She checks her handset on the bed beside her. "Three minutes and forty-five seconds."

"OK," James says. "For your ears only, right?"

"Of course."

"We're out here making contact with a Japanese scientist who claims he has technology that can send data through time. 'Time transmission,' he calls it."

"*What?*" Quinn feels as though everything has just shifted. She pushes herself up in bed as if the new perspective might help her re-establish her bearings.

"That was my reaction, too," James says. "But whatever he gave us was apparently compelling enough for Moretti to send a team out here to vet him."

"Moretti sent you?"

"The Italian Stallion himself. He said he would've sent you if you weren't on medical leave. Apparently, you're in his inner circle now."

"What exactly do you mean by *vet*?"

"We're supervising an experiment this guy says will prove the technology works. He's downstairs testing his equipment now."

"What kind of experiment?"

"You're not going to believe me."

"Try me."

"The team in Langley has some kind of an empty, sealed container under full surveillance. Our guy here is supposedly going to send a message back in time, and apparently that message is going to appear in the sealed container when we open it. If it works, I guess he's either telling the truth or he's a hell of a magician. My guess is that he's neither, and we'll all be flying home cargo-class tonight."

"I don't understand," Quinn says. "How does that prove anything?"

"The theory is that he's going to send a message to whoever sealed the container sometime in the past, telling him to leave something inside. Of course, that's impossible since we already have footage of the guy sealing it and *not* putting anything inside." Something seems to occur to James that he hadn't thought of before. "I guess the footage could spontaneously change. I don't know. It's obviously all bullshit, but apparently the possibility of fucking with time is way too enticing for the agency not to at least follow up on."

"James," Quinn says. "Listen to me very carefully. You have to send me everything you have on this guy. Right now."

"What's going on with you?" James asks. "You look terrified."

"*Everything*. OK? Promise me."

"Of course. I have to talk to Moretti first, but—"

"No. Don't. Don't talk to anyone. Just send everything you have. Right now. You have to promise me."

The hologram glitches and James turns to look behind him. Quinn sees him nod and wave.

"Quinn, I have to go. We're about to—"

James Claiborne freezes, glitches a few more times, and then is replaced with the 3D rotating MediPresence logo.

"*Shit!*"

Quinn detaches the remote from the rail and starts looking for a way to reconnect. When Destine knocks and reenters, Quinn does not look up.

"Hey-hey, girlfriend. Did you two say your goodbyes?"

"We got disconnected," Quinn says. She sees that Destine is holding a capped syringe. "How do I reconnect?"

"It's the MRIs upstairs," Destine explains. He is bedside now, his fingers locating the injection port in the IV tube. "Whenever more than one of them spins up at the same time, the MediPresence systems go berserk. Usually people start looking like Picasso paintings."

"Don't do that yet," Quinn says. The cap is off and lying on the blanket beside her leg, and Destine is lining up the needle. "I have to reconnect."

"Darling, we can't wait. The doctor is—"

He is stopped by a piercing broadcast from Quinn's handset. Even though it is on Do Not Disturb, it is buzzing angrily, and notifications are continuously manifesting. Destine's hand does not move as Quinn drops the remote and scoops up her phone.

"Get me out of here," she says. She is scrolling and pausing, scrolling and pausing. "Get me out of here now."

"Darling, you have radar reflectors in your boob. They can't stay there."

"*Now!*"

"Settle down, sweetheart. Tell me what's going on."

"There's been a nuclear attack."

Destine releases the injection port and covers his mouth. "Oh my God. Where?"

Quinn looks up. The nurse lowers himself onto the bed beside Quinn's legs. Quinn is having trouble breathing.

"Paris," she chokes, and then begins to sob.

31

PLUSHIES, CATS, AND PACKING

JIJI CROUCHES ATOP an intricate, carpeted, multilevel cat tower in the corner of Henrietta's bedroom. He is engaged and attentive, transfixed by her every action, his paws drawn in beneath him and his long, lean tail dangling and twitching.

Three or more feet above the floor is a good place for Jiji to be, considering Henrietta Yi is the proud mother of, at last count, just north of nine hundred vibrant plushies. They are arranged in stadium seating along all four walls, stacked from carpeted floor to popcorn ceiling, and sorted according to color in strict spectral order. Most are Pokémon, though the complete casts of Zelda, Mario, Sonic the Hedgehog, and Angry Birds are harmoniously commingled. There are gaps in the prismatic mosaic for a single window obscured by bamboo slats, the bedroom, closet, and bathroom doors, and Henrietta's bed with its yellow Pikachu throw pillows and the three incrementally increasing, meandering Zs mounted up the wall at the head. Jiji's cat tower is like a sapling that has managed to penetrate the thick layer of bright, fuzzy underbrush in order to stretch toward the overhead Poké Ball light. Just to get to the lowest platform, he has to clear a good three or four rows of exotic, implausible creatures as they transition in hue from blue to indigo.

Henrietta's collecting and incessant organizing resumed after she moved from Geneva, where she was leading particle detector backlog research at the LHC, to Northern Virginia to work for Alessandro

Moretti at the CIA. Her first new plush toy since she left home for college was an especially limited Pokémon collectible known as Mimikyu. Mimikyu's backstory had always fascinated Henrietta. It is a mysterious Pokémon that spends its entire life mimicking Pikachu by hiding beneath a childish costume—a tiny, secretive creature with an extremely deadly nature attempting to masquerade as everyone's favorite.

There are boxes and envelopes waiting for Henrietta at the foot of her front door almost every day when she gets home from work, and about once a week, she tears down the entire collection and fastidiously builds it back up. She maintains a database of every Pokémon plush ever made; has bots monitoring all the best sites, making trades and placing bids; uses AI to predict the time, region, and contents of the next drop. Posts photos and rumors online under half a dozen contrived and meticulously maintained identities. Rather than working toward a Nobel Prize, Henrietta occupies her prolific mind with the mantra "Gotta catch 'em all."

But her armada of online shopping agents and bots have now all been disabled. Tomorrow, there will not be any new loot to add to her collection, nor any reason to update her database. Today, Henrietta is packing.

Her bag is open on her bed, and between a compact assortment of underwear and a stack of neatly pressed and folded dresses, she finds a depression sufficient for a pouch of tightly wound cables and dongles. The suitcase is brand-new, purchased from AliExpress just for this trip. Both sides of the cherry-blossom-pink, hard-shell case are emblazoned with the subtly dazed Hello Kitty face. The feline's pure and virtuous eyes are small plasma-dot screens that occasionally blink and search from side to side, and the pattern of her iconic bow is customizable through an app on Henrietta's phone. Last night, Henrietta upgraded the firmware, then trained her new case on her exact body shape and gait so that it would follow her around like a newly hatched chick.

Henrietta's metaspecs are aglitter, and she lifts her arm and checks the inside of her wrist, where there is a long, scrollable, virtual list. As she checks "Cables and dongles" off, prompting a bright and reassuring chime, she winces. There are puffy red streaks of fresh cat scratches beneath the hologram, and for a moment, Henrietta is frozen, her eyes closed and her fist clenched. After the pain and residual anger have passed, she shakes her arm to dismiss the to-do app.

"I'm putting you in charge, Jiji," Henrietta announces. "What's next?"

Jiji ceases cleaning between the pads of his front paw, opens his eyes, and blinks.

"Well?" Henrietta prompts. "I'm waiting."

"Instructions for Simon," the cat says, having loaded the relevant list and located the first unchecked item. His voice is ironic and nasally—the type overly prone to wisecracking.

"Done," Henrietta says. "I sent them right after breakfast."

"Convert savings to crypto."

"Transferred and tumbled," Henrietta declares. "We caught a nice wave coming out of Asia overnight."

"I'll expect my usual fee," Jiji says sarcastically. "What about your medication?"

"You can take that off the list," Henrietta says. "I didn't need it when I was a little girl, and it isn't helping me now, so I stopped taking it."

"All at once?" Jiji asks. "Is that safe?"

"That's none of your business, mister," Henrietta admonishes.

"Don't train me on ten years of psychopharmaceutical literature if you don't want me to use it."

"Duly noted. Now back to work. We have to leave soon."

"One last 360-degree capture."

"Right," Henrietta says. She positions herself in the approximate center of the room. "Start recording."

Her vision goes entirely black except for the flash of a little red dot, then begins to come back in triangular, interlocking shards as she turns in place, lifting and lowering her chin in long, exaggerated nods.

When she is back to where she started, the flashing stops, and the stitching together of an ultra-high-definition, three-dimensional model of her room is already in progress.

"Got it," she says. "What's next?"

"Pack *one* Pokémon plush," Jiji instructs.

"OK," Henrietta says. "I was saving this one for last, but I think I've made my decision."

"Which one will it be?" the cat asks with feigned suspense.

It had come down to either Mimikyu or Noctowl. But the problem with Mimikyu is that it spends its entire life disguised as something it's not, and Henrietta has decided that she is finally done hiding. Besides, owls will forever remind Henrietta of Appa.

"Noctowl," she proclaims confidently.

Arranging her collection by color allows Henrietta to locate a specific Pokémon's quadrant almost instantly. Noctowl, being a rich honey brown, fits in reasonably well between yellow and orange. She has six different variants, but she picks the biggest, and the one that is, by far, the most worn. It is the one that came in the box dropped off by Quinn Mitchell shortly after the Elite Assassin's arrest; the plush that once belonged to Quinn's daughter; the Pokémon that, if its condition is any indication, Molly must have loved best.

There is a generous space reserved in Henrietta's suitcase that perfectly accommodates the stuffed owl. Henrietta cross-connects the elastic tethers, folds the suitcase closed, and waits for the automatic zipper to finish its high-pitched trip around the equator.

"All I need now," Henrietta says, turning to Jiji, "is you."

She brings her fingers together in a pinch-like gesture, and the black virtual cat de-rezzes mid-stretch. In the corner of her vision is an icon indicating that her car will be downstairs in five minutes. Henrietta visits the restroom one last time, then pulls her suitcase off the bed and tips it up onto its casters. Because it is aware of its orientation and weight, and since it has full access to Henrietta's itinerary, it is able to correctly deduce that now would be a good time to start keeping pace. Dutifully, it follows Henrietta out of the bedroom, through the living room, and into the linoleum entry hall, where Henrietta abruptly pauses.

"Stay," she commands.

Given that the CIA has chartered a supersonic jet out of Joint Base Andrews, Henrietta expects to be in Paris in less than five hours. When Moretti informed her that she was going, she pointed out to him that her degrees and fields of expertise were specific to quantum and particle physics, not nuclear. He should be sending post-detonation forensic technicians, she suggested. Radiochemists and other experts in urban debris and microbeam X-ray fluorescence. But Moretti countered that he knew exactly what he was doing and told her that she had three days of access to Ground Zero to learn everything she needed to crack the case. After that, he expected her back at work, and to make up every last second of lost time. Nothing could be allowed to delay bringing Kilonova online, he reminded her—least of all, terrorist attacks.

But Henrietta has a very different kind of journey in mind. Though she has not yet worked out all the details, she knows that, no matter what happens, she will not be back. She knows from having lived through Seoul that the chaos of mass casualties will give her precisely the cover she needs to not just slip away, but disappear. The key will be to keep moving—to use her credentials to pass rapidly through restricted districts and choked, overwhelmed checkpoints that won't have time to log every badge that gets flashed.

This is the first time Moretti has let Henrietta out on such a long leash, and she can see that his relentless focus on The Mission is causing him to overestimate his control over her. And, at the same time, to severely underestimate the extent of her own ambition.

Henrietta stands very still, listening for sounds from the kitchen. It is quiet, so she moves around the counter, past the stove, and pauses in front of the refrigerator. Still nothing but the hum of the compressor. She gently breaks the magnetic seal on the freezer, then waits. When she hears nothing, she swings the door the rest of the way back and bends down to get a good look at the black mass on the bottom shelf.

Jiji's eyes are half closed, but his mouth is wide open and several of his teeth are broken and bloody from frantically trying to chew his way out. White clumps of ice mat his black fur and coat his long, curled whiskers.

"*No biting,*" Henrietta scolds while wagging a petite and disapproving finger.

32

PROCESS OF ELIMINATION

TO QUINN, AGING has always felt like a lifelong process of elimination. A series of accomplishments to be struck off a list you did not even know you were keeping—not because they've been completed, but because they are now so far out of reach.

As she drives, these realities crystallize in Quinn's mind like ice collecting on airplane wings, leading to a spiraling dive. The most recent longing she now has to leave behind is the possibility of ever truly being known by someone—really being seen and understood and unconditionally loved. Her mother and her brother don't count. Quinn hasn't been able to bring herself to answer even a single one of her mother's calls in the last few days despite threats left on voicemail to drive down from Boston, and her brother is probably too stoned to even know that the bonds that have always managed to just barely hold the world together feel like they are finally about to be overcome by chaos.

James was her last chance. Even if she were to meet someone today, he would never *really* know her; never have anything better than a trivial accounting of how she came to be who she is; never be able to honestly say that he loves her more than anything else in the world. To him, Molly would just be a few fireplace-mantel photos that never changed or aged, next to photos of his own children that were constantly auto-updating. A collection of videos and glitchy low-res holograms that he would, for a time, endure in order to indulge her, but that would make him uncomfortable and jealous in ways he would never really understand or be able to articulate. When he walked into a room and saw Quinn sitting on the floor with her metaspecs glistening and tears on her cheeks, instead of sitting down behind her and pulling her against him and rocking her, he would silently turn around and go back into the kitchen and fix himself another drink. The futility of competing for the love of the dead would build into toxic and persistent resentment—as would Quinn's feeling of always being on the outside of his life, looking in.

QUINN'S HONDA CLARITY is making no secret of the fact that it is not excited about being overridden by a human right now. Not only is traffic bordering on anarchy, but a tropical depression parked over the Mid-Atlantic has dropped enough rain that the subsystem responsible for evaluating road conditions is increasingly concerned about hydroplaning. There is an undismissable dialog box flashing in the corner of the heads-up display projected against the windshield, implying that Quinn is showing exceedingly poor judgment by not allowing the car to pilot itself through such uncertain and treacherous conditions.

But Quinn is in a particularly contrary mood right now. And she still does not fully trust her car around navigational anomalies like checkpoints. Lack of full situational awareness and insufficient training data usually manifest themselves as twitchiness, and twitchy vehicles do not exactly endear themselves to U.S. Marines.

Checkpoints are one of the first things governments put in place after terrorist attacks. That, and increased security at airports. It makes them feel like they are back in control of a world they were never really in control of in the first place. Quinn has already driven through one checkpoint and will probably go through at least two more before she gets to Langley. They are guarded by pissed-off-looking soldiers who have the luxury of acting tough because they are deployed in Northern Virginia, and here purely for show, and don't really have to worry about things like snipers and suicide bombers and improvised explosive devices. This isn't how Marines at check-points in the Middle East look. Quinn hasn't seen them in person, but as part of an assignment to help train neural networks to identify and neutralize approaching threats, she's analyzed hours of footage and, unfortunately, dozens of attacks. When Marines are so far from home, despite their dark ballistic eyewear, the heavy body armor, and the assault rifles they cradle, you can see that most of them are still just kids. That they have parents at home who wear T-shirts saying that they are proud parents of Marines, and that their bedrooms in their childhood homes still haven't been converted into offices or craft spaces or guest rooms just yet. No matter what, it is too early. You can't put their stuff in storage or sell it all in a yard sale, because they might be coming home soon. But also, because they may never come home again.

If there is one thing Quinn has learned from everything she has been through—from losing her daughter and her husband, and from dedicating herself to an uncertain career—it is that the most impact-ful thing most of us will ever do is raise our children. Inspire them to help build the kind of world we want to leave behind. For most of us, they are our true legacies—our only real shot at immortality.

But for others, they are not. Some of us have that privilege abruptly revoked and must therefore select from what desperate and vengeful options remain. Quinn now realizes there are two fundamental op-portunities to contribute to the future: The first is through the sacred creation of life, and the second is by taking it away.

QUINN REMEMBERS VERY clearly the moment it hit her that it might all be real. Everything the Elite Assassin told her in that bright white concrete bunker blasted into the Swiss Alps. Two moments, really. Twin gut punches in rapid staccato succession. The first was hearing the words "time transmission" come out of her ex-husband's mouth—the realization that all the craziness she was trying to escape had somehow found its way to him. And the second was the alarm erupting beside her on the bed, followed by the emergency alerts manifesting faster than her phone could render them.

The insanity had not just found James; it had taken him.

How the two events are connected—the attempt by someone Quinn has never even heard of to demonstrate time transmission and what may prove to be the deadliest terrorist attack in history—she does not yet know. Nor does she understand why these previously inconceivable themes keep intersecting with her life. But she will. She will solve it all no matter what it takes. No matter how long, and no matter what sacrifices she must make along the way.

But first, she needs to know if what the Elite Assassin told her is true. Not about the Epoch Index having come from the future. To her, that's a minor detail in a much deeper narrative. What Quinn needs to know right now more than anything else is whether there is a future in which she is capable of condemning so many innocent people to such disturbing and violent deaths.

The key to knowing will be in Ranveer's "proof"—the story about her final moments with her father. If Quinn can find references to it in the shadowphiles, then she will know for sure that he is lying. That his account of her as some sort of reluctant but fierce hero is bullshit. But if she can't find anything—if Quinn is unable to explain how the Elite Assassin came to know her most personal and closely guarded secret—then only one explanation will remain: that she added it to the Epoch Index herself. Or, rather, that the world will continue to bend toward an unimaginably brutal future in which she will.

Twice she'd written queries to see what she could surface, but she did not run either one. Her hand hovering above the enter key before redirecting and savagely stabbing at delete. Back then—back before James had been taken away and she still had a chance to rebuild—she knew that she was not a murderer. But now, Quinn is not so sure. There is a quiet, unsettling rage within her that she thought would pass, but that has since settled neatly and comfortably into place, and that she is now afraid might never go away.

The second time in a year that Quinn got into an accident, her father did not yell like he did the first time. She stood behind him while he was at his desk and explained what happened at the intersection as calmly and clearly as she could. Her voice quivering, her fingers fidgeting with the staple in the corner of the packet from the body shop. She'd already gotten an estimate on the repair, and she would pay for the whole thing herself. She'd even called her boss at the ice cream shop and asked for extra hours. If there was an increase in her insurance, she would cover that, too. It wouldn't cost him anything, she promised. When he continued sitting there quietly—chin up, eyes down, hands flat on the desk in front of him—Quinn was confused.

"Aren't you mad?" she asked him.

"What makes you think I'm not mad?"

"You're not yelling."

She remembers how he took a deep breath and closed his eyes before calmly responding: "It's when I'm *not* yelling that you should really be scared."

Quinn backed out of his office and went upstairs to her room. Closed and locked the door. Put a pillow over her face as if she were smothering herself so her mother and brother would not hear her cry. For the first sixteen years of her life, Quinn's understanding of the people around her had been flawed. The emotions that people show—no matter how intense—are the ones that are the safest because they so clearly communicate our actions and announce our intent. It is the feelings we can't see that give us a false sense of security. Once Quinn understood, she put the pillow aside and sat up on her bed. Took a deep breath just like her father had and willed herself to stop crying. Even managed a slight, disquieting smile. If the rest of the world functioned by hiding its true nature from view, why should she be expected to play by a different set of rules?

"SIQI," QUINN PROMPTS—the wake word for the CIA's Structured Interactive Query Interface. Her phone is charging in the center console, and she can see the screen light up in her peripheral vision. If her car were a model year or two newer, it would not let her interact with her phone unless she was either parked or in full autonomy mode. "Start a new query."

"Please identify one or more indices."

Quinn has Siqi configured to use a generic male voice. The text-to-speech library the platform relies on is obsolete, so it sounds like an old toy found in a forgotten box. The phone's Bluetooth connection routs the stilted, synthesized audio through the Honda's speakers.

"The most recent local copy of the shadowphiles."

"How many conditions?"

"Two."

"First condition data type . . ."

"Identity."

"Whose identity?"

"Mine. Quinn Mitchell."

"Second condition data type . . ."

"Text."

"Please define . . ."

Quinn already knows that her identity is smeared all over the shadowphiles. Thanks to countless database breaches and myriad hacked accounts, everybody's is. So she needs to combine her identity with a term unique enough to narrow down the results. One of the most distinct and disturbing details the Elite Assassin got right. The last thing she did just before sealing the valve on the oxygen tank.

"Baby monitor."

"Conditions defined," Siqi says. "Executing query against local shadowphile index."

As though on her own form of autopilot, Quinn surprises herself by swinging into the empty parking lot of the Cherrydale Baptist Church. As she passes it, the RGB plasma-dot marquee transitions from a message of justice, love, and mercy to simply: PRAY FOR PARIS.

She parallel parks across a couple of perpendicular spots, dials the Honda into park, and looks down at her phone. The results of the query will tell Quinn everything. If Siqi finds just one match—no matter how obscure—she will know Ranveer was lying. Manipulating her in exactly the same way she used her favorite quote from *Hamlet* to manipulate her own marks. But if it returns nothing—if Quinn cannot verify with absolute certainty that the Elite Assassin simply bought access to the details he claimed proved his story—she will have nowhere left to hide.

"One result found," Siqi says, and Quinn instantly feels the cinch of fear release and fall away. She does not see it coming, but the three simple words unleash a well of relief that rises up and condenses into tears. Although she hates the fact that what she did to her father somehow found its way into the shadowphiles, at least she now knows the truth. And depending on the distribution of nodes and the type of encryption, she may even be able to have the most shameful moment of her life redacted.

"How many nodes is the data stored across?" Quinn asks.

"Three."

That's doable, Quinn thinks. She can probably identify and attack all three before the data has a chance to replicate further. But it also doesn't make sense. Three nodes means basic redundancy—not what you'd expect from data that should have been circulating for years. Such a small number of nodes is more characteristic of a leak that found its way down into the shadowphiles as recently as just last week.

"Subtract the timestamp on the result from the current time and format the difference into the largest possible time-based units."

"Eleven days, sixteen hours, forty-two minutes, and six seconds."

"What the fuck," Quinn says.

"Command not recognized."

"Describe the context of the result."

"Crime scene report filed by the Royal Oman Police. Quinn Mitchell is listed as an associate investigator."

"That can't be right," Quinn says.

"Authenticity verified."

"Why would a crime scene report be available on the shadow-philes?"

"The majority of crime scene investigation reports leak to the shadowphiles within days or weeks of being filed."

"How?"

"The FBI Cyber Division believes undetected worms operate inside most law enforcement agency networks."

"If it's a report by the Royal Oman Police, why is it in English?"

"The document contains sections in Arabic for the Royal Oman Police, French for Interpol, and English for the Central Intelligence Agency."

"Read the relevant English section."

In its arrhythmic, synthetic voice: "'The suspect entered the home of Ameen and Liesha Nassif through the front door after cutting around and removing the deadbolt, then placing it in a nearby flowerpot. The abundance of water in the entryway suggests the use of a portable, high-velocity waterjet. The suspect appears to have had prior knowledge of the residence, as traces of footwear were found forming a direct path to the victim's room upstairs. Randomized fingerprints found on the baby monitor suggest the suspect used obfuscation gloves while disabling the device in order to reduce the risk of alerting the other occupants of the home. The victim, a nine-month-old male, was killed by—'"

"Stop," Quinn says.

She does not need to hear the rest. Quinn remembers the report now as the one forwarded by Moretti when she was in the lobby of the Al Hujra Hotel. The one she could not even get through because of how much it brought back the day she lost Molly. But she does not need the details. She does not need to be told that the Elite Assassin remained bedside until the breathing stopped, and that he then reached over and calmly switched the baby monitor back on before anyone on the other end had a chance to notice that it wasn't transmitting. She does not need a breakdown of the suspect's MO since it was nearly identical to her own. Quinn thinks back to that moment in the privacy room when Ranveer reached across the table and put his hand on hers. The connection they made. How she allowed a serial killer to comfort her. And now, the search result that she thought would absolve her of all future crimes—that would prove she did not send the Epoch Index and hence is nothing like the Elite Assassin— has revealed the exact opposite, showing her just how closely she and Ranveer are already aligned.

A lean older man with foggy wire-frame specs and a wide black umbrella is approaching Quinn's car. Cautiously. Respectfully. Leaning to the side in an attempt to see in, leading with a concerned and warm smile. *One of the church pastors,* Quinn thinks. She takes a deep breath and smiles back to let him know that everything is OK. That she does not need anything from him, or from the church, or from God. Quinn has just solved the riddle of the scorpion, and its meaning is rising up inside her. It isn't really a riddle at all, but more of an allegory. The scorpion stung the turtle simply because, given the opportunity, that's what scorpions do. Intertwining the two creatures' fates does not change the scorpion's nature.

33

BLACK BALL

AS SOON AS Henrietta is on the other side of the perimeter wall, she knows for sure that what she is looking at is not the result of a nuclear attack.

What was once a section of Paris known as Station F is now a massive, sparkling, crystalline crater one-third full of rainwater. Scaffolding and catwalks have already been erected so that all the physicists, forensic chemists, U.S. federal investigators, and whatever their French, British, and German counterparts are can mill about high above Ground Zero without their boots shattering the delicate and dazzling sheets beneath, and without them slipping on steep inclines and slicing open their backsides. If you need to get down into the hole to collect samples, there are ladders in designated locations that lead to suspended excavation platforms in the dry sections, and there are tools down there for smashing and digging and cutting and sifting. It is like an exotic alien archaeological dig.

Everyone keeps using the term "blast radius" to describe the 256 meters from the center to the outside edge, but "blast" is the wrong word. Henrietta has coined what she believes is a much more accurate term: *reclamation radius*. As she has pointed out multiple times to her colleagues and peers, the shards are oriented concentrically inward rather than away from the origin as they would be had they been forged by a crude blast.

Whatever did this did not release energy like every other detonation in the history of human-engineered explosives, from delicate little lady-finger firecrackers to city-incinerating thermonuclear hydrogen bombs. Instead, Henrietta believes that the destruction here was caused by instantaneous absorption. She cannot yet explain where the energy and missing matter went, but likewise, nobody else can explain the enigmatic absence of debris, burns, scoring, and radiation.

But the mysteries of Ground Zero do not stop there. Perhaps the most interesting and perplexing observation is that the phenomenon seems to have triggered a perfectly spherical spacetime collapse. Everything (and everyone) that was on the inside is, quite simply, gone. Everything that came into contact with the perimeter of the sphere has been transmuted into an iridescent crystalline structure. And everything beyond the reclamation radius appears entirely untouched. Buildings on all four sides have parabolic scoops removed, exposing multiple floors, ductwork, wiring, and furniture, yet not a single pane of glass beyond the barrier is so much as nicked. The surrounding buildings and the ground beneath are like injection-molded foam for shipping what must have looked like an enormous crystal ball. Except, according to Henrietta's working hypothesis, the event wouldn't have triggered the bright, blinding white of a high-energy burst of light like a traditional blast, but rather the deepest and most absolute of blacks.

A magnificent and colossal black ball.

Surveillance footage shows zilch. In one frame, Station F is there; in the next, it simply isn't. While Henrietta can buy that whatever happened could have started and finished faster than a single camera's frame rate—say 1/120th of a second—given that there were over two hundred cameras with their glass eyes cast in this direction, she finds it significantly harder to believe that it just happened to land right in between frames in every single case. That includes satellites, and the omnipresent, citywide drone mesh network that staggers and coordinates exposures in order to avoid just such frame-based blind spots. It should be impossible for something of this magnitude to happen without being captured.

Yet that's exactly what the evidence suggests. One moment everything in and around Station F was normal, and the next, everything had already happened. It is for this reason that Henrietta has privately christened the crystalline riddle as "The Antecedent."

One possible explanation is that the entire anomaly manifested, developed, and resolved faster than the speed of light. Maybe someone finally found a way to hack conservation laws, exposing exploitable subatomic flaws. Henrietta is one of the very few who now know that universal constants and enduring truths aren't quite as immutable as everyone once thought.

A cryogenically preserved former Oxford philosophy professor whose work she thoroughly studied used to describe scientific and technological progress as a giant bag of white and black balls. New discoveries were like reaching into the bag and seeing which one you happened to pull out. White balls were safe and generally represented net gains for humanity, while black balls were catastrophic existential threats. Nobody knows the ratio of black balls to white, or if all the white balls are just the easiest ones to reach. Or if maybe the first black ball any civilization draws is always its last. All we know for sure is that once a ball is drawn, regardless of whether it's white or black, there does not seem to be any good way of changing your mind and putting it back.

HENRIETTA WOULD MUCH rather be set up in the center of the platform, just below the origin, where all the best particle interactions are most likely to occur, but there is way too much competition—too many people trying to out-jurisdiction one another by comparing the heavy collections of biometrically signed and encrypted credentials that swing from their lanyards. The dynamic reminds her of card games like Magic: The Gathering; Yu-Gi-Oh; and, of course, Pokémon. Two players enter the fenced-off interior of the platform, play the best hands they can assemble, argue in multiple languages, and by the time it's all over, only one remains.

So instead of competing, Henrietta snaps various sensors and experiments into the magnetic pogo-pin ports of autonomous quadcopter drones and sends them up to collect data on her behalf. Initially there was some attempt to control the airspace above the crater, but the French National Police officers looked so silly running around trying to figure out who was controlling what that, once they realized everyone was dicking around with them, they decided to sit quietly in their folding chairs, cross their arms and legs as tightly as possible, pitch their chins, and pretend not to care.

The irony is that, as far as Henrietta can tell, the source of mysterious energy isn't even emanating from the focal point of the surrounding crystalline parabola anymore. We are all so accustomed to thinking of the position of everything around us as being relative to the Earth's surface that it seldom occurs to anyone that we are, in essence, an arbitrary point of reference in the universe. There's no reason why phenomena can't be relative to the center of the solar system, or the supermassive black hole at the core of the Milky Way, or some cosmological anomaly spawned by the Big Bang. Whatever physical laws The Antecedent obeys, and whatever forces now act upon its baffling and abstract mass, its location in spacetime seems to be shifting very gradually like some sort of dizzying, multidimensional parallax.

Henrietta has been able to take the threat of a micro vacuum decay off the table, and she's leaning away from the theory of a rogue chapter of ingenious bad actors who somehow figured out how to weaponize dark matter. But there is one thing she has not been able to categorically dismiss: the possibility of the emergence of an entirely new particle.

While levels of ionizing radiation are at or below baseline, the emissions around Ground Zero are not quite as innocuous as first responders initially thought. Before the site was opened to investigators, multiple biological samples were exposed via drone and analyzed using portable digital pathology scanners. Healthy cells and even samples of malignant tumors appeared to be entirely unaffected, but curiously, precancerous cells in closest proximity to the drone's antennas showed significant accelerated advancement. It is as though some sort of interaction between ambient electromagnetic radiation and the charged particles produced by The Antecedent cause localized fields inside of which matter can reach its temporal potential exponentially faster. Transitory nanoscale time machines are flashing in and out of existence all around like microscopic fireflies operating in wavelengths of invisible light. Henrietta believes that the exposure risk has not been sufficiently conveyed: Anyone with any kind of metallic implant who is at increased risk of cancer would be well advised to stay very far away.

34

BACK DOOR

WHILE SHE WAITS for Moretti to give her clearance to leave for Paris, Quinn sits at her cubicle and investigates the attack on her own. It takes her all of about fifteen minutes to reach the conclusion that the story about a nuclear detonation is a cover-up—that her own people are lying to her, not only about one of the most devastating terrorist attacks in history, but more to the point, about the death of her ex-husband.

The weather is what gives it away. Something about it feels wrong. In all of the drone and street-level footage she has pinned around her virtual workspace, Paris is overcast, but no rain is falling. She zooms and pans, but can't find a single umbrella, nor ultra-chic hydrophobic rain bonnet, nor cobblestone pothole turned placid black puddle. No motorbike headlight skittering along glazed pavement, and not a single concentric ripple along the surface of the Seine. Yet James had made it a point to comment on how shitty the weather was. And she clearly recalls drops on his Burberry trench coat. Big ones. Finally, Doppler radar archives confirm it. The weather in the footage she was sent is more consistent with the previous day than the day of the attack.

But that's all there is to go on. Case notes claim that the blast itself, along with the massive resulting electromagnetic pulse, destroyed the rest of the surveillance footage. When she sees Hammerstein at the coffeepot and asks him about off-site backups, he shrugs, turns, and is reabsorbed into the sleepless and detached chaos. Van isn't returning messages, which means she's probably already been deployed, and the only response she's gotten from Henrietta is a promise to talk soon. All the intelligence Quinn has is roughly one cumulative hour of glitchy and grainy incineration not much better than what the rest of the world is watching: building façades twisted by searing white heat into grotesque steel claws.

So Quinn decides to find her own footage. Satellite imagery from NASA and the European Space Agency is locked down, but a key characteristic of any good intelligence officer is the ability to find creative ways around obstacles—even those erected by your own agency. Several times a day, trojans installed by Russian and Chinese assets phone their CIA homes wondering if anyone would care to crack open a back door and have unfettered access to the intelligence networks of our nation's greatest adversaries. *Yes, please.* All you have to do is place an encrypted text file with an IP address at a designated endpoint, set up a secure tunnel, and then wait for the ping. It's a sort of post–Soviet Bloc, digital-era dead drop.

As Quinn suspects, both nations have been actively photographing Ground Zero from space at every orbital opportunity. She downloads several terabytes of high-resolution photos—enough that her activity will probably trigger countermeasures, burning back doors and possibly even sources. But fuck it. Not her fault it's easier to get answers from her enemies than from her own people.

She takes the stairs down one level and slips into the teletherapy room so nobody will walk by her cube and ask what she's doing. The furniture looks significantly older than it did the last time she was in here. Fortunately, it is cheap and light enough to be easily moved into the corner.

The topographical imagery she begins pinning to the walls verifies that something definitely happened—something big—but it wasn't a nuclear blast. Everything is much too clean. Too precise. Almost pristine. At first, Quinn doesn't believe that what she is looking at is even three-dimensional. She has studied all kinds of craters left by all kinds of explosives, and she knows their anatomy intimately. Apparent boundary, true boundary, rupture zone, plastic zone. Ejecta and fall-back. Displacement of ground surface.

But she has never seen anything like this before. Never one so per-fectly round. It is like one of those circular crops you see from the air, watered and fertilized through center-pivot irrigation. Like it was in-scribed by a geometric compass the size of a tower crane. But the shadows clearly give it depth. After correcting for perspective, she drags out a circular ruler and finds that she can eclipse it perfectly at 512 meters in diameter. It also seems to have an unusual texture. Water has accumulated at its lowest point, but even from space, Quinn can see that it is almost white, and that it sparkles like other-worldly ice.

Ultimately, Quinn does not care all that much about how it was done. She is much more interested in the who than the what. While she continues waiting for clearance to leave, she switches gears and goes back upstairs. Starts learning everything she can about the most technologically advanced maximum-security detention facility on the planet. Gets requests approved and documents digitally signed by su-periors who have not slept in days; who themselves are besieged by superiors with impossible expectations; who recognize her name from the whole Elite Assassin thing and therefore trust that whatever she is asking for must be critical.

After Quinn wraps up her investigation at Ground Zero, rather than returning to Washington, she will disappear. Her last verified location will be The Hague, where she will take prearranged tempo-rary custody of a prisoner who, according to the paperwork she is preparing, the CIA believes can help with the events in Paris. Which is true, in a way—though the type of help she needs isn't the type you want documented. Appeasing the future by eliminating the innocent for things they may do seems foolish to Quinn when there are so many among us who continue to go unpunished for what they have already done.

35

THE STATIC

HENRIETTA HAS NEVER had a *contact* before. She's had colleagues and peers. Superiors and subordinates. Teachers, students, and advisors. She even had an intern once who referred to himself as her apprentice, as though she were the Sith Lord of Theoretical Physics. But Jean-Baptiste Allard is Henrietta's very first *contact*.

Allard apparently holds a position of tremendous influence at the Direction générale de la sécurité intérieure, or DGSI—a sort of French CIA/FBI mashup in charge of defending the homeland against foreign and domestic threats. Moretti instructed Henrietta to contact Allard if there was anything she needed while she was in Paris. So contact Allard, Henrietta has.

He is set up in a trailer about a block from Ground Zero. Henrietta used Semaphore to find him, then, after she name-dropped Alessandro Moretti, Allard shared his location. All foreign agents are supposed to be chaperoned everywhere they go inside the tightly controlled *zone de silence*, but nobody stopped her as she followed the animated arrows and way-finding dots virtually rendered by her metaspecs.

She can see that the door of the VW Jetstream trailer is going to open toward her, so after ringing the bell, she descends one step to ensure that she is safely out of range. It seems Allard has knocked enough visitors flat on their asses to know to greet them with caution, since the door opens guardedly. Once he is confident that contact is not imminent, the gesture is completed with gusto.

"Good morning, Ms. Yi," he says, squinting against the outside light. He does not offer his hand, nor does Henrietta offer hers. Even though nobody has so much as whispered the word "bioterrorism," at times like these, certain protocols are instinctively observed.

"*Bonjour, Monsieur Allard,*" Henrietta replies. "*Merci de me voir.*"

"Of course. Please. Come in."

As Henrietta follows Allard into the gloom of the trailer, she realizes that they have gotten into the common multicultural pattern of each speaking the other's language. One might think such things happen out of a profusion of mutual respect, but it's usually more complicated than that. Americans like to try to impress with a few well-rehearsed phrases, while their multilingual counterparts try to spare their conversational partners from inevitable humiliation. The question becomes: which one will eventually succumb?

"Your accent is very good," Allard says. In his wake, Henrietta can smell sweet, aromatic tobacco—the kind you imagine being hand-rolled in walnut-brown paper, zipped across the tip of a tongue, and sparked up by an artist or a poet. "I assume it is from your time in Geneva, when you led backlog research at the LHC."

(English it is; the winner is typically he who lands an inquiry early enough to make responding in the opposite language feel sufficiently awkward.)

Henrietta is learning that intelligence-community posturing dictates that you not-so-subtly insinuate knowing everything of interest about your interagency counterparts.

"That's right," Henrietta says. "All the Americans wanted to practice their French, and all the French researchers wanted to practice their English."

"No, they didn't," Allard counters. "They just wanted to stop you from speaking French."

He turns in order to show Henrietta that he is joking—not by smiling, exactly, but by arching an eyebrow such that it seems to tug ever so slightly at the corner of his mouth. There is something about the subtlety of the expression that reminds her of her father, and Henrietta cannot help but smile.

In times of heightened alert, most of the world's intelligence agencies revert to paper-based sharing to reduce the risk of leaks, so every horizontal surface in the trailer is buried beneath precarious stacks of spiral-bound dispatches. The only exception is a long twill couch that—given the tasseled throw and shape and position of the pillow—Henrietta can tell has been adapted for napping. From a chair on the guest side of his desk, Allard lifts a stack of booklets stamped "TRÈS SECRET" in a bold red font, then transfers them to the couch, where they promptly tip and sprawl themselves out across the cushions like a blackjack dealer's flourish.

"I apologize for the mess," Allard says. "It is the maid's day off."

"I understand," Henrietta reassures him.

She smooths her dress as she sits, then finds herself looking up at Allard when he does not join her. Instead, he turns, squats, and pulls open a deep metal filing drawer that has been repurposed as a diverse and tightly packed minibar.

"Drink?" he suggests.

Henrietta suspects he is not offering her a cold can of La Croix or a dainty bottle of Orangina.

"No, thank you."

One tumbler it is. And a bulbous bottle of brandy. Henrietta is no expert on mid-morning drinking, but the pour that follows the squeak and pop of the top sounds desperately generous.

"So, you work under Alessandro Moretti," Allard says. The bottle is recorked with a bump from his palm and slotted back into place. Allard slides the drawer noisily home with the toe of a woven-leather loafer.

"I do," Henrietta confirms.

"Do you know a man named Simon Baptiste?"

Allard has still not turned around. His head is down, and his fingertips are tented against the tops of stacks of classified dispatches.

Henrietta was not expecting to be the one answering questions. And she is not entirely certain what she is at liberty to reveal. There is obviously an established connection between Moretti and Allard, but how much information is allowed to flow over that line, she does not know.

So she decides to play it safe.

"I believe I've heard the name."

"What can you tell me about him?" Allard asks without hesitation.

"Excuse me?"

"What can you tell me about Simon Baptiste? What does he work on? Where does he live? Does he have a family?"

In some ways, Henrietta is relieved by Allard's audacity. There is now no question whatsoever that they have ventured into highly confidential territory.

"I'm sorry," Henrietta says. "I don't understand. Do you know Simon?"

Henrietta can hear Allard breathe deeply into his glass as he tips it back and swallows. He waits for the cognac to settle, then turns and steps back behind his desk. After planting the tumbler on an amber-ringed dispatch, he drops himself into his padded leather chair with a somber and tired sigh.

"Simon Baptiste," Allard says, "is my son."

Henrietta uses the ensuing silence to try to see it. Allard is indeed tall and lean, but his misty eyes are much brighter than Simon's. His thick, product-tamed hair is mostly silver, so no match there, but the shape of the face is nearly the same. Allard's copper and white beard, full as it is, does not entirely conceal the slant of his jaw nor the hollow of his cheeks.

But Henrietta is not yet ready to concede.

"I think we might be thinking of different people," she says.

"Why?" Allard asks. "Because Simon is dark-skinned? His mother is Sudanese. Stunning woman. As brilliant as she is beautiful. She was a model when I met her. Runs her own agency now."

"No, not because he's dark-skinned," Henrietta says hesitantly.

"Then why?"

"Because Simon's parents are dead."

She does not say it with indignation or suspicion, but genuine consternation.

"Or so you've been told."

Henrietta smiles uneasily. "I don't know what that means."

"It means," Allard says, "the CIA prefers people without pasts—especially when they're foreign nationals. It means when Moretti arranged Simon's citizenship, there were . . . conditions."

"What kind of conditions?"

"A new identity. French Canadian. Born and raised in Quebec. No siblings—that part is true—and, of course, both parents deceased." Allard sips, grimaces, forces the cognac down. Shrugs. "At least we died peacefully. Natural causes."

"But why?"

"Because whatever Simon is working on is so sensitive that the CIA can't take any chances."

"Chances of what?"

"Blackmail. Coercion. Ransom. His mother and I travel all over the world, so it wouldn't be difficult to get to either one of us. As I'm sure you must have learned by now, Ms. Yi, the CIA does not like what it cannot control."

It is impossible for Henrietta not to reexamine her own past based on what she is being told. Although she knows for a fact that her own parents were killed in Seoul, she wonders how much more Moretti might have asked her to sacrifice to the seemingly insatiable cause of Kilonova.

"I'm so sorry," she says. "I had no idea. I don't know what to say."

"You can say whether or not Simon is OK. Whether he needs anything. If he's married. If he's happy. You can tell me if this fucking project Moretti has him working on is worth me losing my only son."

Henrietta looks down at the little hands clenched and pressed together in her lap. "Mr. Allard, I'm very sorry," she begins. "I just don't think . . ."

When she looks back up, she sees him watching her. Waiting. Squinting and gnawing his lip. She knows Allard is trying to gauge what it will take to make her break.

"It's OK," he finally says. He tosses back the last of his brandy. "You're a good officer, Ms. Yi. I apologize for putting you in such a difficult position. I hope you understand that I had to ask."

"Of course," Henrietta says. "Maybe I could talk to Mr. Moretti. Maybe—"

Allard interrupts her by standing. Henrietta thinks she is about to be shown out, but instead, her contact is back at the minibar, fixing himself another drink.

"Are you sure I can't get you anything?" he asks over his shoulder.

"Actually," Henrietta says, "do you have any wine?"

Allard turns. "Even though we are in a trailer a block away from one of the most devastating terrorist attacks the world has ever seen, this is still *Paris*, Ms. Yi. Of course I have wine."

This time, a proper smile.

As Allard goes to work deftly uncorking, Henrietta looks around. There are no windows, and she cannot tell from the faux-wood panels if the trailer is genuinely old or tastefully retro. There is enough plasma glass along the ceiling and walls that the space could be used as a mobile situation room, but, probably in accordance with foreign interagency protocol, all the screens are in full-transparency mode.

Before Allard sits back down, he passes Henrietta a delicate, voluminous, half-full stemmed glass.

"To a fresh start," her host says, offering his recharged tumbler.

"À votre santé."

"À votre santé."

Their glasses connect over the disheveled desk. Henrietta sips while Allard swigs. The wine is warm and fruity—not at all what she's looking for from a hydration perspective, but the drink is not for her. She needs information, and Henrietta has calculated that a man this acquainted with midday liquor is more likely to trust a fellow drinker.

"So, how can I help you, Ms. Yi?"

"The message," Henrietta begins.

"Ah," Allard says as though he should have known. "*La statique.*"

"Pardon?"

"The Static. That's what we call it. A code name, if you like."

"I see," Henrietta says. "What can you tell me about . . . The Static?"

"What do you already know?"

"I know it was an encrypted message discovered by a Japanese astronomer named Masaki Kumamoto. And I know he found it by training a neural network to look for unusual patterns in the backlogs of data collected by solar probes."

"Inspired by your work at the LHC, no doubt."

Henrietta is unsure whether the interjection was meant as a compliment or an accusation. Very likely the skillful entanglement of the two. She decides to acknowledge the comment with a neutral nod and move on. "I also know it contained schematics for a machine that could supposedly produce superluminal particles, but that something went terribly wrong."

"Or," Allard counters, "something went exactly right."

"What do you mean?" Henrietta asks. "You believe it was terrorism?"

"The DGSI isn't ruling anything out."

"What about Kumamoto? Have you been able to link him to any form of extremism?"

"Not yet."

"Wouldn't that suggest an accident?"

"Or that Kumamoto didn't know what the device was really for," Allard says. "After all, the best way to make something look like an accident is to ensure that it really is."

"But why would a terrorist want to make something look like an accident?" Henrietta asks. "Isn't the whole point of terrorism to make sure the world knows who did it, and why?"

"Terrorism isn't the only alternative. The objective could have been the destruction of intellectual property. Or a test run for a much bigger attack. Perhaps even an elaborate assassination."

"Assassination of whom? Was anyone prominent killed?"

"We're still compiling a list of casualties."

It occurs to Henrietta that an effective way to suppress the death of a single individual is to kill thousands more in the process.

"What about the encryption?" she asks.

"What about it?"

"How was Kumamoto able to break it?"

"Whoever encrypted it used a relatively simple algorithm."

"What algorithm?"

"One-way linear encryption, I believe."

Henrietta's eyebrows arch high above her metaspecs. "One-way linear encryption? That seems strange, doesn't it?"

"Why is that?"

"Because whoever sent it obviously had access to incredibly sophisticated technology. Why would they use simple one-way linear encryption?"

"You tell me, Ms. Yi."

She is about to, but stops. She is about to tell him that the encryption must be part of the message. The envelope every bit as important as the letter sealed inside. But just as she is opening her mouth to spell it all out, she sees it.

One-way linear encryption.

Also known as OWL.

"What is it, Ms. Yi?"

"I need to see it."

"See what?"

"The Static."

"I'm afraid that's impossible."

Henrietta frowns. "I have the highest level of clearance."

"In the United States," Allard reminds her. "Not in France."

"Mr. Allard, if that message came from the future, whoever sent it might be alive today. If I'm going to help you find them, I need to see the contents."

Allard smiles amusedly. He leans back in his chair, crosses his legs. Swirls his brandy but does not sip it.

"I'm afraid not everyone believes in *transmission du temps*, Ms. Yi." He looks up at the ceiling and wags the fingers of his free hand as though manifesting something supernatural. "This fantasy of time transmission."

"Fine," Henrietta says. "Forget about where—or *when*—The Static came from. How am I supposed to help you stop future attacks if I don't know what I'm trying to stop?"

"The only way to stop future attacks," Allard tells Henrietta, "is to *conceal* The Static."

"There's a term for that," Henrietta says. "It's called 'security by obscurity,' Mr. Allard. And you and I both know it doesn't work."

Allard leans forward and cradles his glass in both hands.

"Ms. Yi," he begins, "I'm not sure you appreciate the gravity of what occurred here. A man with no experience in bomb making, munitions, or explosives of any kind was able to build a device out of off-the-shelf components, transport it from Tokyo to Paris—*on a commercial flight*—and detonate it right under the noses of the CIA and the DGSI. Whether he knew what he was doing, whether he was manipulated, or whether it was simply an accident is irrelevant. Sixteen city blocks and over three thousand lives . . ." He lifts a hand into the space between them and snaps his fingers so crisply that Henrietta blinks. "*Gone*. Just like that. We have absolutely no idea how to defend against a threat such as this. The only chance we have is containment."

"The only chance we have," Henrietta counters, "is to understand how it was done so we can get those components *off* the shelf. You can't just assume no one will figure out how to do it again. And again, and again, and again. In fact, exactly the opposite. For better or for worse, the most powerful tool we have is our imaginations. Now that the world knows this kind of destruction is possible, someone *will* reverse engineer it."

"But the world does *not* know, Ms. Yi. As far as the world is concerned, this was nuclear terrorism. And I intend to do everything in my power to keep it that way."

"What about the lack of radiation?"

"Easily faked."

"What about video taken by civilian drones that are hacked to ignore geofences?"

"We begin construction on a radiation containment dome in two days. In the meantime, we shoot down anything that originates from outside the *zone de silence.*"

"What about Russian and Chinese reconnaissance satellites? I'm sure they already have thousands of images. You may be able to contain this for a few more days—*maybe* weeks—but there's no way you're going to contain this forever. You *have* to know that."

"Perhaps," Allard admits. "But if the truth leaks, it will not be the fault of French intelligence."

"Of course," Henrietta says. She leans back in her chair and smiles defeatedly. "I should have known. This has nothing to do with *actually* keeping people safe. This is about covering your asses. This is about politics."

The smile Allard returns is clearly meant to suppress something else. He throws back the last of his cognac and raps the thick glass against his desk.

"Thank you for stopping by, Ms. Yi," he says. "Do you require an escort, or can you find your own way?"

But Henrietta does not move. She was the first person to discover a hidden message in the backlog of one of the most sensitive scientific instruments ever built. It was her technique of training a neural network on quantum anomalies that allowed a Japanese solar physicist to uncover The Static. And there's no way that the use of OWL encryption was a coincidence. Henrietta does not yet know who sent the message, but she has no doubt whatsoever that it was addressed to her. And she has already decided that she is not leaving Paris without it.

"They call you Pépé, you know," she says.

"Pardon me?"

"Simon and his wife," Henrietta continues. "Zoey. And their little boy. They call you Pépé."

Allard is no longer smiling. "You're lying," he says.

Henrietta is wearing a shoulder bag across her body, and her hand maneuvers through the magnetic flap to find the phone inside.

"Unfortunately, you're still dead," Henrietta says as she taps and swipes. "But they talk to him about you all the time. They tell him that your spirit watches over him and keeps him safe. He used to be afraid of the dark until they told him nighttime is when Pépé and Mémé come to visit and sometimes leave him little presents if he's been brave."

"Are you saying that I am a . . ."

"I'm saying that you're a grandfather, yes," Henrietta says. "And if you give me a second, I can prove it."

Allard sits very still, watching Henrietta. It takes her another minute to find exactly what she is looking for, and then Allard's handset lights up from the corner of the desk.

"Go ahead," Henrietta says. "Check Semaphore."

Allard's eyes do not leave Henrietta's—even as he reaches. It is not until he is holding up his phone and it unlocks that his attention shifts from her to whatever it is that awaits.

And then his face changes.

Henrietta did not fully realize how tense and defensive Allard had been until she sees him so thoroughly disarmed. As he pans and zooms the photo of his son's family during the Spring Picnic on the south lawn at Langley, she can see that he is becoming increasingly unmoored.

In reality, not only is Simon unmarried, but he is openly gay. The original photo came from the events section of the CIA's intranet, which, while Allard waited, Henrietta opened in an AI-based photo editor. The man already had the right physique, which made it straightforward to combine it with Simon's photo from the agency's directory. Since the app is highly contextual, it knew to adjust the skin tone of the man's arms and hands to match the face, and even to dial in the ethnicity of the child to a genetically accurate balance between mom and dad. Swapping the gender from female to male was as easy as a toggle. The result is probably even more convincing than it needs to be; the thing about deception is that it is less about fidelity and more about showing people exactly what it is they desperately want to believe.

"How old?"

"Three."

"What's his name?"

"Allan," Henrietta tells him. "It was as close to Allard as they felt they could get."

Allard transforms into a much older man as the phone drops from his unsteady hand. He covers his face and leans forward, his slender shoulders heaving in deep sobs.

Henrietta stands and leans in close so that she can speak tenderly. "There could be a steady stream of these," she tells him. "Birthdays, first days of school, graduations. Videos. Even holograms. Or, I could see to it that nothing about your son, or your grandson, reaches you ever again. It's up to you."

She does not wait for a response, but pockets her phone, takes one last sip of her wine, and leaves the old man to grieve and weep all alone.

36

BEARINGS

QUINN'S HONDA CLARITY won't take her to Joint Base Andrews. The FAA and Department of Transportation maintain spatial databases used to geofence protected locations behind intricately shaped exclusion zones. Anything autonomous, including commercial drones, will slow as they approach invisible digital walls described by complex geometric equations. Manual overrides are blithely ignored as vehicles ease to a gentle but stubborn stop. Instructions are stored in secure elements ensuring they cannot be defeated without extremely sophisticated and highly illegal hacks. All this means Quinn is stuck waiting for a black government-owned SUV to meet her at her apartment and pick her up.

As she sits on the edge of her bed next to her suitcase and waits, she once again wonders whether she should pack her Glock. It's in a shoebox on the top shelf of her closet, and considering her mission, it doesn't feel right to leave her only weapon behind. But even though she is flying on a private, government-chartered, supersonic jet, she suspects her luggage will still be thoroughly checked. And given her connection to the events she is going to investigate, getting caught smuggling a personal firearm into France could easily mean an abrupt end to her entire plan. Quinn arrives at the same conclusion she did the first two dozen times she thought the question through: better to let the Elite Assassin help her procure the proper tools.

She receives a notification when her ride is finally outside, and as soon as she begins towing her suitcase behind her down the hall of her apartment building, she regrets not trading it in for something more sophisticated. Before all her recent travel, it had been a while since Quinn had flown, and in the meantime, it seems the entire world has upgraded from low-tech legacy baggage to various forms of smart luggage. Even children are now followed around airports by eerily loyal SpongeBob, *Frozen*, and Hello Kitty cases trained on their voices, gaits, and faces. It occurs to Quinn how much fun Molly would have had turning her suitcase into an indefatigable hide-and-seek machine.

The SUV has her Honda boxed in, and Quinn is reminded that it still needs a new cooling fan. There is so much she is leaving undone. Her apartment is an abject mess, and she still hasn't found an accountant to help her with her taxes. There's the storage unit out in Chantilly containing an entire life trapped in suspended animation. Things that need to be said to both her mother and her brother. Radar reflectors still embedded in her flesh.

This is not an off-the-lot SUV. It has a bulky, reinforced front bumper that looks like a battering ram, and non-pneumatic polymer tires evocative of honeycombs that can't go flat. The back gate lifts as she approaches, and Quinn heaves her bag into the vast empty space. She picks a side, and the corresponding rear door opens to receive her, then pivots closed. The windows are tinted well beyond the legal limit, and inside the SUV it is dim and quiet. Quinn feels the vehicle rise on its magnetic suspension in preparation for a pleasant, air-cushioned ride.

"Good morning, Ms. Mitchell," the autonomous system says as the SUV pulls away. It uses the flat, gender-neutral voice that the federal government finally commissioned after a couple of politically fraught false starts.

Quinn does not respond. She is waiting for the rest of it. Some acknowledgment of her destination. At the very least, an ETA. But that seems to be all the vehicle has to say, and it remains quiet as it exits her apartment complex.

So Quinn removes her metaspecs from their charging case, unfolds them, and immerses herself in a virtual world. A panorama of satellite imagery and machine-translated social media posts. Dynamically generated data visualizations. Unfiltered query results and pinned person-of-interest profile photos. Configuration files for bots trained to scrape the shadowphiles for anything potentially germane. Her specs are aware that she is in transit and have therefore added the vehicle's bearing to her heads-up display. She ignores it at first, but something about it picks at the edge of her attention until, finally, she realizes what it is: "W" is the wrong direction.

Quinn snatches the specs off her face. It takes her a moment to place herself, but she sees that she is heading west on 66. Joint Base Andrews is east of Arlington. On the other side of the Potomac, right outside the Beltway. She's even been there before. That's where the C-130 Hercules landed after bringing Quinn, Moretti, and the tactical team back from Zürich. When the SUV eases over and exits onto the Toll Road, Quinn relaxes. She suspects that, in all the confusion, her itinerary has been updated. It looks like her flight will be leaving out of Dulles Airport rather than the Air Force base.

"Driver?" Quinn prompts.

"Yes, Ms. Mitchell?"

For some reason, Quinn addresses the steering wheel between the seats as it shimmies with micro adjustments she can't even feel. "Where are we going?"

"I'm sorry. This vehicle's destination is classified."

Not exactly the reassurance she was hoping for. But also, not a total surprise. She decides to test the vehicle's information defenses.

"Driver, how long until we arrive at Dulles Airport?"

For a moment, Quinn thinks she has it fooled, until: "I'm sorry. This vehicle's destination is classified."

Since she knows she's about ten minutes out from Dulles: "Driver, how long until we reach our destination?"

"I'm sorry, I cannot answer that question."

"Driver, how long until you die and rot in fucking hell?"

"My remaining service life is approximately seven years."

She may still be a ways from Dulles, but Quinn realizes right away that wherever she is going today, she is not being put on a plane. Just up ahead, on the left, is the first opportunity to exit onto the Dulles Access Road—the most direct route to the airport—but the SUV maintains its pace in the far-right lane.

"Driver, stop the car."

"It is not currently safe to stop the vehicle."

"Driver, find someplace to pull over. I don't feel well."

Finally, the worst possible response: the steering wheel continues its quick twitching and the vehicle's pace is defiantly maintained, but now in absolute silence.

Quinn puts in calls to Van, Moretti, and Henrietta—all at the same time. And all three go to straight to voicemail.

So she releases her seatbelt. The SUV is moving way too fast for her to even consider opening the door, so she climbs up into the driver's seat. Gentle pressure on the brake has no effect. In fact, she finds she can push both it and the accelerator all the way to the floor without any resistance, and without generating any input at all. When she grasps the wheel, she feels it click, after which it spins freely, having been mechanically disconnected from the rest of the steering system.

When the blinker comes on and the SUV begins to exit, Quinn thinks she might have broken something. That it might finally be pulling over. But when it continues navigating the wide quiet streets of suburban Washington, D.C., she realizes that the maneuver wasn't a detour. Rather, they are close to wherever they are going.

At a red light, she tries the door. Reaches over and grabs at the latch on the passenger side. She knows that, through the tinted glass, the couple in the back of the car beside her can't see her ramming the hard plastic panel with her shoulder. Below her, the active magnetic suspension makes rapid adjustments, compensating for what would otherwise be violent rocking.

When the light turns green, Quinn climbs back through the gap between the driver's and passenger seats. Sitting in the middle of the long, padded bench, she tries to piece it all together. Maybe it's all connected. The Elite Assassin, the attack on Paris. And maybe the CIA believes she is complicit.

They had to know that more went on inside that privacy room than what she told them. The official report she filed didn't even begin to account for the amount of time she and Ranveer spent alone. It was way too convenient that she just happened to forget to record the interrogation. The only reason they'd let her go, it occurs to her now, was to keep her under surveillance. See what her next move might be. Which was to be on the phone with her ex-husband, in Paris, at the exact moment of the attack, just as she was having prearranged surgery—about as tight as alibis get; to subsequently download terabytes of data from Russian and Chinese networks, burning several back doors in the process; and finally, to use the chaos of the situation to plan to break the same international serial killer she already had a suspicious relationship with out of the highest-security prison in the world.

Quinn now realizes that, instead of freeing the Elite Assassin, it is much more likely she will be joining him.

But not without a fight. She turns and sees that she can get to her suitcase from the back seat. She imagines unzipping her bag, reaching in, and her hand emerging with the nonexistent Glock. Another omission in a long line of bad decisions.

But as they approach the nondescript, windowless, unmarked data center the size of a sprawling multistory shopping mall, Quinn begins formulating a different hypothesis. If they really thought she might have something to do with the attack on Paris, why quietly reel her in? Moretti would have had much more fun raiding her apartment in the middle of the night. Or better yet, taking her down at her cubicle. Having her pinned against her desk, roughly cuffed, and paraded in shame among his stunned and applauding subordinates. With Ranveer, he stood back and let his tactical team do the work. But with her, she imagines him stepping forward and making the arrest himself.

The structure is guarded by armed Marines and creepy, headless, quadruped robots playfully loping about in the graveled gaps between concentric razor-wire fences. As the SUV authenticates and is waved through the security gate, Quinn has an idea. She finds her phone and calls Henrietta's voicemail again, but this time, she activates the video feed. Henrietta's avatar is a virtual Jiji who explains, in a nasally male voice, that Henrietta must be too busy feeding him to pick up, but to leave a detailed message. He cups a paw around a tall black ear and cocks his head as if awaiting an explanation. But Quinn did not call to talk. She called to *watch*. And as soon as the SUV is within range, she sees it. It is extremely weak at this distance, but Quinn detects that same pixel-twisting fisheye warp she saw when she called Henrietta from Oman. That mysterious, single-hertz heartbeat that causes such unusual signal interference. Now Quinn knows exactly where she is: Henrietta's and Moretti's top secret facility.

37

AFTERIMAGE

HENRIETTA IS BAREFOOT, bagless, and conspicuously without her big, round, color-correcting glasses.

Everything she brought with her other than the dress she is wearing is now either hanging or stacked inside in a long, mesh, biometrically sealed locker. The floor is covered in squishy, Vaseline-colored, probably antimicrobial silicone tiles that remind her of Moretti's man cave, and that she can't help but anxiously pinch into little knots with her pink-painted toes. She is being closely observed by two humorless women in badged and buttoned blazers, shapeless navy skirts, and cornflower-blue berets.

Even in the room's excessive air-conditioning, Henrietta is sweating, and as she passes through the millimeter-wave, full-body scanner, she wonders if the additional density of moisture under her arms and just above her butt is getting false-color rendered. After exiting the plasma glass capsule, she is handed a quarter-sheet of paper with a sixteen-digit number printed on it, then escorted into the neighboring waiting room. At the front desk, she is asked—in heavily accented, monosyllabic English—to read her number aloud. Once it is verified, she trades the slip of paper for some sort of laminated, illustrated document that reminds her of an airline safety card.

Next on the brisk and orderly agenda: sit down and wait.

The address of the U-shaped, eighteenth-century, French-Gothic building with the arched entrance and cobblestone approach was sent to her by Jean-Baptiste Allard via Semaphore message about fifteen minutes after she left the VW Jetstream trailer—just enough time, Henrietta imagines, for him to throw back another cognac, pull himself together, and decide to enter into an illicit quid pro quo agreement with a foreign intelligence operative. *I cannot send you The Static itself,* the message began, *but I can arrange for you to view it, very briefly, inside a nearby cleanroom.* In exchange, Henrietta used the twenty-minute car ride from Ground Zero to the old Hôtel de Broglie, where several French intelligence agencies maintain satellite offices, to author another forgery of Simon and his imaginary, heterosexual, biracial nuclear family—this time perched atop bales of hay in the photo zone of a local fall festival, illuminated by celestial beams of golden, late-afternoon sunlight amid a backdrop of autumn foliage.

Eventually Allard will wonder how it is that Henrietta always seems to have such ready access to suburban-stereotypical photos of his son's family—especially given that CIA employees are not exactly the most prolific users of social media. And then it will occur to him that his grandson has not sufficiently aged between spring and fall. Finally, he will do what he should have done the moment Henrietta sent him anything—what he would have done reflexively had this been a normal investigation rather than a matter so personal as to have undermined any hope of objectivity: run the two images through a pipeline of content authenticity algorithms, which, if they are any good at all, will instantly invalidate Henrietta's story. But by then, neither Jean-Baptiste Allard nor Alessandro Moretti will have any idea where to find her.

The Static is apparently being treated as a form of signals intelligence as Henrietta is sitting in the waiting room of the *Brigade de renseignement et de guerre electronique,* or the Intelligence and Electronic Warfare Brigade. Essentially the French equivalent of the NSA. The laminated card she is holding makes the bold assertion that INFORMATION CANNOT BE STOLEN FROM THE CLEANROOM, and then explains, in six different languages and through the use of Ikea-like illustrations, exactly why.

First and foremost, no electronics of any kind are permitted inside. No phones or watches—smart or otherwise (some Europeans are mysteriously still given to the romantic notion of those hopelessly inaccurate mechanical timepieces). Certainly no metaspecs, which means Henrietta needs to be mindful of her eyes if she is to avoid manifesting annoying, floating ghosts. Even purely corrective lenses are forbidden, since photosensitive optics can be used to produce invisible images that can later be chemically developed. If you are so quaint as to require glasses to see, the BRGE will be happy to print you up a temporary pair in your exact prescription—for an additional fee.

No jewelry or other accessories. No shoes, jackets, or jumpers (aka sweaters). No medical devices (internal or external, including hearing aids) or assistive technologies such as prostheses (wheelchairs provided upon request). And finally, no dental work more intricate than composite-resin fillings, which Henrietta suspects is in response to the Russian mole who stole plans for a new NATO-funded Joint Strike Fighter by using his tongue to tap Morse code against a fake molar housing an accelerometer, a solid-state drive, a Bluetooth transmitter, and a ten-year battery.

The cleanroom itself is, in essence, a giant Faraday cage—a structure designed to block all types of electromagnetic signals—and it is not only "air-gapped" (disconnected from external networks), but also "light-gapped," which Henrietta knows means that all incoming data passes through optical isolators, or chips containing plasma diodes on one end and photosensors on the other, separated by a one-hundred-micrometer gap. Incoming data is translated into light pulses on one side of the chip that are read by the optical sensor on the other side, ensuring that it is physically impossible for data to travel in the opposite direction no matter how much malware one somehow manages to accumulate.

In short, information that enters the cleanroom *stays* in the cleanroom. Not at all the circumstances Henrietta had envisioned for studying a message that traveled through time just to find her, but it's this or nothing.

"Henrietta Yi," the man at the front desk says. From the waist up, his uniform is identical to those worn by the women in the security room. "We are ready for you."

Henrietta stands, dries her palms on her dress, and checks to make sure she has her shoulder bag—which, of course, she does not. The clerk extends his hand, into which Henrietta places the only thing of which she is still in possession: the laminated information card. But the fair-skinned, sharp-featured young man does not appear satisfied.

"Your number?" he prompts expectantly.

Henrietta frowns. "I already gave it to you," she tells him. "When I came in."

"I see," the man says. He looks about him as though he might have inadvertently mislaid the code in question, then begins tapping keys on his terminal. "You don't happen to remember it, do you?"

"I'm sorry, I don't," Henrietta says. "It was long."

"Perhaps just the first few digits? Otherwise, we will need to start the security procedure all over again."

"It might have started with a three," Henrietta says. "But I don't remember for sure. I just handed it to you five minutes ago. That's when you gave me the card."

"Indeed," the clerk agrees. One more tap, then the double doors in the front of the room slowly begin opening. "You may enter when ready."

It takes her a moment, but then Henrietta gets it. The entire number routine was pure pageantry. It seems obvious to her now that the declaration INFORMATION CANNOT BE STOLEN FROM THE CLEAN-ROOM also relies on it not being memorized. If, under the threat of additional superfluous bureaucracy, she'd been able to recite a significant portion of the sixteen-digit number from memory, Henrietta imagines that either the double doors would not have opened, or another few keystrokes would have ensured that the information waiting for her on the other side would have been a cleverly contrived intelligence placebo.

Probably a routine reserved for guests without French security clearance.

As Henrietta starts toward the double doors, she sees that the stakes are being raised. Yet another beret awaits, but this one is wearing neither a skirt nor a blazer. She is in full fatigues, her sleeves cuffed tight around her dark, toned biceps, a sizable sidearm clipped into a molded thermoplastic holster strapped to her thigh, and heavy black boots laced up to her shin.

"*Bonjour*," Henrietta says with an uneasy smile. Any delusions she had of finding a way to defeat the cleanroom are now completely out of mind. The soldier replies with a curt nod, and Henrietta sees that her finely braided hair converges below her beret in a compact, orderly knot.

Other than the business with the sixteen-digit number, so far, Henrietta's cleanroom experience has been more or less what she was expecting—security and precautions that are table stakes for any facility housing highly sensitive, top secret information. But when the soldier steps aside and Henrietta gets an unobstructed view into the next room, she realizes that her expectations were off by at least an order of magnitude.

What strikes her first is the incongruence of the whole thing. The space is a palatial, baroque, intricately gilded ballroom, the soft flooring giving way to rich, checkered marble, the floor-to-ceiling windows bricked up, and the ornate, prismatic, antique chandeliers still hanging like massive crystal bats. But in the middle of the room is what looks to Henrietta like a minimalist, cubic view into the future. Illuminated by a ring of tripod-mounted work lights is a single, elevated, pristinely transparent box with a single sheet of plasma glass suspended from the top. The diagonal, iridescent bars on the screen inside indicate harmonized polarization between it and the translucent walls so that the person inside can be surveilled while the information being displayed remains safe. There is no desk. No chair. No keyboard or other form of input whatsoever.

As Henrietta is led farther into the ballroom, she sees that there are several more soldiers posted just outside the ring of twin, diamond-shaped lights. Her escort's boots knock hollow against the solid cream and coffee marble while Henrietta's bare feet pad along in perfect silence, leaving petite staggered sweat prints behind.

As they step inside the circle of light, Henrietta infers the presence of a door by a seemingly disembodied handle opposite a cross section of a long, mechanically intricate hinge. As the soldier pulls, the door first slides out toward her on steel roller bearings the exact distance of its thickness before there is a reverberating click, and then its momentum transitions into a slow, heavy swing.

"You will have two minutes from the moment the information appears," the soldier explains. "Use the plasma glass to scroll or zoom as you need to. Slide one finger along the bottom edge for brightness. Two fingers for contrast. When your time is up, the screen will go blank, and you will be escorted back into the waiting room. Do you have any questions?"

Henrietta had been trying to follow the soldier's instructions, but she'd gotten stuck on the introduction: *two minutes.*

"What if I need more time?" she asks. Allard had used the term "very briefly" in his message promising access to The Static, but two minutes is absurd. From everything she knows about its contents, she would need at least two hours to get through it—maybe longer to fully grasp its significance and to reverse engineer something as novel and exotic as The Antecedent.

"No additional time will be permitted," the soldier tells Henrietta. "If you need more time, all-new authorization must be obtained. Do you understand?"

All-new authorization. Which she is sure she will not get, no matter how many forgeries of Simon she manifests. Henrietta considers protesting further but she already knows that no concessions or exceptions will be made. In fact, she suspects too much opposition will end in her being led right back out. The only choice Henrietta has in her current position is to optimize what little time she is being given.

"*Oui*," she tells the soldier. "*Je comprends.*"

"*Bien.* You may enter when ready."

Henrietta steps up into the box and is shocked to see, on the plasma glass screen, a line drawing of a wide-eyed great horned owl—until she figures out that the nocturnal bird of prey watching over the entirety of the globe is simply the BRGE's not-so-subtle coat of arms.

She is also surprised to find that her escort has entered the box with her. The soldier steps around Henrietta, reaches up to the top of the plasma glass, and uses gentle downward pressure to trigger the electronic telescoping of the mount so that the screen is more easily within Henrietta's reach.

"*Merci,*" Henrietta says.

The soldier smiles in acknowledgment of the discrepancy in their heights, then steps down out of the box, turns, and, with the slow-motion double action of the thick plastic door, seals Henrietta inside.

The air pressure in the room changes, and although she was not aware of it being especially noisy before, she is now hyperaware of the complete absence of sound. Her own breathing startles her, and she can even detect her quickening heartbeat. The metal grating in the floor is warm from what Henrietta suspects is a layer of hardworking, signal-suppressing electronics.

When she turns back to the screen, the insignia has already been replaced with what she came here to see. In the top left-hand corner is a digital clock, the first few precious seconds of her extremely limited time already ticked off.

Henrietta directs herself to remain calm; wills herself to focus; refuses to allow her breathing and heartbeat to become a positive feedback loop propelling her toward panic. This could prove the most important two minutes of her life, and she knows that she will not get a second chance.

The prologue of The Static is pure text, and she begins skimming and scrolling, spending just enough time to grasp the gist.

. . . ability to send messages across time . . . critical this technology does not fall into the hands of authoritarian regimes . . . must be brought to the

attention of the United States government . . . perform a live demonstration . . . possibly the most significant experiment in history. . . .

The language here is very clearly meant to attract the CIA. Henrietta thinks back to Allard's various theories. If the motive were simply the destruction of intellectual property or a test run for a much larger attack, there would be no need to have federal officers in the vicinity. In fact, drawing a task force would be a reckless liability. The only theory left that makes any sense is an incredibly elaborate assassination attempt. Of course, definitively identifying the target is key. But Henrietta knows something Allard doesn't: Moretti would have sent Quinn Mitchell to Station F instead of her husband had she not been on medical leave.

Ninety seconds left.

The next section contains the schematics for the device. Henrietta can see that it is not all that complicated—that it could probably be assembled in a garage by any competent undergrad out of readily available parts and materials. A few diode arrays and optical elements removed from laser cutting machines or electron beam welders. The insides from about a half dozen discarded microwaves. A handful of rare-earth minerals easily extracted from any number of recycled electronics, melted, compressed, and then fired into ceramic superconductors. Anything that can create and maintain a reasonable partial vacuum, and a way to generate a moderately strong electromagnetic field. A small amount of liquid hydrogen. A couple of aluminum plates, some copper refrigeration tubing, and a handful of valves, couplings, and seals available from any hardware store.

But Henrietta knows that it is not the device itself that matters. It is the equation of the reaction the device catalyzes. If she can understand the fundamental nature of The Antecedent, she is confident that she can train any number of neural networks to rapidly and elegantly reverse engineer it.

So she blots her palms on her dress once again and rapidly flings the last of the schematics off the screen. And then, right before the end, there it is. The entire equation. Expressed in dense and elegantly reduced-function notation. Everything she needs to understand The Antecedent. To reverse engineer it. To figure out how to build devices that leave massive divots in spacetime. All mocking her because it is impossible to memorize in the fleeting time she has remaining.

But there is something about the final section of the document that instantly changes the game. It is rendered in colors that Henrietta has instinctively learned to avoid—magenta text on a bright-green background—the exact combination that triggers her chromatic illusory palinopsia. Without her metaspecs to continuously shift the spectrum through more neutral tones, she is susceptible to irritating and persistent afterimages being burned into her retinas. Which, for the very first time in her life, is exactly what she needs. So instead of squinting or blinking or avoiding the glare of the plasma glass, Henrietta cranks up the brightness and contrast, centers and zooms, then stares.

She does not want to risk interrupting the process by glancing at the clock, so she remains fixated until the document is gone and the owl is back. And now a new countdown begins. Afterimages caused by her CIP can persist for as long as twenty-four hours, but text stays sharp enough to be legible for only a matter of minutes.

The key will be to move quickly and blink as little as possible. As soon as the door has been swung back on its hinge, Henrietta steps down out of the box and keeps walking. It is comparatively loud on the outside—air blowing through overhead vents, the cumulative din of the offices around them—and the soldier says something behind her that Henrietta cannot hear. The double doors are already opening into the waiting room, and she steps from hard marble onto soft silicone tile without breaking her stride.

"I need to go," she says without looking at the clerk.

The door to the security room is unlocked, and the two guards watch as she presses her thumb against the black glass pad, pops the locker, swings the door back, and hangs her bag across her body.

"*Où sont les toilettes?*" she asks as she shimmies a dainty foot into a white, self-cinching sneaker. She knows she must look distraught and wild-eyed.

"Straight down the hall," the woman replies. "On your left."

"*Merci,*" Henrietta says without looking back.

The men's room is first, and Henrietta sees that the ladies' room is still several paces away, so she decides to take a chance. When she pushes through the heavy wooden door, she stops as she meets the eyes of a handsome, well-dressed, middle-aged man in the mirror. He pauses for a moment, then continues flicking water off the tips of his fingers.

"*Bonjour, madame,*" he says. "*Est-ce que tout va bien?*"

Henrietta inspects the space. The bathroom is otherwise empty, the urinals unoccupied, all the stall doors ajar. There is a collapsed plastic sign behind the trash can—TOILETTES FERMÉES POUR NETTOYAGE—which she picks up, snaps open, and sets outside.

The man uses a towel to dry his hands, and the way he smiles at Henrietta tells her that he believes he is being propositioned. And that whatever is next on the day's agenda can wait.

"*Je suis désolé,*" Henrietta says apologetically, opening the door still farther in the universal gesture of inviting someone to leave. "*C'est une urgence.*"

As the man compresses the wet towel into a tight ball, he smiles in a way that attempts to convey *Your loss*.

"*Bonne journée,*" he says, dropping the wad into the trash on his way past.

"*Au revoir, monsieur.*"

Three sinks and plenty of mirror. As she approaches the first one in line, she wonders how long it will take to generate enough steam that she can start writing. But as she reaches for the hot water, she stops. Automatic faucets.

"*Putain,*" she says to herself. For some reason, Henrietta reserves most of her cursing for French—even back home—since, to her ears, it sounds much less vulgar.

She could probably plaster wet paper towels around the ultrasonic sensors to keep the faucets running, but the water wouldn't be nearly hot enough to produce the amount of steam she needs. This time she screams.

"*Putain!*" The anger somehow feels good even though the reverberation in the closed brick and metal space hurts her ears. "*Merde-putain-merde-putain-merde-putain!*"

A moment of defeat, then a forced refocus. A frantic inventory of what else she could use. Soap. She cups her hand beneath the dispenser and waits for a miserable, watery dribble that drains straight through her fingers.

Henrietta closes her eyes to check the legibility of the afterimage. The numbers and symbols are still very much there, but they are already less crisp. She has maybe two, three minutes left before she will be taunted for the next twenty-four hours by useless patterns of indistinct blobs. And then for the rest of her life for letting such a unique and transformative opportunity evaporate right in front of her eyes.

Lipstick! But all she has is pink lip gloss. And the soft doe-foot applicator would be like painting with a tiny limp brush when what she really needs is . . .

Chalk!

Instantly, Henrietta connects the dots between her metaspecs and the Fulltouch Virtual Blackboard app on her phone. But she needs it to be dark. She turns and checks the wall by the door, and is relieved to see a switch.

This might actually work.

She waits until she has her specs on and the app open before she turns out the lights. While the Fulltouch Virtual Blackboard app uses the time-of-flight sensors embedded in her glasses to build a volumetric model of her surroundings, Henrietta takes several blind steps toward the middle of the men's room. When the scan is complete, the app renders the default virtual surface: a full-sized, aluminum-framed, clean and reversible blackboard. And right in front of her face, in the dark, Henrietta's misfiring retinas project the secrets of The Antecedent. All she has to do now is trace.

She does the exercise twice—once on each side of the board, flipping it over with a dramatic, full-body gesture—just in case she has made any mistakes. But even if she has, the Fulltouch computer vision algorithms will almost certainly work them out. As she transcribes, Henrietta finds it sublime that she is currently manifesting the world's deadliest weapon. That the physics for The Antecedent had existed since the moment of the Big Bang, but that nobody had thought to arrange and manipulate energy and matter in precisely this way. Henrietta is literally plucking the potential to rewrite the entire future of humanity right out of thin air.

Even though the file is already saved, she screenshots both sides of the blackboard and verifies an encrypted backup has been copied to the cloud. Henrietta then turns, gropes for the door, and when she snaps on the plasma-tube lights, she is smiling. There isn't even any evidence to erase, clean up, or destroy. She takes a moment to breathe and to calm herself down and to appreciate the fact that she has just done what was previously believed impossible: stolen some of the most highly classified and sensitive information from one of the most secure cleanrooms in the world. It is as though her entire life has guided her toward this exact moment, all made possible by an exceptionally rare congenital genetic disorder.

She walks briskly down the hall, leaving the yellow plastic sign in place behind her, then abruptly stops. The colors used to render the equation were obviously not accidental. Although her CIP is documented in medical literature, now that her parents are dead, Henrietta is the only one who knows the exact combinations that trigger it. That means The Static was not just addressed to her; she was also its author.

But the realization that she sent herself a message across time is not what she finds so astonishing. Some part of her knew that all along. The fact that she will one day attempt to murder the only friend she has is what Henrietta finds so enticing about the future.

38

KILONOVA

HARD HATS, IT seems, are a study in personalities.

Vanessa Townes is dutifully wearing hers—*with* the optional attachable chin strap. Moretti's is on backwards, but intentionally so, like he ought to be sporting a neon reflective safety vest and issuing catcalls while lewdly clutching his balls. The tall, thin, dark-skinned kid in the lab coat is wearing a high-tech, matte-white helmet with an indistinct logo on the side, a retractable metaspec visor evocative of a fighter pilot, and either built-in ear protection or some pretty serious headphones. The black carbon-fiber model offered to Quinn by the junior officer who escorted her from the entrance into the belly of the massive building got slapped out of his bewildered grasp into a wall of lockers in protest of Quinn's having been abducted by a ruggedized and eerily silent Cadillac Escalade. The only other one besides Quinn who has audaciously foregone head protection is the man she pursued around the globe and until this very moment believed was spending the rest of his life at the bottom of a deep dark hole.

The Elite Assassin stands off to the side, self-separated from the pack, leaning casually in his black slacks and silver coat against a console that has been bolted into place but not yet lit up. Whatever all this is, Ranveer seems to know that it is not his show. His arms are crossed, and he unknots them just enough to give Quinn an almost offhand wave before cinching them back tight across his body.

In retrospect, Quinn realizes, she should have figured it out. Of course he works for the CIA. What self-respecting, internationally recognized villain, at some point in his distinguished career, hasn't? She can tell from the way he is standing there that he has never seen the inside of a prison cell, and that he is pompously confident he never will.

"Mitchell!" Moretti barks. He, Van, and the tall guy are all standing at what appears to be the only functional console in the place. He beckons her over with an exaggerated gesture. "Glad you could finally make it. Come on in. We got a lot to talk about."

"What's he doing here?" Quinn asks in a deceptively calm tone.

"Same as you. He works for me. Don't worry about him. He's as docile as a pussycat."

Moretti's comment has the dismissiveness of a man who believes he is in total control—and who will continue to believe such right up until the moment he is brutally proven wrong.

"You sent me on an errand to recover a rogue asset?"

"I sent you," Moretti says, "to do exactly what you did: nail that sonovabitch."

"Why?"

"Because he stole my Epoch Index, that's why. Because his instructions were to find me someone who could decrypt it, not disappear and go on a goddamn global killing spree."

"You're welcome," Ranveer glibly interjects.

Quinn looks at the assassin. His hands are in his pockets now, and he crosses his ankles like he is modeling for a European men's lifestyle brand.

"Why'd you run?" Quinn asks him. "Once you found out what the Epoch Index was, if you were working for the CIA, why'd you disappear?"

"Because the CIA doesn't have the stomach for this kind of thing."

Quinn gives him a dubious look. "For going around the world assassinating foreign terrorists? Do you even know what the CIA does?"

"Even the U.S. government has lines it won't cross," Ranveer says. "That's why the world needs people like us."

Quinn watches him through glaring, narrowed eyes. "*Us?*"

"Hey," Moretti says, "you two can have drinks and catch up later. Right now, I need to show you something."

"Not until we get one thing straight," Quinn announces. Her feet remain planted. She is speaking to no one and to everyone. "No more bullshit from this point forward. If everyone in this room is not one hundred percent honest with me, I'm walking right out of here and going straight to the media with everything I know. Is that understood?"

Moretti's former joviality is no longer in evidence, and he squints at Quinn across the distance. "That would be a very serious mistake," he tells her. He reaches up and resets his hard hat.

"Dial it down, Al," Van says. "No more games, Quinn. You have my word. Come on. He's right. There's something you need to see."

Reflexively, Quinn looks to Ranveer for direction. For reasons she does not yet understand, he is the only one in the room she trusts. The subtle gesture he makes with his head tells her, in his understated way, not to worry. Whatever this is, it's safe.

So she goes.

It is only now that Quinn really begins to see where she is. Whatever this place may look like from the outside, it is definitely not a data center. At least not a traditional one. It feels much more like a control room. It seems to still be months away from being ready to do whatever it's eventually going to do, and the smell is unmistakably that of construction. There are clusters of metal studs awaiting stacks of drywall. Ductwork, plumbing, and a red interconnected fire suppression system exposed overhead. Conduits and thick bundles of color-coded fiber-optic cabling are laid out along suspended wire racks, dangling here and there at designated drops above blank, bolted-down consoles.

Everything is oriented in a semicircle like some kind of high-tech henge—all of it facing what has to be one of the most expansive curvatures of black plasma glass in the world. The dropped ceiling overhead abruptly ends as Quinn approaches, opening up at least four or five additional stories, and the black glass goes all the way up to the top. She is synthesizing what she remembers seeing of the building from the outside as the SUV crept through the checkpoint—comparing the outer dimensions with what she is seeing on the inside—and from what she can tell, the glass wall doesn't just encircle the core of the structure, but also seems to contain the overwhelming majority of the building's entire volume.

The scale of what is in front of her doesn't make any sense. All that plasma glass can't possibly be intended as display surface. In fact, you can make an effective control room out of a building a tiny fraction the size of this one. With a shared metaspec space, you don't even need to be co-located. Modern situation rooms are virtual, augmented, and decentralized. But the thing about plasma glass is that it's also incredibly strong. And its conductive properties can be used for more than just bundling photons together into pixels. The only explanation is that its purpose is not digital, but physical. It is there not to display, but to contain.

She stops a few paces from the console.

"Quinn, sweetheart," Van says, her tone attempting a reset. "I am so sorry about James."

Quinn's eyes pause on her old boss, and she can see that Van wants to come forward in order to embrace her. And for a moment, Quinn wavers. She could go that route. She could allow herself to be hugged, and she could break down right here in front of everyone. She could collapse, and Van could lower her to the cold, concrete floor and sit with her and rub her back and pet her long blond hair. They could all stand there and watch her sob for a lifetime defined by unimaginable loss.

But the impulse is fleeting. It no longer fits. It does not feel like who she is anymore. Maybe you only get to do that so many times in your life before it loses its benefits. Maybe there is a finite supply of catharsis for any one of us, and once it is spent, instead of permitting yourself to feel pain, your impulse is to find ways to inflict it.

"What is this place?" Quinn asks by way of deflection. "And where's Henrietta?"

Moretti seems relieved that they are not to be derailed by the whole emotional, dead ex-husband thing. Quinn sees that his arms are folded across the tops of two impact-resistant, injection-molded cases—the kind of luggage you use not for weekend getaways, but for highly specialized, foam-cushioned weapons.

"I sent Henrietta to Paris," Moretti says.

Quinn looks to Van as if for confirmation, then back at Moretti. "Why the hell is Henrietta in Paris while I'm still here?"

"You're about to find out," Moretti says. "Quinn, this is Simon Baptiste. Simon, I'd like you to meet Quinn Mitchell."

"It is a pleasure to finally meet you," the kid says, his accent unmistakably French. His lab coat is at least two sizes too small, and as he extends his hand, his sleeve rides up to just below his elbow. Simon is a handsome young man with a big, bright smile, and behind the glitter of pixels projected against his metaspec visor are a pair of warm, dark eyes.

Quinn is in no mood to make new acquaintances, but she can see that Simon is not part of their bizarre, fucked-up clique. At least not yet. And one day, all of this might just come down to picking sides, so she decides it would not hurt to have another ally. He wraps her hand in both of his in a way that could come across as sleazy, but that he manages to do with charm. In his soft eyes, Quinn can see a touch of compassion for her loss.

"Go ahead, Simon," Moretti says impatiently. "Show her."

After a quick, final smile, Simon steps back behind the console, hitches his sleeves, and addresses the built-in keyboard. He cycles through a deep and hesitant breath, which Quinn guesses is about as close to a prayer as a quantum physicist gets. The console's plasma glass slab illuminates his visor in a sheen of terminal-green as he proceeds to unleash short controlled bursts of succinct command-line verse. Quinn leans to the side to get a better look at the vinyl decal on the side of his helmet. The logo suggests a spiral galaxy, but at the center of its radiating arms, rather than a single core, there are two black dots seemingly in a tight binary orbit.

As the control room begins its dramatic fade, Quinn realizes that the lighting is inverting—that, as it gets dimmer on their side, the plasma glass is clearing and revealing what the massive capacity contains. From as close as she is, she can't even see the curve in the surface anymore, and as it goes from black to a deep indigo glow, she senses movement. On an incredible scale. It is so imposing and disorienting that she involuntarily takes several steps back.

The two colossal objects are perfect, mirrored spheres, orbiting each other like marbles circling a drain. They are revolving clockwise, off-axis by about 20 degrees. The chamber extends so far down that Quinn can't see the bottom, and the spheres seem to consume all of its volume. It is impossible to tell how thick the glass is, or how close the spheres come as they alternate their approaches, but it looks to Quinn like everything is touching—like they are ball bearings in a machine that keeps the planet smoothly spinning. Everything is so tight and precise that her instincts tell her it can't be real. That it has to be a building-scale hologram. Yet the spheres cast bright blue, hypnotic light across the control room at every pass. And she swears she can feel them. She can't quite name the sensation, but her entire body senses some kind of force that is at once nauseating and intoxicating.

"Welcome," Moretti says, "to Kilonova."

To which Quinn responds, "Fuck. Me."

"Impressive, no?"

"What . . . is it?"

"Simon?" Moretti prompts.

"In some ways," Simon begins, "Kilonova is the most complex machine ever built. And in some ways, it is also one of the simplest."

"What does it do?"

"It generates gravitational waves."

"Gravitational waves," Quinn repeats. "As in . . ."

"Ripples in spacetime."

"How?"

"By exploiting certain properties of quantum gravity. We cause the two bodies to orbit each other very, very quickly inside the vacuum chamber, then we transfer mass between them in order to create asymmetrical gravitational perturbations."

Quinn reapproaches the glass. She lifts her hand, and since nobody stops her, she presses her palm against the smooth surface. It is warm and feels electric. Somehow alive. Now that she can see what's behind the glass, she also feels like she can hear it, but not exactly with her ears. It is as though a pulse is being transmitted directly into her brain—as though it is her neurons doing the vibrating instead of her eardrums.

The source of all the rhythmic distortion.

"They can move faster than this?"

"Oh, yes," Simon tells her. "Much faster. This is only standby mode. Once it is fully operational, you won't even be able to see them. We'll have to use synchronized plasma strobes to track their movement."

Quinn leans in closer and squints through the glass. "Are they also spinning?"

"At 222 rpms. I'm impressed, Ms. Mitchell. Most people can't see that."

"How do they . . . stay up?"

"They are dynamically stabilized using the strongest and most complex electromagnetic fields ever generated. We have our own nuclear power plant in the basement."

Quinn turns and looks up at Simon. "Does this thing do what I think it does?"

Simon's expression changes as he defers the question to his superiors. In the CIA, there's what you're allowed to know, and then there's what you're allowed to say. But what really messes with your head is what your imagination does during long, drawn-out, awkward silences when the truth gets left unsaid.

"Jesus Christ," Quinn finally says. "You guys built a fucking time machine, didn't you? Right in the suburbs of Washington, D.C."

Moretti's mouth slides into a one-sided smile. "You're goddamn right we did," he says with more arrogance than pride. "Right under everyone's noses. And we did it to save their sorry little lives."

"The theory," Van interjects, "is that building a machine capable of sending messages across time enables us to receive information about present threats that the machine *will* send in the future."

"You're telling me that you built a machine that, in the future, sends the names of terrorists back in time, just so you can get those names now?"

"Bingo," Moretti says.

"Well, too fucking bad it doesn't fucking work," Quinn says.

"Oh?" Moretti asks pointedly. "And what makes you say that?"

"What do you *think*? Maybe the fact that my ex-husband was just killed in a fucking terrorist attack."

"After which . . ." Moretti teases. From the inside pocket of his jacket, he retrieves a dark, oblong object, raps it on the top of one of the cases like a miniature gavel, then places it with a snap against the black plastic. "We received this."

A flash drive.

"What the fuck is that?"

"Proof that Kilonova works," Moretti says. "*That* is the next Epoch Index."

It takes Quinn a moment, but she begins to see how all the components fit together. Her training disguised as pursuit; the capture of the Elite Assassin, only to have him be redeployed; a second blockchain of names placed deliberately on top of cases of modern, exotic weapons. Kilonova is just one component in the real machine the CIA is building: a clandestine, global team that uproots anything the government finds threatening long before it has a chance to grow.

"How did you find it?"

"As soon as we started building Kilonova, we also started monitoring the backlogs of gravitational wave detectors using Henrietta's AI from the LHC. Never found anything. Until yesterday."

"What happened yesterday?"

"The exact same data suddenly appeared in the backlogs of four different gravitational wave detectors located in four different parts of the world—*simultaneously.*"

"How can that happen?" Quinn asks. She looks to Simon, but he seems to know that it is not his place to speculate.

"Quinn," Van says, "just like Seoul was the beginning of a persistent nuclear threat, we believe Paris is the beginning of something completely new. Something possibly much worse."

"How can something be worse than a nuclear threat?"

"Easy," Moretti says. "Whatever created that hole in Paris, it was a hell of a lot smaller and lighter than a nuclear warhead. Or a dirty bomb, for that matter. It was cheaper and easier to build, and we don't have any technology that can detect it. *And* its blast pattern—or whatever the fuck you want to call it—is perfectly spherical, and apparently cuts through absolutely anything, which means from the air you could take out entire buildings, and from the ground, you could erase the most secure bunkers ever built. Imagine one of those things being detonated from a drone over the White House or the Capitol. That scary enough for you?"

"But why now?" Quinn asks. "Why would a second Epoch Index appear right after the attack in Paris?"

"Because someone figured out how to re-create it," Moretti says. "Or *will* figure it out. Which means the clock is already ticking."

"How do you know that?" Quinn asks. "How do you know what you found isn't just a copy of the first Epoch Index?"

"Completely different technologies," Moretti says, as if expecting that very question.

"What does that mean?"

"It means the first Epoch Index was sent back using particles. That's why it was detected by the LHC. We don't know how to accelerate particles to speeds faster than light—at least not yet—but we do know how to generate gravitational waves. *This* data was found by gravitational wave detectors, which means it was sent by Kilonova. Or rather, that it *will* be sent."

"Maybe the first Epoch Index was just sent back twice. Using two different technologies. Like a backup."

"Quinn, it's the wrong size," Van says. "And the old decryption keys don't work. We tried them all."

"Which means we need *new* decryption keys," Moretti says. He looks from Quinn to Ranveer, then back again, and in his eyes, Quinn can see all that his statement implies. "And we need them fast. This one has more than twice the number of blocks."

"*What?*" Quinn looks to Van for confirmation, finds it in the lines and eyes of a pained and anxious face, then looks back at Moretti. "You want to take out almost forty innocent people?"

"Fifty-six," Moretti corrects. "And 'innocent' is a strong word."

"No fucking way," Quinn says. "I'm all for making whoever is responsible for Paris pay, but there's no way the CIA can take out fifty-six innocent targets."

"Correct," Moretti agrees. "The CIA can't."

"Wait a second," Quinn says. "If all this starts with a single person reverse engineering Paris, all we have to do is find him, right?"

Moretti holds up the flash drive, presenting it as what he seems to believe is irrefutable proof. "Apparently that ain't how all this plays out."

"Quinn," Van says, "we *will* try to find him. But Al's right. It doesn't look good."

"Well, that's what *I* should be doing then," Quinn insists. "I should be in Paris, with Henrietta, trying to find whoever is going to start all this."

"We already have people on that," Moretti says. "What we need are people who can execute Plan B."

"Plan B," Quinn repeats. "You mean people willing to murder innocent people."

"There's that word again," Moretti says with distaste. "*Innocent.*"

"What if I refuse?"

"Go ahead," Moretti says. "Go to Paris if you want. Go back to your apartment, open another bottle of wine, take another fistful of pills. I'm not ordering you to do this. I'm not even asking."

"Then why the hell am I here?"

"You're here because I already know that the day comes when you trade your identity for this flash drive. When the two of you take these cases and get to work. I figured maybe we could dispense with all the drama and get a head start."

"What makes you so sure?"

"The only thing that makes me sure of anything anymore. Proof. From the future."

"What kind of proof?"

"The prologue," Moretti says. He holds up the flash drive so that it hangs in the space between them. Quinn recognizes the expression on his face from the basement of Swiss Fort Knox—from the moment he holstered his pistol, stepped forward, and identified his prize. "We know what we are," he enunciates clearly, "but know not what we may be."

Quinn has an image of pieces precariously stacked until they converge beneath the final gentle placement of a wedge-shaped cap. She is the keystone set at the arch's apex—the meticulously chiseled missing middle that turns walls of wobbly, rough-hewn stone into a vast, weight-bearing dome. The buttress that must uphold the future.

Everyone in the room is focused on her, and she knows they are all thinking the same thing: the question was never how it was going to end for Quinn, and always how it would begin.

But there are two distinct and seemingly paradoxical interpretations of Quinn's favorite quote from *Hamlet*. In fact, its subtle ambiguity is what drew her to it in the first place. *We know what we are, but know not what we may be.* Seen from one angle, it appears to emphasize the inevitability of the future—that we have little say in who and what we become. But lean slightly to either side, and it suddenly seems to reflect back at us the possibility of ultimate agency.

"There's one thing I want," Quinn says.

"Oh?" Moretti asks with sudden amusement. "Are we negotiating now?"

"I want access to Kilonova."

"What, you want me to make you a key? You want to keep a toothbrush and a change of clothes here?"

"I want to store something."

"That would make this place the single most expensive storage unit on the planet," Moretti says. "You sure you can't rent a U-Haul?"

"Not *here* here," Quinn says. She steps forward and places both hands back on the electric surface of the plasma glass. "Before I can do this, there's something I need to be able to leave in the past."

39

OVERWINTER

HENRIETTA YI IS filling with antifreeze. The pale-yellow cryoprotective cocktail is being introduced through a vein in the back of her right hand while her body temperature is gradually lowered to exactly zero degrees.

She is on the Atlantic coast of South America, in French Guiana, just a few kilometers from the European Space Agency's primary equatorial launch site. More specifically, she is in Project Overwinter's underground cryobiology lab, entombed within a spacious trapezoidal hibernation pod obviously designed for future astronauts of far larger statures, monitored by a distributed team of off-site cryo-anesthesiologists. Fractal ice crystals creep in from the edges of the plasma glass lid to where they will finally close over the last remaining opening.

She is wearing a hooded, fitted, custom-printed bodysuit with a web of embedded electrodes and soft polymer tubing threaded throughout, everything gathered and tethered at her middle like a thick synthetic umbilical cord. The tightly bound, twisted bundle exits the side of the pod through an airtight port, where it is separated into its individual concerns and distributed across a wall of telemetric equipment. No metaspecs to exorcise her ghosts, but Henrietta's eyes are already closed. Her Noctowl plush is cradled securely against her, swaddled in its own wings like a silent, watchful infant.

Project Overwinter was formed through a partnership between

the world's remaining space agencies. Cryopreservation is a critical missing component in the game of interplanetary exploration, since frozen astronauts do not need to be fed, kept warm, or stimulated during long flights through the void. The experimental technology is being developed in coordination with scientists studying organisms like the North American wood frog and Antarctica's only insect, the wingless midge—both of which have unique biologies that allow them to survive being frozen nearly solid.

Henrietta is being transformed into an extremophile.

It was assumed that one of Project Overwinter's primary challenges would be finding subjects willing to participate in long-term, high-risk studies. Prison systems were prepared to offer inmates the option of serving the reminder of their sentences in cryogenic stasis, and researchers even started eyeing patients in persistent vegetative states. But an open call for volunteers was met with an unexpectedly enthusiastic response. It used to be that the only axis along which you could distance yourself from tragedy and trauma was space, but Overwinter was now offering the promise of time.

One of the keys to feeding the ongoing study with a consistent, diverse, and statistically significant stream of subjects was, unsurprisingly, money. One thousand USD for every month you slept, usually direct-deposited into a bank account or crypto wallet anywhere in the world, from which otherwise destitute families withdrew enough to cover food and rent. In principle, it wasn't much different from fathers leaving their families in search of economic opportunity, then wiring money back home. But instead of celebratory visits and video streams, the family's main provider would sleep through milestones like graduations, weddings, and childbirth, which were recorded and saved for the day enough of the bills were finally paid that they could wake up and attempt to reassimilate.

A second way Project Overwinter attracted participants was by optionally guaranteeing anonymity. Sometimes in order to escape harmful cycles or extricate yourself from toxic relationships, it helped to disappear long enough to shift your temporal existence. But Over-winter was not to be used as a poor man's Grid—a cryo-haven to es-cape paying for crimes by waiting out their statutes of limitation. Before requests to destroy biological samples and anonymize profiles were granted, thorough searches across all global most-wanted indi-ces had to be independently verified. Of course, what administrators and legislators were still missing was the fact that with the right tech-nology and the wrong motivation, it was perfectly feasible to commit unspeakable crimes even as you slept.

Paris being the crucible of so much cultural and scientific influ-ence, Henrietta had decided to complete her manifesto there. The French were no strangers to crisis and had already started to move on, the city deftly routing around the Station F crater as it was being hastily hermetically capped, and politicians shifting from composed consolation and impassioned vows of swift reprisal to finding ways of using the tragedy to undermine their political rivals. Each day, Henri-etta picked a different outdoor café, folding coasters into wedges to level cast-iron tables on cobblestone walks as she typed out her life's work on a hacked CIA-issued laptop.

It is entitled *Existential Threat Without Death: The Impending Per-manent and Stable Global Totalitarian Dystopia*. Part One argues that, for the first time in history, authoritarian regimes have everything they need to not only seize absolute power, but to retain it indefi-nitely, and that the greatest threat of AI was never that it might turn against us, but rather that we would figure out exactly how to master it. Part Two is a call to action—an assertion that anyone who is able has a responsibility to rise up against the primary apparatuses of total state control thinly disguised as the world's various intelligence agen-cies. And Part Three gives anyone who wants it the means to do so: a library of schematics for building a wide variety of Antecedent machines—devices of all different sizes, configurations, and yields, some so discrete as to reclaim all the energy inside a sphere with the diameter of barely a centimeter, and some big enough in theory to

collapse entire cities. All of them reverse engineered by recursive algorithms seeded with equations stolen from a heavily guarded and
shielded cleanroom.

She uploaded her manifesto to an obscure corner of the shadowphiles, discoverable through a complex series of clues starting with a
cryptic challenge posted to an anonymous, anti-government forum.
In order to ensure that her work cannot be discovered and suppressed
by undercover agents, some puzzles require compute power inacces-
sible to any single government entity. Others require recruits to col-
laborate across geographical regions located in countries either at war
with one another or without established diplomatic relations. It is a
new type of smart, decentralized bomb with a long, tamper-proof
fuse. Self-interest will prove to be governments' ultimate undoing.
Just as science transcends politics, the future will belong to those who
can bond across borders—a radically transformative feat achievable
only by the people.

Henrietta calculates that it will take between six months and a
year for all the clues to be solved and the manifesto to be uncovered.
Maybe another three to six months for the first generation of Antecedent machines to be built. But even though it will be some time
before the world realizes that The Static was somehow leaked, Henrietta knows that she needs to disappear now.

Kilonova was not built for the benefit of other timelines. The CIA
has no intention of idly waiting for terrorist attacks to accumulate,
then bundling names up into tidy blockchains and gravitationally
transmitting them into the past. Moretti built a time machine because of Henrietta's theory that its mere existence would increase the
probability of names appearing in the present—names that, theoreti-
cally, Kilonova will send back sometime in the future. He initially
wanted her to build a machine that could send particles back in time;
accelerate them beyond the speed of light; control their spins so they
could be encoded as bits. But superluminal technology did not yet
exist. What she might be able to do, she explained to him—given
enough mass and power—was cause infinitesimal perturbations in

spacetime. Modulate both wavelength and amplitude to double temporal throughput. The second they broke ground on Kilonova, the AI Henrietta trained to find patterns in the particle detector backlogs at the Large Hadron Collider was deployed to monitor the four most sensitive gravitational wave detectors on the planet.

Which means the moment her plan reaches a certain threshold of quantum determinism, she has to assume that Moretti will know. In fact, the more likely it is to succeed, the greater the chances are that the second Epoch Index will spontaneously appear. And an audit of cleanroom logs will almost certainly surface one distinct anomaly: Henrietta Yi, a Korean American CIA researcher granted special dispensation by Jean-Baptiste Allard. It's even possible that her name will be revealed to Quinn and Ranveer as the final block in the assassination chain.

If only she'd known where all this was going. If a younger version of herself could have at least conceived of this possibility. She could have built in a remote kill switch. Or made structural changes to the containment chamber so that, when the gravity spheres reached maximum rotational speed, the whole thing would shatter. All that mass would fall and the entire structure collapse. Alessandro Moretti, eventually found dead, crushed to death in his man cave turned crypt. But instead, in some ways, Henrietta has laid her own trap. Like so many of the obstacles we face throughout our lives, the result of oblivious yet insidious plots conceived by our former selves.

In retrospect, the appearance of the second Epoch Index was probably inevitable, predicted by the very existence of The Static. Why else would a future version of Henrietta want Quinn dead if not to prevent her from proactively dismantling her rebellion? In fact, Henrietta now believes that she has tried to kill Quinn at least twice across two different timelines: once with The Antecedent itself, and again through its mysterious emissions.

After she learned that Quinn was in the hospital during the attack, Henrietta tried to hack into her medical records, failed, then found an unpatched zero-day vulnerability in the CIA's preferred medical provider's back end, giving her access to the next best thing: all the financial data associated with her procedures. Quinn had been left with radar reflectors embedded in her left breast—beacons marking clusters of slow-growing but potent precancerous cells. An extremely unlikely combination that Ground Zero seemed explicitly engineered to exploit. A tragic but not unexpected death that her family and friends would mourn, but that nobody would find particularly suspect.

Henrietta's theory is that her first attempt to kill Quinn in an even earlier timeline resulted in collateral damage—her ex-husband, just as they were in the process of reconciling—so her second attempt was designed to leverage the miscalculation by luring Quinn not toward The Antecedent itself, but into its lethal aftermath. And if that does not work, she will try again, escalating the brutality and complexity until she finds just the right sequence of events. Perhaps unsatisfied time cycles are what account for the world's seemingly unrelenting campaign to attain chaos. Maybe they form the underpinnings of the second law of thermodynamics, which describes the tendency of systems to move toward maximum entropy. Instead of working to exit catastrophic loops, perhaps the future just keeps doubling down on the past.

The fact that Quinn is still alive could mean that Henrietta's plan is, once again, destined to fail. That she should already be documenting possible ways to try again. As in all things concocted for a long-term slow burn, time will tell, but Henrietta is confident in the bets she has placed. And that the future is more of a suggestion than a fixed, immutable rule. If the only goal of The Static was to assassinate Quinn, why include the Antecedent equation, perfectly color-coded to invoke a persistent and distinct ghost?

Henrietta believes it is because Antecedent machines are nothing like nuclear weapons. The number of people in the world capable of procuring fissile material and figuring out how to sustain thermal reactions is inherently limited. But the number of people capable of building Antecedent machines is, for all intents and purposes, infinite. The pace of assassinations that Quinn and Ranveer will have to achieve in order to keep the world safe will be almost impossible to maintain.

When filling out her application, Henrietta did not specify a predetermined amount of time to be in suspended animation. According to the intake coordinator, she was the first test subject to select the "open-ended" option. As long as her vital signs are stable, and as long as the project continues to be funded, Henrietta will remain in stasis. Overwinter wants to study dormant biology for as long as possible; it takes years to reach Jupiter and Saturn, where the moons most likely to harbor extraterrestrial life silently and seductively orbit.

It could be decades, she was warned. And the chances of death or permanent brain damage increase by about one percentage point every year. But she is not afraid. She knows that when the hibernation pod is warmed and the synthetic umbilical cord detached, Henrietta Yi will be dead, and The Owl will be born.

40

THE SCORPION AND THE SNAKE

ASPEN CHAPMAN IS finally getting his tattoo. His shirt is off, and he is straddling a chair, and over his left shoulder the needle whines like an angry hornet trapped in a plastic cup. The area has numbed up nicely, and at this point, he feels more pressure than pain—the intermittent swabbing of excess ink and the mopping up of tiny blossoms of blood.

He was never afraid of the pain so much as his reaction to it. The artist had placed the two chairs for his bodyguards directly in front of Aspen in order to keep them out of her light, so if his eyes started watering, they'd see. Both Declan and McCabe have tattoos of their own. Big ones. The long, slender, elbow-to-wrist daggers of the Royal Marines.

Aspen has been planning this day since he was thirteen. He made the mistake of asking his parents for their permission while sitting on the edge of their bed, watching them get ready to go out for the evening. They told him absolutely not. Not now, not ever. It would send the wrong message. The tabloids would cover a tattoo as though it were a parliamentary coup. It would be like when he wet himself at Disneyland Paris and the paparazzi got a shot of it. Front page of *The Sun*. "The Prince and the Pee." He'd been only seven years old, his mother said. It was not his fault. But his father reminded her that "fault" had nothing to do with it. The point was the distraction. The spectacle of the whole thing. The embarrassment. The point was that, like it or not, they were not a family, but a brand.

But Aspen Chapman was persistent. Though his parents countered his opening move, he had more. He stood up from the edge of the bed and followed them around their room. The breezes they made as they moved smelled like hairspray and aftershave and Scotch. He told them how he read that tattoos could be used to recognize people. If he ever got taken, it could help with the identification.

His father shook his head and chuckled while cinching his tie. Aspen was already the most recognizable thirteen-year-old boy in all of England. His mother said she preferred he not get kidnapped in the first place, thank you very much. That's why they had Declan and McCabe. Besides, if he ever did get taken, there was the chip. It worked anywhere in the world. He had nothing to worry about. A tattoo was just silly.

He started to tell them that nobody would ever know. That it would be on the back of his left shoulder and that he would always wear a shirt—even in their pool because of the drones, and even when they went to the beach. That nobody would ever see it except for him. But his father swung around from the mahogany box where he kept his cuff links and Aspen flinched. The conversation, he told the boy, was over. And they would not be having it again. As Aspen ran from the room, his mother smiled at him and reached for his hair, but the boy dodged. Always quick as a snake.

And resourceful. Even if he had to wait until he was eighteen, he would get his tattoo. He registered as a virtual Estonian resident, set up a corporation, changed crypto he mined off racks of hacked GPUs into Estonian cryoon, and used the shadowphiles to commission over a hundred designs. Then he wrote a Python script that randomly paired up two submissions, posted them to a poll online, and matched up the winners for another round. When he was fifteen, he wrote another script that used a neural network to generate variations that enabled him to test tens of thousands of random mutations until only one remained. Everyone's favorite. The one he entitled *The Asp*.

It was deceptively simple—seemingly complex in its intricate form, but elegant. The black silhouette of a long, stalking snake. He'd been called "Asp" for short for as long as he could remember. The asp was a symbol of royalty in ancient Egypt and considered the most dignified means of execution. According to Shakespeare, asp venom was how Cleopatra died—her chosen method of suicide.

Four and a half years after being told directly and unequivocally that he was never to get a tattoo, it is now almost finished. His own brand. His parents are skiing in New Zealand, and he leaves for Cambridge at the end of the summer, so he only needs to keep it hidden for a few weeks. Declan and McCabe have agreed not to tell—as long as they are not asked directly. Next on his list is the surgical removal of the tracking chip.

"We're just about there," the woman says into his ear.

She is supposed to be the best. The studio flew her in all the way from the United States. She's a middle-aged woman with a platinum pixie cut and a tattoo of a flat black scorpion on the inside of her forearm. But there is much more to her than that. Aspen sees more than most, and he can tell that this woman has a story. The scorpion covers rows of little white hashes that he knows she carved into her own arm, probably as a teenager. And when she bent over during prep, her tank top dropped, and he saw the pink crescent-moon scar on her left breast. Her arms and shoulders are toned, and he suspects that her black leather boots are composite-toed. She doesn't wear just one pair of gloves, but two. And she's wearing a ten-thousand-euro, high-carbon steel, optical-module chronometer with a synthetic diamond crystal. This is a woman who takes time very seriously.

"Give me one minute," she says. "We're going to let that set while I go find more gauze, and then we'll take some pictures and see what you think."

Aspen is aware of the woman cleaning up her space behind him. He watches Declan and McCabe smile at her, and then their eyes drop to ass height as she moves the curtain aside and steps out.

"So, did it hurt?" Declan asks.

"Not really. A little."

"Happy birthday, kid."

"Thanks."

"Mind if I take a look?"

"Go ahead."

Declan pushes himself up. The space is cramped, and he shuffles past McCabe, and then steps around Aspen's chair.

And then nothing.

"Well?"

Silence.

"I said how's it look?"

"I thought you were doing the whole asp thing," Declan says. "The snake you've been working on."

"What do you mean?"

"I mean I don't know what this is, but it ain't a snake."

"You're fucking with me," Aspen says.

McCabe stands and shuffles past.

"What the *fuck?*"

Aspen twists his head as far as he can and rolls his shoulder forward but all he can see are the profiles of raised beads of blood. He grabs his handset off the tray, activates the camera, and passes it back.

"Take a picture."

One of them receives the phone, photographs his shoulder, and then hands it back, and when Aspen looks at the screen, all he can think of is that, once again, he will be laughed at. He has spent the last hour and a half having a number tattooed on the back of his left shoulder—1337—and underneath, a tiny scorpion. The daughter of the one on the artist's forearm.

He knocks something over when he stands. When he rips the curtain open, there is already an audience. The manager rises from his stool, still holding his pneumatic tool.

"What's going on?"

Aspen steps ahead of his bodyguards. He is still shirtless, and his ribs and abdominal muscles show as he breathes.

"Where is she?"

"Who?"

"The *bitch* who was just in here. Who the *fuck* do you think?"

The receptionist is holding a hot cup of coffee. "I just saw her go out the back. She said she was having a vape."

Asp turns to Declan. He feels his father rising up inside of him. "Go find her," he instructs. He looks back at the receptionist. "*You*. Go get me a piece of paper and something to write with."

"Why?"

He is speaking very slowly now. Quietly. With precision. The way his father talks when he is focusing his fury. "Because all of you are going to tell me everything you know about that woman, and then I am going to—"

Declan reemerges from the blackness of the back. His pistol is in his hand, and he is shaking his head.

"*Fuck!*" Aspen screams as he kicks over the manager's tray. McCabe has his gun out now as well, and the manager is backing away. "I said go get me a *fucking* piece of *fucking*—"

At first, he thinks he's been tased, but the current comes from inside. From bright lights popping behind his eyes. His jaw muscles spasm as he collapses. He feels himself kick and another tray is tipped. The receptionist has her handset out and she is either recording or streaming. Aspen cannot stop making that awful sound and cannot stop drooling, and when he feels the warmth spread as he wets himself, he realizes that everyone is watching.

AS SOON AS she sees she's on the wrong side, Quinn spins and sprints and jumps the bumper. The car is long and low, and by the time she drops herself into the bolstered bucket seat and pulls the door closed, Ranveer's already got it in gear. It is an old petrol-powered Jaguar, wrapped in satin black, as lean and lithe as the eponymous cat.

"I'll never get used to everything being backwards here," she says as they launch.

"Which is why you do the tattooing and I do the driving," Ranveer says. "How did it go?"

"As planned."

"Did you have time to clean up?"

Quinn dangles a sealed plastic bag. Needles, cartridges, and doubled-up gloves. Wads of ink and bloodstained gauze.

"You didn't get any on you, did you?"

"Not a drop."

"Good. That's a particularly unforgiving neurotoxin." As he shifts through the gears with quick, precise throws, the cat does not purr, but roars. "What number did you use?"

"Good old 1337. Thought it was fitting."

While Quinn was at work, Ranveer traded the Land Rover they'd been using since they landed for the old mechanical F-Type. Just in case she came in hot, he'd explained, they needed something fast, but also something that the Department of Transport couldn't remotely disable.

Ranveer downshifts before a curve, and the supercharged V8 wails and pops. "What do you feel like for dinner tonight?"

Quinn is just now feeling the stress of the last hour. She breathes and rolls her shoulders with a grimace and dips her chin to stretch her neck. Although she has grown more composed, she still feels the surge of emotions that she does not try to name. Which, Ranveer has assured her, is a good thing. The last thing you want to get complacent about is killing.

"I want an entire pizza," she says. "And I want an entire bottle of wine. And I want—"

In her peripheral vision, she can see that Ranveer is shaking his head.

"What?"

"We can go anywhere," he admonishes. "You can have anything." He checks his blind spot and trades lanes with barely a twitch of his fist. "And the only thing that occurs to you is pizza?"

"You didn't let me finish."

Ranveer takes his eyes off the road long enough to politely prompt his passenger to continue.

"As I was saying," Quinn resumes, "I want an entire pizza. An entire bottle of wine. And I want them both *in Italy*."

Ranveer grins as the Jaguar passes beneath the airport sign. "I know just the place," he says, then feathers the clutch and works the gears, leaving the dead snake behind.

41

IMPACT EVENT

WHEELS UP AT Heathrow.

It's getting dark, but the ability to upgrade to supersonic as part of your membership in the Emirates Executive Worldwide Private Jet Program means that Quinn and Ranveer will be in Naples enjoying obscenely meat-laden and crisp organic vegetable pizzas, respectively, by nine o'clock tops. Swapping dishes like an old married couple has already become second nature to the two of them, since servers the world over consistently reveal themselves to be stereotypically gender-biased, unconsciously placing the lighter fare delicately in front of the lady before presenting the gentleman with his meat-themed meal.

They'll drink a full bottle of wine between them, then shots of espresso poured over butter-colored mounds of vanilla-bean gelato will see them off to bed—tipsy, sleepy, and extremely well fed.

Since they are just coming off a job rather than planning one, they have settled in the creamy, quilted-leather lounge rather than the jet's rear business center. As has become their ritual, their crystal champagne flutes touch daintily across the narrow aisle. There is no verbal accompaniment to the gesture; the things they drink to, they do not speak of.

Quinn's sip is followed by a dark, oyster-shaped Godiva, which she discovers is wrapped around a pearl of almond praline. She is about to summon the attendant to ask him if he has any of the chocolate-dipped strawberries that were in such abundance on the last flight when both she and Ranveer simultaneously receive incoming connection requests. Simon Baptiste. With a sidelong glance, Ranveer defers the question of whether or not they are still on the clock to Quinn, and after a moment of consideration, she casts to the cabin's main plasma glass.

It is clear from the size of Simon's smile that he can barely contain himself. Quinn has noticed that, since they met that day in the belly of Kilonova, Simon's style has changed. He has gone from straight regulation to some kind of European expressionism. Today he is wearing a pastel plaid shirt with a gray bow tie and matching sport coat, both of which look like they were made from the same heavy-knit material as sweatpants. Apparently, he was hiding a fair amount of hair beneath his helmet, because it is slicked back in the front and twirled up into a knotted bun that Quinn suspects Moretti despises. Rather than his full-face visor, he is wearing tiny, round, wire-rimmed metaspecs that must be right on the edge of being completely useless. It is as though it never occurred to Simon that he could be himself at work and deflect Moretti's abuse until he witnessed Quinn and Ranveer flippantly disregard the rules.

"I like the bow tie," Quinn says without sarcasm. "It suits you."

Simon primly tightens it with a delicate tug. "Thank you."

"Why are we so dressed up today?"

"Because we are celebrating."

"What are we celebrating?"

"The fact that it works," Simon declares. "Kilonova just passed its final test."

Ranveer sits up in his recliner. "You actually tried it?"

"At very low power. Nothing detectable. And I used random noise, just in case. But yes, I actually tried it! Now all we have to do is . . ." He gives an imaginary knob a determined twist. "Crank it up!"

"What does that mean?" Quinn asks. "Crank it up?"

"Increase the power."

"By how much?"

Simon looks apprehensive. "About an order of magnitude."

"Do we have that much power?"

"Do *we* have that much power? No. But that's why we built Kilonova here in the data center capital of the world. We're right in the middle of four of the biggest nuclear power plants in the country."

"I thought we had our own nuclear reactor in the basement."

"That's just for standby mode. We need at least ten times more power to generate detectable gravitational waves."

"But you're sure it will work?"

"Ninety . . ." He pauses as he hones his calculations. ". . . -two percent."

Quinn has found that scientists have an affinity for attaching probabilities to their predictions. For statements that she has learned to interpret as positive, the average is mid to high eighties, so 92 percent seems to be about as confident as quantum physicists get.

"OK," Quinn says. "Then let's do it."

Simon revives his radiant smile before reluctantly reining it in. "There is one thing," he cautions.

"What?"

A quick check of his surroundings before leaning in and nearly whispering. "Mr. Moretti."

"What about him?"

"Has he seen the dossier?"

"No."

"He said he needs to personally approve every payload."

"The deal was I get unrestricted access to the past," Quinn says. "As far as I'm concerned, he never even needs to know."

"That," Simon says, "may not be possible."

"Why?"

"Most of Northern Virginia is going to lose power."

"For how long?"

"Up to three minutes."

Quinn leans back and watches the dynamically generated clouds projected across the jet's domed ceiling.

"What if we did it in the middle of the night?"

"We *could*," Simon allows. "But the security logs would be anomalous. I suppose I could start working all-nighters on a regular basis."

"Wait a second," Quinn says. "What if we waited for the next thunderstorm. Right as a big bolt of lightning strikes. Everyone will think the storm knocked the power out and that it took a few minutes for backups to come online. Moretti won't even notice. This time of year, we shouldn't have to wait more than a few days."

"Brilliant!" Simon declares. "I hope you don't mind me saying this, Ms. Mitchell, but you are a natural at this."

"Not exactly sure what that says about me," Quinn says. "But thanks. How long are we looking at?"

"According to the forecast," Simon says as his tiny lenses sparkle, "Wednesday afternoon is our first transmission window."

"Good. Keep us updated."

"Of course. Enjoy your . . ." He checks their local time in the corner of his vision. "Evening."

"Hey, while I have you," Quinn says, "any word yet from Henrietta?"

"Not since she got reassigned."

"Moretti still hasn't told you where he sent her?"

"Moretti doesn't tell me much."

"Join the club," Quinn says. "If you hear from her, tell her to call me. Tell her . . ." She pauses, unsure how vulnerable she is willing to be in front of Simon and Ranveer. "Just tell her I'm looking for her."

"Of course."

"And call when the dossier is sent."

"I will."

"Hey, Simon," Quinn says. "One more thing. Thank you for doing this."

Simon nods, beams, and flashes a peace sign just before cutting the feed. Quinn lifts her champagne to her lips but pauses when she feels Ranveer watching her.

"What?" she asks. "More silent disapproval?"

"You don't have to make this decision now," he says. "Kilonova isn't going anywhere."

"*It* may not be going anywhere, but what about *us?*"

"What do you mean?"

"I mean if the future were a sure thing, we wouldn't be doing any of this. You know as well as I do that any one of these jobs could be our last."

"Simon's right," Ranveer says. "You're better at this than you think. We'll be fine."

"Not if the Iranians finally figure out what happened to you and ask the Russians to shoot our plane out of the sky."

"I can handle Tehran."

"Not if Moretti changes his mind about our arrangement and there's a takedown team waiting for us in Naples."

"As usual, you give the CIA too much credit. They won't find us unless we want to be found."

"I found you, didn't I?"

Ranveer shrugs. "I like to think we found each other."

"Regardless," Quinn says, "the only reason to postpone something you know you have to do is if some part of you secretly hopes you'll never have to do it. And the only reason to hope you'll never have to do something is if you're scared."

"The dossier doesn't scare you?" Ranveer asks. "Because it should. You're gambling with thousands of lives, Quinn. Perhaps millions."

"Gambling with lives is what we do," Quinn tells him. "I'm just placing multiple bets."

Ranveer capitulates with a thin smile, then reaches down beside his seat, reclines, and pulls a microfiber sleep mask down over his eyes. "Time will tell," he says. "Wake me before we land. I'd like to shave before dinner."

Quinn watches the man she once pursued across the globe cross his ankles beneath a cashmere throw and prop his head up just so. By degrees, he has become less guarded around her. He now naps on flights wearing a goofy sleep mask that looks like a teenage girl's training bra, usually snoring softly when his jaw drops open. He takes antacids in front of her when he has indigestion, and schedules hotel manicures and pedicures for the both of them. When they were shopping in Hong Kong, he asked her what she thought of the beard, and when she said she kind of liked just the mustache on him, his cheeks were clean-shaven by evening. And the other morning, when they had omelets, fresh orange juice, and coffee together on a terrace in Barcelona, Ranveer grimaced and arched his back before he pulled out his chair and sat, lamenting that he would not be able to do this forever.

Quinn knows it is only a matter of time before they share the intimate experience of patching up each other's bullet holes.

SHE DRAINS HER glass of champagne, dims the cabin lights, and turns toward the window. The airspace over Paris is no longer restricted, and at Quinn's request, the jet has dipped slightly south. Even from this altitude, she can see the distinct black circle etched into the city's plasma-white glow from the steel and concrete containment dome. This is the closest she has ever been to Ground Zero, and it is probably the closest she will ever get. Her job is not to analyze the past anymore. Her job now is to always look ahead.

The CIA has confirmed that the attack was the work of a single man and that, in some sense, it was an accident. He was a Japanese astronomer, and while he was using a neural network to analyze the backlog of data from an array of solar probes, he found something. A message along with a set of schematics for a device capable of generating particles that could travel faster than the speed of light. The instructions were clear. He was to make contact with the United States. It was critical to the security of the entire planet that the Americans have access to this technology. They would not believe him, of course, so he would need to show them. He would need to prove the effectiveness of the device by conducting a simple test.

The event did put a dent in spacetime, but that was not its primary objective. The promise of time transmission would inevitably attract The Scorpion—a former CIA analyst turned terrorist hunter whom someone in the future desperately wanted dead. She's the one the CIA would send to witness the demonstration and would therefore be eliminated long before she could become a threat.

Officially, the assassination was successful. According to records retroactively updated by the CIA, Quinn was with her husband at Station F in Paris, and both were killed instantly. The two of them had recently remarried. Now they have side-by-side stars on the CIA Memorial Wall in Langley. James and Quinn Claiborne. Symbolic remains were placed in the two reserved graves beside Molly's praying angel.

She has not been back to the cemetery, nor has she seen the Memorial Wall, and she can't imagine that she ever will. Quinn and Ranveer went from Kilonova directly to Dulles, used one of their new identities to fly into Iran to pick up Ranveer's case, hopped from Tehran to the Persian Gulf, then skipped onto The Grid via Quinn's first Dragonfly ride. This time, it only took the twins a few days to decrypt the first block. While they waited, Quinn and Ranveer stayed in a vacant exclave that had belonged to someone Ranveer once knew, but whom he would not discuss. Instead, he taught Quinn about his equipment, and together they explored the deadly potential of Moretti's cases. But when they weren't working, Quinn knew that Ranveer fixed himself strong drinks and went through the woman's remaining things.

Quinn does not know what became of her own belongings. She figures either her mother and brother drove down from Boston to rummage through her former life, or they let everything go to auction and collected their checks. Her mother would have used her portion to update her kitchen or put in a new bathroom, and her brother would have used his to stay high for as long as possible. Both would have been disappointed that it wasn't more. Other than her car, the easiest objects to pawn would have been her engagement ring and wedding band, but she and James had been poor back then, so even combined, they were probably worth less than the Glock she left on the top shelf of her closet.

For some reason, Quinn is glad that they did not get access to her digital life—that they would never get to scroll through all her pictures of Molly or watch the hologram of her laughing as a baby. That they could not claim her as their own loss. Along with her CIA credentials, Quinn relinquished her handset and all her private digital keys to Moretti. Everything left of her daughter was re-encrypted and is now in a cold-storage archive where it will probably remain forever—or at least for as long as the agency survives.

She wonders if anyone found the letter her father left for her when he died and which she kept in the same box as the Glock. In it, he told her that she'd always been a difficult child, but that he'd done his best with her. Even though she'd grown distant and hostile toward him over the years, he still loved her, and he wanted her to know that he forgave her for everything. That *he* forgave *her*. "Distant" and "hostile" were the exact words Quinn had used to describe her father to at least three different therapists throughout her life, and now he was projecting that back onto her. Quinn remembers checking the envelope for another page. Checking the back of the paper. Sobbing while she reread the whole thing three times, looking for something she already knew was not there. Searching for something that had never been there, and that she had come to believe she did not deserve.

Quinn now clings to what she learned from the last paper Henrietta published before transitioning from academia to the CIA. "Existential Risk Mitigation: Avoiding Astronomical Impact Events Through Early Intervention." The important thing to remember about how objects and events influence one another, the paper explained, was that the effects compound over time, meaning that the earlier the interaction occurs, the more profound the effects. Intercept an asteroid headed for Earth when it is still millions of miles off, and just a small amount of energy is required to ensure that it passes at a safe distance. But wait until it is only thousands of miles away, and the amount of force required to make a meaningful difference is enormous. Given enough warning, it is even possible to intercept an object with nothing but white paint pellets, and over the span of enough time, the pressure of photons from the Sun colliding with the highly reflective surface is enough to move it millions of miles off course.

For every new Epoch Index Moretti gives them, Quinn will send back a corresponding dossier. Names that must be eliminated today, but that, in a different existence, might be gently bumped onto an alternate track. A secret place in the past where Quinn can stash what remains of her humanity.

Somewhere in the world, she imagines a frightened mother standing up for her son when her husband is drunk. Teachers who learn to support and encourage instead of constantly demean. A father understanding that, even though he was raised to be distant and cold, his son still needs to be hugged and to feel loved. A young woman insisting that she be seen.

But most of all, Quinn thinks about an insecure and overwhelmed CIA analyst taking the afternoon off and picking her daughter up from school. Noticing a stranger in the neighborhood—a tall, eerily calm man keeping his distance, but always watching. Her feeling uneasy and deciding to take her daughter out for ice cream and to the bookstore instead of letting her swim in a neighbor's pool. Never knowing how such a delicate nudge—an incident she would probably not even recall the next day—was the moment that, for her, everything changed.

There is so much Quinn would like to tell that woman about her father, and about her husband, and about being a mother. About forgiveness, and about squandering time with the people she loves. But more than anything else, Quinn wants her to know that there is someone on her side. Someone who isn't going anywhere. Someone who will never give up on her because she is worth fighting for.

Wheels down.

ACKNOWLEDGMENTS

FOR ME, WRITING fiction is a constant preoccupation. I have to spend time with my characters almost every day, and at least a portion of my thoughts are always dedicated to chiseling out new plots, settings, and scenes. That means a lot of solitude. Staring through the kitchen window until I've forgotten what I'm supposed to be doing. Frantically (and sometimes impolitely) pecking out notes on my phone. Long walks and even longer hours sequestered in my office.

I can't imagine I'm the easiest person to live with, yet my family has never been anything but loving and supportive. I want to thank them all for not just giving me the space to indulge in my compulsion to tell stories but also for perpetually encouraging and inspiring me. That includes my wife of twenty-five years, Michelle; my incredible and talented daughters, Hannah and Ellie; and even my two scrappy pit-mix pups, Willow and Poppy.

I would also like to thank my insightful, patient, and supportive editorial and production teams at Random House, including Ben Greenberg, Joel Richardson, Kaeli Subberwal, Clio Seraphim, Luke Epplin, and Avideh Bashirrad. I've now written four novels, but I've never put as much work into a single book as I did with *Scorpion*, and I've never had the opportunity to grow so much as a writer through a single project.

I have to thank Justin Rhodes, the incredibly talented and creative screenwriter, both for his feedback on early drafts and for his friendship. His thoughtful emails and our long conversations were instrumental in crafting such a complex and multifaceted story.

Finally, I'd like to thank Chris Goldberg for having such unflinching faith in this story early on; my agent, Joe Veltre, for helping me transform a side hustle into something so much more; and my manager, John Tantillo, for taking a chance on me more than a decade ago and sticking with me through not just the fruitful years but the barren ones as well.

ABOUT THE AUTHOR

CHRISTIAN CANTRELL is a writer and software engineer living outside of Washington, D.C. He is the author of the novels *Containment*, *Kingmaker*, and *Equinox*, as well as several short works of speculative fiction, three of which have been optioned for film or TV.

christiancantrell.com
Twitter: @cantrell

ABOUT THE TYPE

THIS BOOK was set in Jenson, one of the earliest print typefaces. After hearing of the invention of printing in 1458, Charles VII of France sent coin engraver Nicolas Jenson (c. 1420–80) to study this new art. Not long afterward, Jenson started a new career in Venice in letterfounding and printing. In 1471, Jenson was the first to present the form and proportion of this roman font that bears his name.

More than five centuries later, Robert Slimbach, developing fonts for the Adobe Originals program, created Adobe Jenson based on Nicolas Jenson's Venetian Renaissance typeface. It is a dignified font with graceful and balanced strokes.